I0835154

Just Beneath Your Boat

Tales of Aquatic Terror

Just Beneath Your Boat

Tales of Aquatic Terror

Edited by: Thomas Folske

Cover Illustration by:
Alhiya Hoffman, Olivia Davis, and Mia Folske

Back Cover Illustration by:
Milan Simić

Dark Moon Rising Publications | Virginia

70 Foxwood Drive
Rocky Mount, Virginia 24151
Tel: (540) 257-2861

ISBN: 978-1-945987-99-1

10 9 8 7 6 5 4 3 2 1

Printed in the United States of America

At Sea, by Stephen A. Roddewig was originally published in *Halloween Party '23* from Gravelight Press in October 2023.
Find of the Century by Jeff Parsons was originally published in *The Best of the Horror Zine: The Middle Years* by Jeani Rector in 2022.
Among the Waves of Time by Charles Reis, Copyright 2026.
Dark Water by Lillian Csernica was originally published in *The Urbanite* #5, 1995
The Wealth of Dagon by Rob Tannahill, Copyright 2026
Bite of the Ocean by Claire Davon was originally published by Skywatcher Press, in *The Depths Unleashed.*
Bros Before Hoes by LJ Jacobs, Copyright 2026
Scylla by Mawr Gorshin, Copyright 2026
Beyond the Veil of Fog by Milan Simić, Copyright 2026
The Offering by Justin Carlos Alcala, Copyright 2026
The Maw Beneath by Denise Landry, Copyright 2026
The Blue Whale of Catoosa by Blake Hoss was previous published in *Fiction on the Web.*
They Don't Feel a Thing by David McDonald, Copyright 2026
Silence Next The Sea by CJ Hooper was originally published in *Silence Next The Sea and Other Strange Tales* by CJ Hooper
Seaweed Folk by Pip Pinkerton, Copyright 2026
Propagating Wave by Dino Parenti, Copyright 2026
Whatever Happened to Jonathan Obrero by Don Anelli, Copyright 2026
Dillena's Dragon by Matthew Chabin, Copyright 2026
Cotton Eyed Joe by Kasey Hill, Copyright 2026
Broken Bridge by DJ Tyrer was previously published in *Toasted Cheese Literary Journal* Volume 22 Issue 1 (March 2022)
Narrative of the HMS Verdigris by Miguel Fliguer, Copyright 2026
Persy by Thomas Folske, Copyright 2026
Jacob's Dragon by Michael Mortimer was previously published as a chapter in Michael Mortimer's novel *The Town Crier.*
Something in the Water by Margaret Eve was originally published by Scare Street in *Night Terrors Vol. 22*

Table of Contents

FOREWORD

Their razor-sharp teeth can flay the meat from your bones. Their muscular tentacles can crush any vessel crossing the ocean's surface. From the shallow beaches to the darkest depths, they seek to kill anyone and anything in their path.

Stories of deep-sea monsters is a phenomenon that has stretched across the centuries. The year 565 brought the earliest report of a monster in the vicinity of Loch Ness by Adamnán of Iona. In his hagiography, he describes how Saint Columba and his companions encountered a burial by the River Ness. Locals in the area claimed that the victim had been mauled by a "river beast".

Whether or not you believe the story, one thing is certain: death, as well as a fear of the unknown, are natural ingredients to tales of underwater beasts.

As the years went on, stories persisted, often with mariner reports of sea serpents and tentacled monstrosities.

The 19th and 20th centuries enabled us to experience the fear—and more importantly, the thrill—of deep underwater organisms through the gift of literature and film. From Jules Verne's classic *20,000 Leagues Under the Sea* to the unforgettable adrenaline rush that is Peter Benchley's *Jaws,* and its unforgettable film adaptation, people around the world have been able to experience nautical terror.

It is a genre that remains strong to this day, both in film and, of course, in thrilling books. Since water covers over seventy percent of the planet, the potential for great sea monster thrillers is endless. If you ask me, there's no better sandbox for talented authors to flex their creative muscles.

In this anthology, that creativity comes to frightening life. Behind the cover, you will find pages full of savage predators hungry for human flesh.

Krakens! Megalodons! Mosasaurs!

Turn the page if you dare. But be warned: you're gonna need a bigger boat.

—Michael Cole. Author of *Thresher, Scar,* and *Helicoprion.*

At Sea

By: Stephen A. Roddewig

Samuel walked the deck of the sloop, listening to the sun-stained planks creak beneath his boots. His nostrils filled with the thick, humid air of the Georgian coast, the same that made the lines swell and strain against their bearings. With a final scan of the ship, he paused his patrol at the aft deck and turned to watch the waves lap against the hull.

A man of many voyages, Samuel swayed the same as the sloop, matching the lantern swinging from the yardarm above his head. *Spot* was the only ship in the Tybee Roads anchorage, and his lantern was the only light source across the black water below the distant stars. Samuel loosened his shirt collar to let the slight breeze wick away some of the sweat. Nothing brought greater peace than a calm sea and a well-kept vessel.

His connection to sea and ship may have given the first warning. The waves seemed to awaken, swirling out of their rhythm to smack against the side of the vessel. Drawn to the side by the sudden shift—*had the tide changed?*—Samuel felt his neck prickling. What had been peace shifted to unease as he turned his eyes to the horizon.

A squat shape appeared, drifting toward *Spot*. For a moment, Samuel squinted, trying to determine whether the flotsam was imagined, but it drew closer until the unmistakable point of a bow showed in the lantern's glow. *A ship's boat, but where is its master?*

Samuel fetched a spare line and tied a boat hook to the end. He tossed the improvised grappling hook over the gap, snagging it against the boat's hull and hauling in the line. Grabbing another line, the sailor scrambled over the side and tied the craft off to *Spot* by the bow. As he stood in the bobbing ship's boat, he looked for the telltale signs of wear and salt brine of a derelict but found none.

A lantern hovered over Samuel's head. "What have ya got there, Sam?"

Samuel held a hand up against the light. "I saw this here boat adrift, Cap'n, and claimed her for the *Spot*."

The lantern's glow illuminated another puzzling fact: the oars lay in both locks. It also showed no signs of leakage. All in all, a great find for the sloop, as his captain seemed to be nodding, but where had the craft come *from?*

As he scanned the boat once more in the pitching sea, Samuel noticed the only thing out of place in the entire craft: a ship's log laying on the port side. He picked up the tar-bound book, tied closed with string. *A ship's log serves as the central record of a voyage, so how did it come to be in a ship's boat?*

Captain Micken had turned away toward his cabin below. "Make sure you tie her off well now, Sam. 'Tis a fine find. I drink to your sharp eyes."

Samuel climbed back aboard to retrieve a second line to secure the stern. His prize tied off snugly, the sailor returned to *Spot,* ship's log in hand. Though his watch had ended, Samuel did not feel any closer to sleep. His head buzzed with a threat unseen but *felt,* and the log seemed to thrum between his fingers.

Samuel opened the book beneath the yardarm lantern. He had learned some of the written word during his years at sea, though mostly to interpret navigation charts and ship's manifests. Still, the mystery would not leave Samuel's mind, so he settled into his best attempt at reading.

The book had belonged to *The Kingfisher,* a merchant brigantine out of Newport, Rhode Island. The name Winston appeared enough times beneath the entries that Samuel took it to be the master of the ship and crew. Most of the log was a record of *The Kingfisher's* journeys between ports in the Caribbean and New England. As far as Samuel could tell, the last pages contained the same routine recordings of landfalls, weather conditions, and events aboard.

But even Samuel could tell the final three entries had a different sentiment. Some words had been crossed out and smudged in the writer's haste.

Arrived at Tybee Roads toward dusk. Quiet aboard until near midnight, then night watch cries out that a light is emerging from the sea off the port bow. By time I gain the deck, light has vanished, but all aboard hear a ghastly scream. Even those below hear it. They claim it came from beneath their feet.

Rest of night passes without event, but crew is shaken. Kingfisher will be clear of this place the moment the barge from Savannah has finished offloading our cargo. Still no sign of our broker, however, or of any other ships. Lookouts posted on all points to keep watch for the barge—or anything else.

The awful truth is revealed. The mast lookout first spotted the barge. Then he reported that no one appeared to be aboard. Our cheers died in our throats. At once, a chorus of screams, dozens of them, from all around Kingfisher. Green, eel-like creatures slithered up the sides, and I yelled for the crew to fight them off. I reached for a boat hook, but my arm froze under the blazing yellow eyes of the closest beast. I heard splashes—the crew all stepped over the side, one after the other! I ran for the ship's boat. Maybe they will not follow me while they feast, or what other horrible fate awaits my crew. I have only paused my furious rowing so that this record might survive if I do not. Beware the Roads!

The final entry was too full of words not seen in nautical records for Samuel to decipher, but something clearly had happened to *The Kingfisher* while it lay in this very anchorage. Feeling a chill amid the hot night, Samuel looked out into the dark, where a mist was gathering—and stumbled backward.

A pair of masts had grown out of the fog, drifting silently by as the tide retreated out to sea. Could it be the same brig?

By the time Samuel reached the bow for a closer look, the masts had vanished. But as he turned, he swore he caught a flash of yellow from the black waves beneath *Spot*. Yet this anomaly, too, had disappeared by the time he looked again.

Beware. The same word often appeared in reference to shoals and reefs. Samuel made a note to show the log to Captain Micken as soon as he awoke the next morning.

***

At first dawn, Samuel's eyes flew open. The rest of the night had passed without any more boats drifting past *Spot* or flashes in the water—not that he had made a point of looking after blinking and staring over the side for several moments the first time.

Samuel turned in his hammock, feeling a strange object wedged against his side. *The ship's log!* Memories flooded back, and Samuel scrambled through the dark of *Spot's* cargo hold. The dim light flooding through the hatch led Samuel back to the deck, where he found Captain Micken already awake.

Samuel started to greet his captain, but Micken continued facing off to port. Walking to his side, Samuel followed the ship master's gaze. A two-masted revenue cutter was picking its way through the swells toward their sloop on the early morning breeze.

"What in the blazes does he want?" Micken muttered to himself as much as Samuel.

The sun had changed from crimson to gold by the time the cutter came within hailing distance, but instead the ship dropped anchor, and a boat set out for *Spot*. *Wasting no time,* Samuel thought as he straightened his shirt and looked about the deck for anything that needed mending or stowing. As usual, *Spot* lay in perfect condition, except the planks beneath their feet could use a scrubbing in the next day or—

"Ahoy, *Spot!*" The revenue officer broke through Samuel's mental checklist. "Prepare to receive us for inspection."

"So that's it, then?" Micken scuffed his boots where he knew the blue-coated man could not see. "We're part of their monthly search for contraband? Well, they're welcome to search this hold all they want, but I will not let them get in the way of our cargo schedule."

"Not sure we have much say in the matter, Cap'n."

Micken's eyes narrowed, but his retort was cut short by the sound of oars turning in their locks and the soft scuffing of two hulls meeting. With two steps, the officer bounded onto *Spot's* deck, doffing his hat in salute. Captain Micken returned the gesture.

"Welcome aboard the *Spot,* sir. I am the ship's master, Arnold Micken. Might I offer you refreshment?"

"I will politely decline," the man replied, sword rocking in its scabbard as he paced the deck and cast his head in all directions.

"Then may I at least have your name and your business, sir? So as to better assist you," Micken quickly added.

"My name is Lieutenant Killard of the Revenue Service. As to my business," Killard turned back to face them, his eyes flashing beneath black brows, "I am hunting suspected pirates operating in the area. Perhaps you have spotted anything unusual?"

"We only fetched into the Roads this past twilight, so I'm afraid we haven't seen much of anything, suspicious or otherwise."

Samuel felt his brow furrowing. *The ship's boat. Why does he not mention it? Or should I speak of the brig I saw? But can I be sure that wasn't a trick of the mist?*

Killard continued pacing, inspecting every line and bulwark. "How convenient."

"Why, Lieutenant, you speak as if this small ship's crew is under suspicion."

Samuel edged his way to the port stern, only to stifle a gasp. The ship's boat was gone. The lines that had held it only hours before now lay limp upon the shifting surface of the sea. *That's impossible. I tied the knots myself.*

"No one is above suspicion at this moment." Killard whistled, and his two boat's mates climbed aboard. Their coats opened to reveal matching swords and flintlock pistols.

"This is quite unnecessary, Lieutenant," Micken protested. "Search this craft, and you will find we possess little in the way of weapons or contraband beyond a few boat hooks and a signal cannon. Certainly not enough to make much headway as pirates."

"Even so," Killard concluded his lap of the deck and turned to face Micken, "we have reports of a barge gone missing from a local merchant, sent out to meet a trader and offload cargo. I searched the area this morning to find only empty sea save for this ship. Either you are witnesses, culprits, or innocent as you say, but I have no lead else to go on at the moment."

Killard shook his head. "What's more, these are not the first reports of missing boats. I suspect a pirate or other marauder is preying off this anchorage."

"There is something, sir," Samuel found himself saying. Micken's eyes blazed in his direction, but he had already offered the ship's log to the lieutenant. "We found a ship's boat adrift last night. Found this on board."

Killard took the book, though his other hand still lay close to the hilt of his sword. "And where is this craft, now?"

"It seems she slipped free of the lines, sir."

"Call yourself a sailor but you can't tie a knot?" Killard spat over the side. "Still, this log matches the name of the ship the barge was scheduled to meet. The most logical conclusion would be that you made up the story about the ship's boat and seized this log with other cargo from *The Kingfisher.*"

Samuel could feel Micken's eyes burning into his neck, which matched the prickling in his own stomach.

"But then why offer it up?" Killard stroked his chin. "Let's just see if *Kingfisher's* captain had any time or thought to describe what happened."

The sea breeze whistled through the lines as the lieutenant flipped through the entries that Samuel had already judged to be commonplace. Then his hands came to rest on the final passages, and Killard's brow furrowed as his eyes moved between each line. His two blue-clad companions moved closer in the ensuing silence, but Killard waved them away.

At once, he slammed the book closed. "This is certainly something your man has found, Captain. Either you have forged these final entries to cover your tracks… or if the words are to be believed…"

Killard handed the log to Micken, who buried his nose into it to find what could have taken the fire from the lieutenant's accusations. The wind gathered strength, agitating the waves and increasing *Spot's* listing from side to side. Despite the increased motion, Micken remained rooted to the spot as he let the log slide away from his face. He looked to Killard, then back to the words, as if seeking corroboration.

"What he writes of…"

Killard nodded. "I am at a loss. If the man's account is true, then it would certainly explain the disappearances. Yet, I cannot rule out hysteria in such wild words."

Samuel felt the hair rising on his arms as the two talked. He still did not know the true terror the words had contained, but his sense of their intent now returned two-fold. Something was amiss with *Spot*. The wind had slackened to a murmur, yet the ship continued to sway.

One of the lieutenant's men stepped closer. "Sir, what did the log say?"

Killard turned to answer his comrade when a single, shrill note pierced the air. It reminded Samuel of the sound the boom made as they came about, the joint connecting it to the mast screaming the song of metal on metal as it swung across the aft deck. Then he remembered that they were not at sea and the boom was secured. The others had less experience with *Spot* and had not settled on any logical conclusion as they swiveled their heads about.

Then the source of the swaying deck became clear: five green heads slithered up the starboard side, peering at the wide-eyed men before them. Rows of needle-like teeth revealed themselves between slime-covered lips as the creatures dripped saltwater onto the deck. Eels, but the size of men. *Sea serpents.*

Killard and his men backed away, only to hear Micken gasp behind them as more appeared on the port side.

Silently, the three revenue men drew their swords. Samuel only had a boathook, but the feeling of solid wood gave slight solace to his shaking hands. Green heads surrounded them on either side of *Spot*.

"Why do they wait?" Micken asked, clutching the ship's log to his chest.

"Captain, you spoke of a signal cannon," Killard whispered from the other side of the makeshift defensive circle. "If we can alert the rest of my crew aboard the cutter—"

"I'm on it, sir." Samuel broke from the circle.

"Wait, not so sudden!" Killard hissed. Samuel heard a wet sound smack the deck planks as he dashed for the bow. A green mass with a black dorsal fin was snaking toward him, the creature rising as Samuel turned away. He managed two more steps before its teeth latched onto his shoulder.

Swearing through the thousand punctures, Samuel beat at the finned head with the boat hook, but that only drove the teeth deeper. A shot cracked through the air. Feeling the jaw slacken, Samuel cast the serpent off and dashed the last yard to the signal cannon. Before pulling the lanyard to fire the signal, he looked back to find the beast writhing across the deck, black liquid oozing from a bullet hole beneath Killard's smoking pistol.

"Sound the signal, damn it," the lieutenant barked, and Samuel realized he had frozen at the sight. His hand yanked the lanyard, and the cannon rocked back as its powder ignited and barked in the morning breeze.

Killard raised his sword and finished the serpent's death throes. "Now they're in for it." He smiled.

The blunted heads that had only watched now all began to hiss. Four of the creatures leapt onto the deck in front of Samuel, but they ignored the sailor. Killard yelled, wielding his empty pistol as a club in one hand and slashing with his sword. Grabbing the boat hook, Samuel swung and struck the back of one serpent before another sound met his ear. Metal on metal, the screech from earlier. Samuel glanced away from the battle waging in front of him and watched as the Revenue Service cutter rocked back and forth in the distance. Green shapes scaled her oaken sides.

Whether Killard had realized his crew's fate, Samuel would never know. He turned back to find one beast had latched onto the lieutenant's ankle, while another had grabbed his sword arm by the wrist. Beating against their backs with his pistol, Killard screamed to his men for help, but none moved. They only looked at the beasts, and then each walked calmly to the side and dropped into the sea. Micken joined them in the water, and green heads followed them out of sight.

Killard's yelling turned to screaming as a third serpent cleaved off the hand holding the pistol. He stumbled backward toward the edge of the deck.

Instincts that had once screamed at Samuel to intervene quieted now. He turned away from the scene, meeting the yellow eyes that never blinked.

As Samuel looked into the eyes, he felt the world fading away. In the background, a final shout and then a splash. It no longer mattered. His terror, his pain: all melted into peace and gold. He nodded.

***

Moments later, Samuel awoke. *Or perhaps an eternity has passed.* His eyes were met with darkness and pounding pressure. Cold, stinging saltwater surrounded him on all sides.

His instincts returning, Samuel started to kick for the surface, but he found his arms wrapped inside a coil of muscle. Writhing and gurgling, Samuel watched as the finned tail continued pushing him deeper into the murk. The progress had not slowed nor had the serpent's grip weakened, and his lungs had started to smolder from his struggling.

Still, there was one final path of resistance. Whatever the creature's designs, he did not have to go willingly. Samuel opened his mouth and let the pressure force the sea deep into his lungs. Black water gave way to a stiller, deeper darkness.

Find of the Century

By: Jeff Parsons

The schooner tilted low to starboard then slammed to a sudden stop with a jolting crunch.

Thomas Eagen's slight frame was propelled from his bunk, trajectory halted abruptly by the white cabin wall. He crashed head-first, leaving a blood splatter and runoff trickle oozing down the wall. Stunned, he realized something had happened to the ship. Something dreadful.

Feet sliding, floor listing about thirty degrees, Eagen hoisted himself upright. Through his socks, he felt the ship shudder, immobilized yet subject to further impacts. He held on.

Don't sink! his thoughts wailed. He heard multiple shouts from the deck above. He grabbed his shoes and put them on.

He yanked open the cabin door and pulled himself into the long corridor. The luxury yacht was 270 feet in length, so the crew quarters deck stretched like a racecourse ahead, making his walk to the closest set of ladder stairs a struggle.

The ship rolled, as if trying to shrug him loose, sending him into a metal hallway mirror etched with the oak-leafed frillery of the Duchaine Company crest. Looking back at him, he hardly recognized the face there: short grey hair, unkempt, blood oozing from a purple welt on the upper forehead, brown eyes open wide.

Pushing away from the wall and scrambling on the angled floor, two disparate sounds competed to alarm him as he reached the steep ladders: shouts from above and water from below. He took the steps quickly, lifting himself using the handrails, anxious to reach the outside air.

Finally, he reached the freeboard deck. The night was overcast with dense clouds. He could see the yellow safety lights spaced along the white composite walls shining softly onto lacquered, golden floorboards.

On the starboard side, the ship's green navigation lights showed frothy Atlantic Ocean waves smashing against the hull closer than they should. The deck was slippery from the spray of waves, but pushing from a wall guardrail, he managed to grab hold of the higher portside rail.

He moved to see the mayhem occurring at the bow. At the foredeck, the captain was struggling at the railing, using one of the long boathook poles to push against something in the water. It looked to be a dark gray, lumpy mass below the ocean's surface. Around it, the water rippled as if boiling with anger as many large, snake-like shapes writhed within.

Eagen realized that the shapes were actually the suckered limbs of a giant squid. *Oh my god,* he thought. *It's a kraken. The old legend is real.*

Darting among the tentacles of the giant squid were some sort of speedy creatures. The unusual animals leaped above the waves, greenish-blue and dolphin-like in their movements, yet their shapes were like nothing Eagen had ever seen before.

One of the tentacles of the kraken lashed out from the water, looped around the captain's body, and lifted him into the air. The limb pulled the captain below the churning water, all in one smooth motion, abruptly cutting off the man's agonized scream, almost as soon as it began.

The enormous end of a curled tentacle rose again. Along its suckered length, globs of white foam fell to the sea. The ship groaned, then inched forward, righting itself unexpectedly as the anemic wind in the sails pulled it away from the gigantic squid.

The ship creeped away from the danger. Overhead clouds parted momentarily to allow more moonlight to reveal the creature that the yacht was leaving behind. It was a sea monster by any reckoning, easily as long as the boat, its baleful head rolling above choppy waves, limbs flailing, reaching, and grasping.

The squid smashed into a school of those strange, dolphin-sized creatures that were equally bizarre, both discernable enough for lasting nightmares.

The clouds shifted again and darkness descended with a newfound creaking in the ship. From the front, the second mate and engineer raced past Eagen.

"Captain's gone!" the second mate, a man named Oswin, screamed as he ran. "Need to check the aft end!"

Eagen chased after him and found two men assessing a two-foot-wide swath that smashed deep into the open spaced lounging patio, only stopped by the battered engine below.

Oswin spread his fingers through his curly black hair. "Priest, you need to get this engine into high gear, fast!"

"It's damaged by that *thing*. I'll go see what I can do to get it cranked," the engineer said.

"Take him with you," Oswin said, pointing towards Eagen.

"What!" Eagen stuttered. "I'm an Accountant out of Halifax! What do I know about a yacht engine?"

"Not you. You're practically useless. Behind you. Him—Weinraub," Oswin said, indicating the deckhand. Oswin walked away with the engineer and deckhand. Eagen was left alone on the stern.

Eagen prayed that the squid monster was not chasing them. He risked a glance at the ocean, but it seemed empty of monsters. The flap of canvas high above reminded him that the ship was still sailing, even though the three sails barely fluttered in the mild wind.

The engine! Please let it get us out of here!

And then suddenly, one of the strange, greenish-blue creatures leaped from the water and landed on the deck. Eagen stopped in his tracks. The details were sketchy in the shadows between deck lights, but the slender creature had limbs and a long tail that flailed about like someone having a seizure from a head wound.

His throat constricted and his stomach squeezed as if he'd soon vomit. He felt completely overwhelmed.

The deckhand Riley was suddenly in front of him.

"Help me throw it overboard!" Eagen yelled.

"Are you really that stupid?" Riley said. "I've never seen anything like this thing. It could be a new species of some kind. We could make some money off of it once we get to shore."

"*If* we get to shore," Eagen said.

"I'm a betting man," Riley said.

"Bad idea," Eagen said. "You're on your own."

Eagen raced away and went down through the aft cabin access door. He entered the aft stairs, amazed at the damage inflicted by the kraken. Burned grease lingered in the air of the engine deck. Water sloshed over his socks and wicked up the bottom of his khakis. The storage deck below was taking on water and flooding upward.

When Eagen approached the engine room, Oswin and the deckhand were listening to Priest as he secured the bulkhead door, sealing off the destroyed engine room on this level, even though water still cascaded into the room.

With the door closed, the noise level dropped considerably. It was easier to hear Priest's dour words. "...diesel's a no-go, propeller shaft snapped, flooding faster than the pumps can handle, slowing us down..."

Oswin cursed. "Sails still working but not much wind." He glanced towards Eagen, then spoke to Priest. "Still have electrical, but for how long?"

"I'll check the generator room," Priest answered. "This whole deck has tears in the hull. Worse below."

Weinraub spoke from behind Eagen, "Sounds like we're fucked."

Priest said, "It's time for an SOS."

Oswin tugged on his scraggly beard. "One has already been sent. Now find out the situation on the generator. Seal what you can. Give me a status. I'll be in the radio room talking with Duchaine."

Weinraub said, "Oh, wait, Oswin. I saw one of those leaping dolphin things, uh…whatever it is…it's certainly not a dolphin. It somehow landed on the deck. Riley took care of it. He locked it up in the business suite."

Oswin barked, "I can't worry about that now. You said that Riley locked it up. Fine. Priest, get to work!"

Everyone left him. Again.

Eagen was alone in a corridor of a ship taking on water. Farther away from the water would be better, he thought. The business suite was two floors up. He considered going to see the dolphin-like creature. After all, it was just a fish…well, a water mammal anyway, and it was locked up. He hesitated for a moment in indecision. He felt useless.

Eagen wondered if he could do something about the sea creature. He had read books all his life…maybe he could somehow identify it. It would make him feel less useless. He finally decided.

His muscles ached as he slogged up to the next deck. There was a cabin that had its door left open. *That one.*

Eagen was surprised to see Riley inside. He would have thought that everyone would be trying to fix the ship.

Riley sat in a plush wingback chair close to the door, facing into the large room. He glanced at Eagen sideways. "You won't believe what we found. No, let me rephrase that. You chickened out. What *I* found."

"Where is it?"

"It's in the water."

"In the jacuzzi? Uh, I mean the spa?" Eagen edged closer to the water.

Just below the water surface, a greenish-blue hand was chained to the silver-colored support bar on the entry steps. Diaphanous webbed skin spread between clawed fingertips.

Edging closer to the aqua-tiled spa rim, Eagen saw that it was almost humanoid, with a streamlined head. It floated face down, the water ebbing around gills where ears should have been. Spiny fins went from the crest of the head down its back, to a drooping dorsal fin, before extending further along a long tail, tucked between a pair of legs. It had dark, cobalt-blue skin on the backside with a lighter blue-green underneath. There was no hair or fur, but no scales either.

"It's not awake, right?" Eagen asked.

"Nope."

"Any idea what it is?"

"Surely something never discovered before. Not mammal, but

not fish. If we can get it back to port, we'll all be famous. This here critter is the find of the century. Worth a fortune."

And then the sea-creature woke up.

The creature's huge
forward-facing eyes suddenly peered from the spa lip. It brought down a mouthful of sharp, conical teeth on the metal chain with a grinding, rending screech that had no effect upon the high-tensile steel.

Eagen jumped back in fright.

"Calm down," Riley said. "It can't get out of the restraints. I put them on it myself."

The creature stopped trying to free itself as suddenly as it had started. Lowering its trapped hand, it stared down its captors with deep eyes that didn't blink. Slowly, it slipped back under the spa water, chain rattling along the pole, its manacled hand still close to the surface.

Riley was still calmly seated in the chair. "You know, maybe those critters weren't being attacked by that kraken. Maybe *they* were attacking *it*."

Eagen was horrified to imagine that any being that had the guts to attack a giant squid was in the same room as him. "Look! It's changing!"

Within seconds, the creature's color drained from its body, making it possible to see through it to the background. Parts of its body, eyes, skeleton, and stomach remained, albeit almost invisible as well.

The lights dimmed, then went out.

Darkness.

"God damn it, the generator must be going out," Riley said. "We should have battery backup in a minute. Stay here." Riley's footsteps stumbled off into the darkness.

Eagen's throat constricted, making it difficult to swallow. His pulse quickened with fear. He had to get out of there! He turned to find the door but couldn't see it.

And then a small emergency light clicked on above the door. Feeble as it was, the lurid red illumination was infinitely better than the darkness. Eagen almost cried with relief. He ventured a glance back at the creature.

It had risen above the water again; so quietly. *Was it readying to attack? Or maybe it didn't want to startle me.*

It studied its cuff and chain, then looked sideways at him. Its eyes grew wider, each the size of grapefruits, as it cocked its head. He'd seen that behavior before from his golden retriever, as if saying, "What now?" True to form, it exhaled through a tiny nose with a long exasperated snorting whistle. He half-expected it to wag its tail.

It's intelligent. Kinda cute in its own way.

He yelped like a startled puppy when a pounding echoed on the hull below decks. His eyes darted across the floor, tracking the sound's erratic movement. More pounding from diverse locations with accompanying sharp cracking.

What is that?

Suddenly he realized that sounds were not just emanating from the floor, but from the sea-creature as well. A deep clicking purr was coming from it. Its body had returned to the bluish-green color, except repeating bands of white slowly covered its body from head to tail. Its clawed hands writhed, almost in sublime pleasure, maybe in anticipation of an attack? Unbidden, he visualized those cold wiry hands wrapped around his throat—would he bleed out first or simply choke to death? And those teeth…

Wait! Maybe it's reacting to perceived danger and not to me personally.

"Eagen!" he heard from the hallway, causing his heartbeat to skip and the creature to dive below the water surface, invisible again.

The deckhand stood at the cabin door, both hands spread against the upper frame for support, breath ragged. It was

Matson, an American with fiery red hair and a beard that reminded Eagen of braided Viking warriors of old. "Rescue ship on its way. Frikkin company wants the creature safe, and Oswin—"

"Rescue! What? Are you saying the ship's going down?"

"Where the hell've you been? Haven't you heard all that screaming? We've lost the captain. Everything's shorted out 'cept emergency power; engine's crushed, taking on water…for fuck's sake, Eagen, get a clue. Oswin wants us on deck!"

Arriving at the freeboard deck, he was surprised to see that the wall and floorboards were stained with a spray of sticky fluid. *Blood!* A nearby rectangular life raft package, not activated, was askew on a wall bracket.

Whose blood?

More thumps upon the ship, moving forward along the hull.

Oswin came around the curve of the forward superstructure at a run. Short of breath, he said, "Where were you! Matson, take port, Eagen, starboard. I'll go to the bow. Shout out if you see anything." With that, Oswin ran to the bow.

Gathering up his courage, Eagen forced himself to the starboard railing and held on for dear life. In the clouded, opaque light, he noticed that the ship crept forward in the water about as fast as a man could walk, and the churning sea seemed closer than before. They were taking on more water than he'd thought!

He wasn't sure, but he thought he saw speeding blurs flash by in the frothy black water. *Those creatures put more holes in the hull?*

He looked to Oswin for guidance. Oswin bent over the bow's starboard railing, head jerking in surprise to track the cracking sounds. Standing, Oswin moved towards the port side. Suddenly Oswin was catapulted overboard! He was lost in a mass of limbs rising from the depths.

Eagen gripped the railing tightly, howling in surprise when he realized that the kraken was back. Its maw now encased the bow of the ship.

Two deckhands sprinted forward with boathook poles. The swift crunching smack from a tentacle sent them spinning lifeless into the ocean. A serrated bone spear bounced off the tentacle and skidded along the deck.

The dolphin-creatures had returned to the fight. There weren't as many of them as before. Their trilling squeals penetrated his head as they attacked and died.

Shaken, Eagen pushed away from the railing, realizing he could be killed. He backstepped to the relative safety of the cabin deck.

Matson was already there, almost hyperventilating, "You see that?"

Eagen could only grimace like a death's head skull; words eluding him.

Matson motioned for him to quickly follow. "We're in a shitload of trouble! Oswin said a company ship is outbound from Halifax. That's too far away. We won't be afloat much longer. I'm going to send a general SOS. Something should be closer."

"What?" Eagen asked, still not comprehending the situation completely.

Matson griped, "We need to check on that thing we caught. Come with me. Goddamn Duchaine doesn't want anything to happen to our guest, even with all that's going on. They're claiming it as salvage or whatnot." When they arrived at the room, he said, "Good. It's still here."

The creature seemed to be standing erect, cuffed hand held aloft to the uppermost arc of the spa's support rail. Fully colored, its gills and flat mouth fluttered with each breath. It watched them with calm, unblinking eyes while the pounding racket echoed throughout the ship, the kraken becoming far more aggressive, as if demanding to be let in.

"Why don't we let it go?" Eagen asked.

"Because I suspect the others know we have it. I believe that our having this creature is the only thing stopping the rest of those monsters from coming aboard and overwhelming us." He watched it with an expression akin to disgusted fascination. "That is, once they're done with the kraken…if they win. If not, the kraken finishes us off. Suck it all, we are truly screwed."

"But the ship is sinking, so we don't have much time anyway. Why keep it chained up?"

"You know, they said you were crazy. Don't prove it. Stay here. Watch our guest. I'll go make the SOS." Matson abruptly bolted from the room.

Crazy is right. Not getting me out there. He couldn't hear any more of the crew screams, but judging from the squealing outside, the battle kept on raging. A rasping grind vibrated in the hull, traveling up from his feet to his tense back.

Balance unsteady, Eagen plopped down on a chair, uncertain what to do, the inevitable closing in.

A persistent beating began on the nearby hull at the waterline. The creature watched his eyes flinch slightly with each attack. Curiously, it began to mimic his reactions. Or, it had the same feelings of dread.

The creature's kin were undoubtedly taking terrible losses. *Maybe it could sense that. If the kraken wins… I'm a dead man.* His fists clenched. *Maybe the creature could help?*

An explosive blowout breech occurred on the other side of the ship in the lower decks. Loose items in the room slid on the floor to the hallway door and wall. The ship lurched with a teeth-rattling shake.

If it's the last thing I do, I have to free this creature. It'll be stuck in chains if the ship goes down. And we need all the help we can get! Screw Duchaine!

Eagen stood, stumbling, floor at a tilt, reminding him of when all this insanity had started. He remembered seeing a key in the room's kitchenette. *There!* On the marble countertop near the fridge! Maybe it fit the lock holding the creature's chains together? He scooped it up and turned towards the creature, movement jolted to a halt—it was observing him with the intense focus of a predator. And its color drew his breath away. The captive was a stark coral color, as visibly bright as possible, upright, one hand still chained to the spa support bar.

The key! I have to try.

The creature's eyes blinked once as Eagen, trembling, slowly approached it. He held up the key and pointed to the lock, nodding with what he hoped was a reassuring manner. With emotions as obscure as light at the bottom of the sea, the creature remained motionless while he opened the lock and disengaged it from the chains wrapped around the pole.

Task complete, he withdrew to the kitchenette, careful not to get between the creature and the exit door, where its freedom awaited.

The captive creature watched him intensely as if judging his intent and future movements.

Reaching up with its free hand, its delicately clawed fingers pulled the chain length through the cuff holding its wrist. Both chain and cuff fell with a splash into the water.

A short, high-pitched squeal resonated from the creature. It opened its mouth and some kind of sonar-communication reached into Eagen's brain like tickling fingers, intensified by an answering response from afar.

The creature's color reverted back to blue-green as it sized up Eagen. Without a further look, it left the room in a loping gait, thin body hunched over, spiny finned tail held aloft for balance, long and dexterous like a sassy cat. The creature's footsteps splashed away.

Eagen, who'd been holding his breath, exhaled with relief.

The ship creaked, tilting more to port, while he waited, mind wandering in a panic. Unknown time passed. It could've been a minute or ten minutes or a half-hour, he didn't know, he'd been stuck in a morass of uncontrolled worrying until his thoughts ended with *if they win, maybe they'll leave me alone.*

There was no more trilling from the dolphin-creatures. The battle seemed to have ended. *I'm still alive!*

A sharp pop and something gave way deep in the ship's keel.

The kraken!

The ship lifted sharply but suddenly it was pulled down to port...sinking!

Eagen struggled to walk on the steep slant to the door. He saw that chilling water was now everywhere. It was up to his shins and rising quickly in the hallway. It overflowed from the jagged slice in the rear and from some new leaks jetting from the closed cabin doors in the front.

The murky water left a residue of inky stains on his khaki pants by the time he pulled himself up the stairs to the main deck cabins.

Need a lifeboat, he thought, realizing he felt far less disturbed than he should be at the imminent sinking of the boat.

On the way outside, one of the cabin doors popped open; once immaculate, the room was now in disarray, a keen reflection of current events.

The water was swirling halfway up the stairs he'd just used.

He grabbed onto the corridor support railing as the deck suddenly shifted again, this time righting itself close to level. As he ventured outside, the floorboards shivered, much like him, feeling the slight wind hit his soaked pants.

The moon hid behind scattered clouds, but he could still see the life raft package partially disengaged from the wall mount, hanging askew, nearby blood spatter smeared by the sea spray.

His head shifted about, looking around him, seeing no kraken. No creatures. No shipmates.

The ship's forward superstructure was a shredded mess of composite and metal. The remaining front of the ship stretched unnaturally as if grabbed, twisted, and snapped off completely, leaving a gaping hole. The bow was gone.

Water surged up the stairs inside the cabin deck and ocean waves lapped at the main deck. The ship was going down fast.

Trying not to overthink about what was going on, he focused on tugging the life raft package from the wall, unsuccessful until he lifted the covering bag's strap handle caught in the mount. Releasing the bag, which he realized was surprisingly heavy, it fell into the water pooling on the deck. He couldn't see the instructions, only a big yellow arrow pointed to a rip cord.

Pull it here? He wasn't sure if he'd need to do it now or throw it overboard then pull the cord.

The point became moot as the water rose above his shoes, soon to set him swimming.

Upper teeth pressed into his lower lip, he pulled the cord. The loud pop of the raft expanding from the carry bag caused him to step away with a stuttering heartbeat.

The raft was fully inflated by the time the water reached his knees. He entered it, careful not to overturn it, feeling isolated in its middle—it must've been built for six people. Inside, tied with a nylon rope, sat a smaller red rectangular package and two small paddles.

Need to get away! The ship's sinking might pull him under if he was caught in the down draft. He slid across the rubber bottom and, hands fumbling, unlatched one of the paddles. Scooting to the side, he began paddling. Using the plastic oar was highly ineffective, but a rush of water geysering from the cabin deck sent his raft cascading over the submerged rail and spinning away from the ship with a drenching splash. Swiping away stinging saltwater from his eyes, he scooted to the new backside of the raft and paddled as fast as he could.

He glanced back. The bridge structure disappeared before his squinting eyes, and with a great release of trapped air, his last hope of security sank beneath the waves.

The raft drifted backward despite his frantic paddling. Luckily, the pull eased off to nothing by the time the raft entered the sinking location, surrounded by bobbling debris such as seat cushions, assorted clothes, a beverage cooler, and many other loose items. Eagen turned away when he saw a floating body.

Choppy waves, obscure as obsidian glass, rocked and slapped his bobbing raft. The pontoons filled with pressurized air were the only thing protecting him from sinking as well. Surrounded by water, childhood memories returned unbidden: he'd fallen off a tube float into a river current that dragged him down, choking on water even as his father rescued him. He hated the water ever since.

Again and again, he did whatever Duchaine asked, but this was ridiculous. On board, his purpose had been to perform accounting for the ship's purchasing in Italy, upgrades in England, and ongoing operations and maintenance, while traveling to Halifax. *What was I thinking, coming out to sea?*

The embrace of the ocean chilled him, and his clothes were saturated, so there was no chance of getting warm. Smothering darkness was all around; he couldn't recognize details of the debris further than thirty feet away.

Matson said he'd send out a general SOS. Had he managed to complete that call? He sighed, almost sobbing with despair. So many lives lost. Scared witless, he was adrift in a foreboding, merciless sea.

Moonlight appeared. He saw no more shipwreck bubbles in the water. The graveyard of floating debris marking the location already being dispersed by the relentless low rolling waves.

And then he saw them.

Moonlight reflected off a set of eyes just below the surface. Many sets of eyes. They were spread out at varying distances, some as close as an arm's reach from the raft's edge. The eyes surrounded him.

The creatures! No no no no!

Heads crested above the rippling waves. The creatures watched him with an eerie still silence, possibly over a hundred of them.

He heard a tiny moan, then realized the sound had come from his own lips. He tried to swallow but couldn't. Sweat broke out, making the chills worse.

A dot of light appeared on the horizon, almost as far away as the stars above. *Rescue ship? Too late.* He squeezed his eyes shut, awaiting the inescapable attack.

They were quiet, so quiet; he heard no approaching noise. Rapid heartbeats passed. Nothing.

Cracking an eye open, he saw that the creatures were gone. Except for one. One that had a discoloration on its forehead.

Smaller than most of the others, it nodded to him, then slipped beneath the waves.

He'd been spared.

He had observed the sea-creature in the spa and felt it had intelligence. He had saved it. Perhaps it was capable of empathy.

The light from the rescue ship on the horizon was closing in, but it seemed excruciatingly slow. It would be a long wait; plenty of time to think about what had happened and what he'd say about it. Maybe some things were best left unsaid.

Among the Waves of Time

By: Charles Reis

Hallie lay on a beach towel on the deck of a forty-foot sport fishing boat as waves gently sloshed against its sides. Wearing sunglasses and a red bikini, the twenty-nine-year-old smiled while absorbing the light. As it peeked through the clouds, the sun glared down, creating sparkling crystals that dotted the water.

A shadow appeared over her. "You're going to get skin cancer if you keep that up," Phil said. An open Hawaiian shirt showcased his muscular body, revealing a U.S. Marine logo tattoo on his upper right chest. Blue shorts finished off his outfit. He held two beer bottles and handed one to Hallie.

She placed the bottle down. "It's worth it! I'm sick of the cold New England weather." Every year, they took a trip to Miami after Christmas for a week of fishing, a hobby they both loved.

He sat next to her and took a sip. "Maybe we should move to Florida. The security firm has several branches in the state I could transfer to, and I'm sure you'll find plenty of schools in need of a music teacher. That way you can get all the sun you want, and you'll have a longer growing season for your garden."

She smiled. "Nah, you'd miss your buddies at work, and I'd miss my students and church family." She sat up. A calming wind cooled her warm skin. "We're not getting much fishing done. Where are we?"

He rubbed her back. "Northeast of San Salvador… inside the Bermuda Triangle!" He snickered.

She ripped off her sunglasses and looked at him. "You took me into the Bermuda Triangle?" She had watched many programs and read several books that dealt with the strange events that surrounded this area. Theories ranging from freak storms to alien spaceships to Atlantis were associated with the disappearances. Although she wanted to remain logical, she couldn't help but worry they would fall victim to the Triangle as well, like so many other planes and ships.

Phil raised his eyebrows. "Come on. You don't believe in that mystical shit?"

"Honestly, I'm not sure. I mean, how do you explain all those ships and planes that vanished?"

He rubbed her shoulder. "Peaches, that's just sensationalist nonsense. Trust me." He glanced down at Hallie's beer bottle. "Hey, you're not drinking?"

"I'm giving it up. At least for nine months."

Phil tilted his head and had a blank look. After several seconds, his mouth barged open. "You're pregnant!"

She nodded. He wrapped his arms around her waist. With flushed cheeks, Hallie closed her eyes and squeezed him.

He let go and touched her stomach. "How far along?"

"Ten weeks."

He grabbed her hands and helped her to her feet. "Can't wait to tell my mom. She's been begging for grandkids." He spun Hallie around as if they were dancing.

"Good job, momma's boy."

He laughed. "You know it."

After the spin, she placed her arms over his shoulders. "I wanted to tell you at a special moment." She smiled, thinking about all that God had given her. Then she glanced out over the water. "And nothing's more special than being in the Bermuda Triangle."

Phil gave her puppy-dog eyes. "We can head back, it's only two hours to land." She nodded, then gave him a kiss while caressing his short red hair with her fingers.

A cold wind brushed over her skin. Lightning flashed, followed by the rumble of thunder. They looked north; orange clouds rolled in, pushing away the blue skies. The waves grew and smashed against the boat.

"Fuck a duck! We better go, that storm don't look right." Phil rushed to the boat's wheel under the hardtop. A low whine resonated from the engine as he turned the ignition key.

As goosebumps covered her flesh, she wrapped her arms around herself. "I hate being right," she said to herself. The clouds quickly overtook the sky, shrouding the area in a darker shade. The wind tossed her black hair. Cloud-to-ocean lightning created a jagged electric forest that surrounded the vessel. The drum-like rumbles and booms forged a war-like melody. She tasted the saliva flooding her throat as the anxiety increased.

Her body trembled as she grabbed the railing to keep her balance as the boat rocked. Far above their spot, the clouds rotated into a whirlpool so large it could easily swallow their entire location. The vortex seemed to stretch upward for miles. The fear that their boat would be swallowed by the clouds entered her mind.

"Get us outta here!" she pleaded.

A whine emitted from the engine. With each passing second, it grew louder, turning into a piercing disturbance. Phil let go of the key and took a deep breath before trying again. The engine still wailed. He pounded his fist on the wheel. "Get your life jacket on!"

Orange light shined from all directions. The glow grew brighter than the sun and encased the boat. Hallie's scream ripped through her throat like a vine of thorns. She squeezed her eyes shut. She covered her ears with her hands over the loud booms pounding on her eardrums. Her heart slammed against her chest to the point she thought it would rip through. She gripped her hands together in prayer. Like smoke in the wind, the light vanished.

She opened her eyes. The bright sun greeted her, although she found it strange with the absence of clouds. The boat relaxed in the calm waters. Hot sticky air brought sweat to her skin, but a gentle breeze fondled and cooled it. No one moved for a moment.

"I've never seen a storm like that." With his hand on his head, he focused his eyes on the sky.

After she opened the cooler, she grabbed a bottle of water and then sat in the passenger seat. "Can we go?" As she drank, the water soothed her burning throat.

Phil placed his hands on her shoulders to rub them. "Peaches, it's over. Everything's fine now."

"Great… but I still want to get out of here." She took another sip. Water spilled from the bottle's open neck because of her shaking hands.

After nodding, Phil returned to the wheel. When he turned the key, the engine revved up. Hallie wanted to cheer at that sound.

Phil tapped on a small screen on the control panel once, then twice. After the third time, he shook his head. "Fuck a duck. The GPS is out."

"Great! This is like a horror movie!"

"Chill, everything else works. I know where we are. We'll get back with no problem." After he grabbed the wheel, he glanced to his left. "Peaches, come look at this!"

She squeezed the empty bottle and tossed it to the floor. After she stood up, she crossed her arms. "What?"

He pointed. "A shark." Looking like a black blob the size of a car, the shark glided in the light blue water around fifty feet from the boat. The tip of its top fin broke the surface. Its swinging tail was visible.

"I wanna get a video of it, then we'll head right back."

"Fine, but hurry." While Phil searched his bag by the captain's chair, Hallie focused on the animal swimming parallel to the vessel. She uncrossed her arms and filled her lungs with salty air. Her muscles relaxed. Except for in an aquarium, she'd never seen a real shark before. "Nature at its best," she whispered to herself. She kept thinking how nice it would be to take this shark video and add the theme to *Jaws* over it. The idea of playing it for her students had her smiling.

Phil stood next to her holding up a tablet. He tapped the screen to record. "Everyone back home will love this. I'm seeing a shark, I've experienced a freak-ass storm, and I'm going to be a dad. What could make this day any better?"

Hallie reached up and squeezed the back of his neck. "A happy wife back on land." She smiled, and he rolled his eyes.

Underneath the shark, a large dark mass formed. Within seconds, it grew twice as big as the fish. Hallie stared at it as she wrapped her arm around Phil's waist. The water burst into a geyser when a gigantic dark gray creature breached the surface. The shark dangled in the mouth of a lizard-shaped head with small black eyes. Small scales covered its skin.

As the creature launched further into the air, it exposed four long, thin flippers and a white-colored underbelly. It let out a deep trombone-like moan as it dove headfirst back into the sea. Its long tail with a crescent-shaped fin submerged back into the water after it.

The high waves drenched the deck and rocked the boat. Hallie screamed and stumbled a few feet back. The creature propelled itself under the boat, turning the waters black around the vessel. Ripples formed on the sea surface as the ominous shadow moved past them.

Hallie screamed. Phil dropped the tablet and placed his arms around her. He rubbed her back as she laid her head on his shuddering chest. Her fingers dug into his flesh.

"Shit. What the fuck kind of whale was that?" he asked. The shadow dwindled in size as it propelled away. It shrank until it finally vanished. Only the blue remained.

"I think it's time to go home!" Tears joined the saltwater that soaked her face. She pressed her eyes shut. They held each other until the boat steadied. Thinking about the animal, she believed it looked similar to the water dinosaur in *Jurassic World*.

"You don't have to ask me again."

***

For over an hour, Phil piloted the boat. During that time, neither spoke. Jules Massenet's *Meditation* played from a radio to drown out the motor's buzzing. Its melody calmed Hallie, allowing her to place the past events into the back of her mind.

Hallie sat in a cushioned chair in the back of the boat wearing a long white t-shirt with a Pomeranian puppy printed on it. The wind whipped her hair into a frenzy. The further away from the Bermuda Triangle they went, the calmer she became.

To keep her mind away from past events, she used a pen to write on a small yellow notepad. On the top of the page, she wrote "BOY" and "GIRL" with several names under each. Under the "BOY" she circled the name "ROGER", her dad's name, while under "GIRL" she circled "ELIZABETH", Phil's mother's name. While she figured she was jumping the gun by doing this, it made her happy. She had only told Phil, but the anticipation of telling their families had her heart beating fast.

She stood up and wiped the sweat off her forehead. "Geez, it sure got even hotter." She moved in closer to Phil and placed her hand on his shoulder. He didn't answer. His body remained motionless. His grip on the wheel turned his knuckles white. She looked at him. "You okay?"

He idled the engine and let the boat drift. He shook his head. "This isn't right."

Hallie noticed on the horizon a green landmass with distant cloud-covered mountains. Bright white beaches aligned the shores and flocks of large birds circled above. The natural beauty of the Caribbean never ceased to amaze her. The birds, however, were larger than any she had ever seen.

Straightening her back, she smirked. "Hey, we're almost there." She rubbed his back.

"We shouldn't be. We still have an hour to travel." His body remained still as if posing for a photo. His chest swiftly rose up and down. "Also, that doesn't look like San Salvador or any place in the Bahamas. Fuck, it's not even Florida."

"Maybe that storm took us off course. Maybe that's Cuba."

"Maybe." He grabbed a beer bottle and took a long drink.

Hallie's stomach fluttered. She tightened her mouth and gripped her fingers while sitting in the passenger seat. She stared at the land while barely blinking. If she wasn't pregnant, she would have gulped down several bottles of beer.

Phil looked at a screen. "Fuck a duck. The GPS is still out." He paused, then he grabbed the radio microphone. "Mayday, Mayday, Mayday. This is the Peachy Queen. We are lost. Our GPS isn't working… we're close to land, but I don't know where we are. Someone, please answer. Over." Over a minute passed, but only static emanated from the radio.

"I say again, Mayday, Mayday, Mayday. This is the Peachy Queen." Phil said in a rattled voice.

As he repeated the message, Hallie rummaged through the bag and retrieved her phone. She tossed it back into the bag when she noticed it had no bars. She placed her elbows on her knees and her hands on her forehead. As the freak storm played out in her mind, she remembered a theory about the Bermuda Triangle that vortexes caused the disappearances.

The boat jolted. Bottles and other items crashed to the floor. Splashes of water flung into the air from the right side. Phil lost his grip on the microphone as he grabbed the wheel. Hallie tumbled to the floor and hit the side of her head. She pressed her finger to the sharp pain in her temple.

A loud boom occurred, followed by a horn-like moaning. The vessel launched two feet to the right, crashing back into the water seconds later. Water rained down. Phil smashed into the floor.

Hallie groaned and curled into a fetal position. While saying a prayer, she wrapped her arms around her stomach. From the age of eight, she attended Christ Church in Arkham regularly, becoming the music director years later. Prayer was the natural thing to do.

The moaning played in short tunes, intensifying with each play. Another boom accompanied a boisterous crack. The engine stalled as the boat jumped three feet to the left. From the corner of her eye, Hallie spotted a dark blue, fat tail rise from the water. It rushed back under the surface.

Phil crawled to Hallie and wrapped his arm over her back. The vessel received another hefty bump, followed by another cracking sound. The boat bounced in the water. As the sky appeared to move back and forth, Hallie took his hand and squeezed it.

The boat ceased rocking after what felt like an eternity.

A minute of silence passed. "Stay there," he whispered. Phil slowly stood. He took small steps towards the side and stopped a foot away from it. He slouched forward and looked over it, then hustled to the other side and peered over the railing. "There are cracks in the hull."

She stumbled to her feet. "How much time do we have?"

"Ten minutes if we're lucky." He turned the key. The engine let out a short whine before sputtering into a grind. When he tried again, the engine achieved a final whimpering act. He kicked the control panel. "Fuck a duck! The water's already in the inner board. It's going nowhere."

Hallie rushed to the chairs and retrieved two life jackets. She and Phil put them on.

"Can we make it to land?" She didn't know what kind of aquatic life decided to tango with their boat, but that mystery had her heart throbbing. Although she'd loved to have an alternative to getting into the water, she knew they had no choice. They were ending up in the water regardless, so they had to act fast. With sweaty palms, she clicked the waist belt.

He clicked his. "It's just over a half mile away. The tide is low, and we're good swimmers, so we should be fine. I just hope that pissed-off whale is gone." He looked at her. "I'm so glad you know Spanish."

"Me too." Studying music in Spain not only allowed her to learn about the rich heritage of the country's music, but she quickly learned the language. Looking at the land, Hallie took some relief knowing she had that skill if it was needed.

While taking long, drawn breaths, she hoped it was just a whale that had hit them.

A splash erupted from the waters and something with dark gray skin rose. Phil grabbed Hallie's shoulders and pushed her to her knees between the seats. "Stay down," he whispered. He placed his shivering arm over her back.

A large creature resembling a snake examined the vessel as it towered from the water. Its sofa-sized head rested on a neck that stretched to the height of a two-story house. The sun's rays glistened in its black eyes. It opened its pointed jaw to reveal rows of long, thin teeth.

She covered her mouth, staring at the creature as it let out another horn-like moan. She repeated to herself that she had lost her mind, or was stuck in a nightmare.

The creature tilted its head side-to-side and snapped its jaw. It bit down on the stern and the boat shook. Then it pulled back and swayed its head.

"Don't move, it hasn't noticed us," Phil whispered into her ear.

A beer bottle rolled from under the captain's seat as the stern lowered. Its drumming noise attracted the creature. The bottle slammed into another seat near the back. The creature moved in closer and sniffed it. It jerked its body and a tail sprouted up. Water showered the deck as the boat jolted. It shifted its attention towards the couple. It maintained its stare, but it didn't react to their presence. Instead, it just remained still, like it had become a statue.

The couple held their breaths. Hallie's eyes watered. Her body trembled while she struggled to hold the air in. Each second felt like an hour. The fight to keep from exhaling drained her energy. She knew that if she breathed, this creature would notice and attack.

The animal turned its head away. The couple exhaled.

"That can't be a dinosaur," she whispered.

"I don't know what it is, but we gotta get the fuck out of here," Phil said, stretching his arm towards his seat and retrieving his flare gun. "I'll distract it, then we'll haul ass to the shore. Just swim as fast as you can and don't worry about me." He caressed her cheek. "I have two that I'm more concerned about."

Water reached over the side of the stern and more bottles rolled down. With no other options, Hallie knew they had to do this insane act. She frowned and wiped the sweat off her face. The idea of a possible life without Phil made her stomach turn. She cupped his cheeks and pulled him in closer. She pressed her lips to his as his sweaty cheek drenched her hands.

"Just... make it yourself," she said.

"I love you, Peaches."

"I love you more."

He leaned back. "Ready?"

She took a deep breath and her heart accelerated like a drum. She whispered a count to three, then nodded.

Phil pointed the gun at the creature. "Semper fi, motherfucker!" He pulled the trigger and the flare traveled across the air. The blaze collided with the animal's neck. It snapped his head, and it cried like a trumpet blast. Then it retreated below the surface.

"Go! Go!" Phil screamed.

With adrenaline pumping through her veins, Hallie lunged off the floor. Her mouth had filled with pressure from clamping her jaw. She grunted as she leaped onto the boat's gunwale, bounced off it, then plunged into the sea. The warm waters soothed her skin as the race began. She kicked up water and swung her arms overhead to push herself along. The water in her ears generated a muffled hum. Water shot up her nose. She coughed and her nostrils hurt. She looked back and forth from deep waters to the high sky. Her arms and legs burned.

She stopped and spun her head around. "Phil!"

"Don't stop!" he shouted from several yards away. His body bounced in the waves. In the distance, the bow of the boat pointed upward, with the stern submerged.

She returned to her swim. Her lungs strained from each stroke. Saltwater gagged her airway. Mild cramps seized her legs, but she ignored the pain. She played within her mind,

Beethoven's *Moonlight Sonata*. With her mind focused on that, she suppressed her fear, which allowed her to swim without a hitch.

Hallie halted again, wanting to be sure Phil was close. Wiping the hair from her face, she searched for him. An endless ocean lay before her, but nothing else. Her panting and shaking increased.

"Phil! Phil!" Her cries cracked her voice. Her words tore through her throat. She flicked her head back and forth. "Phil!" The swishing of water and the whispers of wind traveling over the surface greeted her back. She spun her body in a circle. The restless waters doused her face. She begged God to show her where he went, repeating the prayer over and over in her mind.

Three yards away, the creature's neck rose from the sea with Phil between its jaws. Its teeth punctured his body. The sun blazed like a halo from behind its head. Her husband's head, arms, and legs swayed as blood rained down. Several seconds passed, and then it submerged and vanished from sight.

The intensity of Hallie's screams scratched her vocal cords. Her eyelids twitched and her muscles convulsed. Terror devoured her conscience. The pain strangled her heart, but his words kept repeating.

"Just swim as fast as you can."

She returned to swimming. Her arms and legs moved slower with each passing second, but her thoughts filled up with her special moments with Phil. She remembered the day they met at a coffee shop in Arkham, Massachusetts, after communicating through Tinder. He had arrived in his Marine uniform, looking very attractive. They talked for hours. The day he returned from a one-year deployment in the Middle East erupted in her mind as well. She had held up a welcome-home sign at Logan Airport, but when she saw him, she dropped it and ran to him. There was his marriage proposal at an orchard in New Hampshire. The sun peeked out through the clouds as she picked her favorite fruit, peaches. Every summer she did it, bringing Phil along. That day,

Phil got on his knees while presenting a diamond ring on top of a peach. With tears in her eyes, she dropped her bag of peaches, wrapped her arms around him, and they fell to the ground.

The memories brought her sorrow but fueled her swim. *"Just swim as fast as you can."* Faster and faster she went. Water entered her mouth and the salt battered her tongue. Her heart pumped blood through her limbs and muscles to fuel them to work overtime.

The tides forced her along until her hands and feet scratched the ground. Hallie wobbled getting to her feet. She glanced up. A dark tropical forest with four-story-tall trees waited a few yards away. In the background, green mountains stretched into the clouds. Chirps, buzzes, and squawks from the jungle joined the music of the ocean.

She walked with a slouched back and lowered head. Several small waves hit her legs and pushed her forward. Her arms dangled like willow boughs. A minute later, her bare feet touched the hot sand. After several steps, she collapsed onto her hands and knees.

With her drenched hair draped around her face, she stared at her wedding ring with the engagement one below it. Her crying accompanied the shaking in her hands. The view of Phil's body in the air as his blood hit the water replayed in her mind.

She closed her eyes and shouted. "Help! Anyone! Help!" The strength of her scream surpassed the power she gave when playing the saxophone. She lifted her head and the sun warmed her skin. She repeated her cries in Spanish. *"Ayuadame! Ayuadame!"*

Long, heavy breathing, resembling air flowing through a tunnel changed into a deep, rumbling moan, as it came from a distance to her left. Her heart pulsated and she felt every pump of blood. She held her breath and dug her fingers into the sand. Although she didn't want to, she turned her head and raised her eyelids.

Twenty yards away, where the beach greeted the forest, a Tyrannosaurus stopped in its place. The fifteen-foot tall creature kept its reddish-brown body parallel to the ground and its long tail extended. It watched Hallie using its yellow eyes. Its chest rose, forging the airflow sound. When it decompressed, the rumbling moan commenced.

Hallie's stomach fluttered to the point where she thought she'd vomit. Sweat covered every inch of her face. She slowly rose to her feet while maintaining her stare into its eyes. Tremors erupted over every inch of her body. She took a small step backwards.

The dinosaur fluttered its nostrils. It stepped forward and swung its tail to the back. Loud booms accompanied the rumbling ground. The Tyrannosaurus stopped and tilted its head.

Although her mouth twitched while hanging open, she made only a short gasp. Her shaking arms remained at her sides. She took two steps backwards. Her eyes watered as they were dry from not blinking. "Was it true that the Tyrannosaurus saw only movement?" she wondered.

It took another step forward, leaving a footprint in the sand. The claws dug into the ground once its foot slammed down. It opened its mouth and revealed rows of foot-long teeth. A deep bellow spewed out as its thick pinkish-white tongue vibrated.

A scream punched its way up Hallie's throat. Frantic thoughts about surviving the surreal terror swirled within. She readied herself to run and hoped the adrenaline would pump through her weakened muscles.

Shouting resonated from the jungle. Hallie whipped her head towards the noises and witnessed two late-twenties men vaulting from a group of large ferns. Dressed in brown, vintage, pilot flight suits, they aimed their pistols at the animal and fired several times.

A few small spots of blood formed on the dinosaur's chest area as the men kept firing. Deep bellows flared up from the T-

Rex as it turned and ran away. Thunderous booms formed from each of its steps, but they gradually reduced in intensity the further away the creature got. Moments later, it vanished over the horizon.

One man, wearing a leather pilot helmet with large goggles pushed up over it, rushed over. "Are you alright?" Although weak, Hallie noticed his boyish looks and narrow face. Glancing at the name patch on his jacket, she read "C.C. TAYLOR, LT USNR" below gold embroidered military wings. She breathed a sigh of relief knowing they were the American military.

The other man, with blue eyes and dirty blond hair, placed his hand on her shoulder. "Ma'am, we have to get you out of here before that thing comes back." On his patch, below an icon consisting of an eagle, globe, and anchor, read "E.J. POWERS, CPT USMC". While they were strangers, she felt safer with them. With Powers being a Marine like her Phil, she felt at ease. She nodded and crossed her arms. They walked down the beach in the opposite direction from where the T-Rex fled. The men followed beside her with their weapons in their hands.

Hallie's feet warmed up from each step in the sand. "Is-is it s-safe to be out on the b-beach?"

Taylor responded, "It's better than the jungle. There are more of those animals in there."

"Animals," snickered Powers. "Just say it, they're dinosaurs. I've recognized them from several books. Our planes nearly hit some Pterosaurs, we were chased by a herd of Triceratops, and we just saved her from a Tyrannosaurus. So say it, dinosaurs!"

"Absurd! They can't be that!"

For Hallie, it didn't matter. She walked with her eyes glancing at the ground. It didn't matter if it was an animal, dinosaur, or monster, only that her lover, her unborn's father, was dead. Now, she had to survive to preserve their child.

She re-focused her thoughts. "I-I see from your name patches your m-military."

"Yes," Taylor said. "We flew out of the Naval Air Station in Fort Lauderdale for a flight exercise."

"Then some storm hit us. Now we're trapped in this Hell," added Powers.

"Lieutenant, language. There's a lady here."

"My apologies, Ma'am. I'm just confused. I don't know what island this is, but Sir Arthur Conan Doyle would be excited."

"Anyway, our entire squadron had to do a water landing a few miles from here. By God's good grace, all of us survived. We split into smaller groups to explore this place. That's when we heard your cries." He nodded at her. "And just in time, too."

"My husband and I," Hallie paused, taking a deep breath and wiping her eyes. "We sailed out of Miami. A storm hit us and... my-my husband... a-a dinosaur got him." She looked down and cried.

A frown formed on Powers' face. "I'm sorry for your loss, Ma'am."

"Thank you." Hallie looked up and sniffled, rubbing her face with her hands.

She kept walking but also focused on their attire. She tried to make sense of it. Through her years with Phil, she met many people from different branches of the military. The only time she had seen anyone wearing anything like what these men wore were from World War II re-enactors. Also, she remembered something from the Bermuda Triangle documentaries and books about a military flight that vanished in the 1940s.

"Um, what's the date today? My memory is fuzzy."

"December 5th," Powers replied.

Already she knew things were off with them. She and Phil sailed from Miami on December 29th. "What year is it?"

Taylor scrunched his face. "You don't know the year?"

"She lost her husband. I'm not surprised that she's hysterical," replied Powers. "1945, Ma'am."

Hallie stopped, bent over, and placed her hands on her knees. "Flight 19," she said to herself. She hyperventilated as she dug her nails into her skin. First dinosaurs, now men who disappeared over seventy years ago. The Bermuda Triangle claimed them, and they were never seen again. This meant she wasn't going to escape either. "Why did God allow this? Was He punishing me and Phil? Why is He punishing my baby? Maybe this had nothing to do with God. Maybe He simply doesn't exist." Never before had she questioned her faith, until today.

"Ma'am, are you okay?" Powers asked as he placed his hand on her back.

"I know about you. You all disappeared in the Bermuda Triangle over seventy years ago." She straightened back up and looked at them. "I'm from the year 2016."

Taylor shook his head. "Pardon me saying this, but have you flipped your wig? And what's the Bermuda Triangle?"

She didn't blame him for feeling that way. It sounded insane. Even she entertained the idea that she had lost her mind. In many ways, she wanted to be a victim of a mental decline, it would likely mean Phil was still alive. But her senses didn't deceive; her mind wasn't damaged. Everything really happened.

"With all due respect," Powers said as he turned to Taylor, "I've heard many stories about odd disappearances in these waters. Look at the evidence! Strange storms, dinosaurs, those ships we flew over."

Hallie looked at him with raised brows. "Ships?"

"Well, Ma'am, they were old, wooden tall ships. They reminded me of the kind in that *Captain Kidd* pirate movie I saw last week." While Hallie never heard of the movie, she knew what pirate ships looked like.

"What are you trying to say?" Taylor said in a raised voice.

Powers scratched his chin, then looked at Hallie. "Ma'am, you mentioned the Bermuda Triangle. What exactly is that?"

"Um, it's what people in my time call an area of the ocean where many planes and ships have vanished." A cold chill went through her body just talking about it.

"Hmm, so that's what they call this cursed area in the future."

Taylor laughed, "You're mad. You're both mad."

Powers placed his hands on his waist. "I know how this must sound, but I think those storms sent us to another time. And judging from the plants and animals, the prehistoric past."

Hallie glanced at the forest. With her knowledge of gardening, she recognized some plants, such as oak and magnolias, but others seemed out of place. She spotted several with short, rough, barrel-shaped stems topped with a crown of pinnate leaves. A few others she found stood about nine feet tall, with multiple fern-like leaves sprouting from a rough-looking sturdy stem.

To her, the evidence pointed to the fact that the storm really did bring them millions of years in the past. Her husband would have agreed with her and Powers. She tried to comprehend that Phil died millions of years in the past, but wouldn't be born until the far distant future. "Is Phil really dead since he hadn't even been born yet?" she asked herself repeatedly.

"You both seem off the cob. Let's regroup with the others and get their opinion." Taylor marched ahead. "Time-travel! Nonsense!"

Hallie stayed close to Powers as they followed behind Taylor. She kept her eyes low and remained silent. With no one speaking, she listened to the rhythmic crashing of the waves. It reminded her of the beaches near Truro in Cape Cod, a favorite spot of her and Phil's.

Powers spoke, "Ma'am, um, may I call you Hallie?" She nodded. "Hallie, tell me about the future?"

For the next ten minutes, she talked about it. Space travel, computers, social progression. During the talk, she suppressed her pain, even though she thought about Phil several times.

"Germany and Japan are our friends now?" Powers smiled. "You gave me hope for the future."

"Hope," she said. "Such a foreign word right now." She crossed her arms.

Several seconds of silence passed before Powers spoke, "Tell me about your husband?"

She glanced up into his eyes, her cheeks dirtied from tears. "His name is… was… or will be… Phil." She wiped her cheeks, then grinned. "A Marine like you."

"A fellow Marine? I like him already."

She placed her hands on her stomach. Her child was all that mattered now, the continuation of Phil. They both had to survive. She tried to grasp onto hope, but the grip loosened with each passing moment. She had to accept the frightening possibility that God didn't exist, and that she was on her own.

"There's a ship!" shouted Taylor as he pointed to the ocean.

Hallie spotted a bulky cargo ship about half a mile from the shore, black smoke billowed from the thin smokestacks located in the back. Metal beams formed a large rectangular scaffolding-type structure in the center of it.

Powers took out black binoculars from his flight suit and used them to examine the ship. "Damn! I can't believe it!" He dropped his hand with the binoculars; his mouth hung open. "It's the *Cyclops*."

Taylor turned to Powers. "The *Cyclops*? Didn't that disappear years ago?"

For a brief second, Hallie had a glimmer of hope for a rescue. It faded into oblivion when she remembered the name. It too vanished within the Bermuda Triangle. "Was it in 1917? No, it was 1918," she said to herself. Much like Flight 19, it was never found. That proved that no matter how much praying or hoping, she would never go home again.

A distant but sustaining, deep, tuba-like tone emerged. While the men remained oblivious, Hallie tried to focus on it. It didn't seem to be an animal since it remained steady and consistent.

"We're coming back to the same point in time," Powers said. Hallie turned towards the forest to face the direction of the noise. It grew louder with each passing moment.

"That doesn't make any sense," replied Taylor.

Trembling, Hallie gripped her hands and looked up in the sky. The sound increased in strength to the point that she wondered why Taylor and Powers hadn't reacted to it. She thought that maybe it was a jet, but her instinct told her something much worse approached.

"There must be something special about this day." He looked up at the sky. "What is that sound?"

A large meteor glided above the clouds, blazing brighter than the sun. A tuba-type sound hailed from the meteor as it traveled through the air. No one moved. Hallie didn't blink or breathe, she could only watch it speeding towards the ocean. She kept her eyes fixated on it. The fireball became smaller the closer it got towards the distant horizon.

It reached its final destination. A flash of white light engulfed the region. Hallie closed her eyes as the brightness flourished. She knew what this was, the event that marked the end of the dinosaurs. There was no escape from it. Several tears exited from between the eyelids, rolling down her cheek. As she balled her hands, she contemplated that maybe this meteor cursed the area, creating a gateway between the past and the future known as the Bermuda Triangle.

The flash disappeared, so she slowly opened her eyes. A massive flaming bubble developed in the distance, gradually growing in size. From it, fiery projectiles ejected into the sky like missiles. The clouds scattered as if someone blew on them. A line of ripples rushed over the surface of the water as the shock wave gunned for the land.

She couldn't move a muscle, nor did she listen to the men calling for her to run. Her focus remained on the view. Strangely, Hallie found it beautiful. While there was no escape from the destruction, at least she got to see the Apocalypse of the Era of the Dinosaurs and the Genesis of the Age of Humanity.

The shock wave reached her. The force slammed into her like a gust of wind from a hurricane. Sand blasted into her face and irritated her eyes. She tried to maintain her balance but lost it and tumbled over. Upon hitting the ground, she slammed her head on a hard object. Blackness overtook her vision as she entered the unconscious world.

There was darkness; there were no feelings or thoughts, just emptiness. It was as if time no longer existed. Moments later, she slowly returned to a normal state. As she regained consciousness, someone shouted "Hallie! Hallie!"

"Phil," she grunted. She opened her eyes, but her vision remained blurry. The dark silhouette of a man stood over her as she lay on the ground. "Phil." For a moment, she believed everything was a dream. Phil was alive and they were back in Florida.

"Hallie, we got to move!" he shouted. Her vision cleared and revealed Powers kneeling over her with his hands on her shoulder. Any remaining glimmer of hope vanished. She felt like a fool for not accepting the reality that Phil was dead. Her lips quivered as Powers took her arms and helped her to her feet. She glanced at the ground and saw the driftwood she had hit her head on.

Powers shouted over the roaring wind that ravaged the beach. "We got to get inland!" The jungle swished and moved in a violent dance; her hair whipped around from the hurricane-force gust. Far above, hundreds of small fireballs descended in all directions in the red sky. The *Cyclops* bounced around in the rough waters. The fire bubble stretched for miles into the heavens and overtook much of the horizon.

"Why?" she said as she sat back down in the sand, wrapping her arms around her legs.

Taylor screamed, "Is she mad?"

"There's no escaping this." She pointed at the ocean, which looked like it continuously expanded upward into the air. "Look what's coming." She didn't have to worry about the fires or the freeze that would follow the impact. The approaching mega-tsunami meant any chance of survival evaporated.

She embraced the inevitable.

"She's right," said Powers as he sat beside her. "We can't outrun that."

Taylor shook his head. "I-I can't stay. The others... I'm responsible for them... I-I have to find them." Powers nodded at Taylor, who then turned and ran down the beach. Hallie believed his actions were futile and that he wouldn't find the others in time, but understood that he had to try.

A flock of flying dinosaurs with pointed beaks, long necks, and lengthy wings shrieked and headed away from the growing wall of dark water. The tsunami approached the shore, extending several hundred feet into the air. The *Cyclops* traveled stern first up it, becoming almost horizontal as it did. The ship flipped over when it reached halfway up, crashing into the water and disappearing within the wave.

Wrapping her arms around her stomach, Hallie rocked back and forth. Sadness drained through her, leaving behind a hollow soul. The real agony stemmed that her child would never experience what it was like to smile or to cry or to laugh. There would be no family gatherings or holiday celebrations. It was a far crueller fate than what she and Phil suffered.

"My loved ones aren't even born yet. Will the good Lord make me wait millions of years to see them again?" Powers asked.

She hesitated for a moment. "I'm sure God wouldn't do that." If he had asked that before all of this, her statement would have been truthful. Instead, she not only doubted his grace and love, but also His existence. She said within her mind that "Any all-knowing, all-loving God who allowed this couldn't possibly exist." Regardless of her feelings, she wasn't going to rob Powers of his only comfort.

As the wave reached a few yards from the shoreline, it rumbled as it rose higher into the sky. Hallie grabbed Powers' hand, gripping it so hard that her knuckles turned white. She felt him squeezed back, and then she closed their eyes. She hummed to Beethoven's *Für Elise* and pretended Phil held her hand. She kept the hope that an Afterlife existed and he awaited her arrival. It might have been a futile thought, but she wanted to hold onto that thought.

The wave struck.

Dark Water

By: Lillian Csernica

I'd been working at the parking kiosk by the beach for about a month when I started to notice little things. Clumps of seaweed spaced like footprints, leading up to the edge of the sand in front of the kiosk. Seashells piled by the bench where I ate a sandwich before my shift. If I walked all the way down to the breakers, I'd find something washed up there, a diver's watch or a sports bottle or some other useful item.

At first, I figured I was just lucky. It kept on happening, and only to me. When I asked the guys on the day shift if they'd noticed anything weird, Chuck and Dave just gave me funny looks and laughed, telling me I was crazy. Maybe they were right.

The kiosk sat at one end of the lot, next to the exit lane. Tuesday night I chained my bike to the rack behind the kiosk then stepped inside and set my book bag on the shelf under the counter. My supervisor Roy had thumbtacked a memo to the bulletin board on the back of the door, reminding all of us to check the far corners of the lot. We'd had trouble in the past with bums sleeping over, kids necking, people doing drug deals. Lately I'd been avoiding those corners. They were closest to the beach, right where I'd find the seaweed tracks. Now, I'd have to go all the way out there.

I turned my chair sideways and faced the cars. The radio and my textbooks kept my imagination busy. Only a few people came in and out of the lot. Roy had warned me how slow it would be Monday through Thursday nights. That was all right with me. The shorter junior college summer schedule meant tests were already coming up.

The fog rolled in, blurring the parking lines just enough to make the kiosk feel like an island about to be swallowed by the sea. At closing time, I had to check the lot for any last cars and hang the chain across the entrance. That meant walking all the way out to those corners. With a queasy flutter in my stomach, I stuffed the kiosk's flashlight in my jacket pocket and stepped outside.

The waves crashed against the beach. They sounded louder, closer. All that stood between them and me were a lot of empty parking spaces. The fog was so thick it stuck to my face like spiderwebs. The salt taste made my stomach churn. I settled for shining the flashlight's beam into the far corners, looking for the red gleam of taillights. I didn't see any, so I circled back around the kiosk to the entrance. I fastened the clasp at the end of the chain to the pole on the other side of the entrance, then started walking back toward the kiosk.

The chain rattled. I spun around. Through the misty columns of light thrown by the streetlights, a thin shadow floated toward me. A hand, long-fingered and bony, reached for me. I jumped back.

"Have I startled you? Forgive me." The hand was attached to an older man wearing a blue blazer over a gray sweater and slacks. His smile was friendly, but the angle of the streetlight hid his eyes. "I'm William Corbett. My friends call me Bill." He sounded like one of my professors. "I take it you're the new night man?"

"That's right." His hand was still out. I shook it. "Jim Thompson."

"A lonely task this is, but fine if you like the sea."

"I don't."

"No? What a pity. May I ask why?"

I shrugged. If Chuck and Dave thought I was crazy, I'd better not tell anyone else. "I just--I feel like it's coming to get me. That's all."

"How sad. The sea is your friend. Your brain swims in it with every pulse of your blood."

That thought was so repulsive I clenched my eyes shut against it. Bill chuckled.

"I suspect you have a touch of thalassaphobia. That's the morbid fear of the sea."

"What do you know about it?"

"Quite a lot. You see, my wife was just the opposite. She loved the sea, and it loved her." His voice hardened. "It loved her to death."

"Oh. Well. I have to go now." I backed toward the kiosk.

"Are you tired of being a slave to your fear? I can cure it."

That stopped me. "Are you serious?"

Bill pulled a gold card case out of his breast pocket, opened it, and held out a business card. I took it. He had a string of letters after his name, the address of an office in the expensive part of town, and three phone numbers. I recognized one.

"You work at North Valley?"

"On a consulting basis. Students are referred to me when their difficulties fall under my specialty."

"What's that?"

"Anxieties and phobias. Rather a lucky coincidence that we met, yes?"

"I don't know. I mean, I can't really afford--"

"Please." Bill held up one hand. "Thalassophobia is relatively rare. I'd welcome the opportunity to learn more about it."

"You really know something that will work?"

"We can certainly give it a try. Say tomorrow night, after your shift?"

"Okay."

"Until tomorrow, then." He walked off across the parking lot.

I stared after him. The clothes, the fancy card, all those degrees.... He had to be for real. Maybe I did have this phobia thing, but at least I wasn't crazy.

***

My Wednesday shift crawled by. The stink of the sea made me think of the nasty little monsters that live in coral reefs. In the back of my mind, I'd always thought something evil lurked down in the dark water, waiting for a chance to grab my ankles and drag me under. Its fishy lidless eyes watched me. Now I knew there was no monster. It was just this phobia thing.

By ten-thirty the lot was empty. I fastened the chain across the entrance and hurried back to the kiosk, keeping an eye on the blurry shadows. Bill was waiting by the door. He pulled a flask out of his jacket pocket and handed it to me.

"Take a good dose of that."

I took a sip. The Scotch burned a trail down my throat and warmed my stomach.

"Now," Bill said. "Let's get you out where we can do you some good."

He led me along the empty boardwalk and up the pier to the railing. Bill stared down at the water, then up at the stars.

"It's a marvelous world we live in, Jim. The more we make friends with it, the more it reveals its marvels to us."

"Some marvels I'd rather not see."

"You have to confront your fear before you can conquer it." Bill stared out at the water. "The sea waits to conquer you. Any slip, any carelessness, and it will strike."

"You mean--your wife?"

"We were out in the Caribbean, on a friend's yacht. Rosalind insisted on going for a swim." Bill's breath hissed out between his teeth. "The seaweed trapped her. Before I could dive in and cut her free, it was too late."

"How awful." The weird look on his face made me nervous.

"The sea embraced her like a lover." Bill glared down at the waves. "A cold, merciless, demanding lover."

I might be crazy, but this guy was nuts. Bill snapped out of it.

"Let's get started. Close your eyes and listen to the water. Can you hear the breakers?"

I nodded.

"They crest, and break." Bill's voice eased down to a deep whisper. "Crest, and break. Just like your breath. Feel the rhythm of your breath, Jim. Sink into it."

I listened. My breath slowed until it matched the sound of the waves. I still felt on edge, but more about Bill than the water.

"Listen to the tide, Jim. Listen to your heartbeat, pumping all that salt water through your veins." His voice rolled over me, heavy and soft. "Hear the gentle tide inside your body, and the gentle tide outside it too. All the same, Jim. All the same. Your heart and the sea's, beating together."

I listened, feeling calmer.

"The sea is your friend, Jim. You do want to be friends with the sea, don't you? You want to be happy and calm, like you are right now."

"Yes...."

"Reach out to the sea, Jim. Show it you want to be friends."

My right hand moved a little. I thought of Bill's wife trapped in the seaweed, and those seaweed tracks outside the kiosk. I tensed up again.

"I can't."

"Tell me why, Jim. Why does the sea frighten you?"

"I keep finding things." The answer came out before I could stop it. "Little stuff, just shells and tracks in the sand and little presents. I thought maybe they were for somebody else, but it just keeps happening."

"That's how it always starts. The sea gives, but it always wants to be paid back."

Before I could ask him what he meant, Bill pushed me closer to the rail.

"I suspect your fear of the sea might be just a symptom of something deeper. Think, now. Think back to when you were a little boy."

His voice weighed me down again, sending me back through memories. I remembered salt stinging my eyes and a bad taste in my mouth as I threw up. Then it all came back. I was six, at the beach. My father hoisted me up over his head and carried me way out into the waves. We were both laughing. Then he threw me in. I kept fighting my way to the surface, screaming for help. Dad just stood there and yelled at me to swim. Finally, my sister swam out and carried me back to shore. Old shame and anger flooded me, hot and ugly. I shoved away from the rail. Bill's hands on my shoulders kept me there.

"I'm right here, Jim. Everything is fine. Tell me what you're thinking."

"My father--he thought it was so funny. He threw me in and left me there." Tears welled up, choking off my voice. "I was screaming, thrashing around. He just stood there laughing."

"I see. Could it be, Jim, that your real problem is your rage at your father?

I stopped straining. That made sense.

"What you're really afraid of," Bill said, "is what might happen if you turned that rage loose."

People thought I was easygoing, but that wasn't true. I'd had any bad temper beaten out of me early on. My sister and I weren't allowed to get angry at Dad, could never show any sign of it. I started to cry harder, feeling stupid and awful and better all at once. Bill patted me on the back.

"You've achieved quite a breakthrough. All that's left now is to replace your old fear of the sea with good associations. When I tell you it's all right now, you'll have no fear of the sea at all. Understand?"

I nodded.

"Wake up now."

Bill snapped his fingers right in front of my face. I jerked back. My eyes opened.

"There now," he said. "Have a look at the water and tell me how you feel."

I glanced at the water and shrugged. "No problem."

"Excellent. Shall we try again tomorrow night? We'll have an opportunity we must not miss."

"An opportunity for what?" There was something about his smile, too much eagerness, I didn't like it.

"The moon will be full. The power of its light will chase the darkness out of the water and cure your fear."

That didn't sound like anything I'd read in my Psych texts. "Sounds more like magic than psychology."

Bill gave me an odd look, then laughed. "There's a little of both in each."

Something still bothered me. "I can see how Dad being a jerk started all this, but what about the stuff I keep finding?"

Bill waved that away. "It's probably nothing more than a mild delusion. You wish your father would apologize, perhaps by giving you toys. Since you can't confront him directly, you've transferred that wish to the sea itself."

That made a strange kind of sense. "Look, I'd really like to thank you for your help. Can I buy you dinner or something?"

He shook his head, smiling that same disturbing smile. "Tomorrow night will settle a number of debts."

***

After closing, I met Bill at the end of the pier. Over his sweater and slacks he wore a poncho of black silk. Seagull feathers, fish bones, chipped seashells, and bits of colored glass decorated it. As I got closer, I could see silvery symbols embroidered onto the cloth. Bill had on a necklace of cowrie shells. A flat circle of mother-of-pearl hung off it. More symbols were scratched onto that.

"Hey, Bill," I said. "What's all that for?"

"The Orb of Dreams and the Sphere of Conquest stand side by side in the heavens, with Venus suspended between them. On such a night can miracles occur."

"What are you talking about?"

Bill blinked at me, then chuckled. "Psychodrama. Shamans have been curing people with it for thousands of years."

He made it sound perfectly natural, but something about that get-up bothered me. He'd put a lot of time into it, so he couldn't have made it just for me.

"First, a toast for luck." Bill handed me his flask. I took a swig. The Scotch had a peculiar gritty edge to it. He probably got sand in the cap. I handed it back.

"Now watch the water," he said. "See how it swirls. Follow it, around and around. Sink into the rhythm of the water. Feel it in your breath, in your blood."

The Scotch filled me with its fire. The heat moved out of my stomach and along my arms and legs, up into my head. My tongue felt thick. My eyes swung back and forth with the current. The swirl of the water wobbled and blurred.

Bill pulled me away from the rail and made me sit on the bench near the stairway that led down to the fishing platforms below the pier.

"Stay right here." He hurried down the stairs.

Something was very wrong. I tried to stand up. None of my muscles even twitched. Hypnotism was supposed to make you suggestible, not turn you into a robot. What had the old man done to me? The Scotch. It had to be whatever made the Scotch taste funny.

"Please." Bill's voice came from right below me. "I've waited so long. The stars, the tide, everything is in place."

The waves hit the pilings with a hiss like steam shooting out of a bad radiator.

"Haven't I served you? You've taken everything, my youth, my love, my life itself!"

A slow hiss answered him.

"You thought you'd trap him with your petty trinkets, didn't you? You'll have him, all right, but only if you give me what you promised!" Bill hurried up the stairs and put a hand on my shoulder. "Come along, Jim. It's all right now."

I felt no fear of the water, but I was terrified of Bill. Even so, my body stood up and followed him. I felt like an engineer trapped inside a runaway train. I took one step after another down to the slimy, barnacle-crusted platform. It rocked a little with the strength of the rising tide.

"Come here, Jim" Bill grabbed a fistful of my jacket and jerked me right up to the platform's edge. "Look at the water. Let it see you."

The water down here was dark, dark enough to smother the moonlight, dark enough to make every one of my coral reef nightmares come alive. My heart nearly pounded a hole right through my ribs. I begged my frozen muscles to run.

"Luna and Venus link arms in the heavens," Bill chanted. "Lovers return from graves long filled. The gates of death swing wide on hinges oiled by blood your priests have spilled!"

A larger wave sloshed onto the platform. Little wavelets ran toward my shoes. Nodding, Bill cackled. He made a paler shadow against the dark water. The bits of glass on his poncho glittered at me like lidless eyes. Those fishy lidless eyes. . . . Raw panic exploded inside me. Straining as hard as I could, I dragged one foot back from the edge.

Bill stared at the water, looking confused, then furious. "Here he is, just as I promised. Now give me Rosalind!"

The water did nothing but stroke the toes of my sneakers. Bill growled and thrust a hand under his poncho. He pulled out a fishing knife. The waves heaved beneath the platform. My moving foot skidded in the slime and I fell over. Bill staggered backward, teetering on the platform's edge. A wall of dark water rose up behind him. I stared at it, praying it was only the drug in the Scotch making me see things. The dark water crashed down over Bill. For a second I saw him trapped inside it, slashing at the water with the knife. Then it sank. I dragged myself to the edge of the platform and watched Bill disappear into the gloom. He fought all the way down.

I rolled over and sprawled on my back, still sluggish. The panic screamed at me to get away before the water grabbed me too. I tried to sit up. A stronger wave splashed across the platform. Something rattled. Bill's cowrie shell necklace. Another present, from the sea.

The waves lifted the platform again, gentler this time, like they were rocking me. I touched the necklace with a cautious fingertip. The sea had never hurt me. That was just my father being a jerk. The dark water had saved my life. I sat up and dropped the necklace down over my head. The mother-of-pearl circle gleamed. My heartbeat slowed, beating in time with the waves that kissed the pilings and drew back like shy lovers.

The Wealth of Dagon

By: Rob Tannahill

It was January, and we were living it up in the Philippines, eating Crispy Pork Sisig and Bistek Tagalog over Yuengling's and coffee at The Deck, one of the more Westernized restaurants in the Zambales Province. For brunch or lunch, it was the perfect place to dine, in our most humble opinion. *Our* is myself, J. Phillips LaBeouf, my photographer, Alfie Banks, and a fisherman with whom we'd made fast acquaintances by the name of Manolo Ong. The days were purely human, lightly toasted, with everyone enjoying the cooler temperatures while they could.

Alfie and I were journalists. Him photo, me literary. Well, we were *aspiring* journalists, neither of us had been out of college for very long, meaning both of us still had yet to be picked up by a major rag. Freelance, they call it, and we held a dear hope that we might one day stick our lances into the middle of a great international story. Tensions had been high between the Chinese and the Filipinos for a long time over the waters about 220 kilometers off the coast of Luzon, which is where we were. We figured it wouldn't be long until we got our wish.

Until then, we filmed fishing, which more people like watching than you'd care to believe. Right now, the shoal would be rich in fish, and, although none of us were marine biologists, we spoke enough Tagalog (or they spoke enough English) for us to hear some pretty serious rumors bouncing around the fishing communities, rumors that the Chinese would attack any Filipino boat caught fishing the acreage of the Panatog Shoal this season. To which the Filipinos quite predictably replied: *Putang ina mo.*

"Interesting things on the horizon, do you think?" Alfie asked.

"Bound to be dangerous," I said.

"Danger's where the money's at!" Alfie said, raising his beer.

"Next, you'll be telling me we need total coverage," I said. "Don't worry, Alfie. You're getting your wish." I was and was not excited. The Chinese, despite Donald Trump's bluster to the contrary, were no laughing matter when they got angry, especially in the middle of the ocean, where there is nothing.

***

Before the thing happens, and this is doubly true if you're a writer, you view it as an adventure; when the thing happens, if it is noteworthy, it is probably dangerous enough that you wonder at your own intelligence quotient just before the shit hits the fan. When said shit splatters, you're too busy trying to get out of the sewage alive so you can write about it, and sometimes you make too much money to consider maybe not risking your neck over a few thousand words. After you publish, you start searching for the next sticky situation, or maybe you're dying to be published. The only thing that can save you is...good copy...we were about six miles off the coast, far enough that land was no longer visible, with no chance of outrunning the much more powerful boats on the water, should any come along. None had. More than likely, none would. I *thought* I wanted them to. Damn good copy that way.

The sea, though not truly boundless, might as well be when you're on a boat in the middle of nowhere. When calm, the waves are hypnotic. You can't tell if they're rolling or slithering as they flow toward the darkness just beneath your boat. This beauty makes it easy to forget the risk you're taking by being many kilometers away from the safety of land. Storms correct that forgetfulness pretty quickly when they come, and you find yourself hoping any rain is a standard rain and not something more like a white squall. These things are all true, but we weren't thinking about any of them. We ought to have, bud, those things and even more...things it's generally out of my purview to even imagine.

Manolo sailed as if he'd been born part fish. The sea was just an extension of his life. Casting nets, setting the big hooks, dumping huge piles of wriggling fish on the decks, where he and his crew would pack them in ice, and clean and fry them and prepare them in diverse ways. Alfie snapped photos of the sea, the sky, of us, and of the fish when he could. He, like many of the people of his atoll, built the boat himself. Though it appeared to be made from a great mass of sticks and rusting steel, the boat was tough. I'd seen his ramshackle boat handle a fifteen-foot swell, and Manolo wasn't at all afraid to take it out during storms.

Manolo stood directly on the nose of the boat, swinging a long, sturdy paddle into the waves. This would spook the fish into the nets. He did this for about twenty minutes at a time, then we all pulled the nets and the traps back into the boat. One of them was covered in squid eggs. He shrugged at things like that. "That's fine. Eggs are good. We can use them as bait." He pulled a handful of them away from the cross-hatched struts holding the trap together and set them to the side.

Alfie pointed away from the sun. "Oh, shit."

On the horizon, three ships sailed in our direction, not fishing boats, but the gray and black brutal design of warships. Manolo squatted, reached into his toolbox, and raised a pair of binoculars, looking through their cylinders. "Chinese Coast Guard," he said. "Number one assholes. One, two, three ships."

If things went south, it'd be automatic rifles versus filet knives. Good copy, indeed.

When they got close enough, the bullhorns came out. Terrible English surfed over the top of the waves, invading our ears with, "Sweep and clear exercise! You are trespassing. This boat, you, has entered Chinese waters in violation of..." Manolo shook his fist at the boats, now close enough that we could almost see the faces of those on board. "...of whatever I fucking say!"

"Are they going to board us?" Alfie asked.

Manolo threw the anchor overboard, cursing in Tagalog.

"Don't give them any ideas," I said.

The starboard side of one boat strafed Manolo's boat, barely tapping the outrigging. It was enough to set the three of us wobbling across the deck. Three Chinese soldiers held us at gunpoint from the deck of their own boat while another one climbed aboard ours. Manolo and the captain spoke heatedly to one another, debating who was trespassing, where, and why, and I had to hand it to Manolo...he had balls of steel, arguing with an armed soldier.

By the time the admiration registered in my head, the Chinese captain drew his pistol, hollering in Mandarin. Manolo backed up, raising his hands higher, saying, "OK, OK," nodding his head ferociously like a nervous bird. The captain gestured to the cabin with erratic little shifts of the pistol barrel, and Manolo led him inside.

My gut dropped. I coughed, the pit of my throat suddenly scratchy with something I could not clear. I glanced at the soldiers whose pistols were still trained on us, just long enough to ascertain their attention, not long enough to make eye contact. The staccato of ancient languages floated from the boat's cabin.

Two shots rang out.

"Oh, God," Alfie said.

I said nothing.

Manolo, still at gunpoint, emerged unharmed from the cabin with the captain in tow. The captain was holding a red flare gun. Manolo had a box of flares in his arms. The captain gestured, and Manolo walked to the starboard bow, handing the flares up to the first mate. Or I guess he was the first mate. The first evil cunt if you ask me.

The captain screamed something I didn't understand in Manolo's face, then said, "So, that's what you get! Our waters! You stay out, fuck. You all. Fuck. Stay out, eat the asshole of a fish, do it at home with your shit-shoveling ancestors. We will escort you." He trained the pistol on Alfie and me. "You two! Throw your phones into the ocean!"

"What?" Alfie said.

The captain strode forward, raised his pistol, and brought it down on the bridge of Alfie's nose. The soft photographer howled and went to his knees. Blood spilled from his nostrils, and he craned his head back, pinching off the blood. With his other, trembling hand, he pulled his phone out of his pocket and reluctantly threw it into the ocean. I did the same thing. I would have been better off being shot, but I didn't know that at the time. There was a splash as Manolo also threw his phone into the vast blue expanse.

The soldiers kept their pistols trained on us as the captain boarded his own boat again. Something bumped into us, hard, sending Alfie and me to the deck. Manolo managed to stay on his feet, his teeth grinding. The two skiffs accompanying the captain's boat flanked us on either side, pushing Manolo's boat further out to sea by the outrigging.

I wanted to say we could just wait for them to finish having their fun, then radio the Philippines Coast Guard for rescue. Part of me already knew that wasn't an option. Alfie asked in my stead, and Manolo said, "No. Motherfucker shot the engine and the radio. We're fucked...unless someone comes along."

"We can't sail?" Alfie asked.

He shook his head. "Right now, who can say. Possibly. Maybe I could make a sail. We can do nothing until these fascist imps disappear. Until then..." He shrugged, sat down on one of the boat's flat seats, then buried his face in his hands. Up, down they rubbed, lingering on the eye sockets, his fingers curling over the crown of his head. I thought Manolo was going to push his eyeballs straight through the back of his skull. A small growl escaped his throat, but he cut it off. The Chinese were still close.

Helpless, we floated with them across the top of the ocean, a mile, two, three, maybe four. Finally, a honk came from the captain's boat. The man himself emerged from the cabin, a huge grin splitting his face, and he said, "There you go. Our waters, stupid. You want to be out here so bad? Die out here. We will not call anyone for you." He saluted us with a middle finger.

One of his crew ran to him, an AR-15 in his clutches. The captain took the automatic rifle and aimed it at the deck. We all ducked for cover, and the *rapraprap* of fast, hot rounds rang out. Our ears joined in the ringing, and when it was over, we were all still alive. The Chinese boat was also still alive, but with pernicious laughter rather than delicious (if short-lived) relief. Manolo screamed, holding his head in his hands and rocking back and forth. I searched for the place with the most bullet holes and saw that the anchor had been blasted into smithereens. Alfie sat down and wept quietly, rubbing tears away from his eyes, cursing himself for snotting up his broken nose.

Shortly after, the Chinese boats were gone, and we were adrift. Manolo and I made eye contact. He shook his head one more time, then got up, grabbed his iron skillets, and did the only thing he knew to do: cooked for us. "Everything will be fine," he said. "In a few hours, we will either float to another peninsula, or another boat will be along."

***

Three hours later, the sun was setting. We had yet to see land. Manolo checked his maps, which said we ought to be ashore by now. No comfort there.

Alfie's broken nose swelled up one side of his face. He had not said a word.

Manolo walked to the front of the boat and stood on the nose as if he were about to scare more fish into the nets, but rather than pick up his paddle and get to work, he threw his arms out and screamed. Alfie smashed his palms over his ears to block the noise. I winced, keeping an eye on Manolo. If he'd gone mad, we were in trouble. Neither one of us knew how to sail. I opened my mouth to ask...something, why are you screaming, what are we going to do, you're the only one who knows the sea, something along those lines. But his scream stopped mid-crescendo, becoming a chant, and not your basic OM. I'd never heard a chant like this. Until the end, all I could make out was gibberish. Finally, he spoke, and I understood, not a word but a name.

Dagon.

He ran through a few more cycles, then quieted, leaving us again with only the soft rustle of the waves. Alfie locked eyes with me, his mouth open, aghast at the whole situation. By now, he had to be dying for a drink like I was, but neither of us felt like asking Manolo if there was any booze on the boat. Turned out, he didn't have to, for Manolo stepped down from the prow, hurried into the cabin, and we heard a few things moving around from within. Manolo came back out holding a bottle of rum.

Grinning, he sat down next to Alfie and popped the cork. After pulling directly from the neck, he handed it off to Alfie. "Don't be scared, amigo," he said. "At least he didn't think to ask for this."

"Not scared of rum," Alfie said, drinking. "I'm very scared of our having been set adrift. What the hell happened to the Coast Guard? I'd have thought we'd have seen our own military at least, aren't they out here? Aren't they supposed to be protecting your people from this fuckin'...piracy shit?" He scoffed. "Beaten by pirates."

"Yes," Manolo said.

"The military is as the military does." I took a drink of my own. "Alfie, there's a far remove between *is* and *supposed,* both in the dictionary and in life." I had one more little sip, then handed the bottle back to Alfie, who handed it to Manolo.

Manolo waved it off. "Y'all go ahead," he said, and I chuckled at his usage of the colloquial *y'all*.

The alcohol kicked slowly in, warming my core, lightening my mood. We were going to be fine. I was still sober enough to be uncertain of that and getting drunk enough to believe a true, mildly relaxing fact; whether I was sure or not of my own safety didn't matter. Unless I intended to put a bullet through my own head, I had to smile. There was just nothing else to do.

As the last hints of light faded, I watched the end of the day's colors play across the sky. A black spot spread across the water, spilling from underneath the belly of the boat.

"Manolo Ong! We're dumping fuel!"

The fisherman didn't hear. He was busy, leaning up against the side of the cabin like James Dean, the bottle of rum clutched in his right hand. He raised it carefully to his mouth, glazed eyes locked on my own, and I counted three bubbles rolling through the amber spirits sloshing behind the glass before he lowered the bottle again to his side. He belched, shaking his head, one bubble clinging to his lower lip. "S'not fuel, fool. That's a helper. He's going to help me get home." A wry smile flashed briefly, his eyes glinting. "But food first."

Alfie joined me, leaning over the deck. "What the hell is that, Phil? It looks *WHUF--"*

My photographer spilled over the side of the boat, landing in the center of the black, tarry mass. His body punched through the middle of it; instead of disappearing into the depths or conversely, bobbing up like a buoy, only the top half of his body disappeared into the mass, his legs sticking straight up in the air. One arm lay flat across the black top.

His legs wriggled.

"Alfie!"

Manolo giggled. "Whoops." He barked laughter.

"Did you fucking throw him overboard?" I reached for Alfie's legs. Manolo snaked one lithe, industrial cable of an arm around my neck, squeezing, and jerked me away from the deck. He threw me across the boat, and I banged my shin on the side of the cabin hard enough to chip the bone. Flipping sideways, I slammed into the deck on my shoulder, which promptly slipped out of joint.

Underneath my screams, I heard Manolo's laughter.

"You sound like your friend," Manolo said. "Buddy. My buddy, my pal, ole Phillip, yes?" Manolo took another drink, then set the bottle gently next to me. Behind him, I could hear gurgling, thrashing, and crying as Alfie fought with the creature. "Alfie makes a good meal." Manolo leaned over the deck. *"Abhoth, jolo va,* white meat is tasty, no?"

Howling, I rushed Manolo, wrapping my arms around his torso and wrestling him to the ground. He was tough, but he was three sheets to the wind. I had very little trouble getting him into a side-mount. I socked him once in the nose, drew back for another punch, and felt hot pressure smash against my groin. Manolo hawked laughter into my face. His hand manifested on my throat, its fingers curling into my larynx. I brought a hammer fist down on his forehead, bouncing his skull off the steel flooring. His eyes rolled and fluttered. His hand relaxed, and I tore it away from my throat, then kicked myself away from his now-limp body.

Maybe I still had time to help Alfie. Only about a minute had passed. When I leaned over the deck, I saw his leg still sticking up, and I snagged hold of his exposed ankle. There was no time, and I jerked as hard as I could...I could still pull Alfie out! He wasn't making any noise, I flew backwards, stepping once, twice, then tripped over Manolo's traitorous ass, spilling back to the steel floor.

Alfie's leg was jutting bloodlessly from my clutches like a giant ham hock.

"GAHH!" I threw the disembodied leg away and got back up. Panting, I gingerly stepped toward the stern, knowing what I was going to see, not knowing if I could handle it. *I'll get you a story before it's all said and done,* Manolo had said back at The Deck, and he'd spoken the truth. I just had to live through it to tell the tale.

Satiated, the living oil slick swam, slipped, or slid away with Alfie's remains still sizzling over its top, now giving off smoke as it digested poor Alfie. I thought obscenely of a floating gas grill and snickered, then laughed, then cried, then slapped myself in the face and shut the fuck up. When I turned around, thinking another drink might do me after that, something hard and meaty hit me in the face. My head whipped back, I bent my knees, and planted one fist into the deck, then looked up. Manolo stood over me, Alfie's leg clutched in his hands like a baseball bat. He swung again. I ducked, and when I came back up, I delivered an upper cut to his stupid balls, returning the earlier favor he'd done me. He took a step back and doubled over, dropping Alfie's leg. Without thinking, I snatched it off the deck, leaned back with it, and gave the best Barry Bonds swing a man could give, catching Manolo right on the temple with Alfie's heavy thigh.

"OOF!" Manolo canted left and fell, catching himself before his face could be further damaged by crashing into steel. I snap-kicked him underneath the chin. His head snapped back so damn hard I thought I'd broken his neck. He was out cold. I checked his pulse...still alive. Good. That's right, good. I, unlike this asshole, was not a fucking killer.

"I thought you were my friend," I said, rolling him over on his belly. "You go easy, now. Just let me tie you up, or I'll smash your skull underfoot. I shit you not. You call people assholes all the time. Who's the asshole? You are! We were friends!"

Manolo growled at me, spitting. "Ah, you are friends sometimes, others you are food. It depends on the situation. Friends until the Chinese came along. No one came for us, why? That is not the usual way it goes out here, is it? Where's the peninsula, bro? That is also unusual. It's supposed to be right fucking there. It is not. And the captain told me that Dagon required food."

"What?"

"I told him you were my friends. He shot the radio and the engine and told me I had no friends if you were my friends." Manolo groaned. "Everything is broken. Kill me. I'm not sailing you out of here. We die together."

"You're not going to die. The Coast Guard will be out here to pick us up soon. You'll be missed. And. *I* will be missed! So, stop it. They'll come looking."

"No. No one is coming. Night is not ending. Where we are, it never ends." Moving at the speed of tachyons, Manolo, despite both of his arms in a state of truss behind his back, got to his feet, took three steps, and took a nose-dive off the port bow.

***

By the time I was done screaming, I was hoarse, and the sun had only started painting space away from the night. An alien part of me I did not even know existed tried cajoling me with blandishments like: *Go on and cook some fish, try to enjoy yourself.*

I had no idea how to sail. I could try to use Manolo's fishing paddle. I could drift until I reached Australia or somewhere, surely one or the other Coast Guard would come along...was bound to...nothing was really bound to even if it might or might not...these were the things going through my head as it got gradually lighter and lighter outside.

It was a touch beyond the break of dawn. The water, still almost black, rippled. A bubble appeared. Two. Four, then, like cell division, they came rapidly, and the ocean slapped the underside of the boat. Waves pushed me up, then back, then down, and I feared they would capsize this very flimsy vehicle. The ocean felt like the wave pool at the water park of my youth, splashing everywhere. Steel clanged, things were falling over, and a pile of fish slapped me in the face.

I forced myself to crawl to the starboard bow and peek over the edge. Several white islands surrounded the boat, or at least that's what my mind told me they were at first. Not rock but bone, these were teeth, and I was trapped, swirling in the whirlpool of Dagon's mouth. The boat rocked, flipping forward. I flew, knowing this was the end, this was how I die, eaten by an antediluvian creature, unknown to science, called a god.

My body collided with wet, mushy ground, and I slid, down, down, rolling wrist over face over heels, tucking my legs, wrapping my arms around them, the only thought in my head *oh shit,* then I hit more mush. I slid up again, thrown up the side of a fleshy half-pipe by inertia, then splashed back into the swampy floor.

Wood rained down, slamming into the bottom of what had to be the belly of the beast that had eaten me. After the wood, the traps came, the nets, hunks of steel, pots, pans, paddles, and, as luck would have it, the remains of the bottle of rum, smashed to the floor of the god's belly.

When it was all over, I ventured into the swamp to inspect the wreckage. You're damn right I grabbed the bottle of rum, why not? I wasn't going to have much oxygen, surely, meaning I'd be dead very soon. With that in mind, I searched for something sharp with which to euthanize myself when it came to that. I intended to be drunk first, and there was just enough rum left to do the job. The ignominy of it all was occurring to me when I saw something that gave me a spark of short-lived hope, just enough to make sure that in some form this story is told.

I found my own fucking cell phone.

It's amazing, the things that swim in the ocean, don't you agree?

Manolo kept enough food around to last for a week. I found a portion of it, and if I were conservative, I might be able to make what I found last for two weeks. I, however, will not last two weeks. My hex back on Manolo is that this cellphone, which now contains this story, finds its way to a sandy beach. It could happen. I've got to believe it will happen...I am dying horribly. It's a slow burn, the stomach acid of a god.

Bite of the Ocean

By: Claire Davon

At five feet, the water was cool, but sunshine still warmed the surface area. The ship—what was left of it—was still visible. As I plunged further underwater, I could still see it.

...the octopus rising from the depths, each tentacle bigger than a man, with suckers that latched onto the shipboards to tear it apart...

At fifteen feet the water was cooler and my hazy view of the vessel faded, yet the bits of detritus were evidence of what was still happening above.

My Finnish ancestors talked of the Iku-Turso, a giant creature every bit as big and lethal as the Kraken. It lived in the deepest ocean, in legend, banished there by Väinämöinen. We did not trust that any oath to a human could hold such a monster.

I told the tales at night, over glasses of rum, to anyone willing to listen. If any of my fellows still breathed, they might credit my stories now. I would go to my watery grave knowing I was right, and giant beasts did lurk in the briny depths.

For all the good it did me.

The first sighting of the behemoth had been mistaken for a dolphin, though the tentacle had not behaved like one.

The second spotting had not. The sailor was shouting and pointing, and the captain began crying out furious commands. The Iku-Turso, a hundred feet long—or bigger—cruised beneath the water, the shadow of its massive form visible below the waves.

At forty feet the sun was a distant orb, its light wavering. No sea life was near.

...It rose from the ocean, most of its body still unseen. Its giant head, like an octopus but also not, surfaced. The beast was ten times—a hundred times—the size of the biggest of known octopus. It swam into view, fixing on the boat...

I didn't have long. Hypothermia would set in almost at once. If I didn't drown first.

At sixty feet the sun was gone, and the fish had started to return. Little of my prior vessel made it to this depth, but I suspected the heavier items would soon be returning to Davy Jones' Locker. My lungs weren't behaving as expected. It was strange. I was falling faster than I should, perhaps helped by the devil's shove into the waves, but I still needed to breathe. All creatures needed air. Perhaps the Iku-Turso did not, not the way I imagined it.

The creature had planned its attack with an intelligence that scared me. When it got to our boat, it stretched a giant tentacle up and ripped our spar off, tossing it into the water like that careless jerk Nathan had thrown his trash overboard.

Its next foray slashed through the deck, ripping a hole across the top. The ship tilted, shifting toward the water. Reggie, in the act of aiming his rifle, was the first to go into the drink. The monster reached out with a casual air and plucked him out of the water before throwing him into the distance, in a toss that would make any baseball player proud. I heard him scream as he flew through the air, crash landing in the water a hundred yards away from us.

He didn't move.

I doubted he would ever move again.

"Get it, men!"

Several of the sailors began firing at the beast. Its eyes swiveled toward the commotion, focusing on the spot where it had torn the deck. A second tentacle lashed out, widening the hole and pushing us too close to the water. We were still upright, but wouldn't be that way for long.

I came back into myself, the memory fading. I continued my plunge into the cold water. I was sinking like I was a safe. I should have plunged into the waves and then floated back up again, instead I plunged to the bottom.

At a hundred feet down, I couldn't make out the surface, but I could now sight the belly of the beast. My heart quailed. We had never had a prayer against a monstrosity that big. My skin was cold and my nose and ears numb. I wasn't sure how I was even still conscious. What was happening wasn't possible. I was in good shape, but nobody could hold their breath for this long. Slippery bodies glided around me. Faint illumination dotted the area, no doubt from fish I couldn't make out. I'd never been much of a man for the names of fish anyway, unless they were delicious ones decorating my plate. A fish was a fish, the only difference was in how it got prepared by the cook.

A cook who was somewhere dead above. Or still drowning in the remains of the boat. Just like the rest of the crew.

...The ship listed to one side, water filling the gaping hole the Iku-Turso had created. It shifted one of its giant tentacles and tore another hole, suckers sliding across the weakening boards and separating them from their companions. Chips of wood flew. Anything that wasn't secured on the deck—including sailors—slid into the brine.

I was perhaps two hundred yards down. I had lost all sense of time and space. I detected movement nearby and was tossed by what must have been a dolphin. Its fierce teeth nibbled on my ankle and I tried to shout, but could make no sound.

I should be dead and drowned. It had been...I couldn't say how long.

I went into the water with that last salvo, following the doomed Reggie and several sailors still firing in a vain attempt to save us. Their guns joined the detritus on the surface, briefly accompanying the remains of our now unseaworthy boat. I began sinking at once, my trajectory carrying me far below the surface like I was one of the cannonballs shot from the cannons, now plummeting to their end. I expected to bob up. Instead, I continued to fall, heading straight for the bottom.

I would be dead long before I got there. At this part of the ocean, the floor was still hundreds of yards beneath me, at least. I hadn't kept track of where we were. We could be at the place where the distant bottom descended into black holes that went on to who could say where. Those areas would never be seen by man, but by creatures like the Iku-Turso. We weren't in the right part of the world, but maybe this area had a place like the Mariana trench or one of those crazy abysses. I would fall and fall and fall until I was a skeleton nibbled by fish, eye sockets staring forever into a foreign landscape.

I'd lost track of the battle. In this cold, dark place, my extremities were chilled beyond measure. My fingers and toes were gone, if I, by some miracle, were to survive. But I wouldn't. I was far past the point of being able to get to the surface, even if I stopped falling.

...the screams, oh the screams. I clung to a spar and missed being thrown into the deep by inches. The men howled in the deep until their voices tapered off...

The slowly sinking boat was not long for the world. The Iku-Turso raised one massive arm and slammed into us again. The already weak boat buckled, and the shudder as it smashed into the craft was too much for the piece of wood I hung onto. I followed my mates into the drink, along with what remained of the crew who had been able to maintain their hold on the deck.

I had time to register what was happening. The sea was thick with debris that had once been a seaworthy boat heading for the Americas, for home, just a short time ago.

I'd been looking forward to a respite from the sea.

In those first chaotic moments, I saw the Iku-Turso slamming on the boat repeatedly. The men had stopped shouting. I glimpsed old Willie, that sailor who had no life but the sea, floating dead nearby. I viewed pots and pans bobbing and bet that the cook, now likely drowned, as he was not a good swimmer, would be following them. If any of us survived this rampage, the ones who remained would be marooned, with naught but the faint hope of another voyager coming by to rescue them before they died from exposure. In this wide-open area of the sea, that chance was as remote as the land we were heading for.

Then I began to fall through the waves. I didn't float as the others did, and had no time to wonder why.

...giant beast slamming down, and then pulling its arm back up...

The sensation was all so familiar. Something about the beast reaching for me triggered a recollection that pricked the back of my mind far down in the deep blue sea.

I blinked, sunlight piercing my eyeballs. But that wasn't possible. I was too far down, drowning/not drowning, my body chilled beyond hypothermia. I had no way to view the sun, not here. Yet the light was penetrating my closed lids like a nimbus.

I gasped, understanding everything when I opened my gaze to daylight and blue sky, and the water churning. A few voices were still screaming, their throats raw from their efforts.

I had never gone into the ocean. I had been hallucinating sinking so that I would not have to face this reality. The Iku-Turso, its huge eyes fixed on me, had me in its grip, one sucker-filled tentacle wrapped around my body, holding me tight. I had watched it approach me with fascinated, absolute horror, which must have been when my mind went elsewhere. Better that than this. I don't think I tried to get away—which would have been futile anyway—but I had no recollection of the time between when the horrid appendage approached me, and now. I'd rather be back with my pleasant memory of going to my death in the dark. Not this, where the stench of the creature filled my nostrils. I wriggled and squirmed but could not break free. The thing was crushing my chest. I struggled for air, but it soon wouldn't matter. The ship lay in pieces, now just flotsam. The heavier items, and some of the men, were already beneath the waves. Just like I believed I had been seconds ago.

That fate was better than what was about to happen to me. I'd supposed drowning would be bad, but this was worse. Barnacles dotted the beast, some scattering away as it maintained its terrible, inexorable squeeze of me, one Santeri Harju. I wished I could drown like them, but this sailor could not escape his destiny.

"For the love of god, have mercy."

The shouts of my doomed companions pierced my ears. One, maybe John, had located one of the life preservers and struggled into it.

That would prolong his life, if the Iku-Turso didn't gobble him up next. Or doom him to a horrible death. Better he goes into the waves, as I had been thinking I was doing. His inevitable death would be caused by the Iku-Turso, but not the same way mine was. Not this direct.

As if in response to my plea, the arm pressed me tighter and brought me closer, but didn't kill me. It took my breath without crushing my chest. Maybe it had some soul in it. Maybe this creature had some mercy. If I could find the right words, maybe I could be free. Free to drown, perhaps, but not to be devoured by a giant sea monster.

I dug for speech, and found it, despite the fact that my larynx was raw from screaming, just like the sailors who had now fallen silent.

"Please, whatever you are and whatever you feel, let me die, but don't kill me this way. It's too horrible."

The sea rolled with waves that came out of nowhere, swamping what remained of the boat. The Iku-Turso undulated, its body waving. If I wasn't mistaken, the creature was…laughing?

"Let me go. Let me die in peace and not by you. Please. You've killed us all, can't you let me live? I'll be dead on the morrow, or the next day, but that will be God's will when it happens, not yours. I don't want to be crushed to death."

Instead of answering, it squeezed until I could no longer speak. My arms were bent and pressed to my side so tight, I feared the left one, which was at an angle, would soon break. It might, even now, be broken. My chest was caving in and my organs were in danger of exploding inside my body. Perhaps they were already destroyed.

Oh, for the sweet solace of the dark, frigid water, where unfamiliar creatures lived. I shut my lids, trying to will myself back into that hallucination. It would not come.

The waves continued to rise and fall and the dark form rocked. It squeezed tighter, not enough to kill me, but to cut off my wind, and any future breaths. It had no pity, no remorse.

Our gazes met and I detected a sort of intelligence in those giant orbs. The Iku-Turso had targeted our boat. For whatever reason, whether out of malice, or boredom, or some motive I would never understand, it had come for us. It had followed us, or perhaps risen from the deep, until we were vulnerable, without hope of rescue. It had done this on purpose. I was wasting what little breath I had pleading with it. I could wriggle and try to scream for the short time left to me, but I knew I was a dead man.

A peace similar to that I had experienced when I imagined I was plunging to the bottom of the sea engulfed me. Now that my life was measured in seconds, I knew true serenity. This was the end. I had no more story to tell. This was the last thought I would have as the life was being squeezed out of me—and that death tasted of salt.

Then I knew nothing else as I slid down the creature's gullet, and into oblivion.

Bros Before Hoes

By: LJ Jacobs

1.

The main criticism about films and books set in the modern era, is the easy access the characters have to mobile phones.

The mobile phone is a tension killer to a suspense story.

For stories to work in modern times, mobile phones must be written out as soon as possible. Writers today must create a plot point (usually at the start) when each character's mobile phone conveniently loses its charge, is lost or stolen or is simply the victim of a poor signal.

The story that follows doesn't have a mobile phone problem. This is because it takes place in the 1970's.

It's a period piece if you like.

But should I be thankful for the absence of a mobile phone so that my tale can have some proper tension?

I would say a resounding yes, if it wasn't for the fact that it's a true story!

Every day since the creation of the cell phone, I've often wondered if help could have been reached for Kate and I, that fateful day back in '74, if only one of us had had easy access to a mobile.

Before the godawful horror that befell us…

I guess that's one of those questions that'll continue to keep me up at night and haunt me to my fast-approaching grave.

2.

Adam and I had been best friends since childhood. We went through school together and enrolled at the same university, opting for the same degree in sport education.

Adam wanted to be a senior year football coach, and I wanted to teach elementary school.

Then Adam met Kate (another student in our year) and things began to get serious between them. He'd never had a serious girlfriend before, and you could tell by his eyes and demeanour how much he worshipped the ground she seemingly hovered above!

She was, as they say, a babe!

Then came the night of the beach party.

All our year gathered at one of Florida's best seafronts to dance, eat, and maybe indulge in some heavy petting behind a convenient dune. Although heavy petting was as far as it went, because of the local foot fall. It was a well-known area for dog walkers as well as for us students.

Some of us brought barbecues to the party and others brought meat, baps and coleslaw.

Everyone pitched in with the alcohol, though. That and marijuana were the two things no one could do without when a party was involved!

We were all having a great time before Adam decided to head off to bed early because of food poisoning! He thought he may have eaten some pink undercooked chicken that had managed to get past the quality control of its cook. He looked as pale as a corpse and couldn't stop vomiting. By the way he was shifting from one foot to the other, I suspected his arse also wanted a piece of the action. He looked like he was desperately trying to hold back a flood of diarrhoea.

He told Kate to stay and enjoy the party.

She protested, but Adam insisted!

-You're having fun, babe, he said, shivering. -Don't worry about me. I'll see you tomorrow… He looked over at me. -Will you make sure she gets back to the dorm ok, Zack?

-Sure thing, I said, putting my arm around her shoulders…

But that wasn't where the night ended for Kate and me, as she invited me into her room and I, like the fool I was, followed.

It was because we'd hit it off at the party, and not having Adam around had created a vacuum that I was more than willing to fill.

There'd been flirting, eye contact, and soft leg stroking at the party. All this, combined with potent alcohol and weed, proved the perfect combination to get us horny and carefree enough to not only deep kiss behind a dune, but also to bring it back inside for some bedroom gymnastics.

And, boy, was the sex great!

She did things to me I didn't know such a conservative looking girl would know.

Not once, while in the throes of passion, did my best friend come into my mind. Like a dog in heat, I only wanted to conquer the body of the gorgeous woman before me.

And conquer it I did!

Only later, after an awkward early morning departure, did the betrayal of my best friend play heavy on my heart and mind.

What had I done?

It was shameful. But it takes two to tango, and Kate was just as guilty as I was.

We decided not to speak of the affair again, both agreeing it was a silly mistake.

I threw myself into my studies and Kate and Adam continued as a couple. But like most temptations in life, we were soon drawn back to what pleased us.

Drunken calls were made in the middle of the night, when we would reminisce about our physical and emotional connection. Kate said it was lovely to finally experience an orgasm with another person, and to also to be hugged afterward the act - something Adam had never done.

It pleased me that I'd pleased her.

One day, sober and coherent, I called Kate again and asked her outright if she wanted to be with me instead of Adam.

She replied, -More than anything. 'It's you I love, Zackary! And, I suppose, always have…

We met up two more times before finally deciding to confront Adam and tell him the cold hard truth.

Kate and I wanted to be with each other.

He took it well.

Too well, I now know.

For behind the cool exterior, he was thinking about the betrayal.

Not so much by Kate, but by a guy whom he considered his brother.

3.

After a few weeks of seeing each other, Kate and I were finding it harder and harder to find privacy. The academic year had begun in earnest, and everyone wanted to stay in their rooms to study.

Adam, aware of the trouble we were having to be alone, took me to one side and whispered, -I know a great place you can go, and it's in the middle of nowhere!

I was slightly taken aback by his amiable and helpful attitude. I knew Adam to be a man who'd held grudges in the past - grudges that were sometimes concluded with violence - but thought that maybe he'd grown as a person since being in the semi mature world of university. I also knew his suggestions would be worth hearing, since he knew the area well, thanks to having family links here.

-Thanks, man, I said. -Where is this place?

-Not far from here is a private lake, he said. -The land it's on is currently unoccupied and for sale, so it's perfect for some sexy privacy. It's surrounded by a high link fence, but there is a hole you can get through from the main road. I'll write out some proper directions for you! There's a small motorboat there that's been left behind, so you can go out on the lake and then be totally alone with… Kate.

Adam gulped, seeming to briefly recall his feelings for the woman in his mind's eye.

After a brief pause of staring into the distance, Adam suddenly smiled. He was out of his head and back in the room. -Go there tomorrow night. I'll even leave you both a little surprise in the boat.

I didn't know what to say. I walked over to my best friend and simply hugged him. He didn't react at first, then I felt him lean in, and his arms tightened around my back.

-Thank you, I finally muttered. -Thank you for being so understanding and so thoughtful these past few weeks. I know it hasn't been easy. We don't deserve you. I don't deserve you…

4.

Adam gave me the directions to the lake, and Kate and I went there the next night in my dad's old Plymouth.

As expected, the property was fenced off, but there was indeed a hole where Adam said there'd be one, and it was very secluded like he had promised. I stopped by the side of the road and turned the lights off. Though it was summer, darkness was creeping fast because of the late hour.

Adam said to come at this time as it would guarantee no interruptions…

-Are you sure about this, Zack? asked Kate.

-Absolutely, I said. -Adam said it'd be the perfect place for a bit of quiet time, as no one is currently living here and there's not another house around for miles.

-Ok, Kate relented.

As we got out the car, the intense heat of Florida's summer evening hit us. It felt wonderful and comforting. I turned on the flashlight I'd brought with us, and we headed for the opening in the fence. Kate still looked unsure but followed me through the hole anyway.

The tiny wooden motorboat was on the shore.

It had a gas lantern on board, and a hamperwith a conveniently placed on top of it. I turned the lantern on, put the torch in my pocket, and read Adam's scrawly handwriting.

Open hamper for surprises.

Have a good evening, guys.

See you soon…

Adam.

In the hamper was a small picnic blanket, some nibbles, and a bottle of champagne with two glasses.

There was a strong smell of petrol coming from the sandy ground, but I paid it no mind because my focus was purely on the hamper, and the little adventure Kate and I would soon be having.

-Something's not right, said Kate, once we were heading out. -Don't you think so? Why is Adam being so nice to us after all we did to him?

-He wants to show us there's no hard feelings, I said. -He's a good guy.

-You said yourself he bares grudges, said Kate.

-That was before we started university, I reassured her. -He seems to have mellowed now. He's turned into that rare type of friend who'll forgive anything. As good as family, if you like.

As we approached the centre of the lake, I turned off the engine and let us drift. It was a pleasant rocking feeling, like being cradled. We lay down with the champagne and, as had been the plan all along, made love in peace.

The only sounds we could hear were the crickets chirping., before our panting, moaning, and cries of ecstasy filled the air, giving those singing insects a run for their money.

Afterwards, we held each other. This was not only out of a deep sense of love but also necessity, as we began to feel the cold. Kate felt it more than I did. She was shivering uncontrollably. I think it was because she was wearing less than me.

-Let's get you back, I said, finally.

Once we were both fully clothed again, Kate sat on the cross seat as I pulled the starting cord on the motor. It spluttered to life, then choked off just as quick.

-What the? I muttered.

I tried again.

Nothing.

The engine was as dead as a nineteenth century poet.

How strange!

I then looked at the floor. Our picnic blanket was ringing wet. Water had begun to pool in the base of the boat. There were bubbles popping on the surface in at least twenty places, like small impotent fountains. They could only have been caused by small holes drilled beneath the boat - small holes that were letting in more water that we could scoop out.

Out of curiosity, I quickly put my hand to the main body of the motor. I felt an oily discharge there. It was then I remembered the petrol smell at the shore. The engine had been leaking out this entire time!

-No petrol and a leak! I shouted.

Kate started to laugh nervously.

Suddenly a loud bellowing roar filled the air.

Kate's look of nervousness turned to terror.

It was the sort of look a rich person in Paris might have given, kneeling at the foot of the guillotine.

-What the fuck was that? she screamed. -Are there gators in here?

-Of course not, I said. -Adam wouldn't suggest a lake filled with gators.

Kate looked at me wild eyed. -Or would he? she said, softly.

I straightened and scanned the boat for a moment. Everything was pointing towards a macabre ending. As my feet got more sodden, I finally concluded that Adam, my so-called best friend, was capable of anything!

-If there are gators in here, I said, -then we won't be able to swim.

-No shit, said Kate.

I hurriedly looked for a pair of oars.

Surprise, surprise... There were none to be found.

-No fucking oars, either! I cried. -He's killing us! He's sabotaged the boat. We're out of petrol, there're more holes in the floor than a colander, no oars, and we're slowly sinking.

Kate stood and wailed a loud, -No! Oh, God, no! Help! Someone help us!

I grabbed her and held her tight to stop her panicking. Her wild sudden movements were sure to get us in the water quicker than any slow leak ever would.

-Calm down, I said, soothingly. -We'll find a way out. There may only be one gator in here for all we know. And gators aren't as aggressive as crocs! They may be more interested in sleeping!

I eased Kate back down and knew what had to be done. I crouched to the side and slowly began to paddle the boat with my hand.

As Kate sobbed loudly, I cautiously began to pull at the dark murky water, where anything could have been hiding.

The boat started to move. We were making progress - even if it was at a snail's pace.

Then, suddenly, quicker than a mousetrap, my hand was seized by a long toothy snout. Before I could even scream, the predator had gone back under the dark water, taking my hand with it.

Blood spurted like a fountain from a frayed meat stump. As I turned in panic to face Kate, I sprayed her whole upper body with my life fluid. She jumped up and squealed in what can only be described as pure terror.

While she was losing her shit, I pulled my belt free and desperately tried to tie a tourniquet around my wound. I tied it using my good hand and my mouth.

Mindful of capsizing us, Kate sat back down and mumbled and rocked like an asylum patient. I sat next to her and put my good arm around her.

-Oh, Zack, what are we gonna do? she sobbed, putting her head on my shoulder.

The water in the boat was up to our shins now.

-Th-th-there's a ch-ch-chance it's a lone gator, I said, with a shiver in my voice. I was in deep shock, and feeling lightheaded from the blood loss.

-Your poor hand… said Kate.

-It's fine, I said, -L-let's not w-w-worry about that now. Let's try and work s-s-something out. If there's only one gator, we could maybe distract it by throwing the hamper in the water while we… I gulped… -While we make a swim for it.

She looked at me, wide-eyed in disbelief. -But that's…

-A risk? I finished for her.

-More like fucking suicide, she screamed.

-Maybe, I said, -but if we both just sit here until the water's up to our chins, then we're both gonna perish anyway!

There was a short pause, then I said, -I'm sure there's only one gator, Kate. Let's be brave and do this.

Suddenly the bellowing roar came again, almost like it was mocking us.

It was joined by a chorus of other roars.

-Fuck, screamed Kate, -there's more of them!

-We've got to go, Kate, I pleaded. -Don't think about them. Just think about the damage I'm gonna do to Adam once we're back at campus! I'm gonna fuck up the jealous prick so bad!

We slowly lifted ourselves up. The boat started to capsize, but we managed to steady it with corrective shifts and leans. I grabbed the hamper and readied myself to throw it. With my injured limb and the loss of so much blood, I didn't have much energy left. I only managed to flop the hamper off the side of the boat.

It was a pitiful effort.

At that moment, a beam of light hit us, followed by a, -Hey, traitors, how ya both doing?

It was Adam.

Adam the psychopath!

-You bastard, Adam, I screamed. -Don't just stand there! Help us! How could you do this to us man?

-You're a crazy arsehole, screamed Kate. -Get us out of here!

-You both should have thought of that before betraying me! You especially, Zack. We've been friends for years! But… I still love ya, which is why I'm offering you a way out. All you've got to do is sacrifice Kate by pushing her in. Let's face it, she's only a spoiled brat who is the product of her parents' privilege anyway, so who's gonna morn her for long? Did she give you the story about you being the only one who had ever given her an orgasm? It's a load of crap - I found out she's fucked most of the guys on campus, and some of the girls, too - especially the ones with purple hair, tattoos, and tit piercings. While the gators are tearing her apart, you can swim back to me - your best buddy - then you'll always remember one of life's most important unwritten rules.

-What if I don't? I said.

-Then you'll both die.

I looked at Kate.

-I'm sorry, Kate, I shrugged.

-No, Zack! Don't even think about it! she wailed.

-I'm so sorry, I repeated, sobbing.

-Zack, noooooo!!!

-I want to live, Kate.

-But so do I!!!

I pushed her with all my might, and she hit the water headfirst. As soon as the frenzied snapping and rolling started, I jumped out the other side and swam to the light coming from the shore - along with the uncontrollable laughter…

5.

As soon as I got to the shore and up close to a still laughing Adam, I started screaming and throwing random punches that had no strength behind them. Adam easily wrestled me, facdown, into the dusty ground.

He lay on top of me until I became deathly still, though I was still weeping.

-We both know you can't kill me, like I can't kill you, he said, coldly, -so let's cut the caveman crap. Your sin is now absolved, Zacky Boy. Congratulations, you've learned an important lesson and the unwritten rule.

-What unwritten rule? I asked, my forehead still pressing into the sand.

Adam laughed. -Bros before hoes, bud. Always. Bros… before… hoes!

He helped me back to his waiting car. He said he'd walk back for mine tomorrow.

He promised to take me to the emergency room. The doctors and nurses wouldn't question me about a silly old gator wound, they were as common as racism down here in the south, in the seventies.

I watched as Adam sealed the gap in the fence, then stooped and picked up a sign that looked like it had been discarded facedown earlier.

He hung it over the repair.

It simply said,

DANGER! KEEP OUT! ALLIGATOR FARM

Scylla

By: Mawr Gorshin

"What a beautiful day to go sailing!" said Caleb Disch, CEO of Scylla, a chemical company heavily involved in plastics manufacturing, as he steered the family yacht out just far enough into the Pacific Ocean to make the California beach barely visible in the background. "Can you believe those two kids of ours, sitting downstairs in their cabin and playing Switch?"

"Yeah, it's ridiculous," his wife, Sarah, said as she gazed upward. "Such beautiful blue skies, hardly a cloud in sight, and such beautiful blue water down below—" She looked down at the ocean, but saw a few pieces of plastic floating by the side of the yacht. "I guess I spoke too soon."

"What was that, honey?" Caleb asked.

"Oh, uh, I was just thinking about something I read in the paper yesterday," she said. "I'm sure you know about the protestors picketing outside the Scylla building with their placards, complaining about all the plastics that have been dumped in the ocean?"

"Yeah, I know all about that. Damn kids. Bleeding heart liberals, they're such a pain in the ass."

"Well, I don't mean to take their side against you, dear, but according to the article I read, they do have a few good points. Marine animals eat some of the plastics, thinking they're food, then the plastic blocks their digestive tracks, preventing real food from reaching their stomachs, so they die of starvation."

"Oh, please."

"Some of these animals get entangled in the plastics, or suffocate from having them around their necks, or toxic chemicals get released and contaminate the water—"

"Oh, Jesus Christ, Sarah! Do I really need this guilt trip? I mean no harm to the sea animals. It's just business. Scylla is in competition with other corporations, fierce competition. We need to keep our profits up if we're to keep our heads above water, excuse the expression. We're kind of stuck between a rock and a hard place here: we either care about the animals and lower our profits, making us lose out to the competition, or we keep our profits up to stay successful, and some of the animals may have to suffer. I'm sorry about that, but that's just the way it is. Besides, there are people who go out into the oceans and clean all the plastic out, they clean up all the other pollution as well. As I see it, that's good enough."

"Whatever," she said with a sneer and a shrug.

"Look, let's just enjoy our weekend, OK?"

"OK." Sarah looked down at the water again and noticed more pieces of plastic. Now they were moving through the water fast, almost like fish, all 'swimming' in one particular direction, the opposite of that of the beach. She shuddered a bit, then remembered the kids. "Hey, Stella! Cary! Will you two please put those damn video game machines away and come up here? It's so ridiculous, you two always down there when we're supposed to be up here enjoying all this beauty. Get up here, now!"

"Alright, alright," the voices of their two teenage kids could be heard saying together. A minute later, the two of them were up on deck.

"There," their dad said. "That wasn't too painful, was it?"

"No," the two of them moaned in unison.

"No," their dad mocked. "Take a look around, won't you? Have some appreciation for the beautiful world out there surrounding us."

The two teens looked all around the yacht and saw only water.

"Dad, where's the beach?" Cary asked.

"What are you talking about?" he said. "It's back there—what?"

The beach that had been barely visible just a few minutes before was now nowhere to be seen. Both Caleb and Sarah noticed its disappearance for the first time.

"Umm, where are we, Caleb?" Sarah asked. She looked down at the water again and saw many more plastic pieces 'swimming' in a long line, in that same direction, to their mysterious destination.

"How could this have happened?" Caleb asked. "We left our motor off the whole time. We dropped our sails as soon as we got to where we wanted, so we could still see the beach and know where we were... How did we get out so far? The waves have been reasonably still."

"We are totally lost," Stella said. "I'm scared."

"So am I, sweetie," her mom said, stepping forward and hugging her tightly.

"We're not lost," Caleb said. "Let's just cruise along for a few more minutes and I will find my bearings. We know California is East. I just have to figure out how to navigate the damn compass."

Far off into the horizon, they could vaguely see where all that plastic was being collected. It was in the same direction their yacht was heading. They all squinted their eyes, trying to make sense of what they were seeing.

As they got closer, they had a better idea of what was happening, but they had no way of explaining it. "What the hell?" Caleb said.

All those pieces of plastic were whirling together, as if to form a whirlwind.

"It looks so...supernatural," he said, trembling, so awestruck by the spectacle unfolding before him that he didn't even think to try to start the engine or flee. "How could that be happening? My God!"

The whirling pieces of plastic seemed to be melting together to form some giant thing.

A living thing.

"That can't be!" Sarah said, her jaw dropping all the way down. "It's impossible!"

The shape of the form was growing clearer…but still, totally incomprehensible. The family saw the shaping of a giant sea monster: four eyes, six long, snaky necks with grisly heads, each with myriad rows of sharp teeth, and a dozen tentacle-like legs. Something was forming near its middle, looking at first like a ring of large balls, before the balls each took on a distinct shape—that of dogs' heads.

"What is that?" Caleb asked, his voice cracking like that of a pre-teen. "A plastic Kraken?"

"We must be dreaming," Sarah said. "I-I must be having a nightmare. This can't be happening. Why am I not waking up? I should have woken up by now! This is only a dream."

"It looks like something out of Dungeons and Dragons," Cary said, his eyes wide open.

"Or out of Greek mythology, or something," Stella said in a tremulous voice, her whole body shaking.

One of the snake heads looked down at Cary, three rows of teeth grinning hungrily right at him. Cary just stared up at it, into its eyes, mesmerized by them, frozen in his spot.

Suddenly, the head shot right down at him like a lightning bolt and grabbed him in all those rows of teeth. His blood sprayed everywhere. He was dead before he even had time to scream.

His family began screaming, though.

"Oh, my God!" Caleb shouted, his eyes watering. "My son!"

"Cary!" Sarah screamed. "My baby!"

The yacht drew closer and closer to the giant monster, which was looking down at the boy's sister now, seeming to salivate, making it apparent that it considered her appetizing. Its eyes stared into hers. Frozen in fear, as was the rest of the family, Stella could only stare back into its eyes.

Another of the serpentine heads dove down at her and grabbed her between its teeth. Again, her blood splashed all over the place, and she had no time to scream.

Caleb and Sarah began shaking in shock and bawling loudly. Other than their shaking, however, they were still too terrified to move, too frightened they would draw attention to themselves, and thus were rooted to their spots, unable to act, unable to help..

Now, the eyes of the monster were looking down at Sarah. She couldn't resist looking back into those hungry eyes. Caleb watched her looking back at it.

"No, no," he pleaded. "Not her, too. Please, let me at least have her! *No!*"

A third head swooped down on her and took her up into its teeth, which stabbed deep into her guts and rained her blood all over her newly widowed husband and their yacht. Her body was given to the dogs' heads, though, while Caleb watched in horror as they tore her body in half, then ate and swallowed the two pieces.

"Why?" he screamed, his teary eyes looking up at the monster. "Why are you doing this?"

A deep, booming voice came seemingly from the ocean itself, ringing in his ears with an almost deafening loudness. *This is your just punishment for polluting my oceans with your plastic.*

"But paying to have the plastics disposed of without polluting would have eaten too much into Scylla's profits! They would have just fired me and got someone else to do the same thing. That's putting me into a place where I have no good options!"

Putting you…between the devil and the deep blue sea? the voice taunted. *You must pay for your greed.*

"But my wife and children were innocent!" Caleb shouted back in sobs. "Only I am guilty of polluting the ocean, not them. They were innocent!"

All of the marine life in my ocean, my children, were innocent, too. Your greed showed them no mercy. Therefore, you will be treated likewise.

"What are you?" he asked. "A god? A devil? I don't believe in any gods or devils."

I am Priff, Crim of the water, the bass voice said. *I am here to avenge the sea animals. My brother, Weleb, Crim of the air, aided me in bringing your yacht here to make you pay for your greed and wickedness.. It does not matter if you think us god or devil, all you need to know is that you must suffer.*

"You killed my family... I can't suffer anymore. Please have that thing kill me too!" Caleb shouted, still weeping. "I don't wanna live if I don't have them."

You shall not die by Scylla, as they did. That would be too easy for you. You must die another way.

"What do you mean, I won't die by Scylla? My *company* is Scylla! My company didn't kill my family. You did!"

Your company did *kill them; they died from your greed. There is more than one kind of Scylla in the world. But neither Scylla will kill you.*

Caleb watched as the yacht began to pass out of the grasp of the creature, of Scylla, who just let it float right by.

He could do nothing other than shake and weep. "Why? Why did they have to suffer for what I did?"

He heard the whooshing of water ahead. He looked out, far in front of the yacht. He saw the water opening out into a giant, circular, swirling hole.

The yacht drew closer, circling the giant aperture.

He thought he could see, sticking out of the rushing water, circles of teeth...teeth made out of...*plastic?*

Those teeth looked strong enough, whatever they were made of, to tear his body to pieces. As the yacht reached the rim of the toothed whirlpool, he stretched out his arms and welcomed his fate.

***

A week later, Kelly Biss, CFO of Scylla, took her family out on a yachting trip as well, also just off the Californian coast.

As their boat went out to sea, she wondered about the Disch family, who had gone on vacation, to an undisclosed destination, and never returned. Last she heard, they were starting an investigation.

"Poor Caleb," she said to herself, closing the last social media update about the Disch family, which disclosed no new information. "I really do hope he's okay."

One of her kids, standing beside her on the side of the deck, looked down at the water.

"Mom, look!" The girl said. "Down there." She pointed.

Both of them saw pieces of plastic…swimming…in a line, straight out ahead of them.

Beyond the Veil of Fog

By: Milan Simić

Lighthouse keeper's testimony... first scrap.

Mother... Father... my purpose is finally known. I grieve that ye cannot behold me at this time, for the Black Gods have taken me under Their nurture. Therefore I made this. Ultimate creation in Their name... an idol of reverence, to glorify Them. I hope they shall forgive for the sudden weakness within me. Fear overpowered my common sense. Though, I believe they spared me for a purpose. I do not know how I came to be here. Why am I this old, when the path I embarked upon was the path of a boy? Was I out there for years? Have I lived here for all this time? I know nothing anymore. When I came here, I was afraid... but no longer. Fear is the fruit of ignorance. Fear prevents action. Fear is weakness for those who know they are going to die. I know that beyond this reality dwells another one. I have seen it with my own eyes. I have witnessed all the loathsomeness of this world in one clear vision. I have seen death, i have seen life, and I have seen the ebbing of hope with pure madness dripping in, filling the void. It was in that moment I called out to Him, begged Him to show me wisdom, to show me visions of this new world and vile insanity of sour truth. And truly I did see that wisdom is better than folly. The wise have eyes in their heads, but the foolish stumble in the dark; yet I also came to know that it is the same for all, for in this place, the choice is meaningless. Wisdom and insanity merge into one, and cherubims of Theirs, like tarry shadows, dragged their ungodly feet through the black mire, which was inaccessible to the pure feet of the unbelievers.

Mother... I hope thy posthumous smile means that you have perceived the realm beneath the crimson sky in all its grandeur. He takes the mind. He takes the sole embodiment of what makes a person from your head, and in its place, He leaves deep scars of eternal knowledge.

That we are all transient, mortal, and insignificant, and only he who bows down to the Black God from the abyss shall live forever. And just as the fish from that sea received wings, to exist in both water and sky, no longer to be bound with the singular reality its creator had intended. It lifts it's head beyond watery world, inhales the air, and soars the path of the drippy heavens, while the others remain in darkness, condemned to perish in uniformity. So too the wings were granted unto me, but I was afraid. I fell after the first ascent. Father… be proud, for I shall again reside in the sky. I shall fly in the fantasy of diversity. I will be eternal.

1.

I just watched as he struggled and opened his mouth, into which black liquid flowed. Then he sank. I thought the water would bring him back, but it didn't. It remained calm, dark, and mysterious. I don't even know when I started running towards the boat. I was crying. I pushed the boat away from the viscid shore and jumped into it. The shapes were somewhere behind me, letting out their malicious screams. The last memory I took from there was forever imprinted in my mind. A deformed face, turned into a mask of fear. The expression on that face didn't scare me as much as the fact that it was my own face. It began to open its mouth and let out a scream. I just watched as it struggled and spread its lips, from which a scream should have come. My vision became blurry from the rush of foul water covering my eyes. It wasn't the grimace on that face, or the very form of primal fear that scared me, but the fact that the fear was directed at me. Why? What is happening to me? Then, my own screech, though under water, pushed me out of this reality and into the embrace of thick darkness. As the small boat lazily drifted away from the sick shore, I began to pass out. as I drifted further from the ill shore, I lost consciousness before I could answer to that final question.

2.

As long as I can remember, I have been obsessed with the sea. That vast, endless mass of water stirred feelings in me that I cannot explain. I could watch it for hours, captivated by its mystery. I gazed as that vast expanse of blue changed shape, gently rippling, curling, rising at the slightest breeze, reaching a mountain of waves, only to crash back down, breaking against its smooth surface, returning to its original, calm form. They say the Moon affects this. What people call tides. No. The Moon has nothing to do with it. The sea breathes. It is alive and those are its sighs. Also, it is merciless. It rarely gives back what it takes. And if you do manage to steal something from it, it will never be the same. Try it. Throw a small pebble into its embrace, and then try to find it again. It's practically impossible. And don't even get me started on people. The sea takes, but it never gives back the same.

I could stand for hours and watch it in secret. I was shy... afraid. I imagined with such passion that I saw the product of my thoughts right in front of me. I looked through the window at the clear water and saw how it dried up and, like a drain, disappeared, flowing down into countless cracks deep in the earth. I waited to see what would be revealed when only the empty riverbed with its muddy bottom remained. I saw fish jumping, struggling for life, I saw algae from which salty water still dripped, I saw bones... white, covered in moss, fused with stone. Next to the lifeless seaweed, I saw countless artifacts and lost personal belongings, then I saw the remains of cities. I saw people, in the way they truly are, exposed, stripped of their outer shell. I also saw their despair frozen in fossilized faces, while their lungs filled with salty water. I stared like that, until one day I saw something that couldn't be.
Down below, there *I* stood, me, covered in algae and tar-like black slime. I stood frozen, looking at this version of myself through the window. The other I, in the dried-up riverbed, tried to say

something, opening my other mouth only for a large, slimy eel to crawl out of it, before slithering away into one of the cracks in the earth. I don't know if the other I was laughing or crying. I only saw this other myself spread arms and call for me to come down. Then he grinned, lay down, burrowed into the mud, and disappeared. One thing is certain. The sea takes, but it never gives back the same.

3.

I was ten years old when it happened. The cold water of the turbulent sea took me. However... that is not entirely true. It took my faithful copy, my image and likeness— the weaker, more disinterested, far more fearful one. My twin brother drowned that evening. At least, that is what they claim. The body was never found, apart from a left shoe in which was some blood and a small, confused crab in it, which had washed up on the rocky shore. They say so, but I know it's not the truth. The sea claimed him as its own. I was angry, furious, disappointed, and above all, betrayed. I wept bitterly. That betrayal hurt me. I did not cry for the loss of my brother, but because the sea had chosen him instead of me. He did not even like the water... While I dreamt of it. I was meant to be the chosen one. Not him. And that is why I wept.

I was nine years old, however, when the light started. At first, it seemed to me that I was dreaming... that I had not seen clearly, but the light began to appear more and more often. It would begin to shine in the evening... briefly, almost timidly, then gradually more frequently. It seemed to only come at the moments when I gazed through the fog. I could have sworn it was communicating with me. I gathered my courage one night, and started sneaking out when father and mother had fallen asleep. I would stand on the pebbled shoal and watch. Far in the mist, across the wide sea, there shone my personal point of mystery. Personal, because I knew that the light was meant for me. This deepened my belief that the sea guarded its secrets jealously. One evening, I called my father out and tried to show him, but in the distance, there was nothing, only night, breeze, and fog. I tried to convince him that the light was real. That it moved gently, flickering and fading intermittently. He told me it was impossible and that the way I described it could only be an old lighthouse that hadn't been in use for decades. A lighthouse... It was the first time I had heard of such a thing. It sparked within me a glimmer of what would later become a flame of curiosity. I wanted to know more. I was hungry for the story, but my father just stared grimly into the night. He said nothing. And again, I wept.

4.

From that day on, my father was never the same. Granted, he was never talkative, but from that day onward, I never saw him smile again. The only emotion that grew stronger was his love for drink. He was a giant of a man, with sinewy, gnarled hands from throwing fish nets all day, and a thick, graying mustache, yellowed beneath the nose from strong tobacco. His facewas creased from years of squinting at the sun.

Every evening, he would arrive home, accompanied by creaking sound of heavy doors and the barking of yard dogs, bringing with him the day's haul. We would eat in silence, mostly fish, but sometimes other types of meat he had traded for or bought at the market. After dinner, he would sit by the fire and light his large wooden pipe, smoking it deep into the night. Now, the shadow of that man would sit by the cold, ashy fireplace, staring somewhere far away, across the sea, beyond the blurred mountains, empty rum bottles rolling around by his feet making the only occasional sound in the grave silence. He would just sit there, gazing at something only he could see, beyond the veil of fog. It was as if he no longer noticed me, As if I had become invisible to him.

That day had also changed my mother. Once always chatty and kind-hearted, now she was just silent and detached. Silent, but smiling. It was not a warm, loving smile though, but a twisted, artificial grin. A housewife by nature, she was a noble woman, raised with patriarchal values. She would do the usual things around the house, like scrubbing, cooking, washing clothes, and her respite came in knitting woolen socks for us. Small in stature, with narrow shoulders, her head covered by a scarf that always hid her neatly tied hair, she looked as though a gentle breeze might carry her away from the earth, but her endurance had always been extraordinary. There was no task that would, even seemingly, ever wear her down. Every morning, before dawn, she would accompany father, before the roosters had sung their mournful dirge of everyday life, and every evening, she would wait for him, when darkness had already taken full command. She would strip off his heavy coat and deep fisherman's boots. Now, the shadow of that woman sat by the cold, grey fireplace, smiling emptily, knitting her braid again and again, until her fingers began to bleed. She ate nothing and drank little water... she aged decades in just a few months. She would only sit and smile, enigmatically silent, gazing somewhere far away, beyond the blurred mountains. She no longer noticed us anyone. We had become invisible to her.

5.

"Father, tell me about lighthouse?" – I asked him one evening.

My curiosity was so strong that it felt like an itch beneath my skin. There had to be something more to it. I knew it was trying to make contact with me. The light signals were becoming more frequent. Whenever I raised my arms on the shoal, bathed only in the light of the moon, it would respond to me. We had our own personal signal. Last night I raised my hands twice, then lowered them, then raised them once more. The light then flickered in that same sequence. Twice briefly, then again.

"The lighthouse hasn't worked for years, I told you. There's no one to tend it." He muttered in his gruff voice beneath his thick mustache. I only saw the corner of his lower lip move.

"Tending it? I don't understand." – I truly didn't.

"What do you think? That the building is alive, hm? There must be a man who lights and extinguishes the light." My ignorance seemed to amuse him. "Now, enough. It's time for bed."

"When was the last time someone worked there, father?" Now, I was really interested. Sleep was the last thing on my mind.

He sighed deeply. I watched his broad back expand with the intake of air. Then he turned around, sat down, emptied his tobacco pouch, and looked at me.

"Fine… I'll tell you the story of the lighthouse keeper, but after that, I don't want to hear another word from you. You go to bed, and that's the end of the story. Understand?"

"Yes, father." I gazed at his rough, weathered face. The fire danced in his pupils. This was the beginning of my journey, though I didn't know it yet.

The Story of the Lighthouse Keeper

They say that on that night, there was a storm the likes of which even the oldest among them could not remember. It seemed as though the earth had sent its vengeance upon the people. The storm raged through the entire night, turning the sky and the land into one, as the wind mercilessly tore apart and carried away everything before it. There was no electricity, no place to hide. The was only fear and prayer. It felt as though a new flood was imminent. However, by the next morning, the earth forgave us. Our prayers, it seemed, had been heard. The first ray of the sun hinted a ceasefire, but with that ray, the water sent us a strange man as well. He appeared to be nothing less than a messenger of the sea itself, with a ragged, long, untidy beard, and dressed only in torn cloth. He looked like the storms very incarnate. No one knew who he was, nor from where he had truly come. The dialect he spoke was unintelligible, and the images he drew in the sand created an unsettling sense of discomfort to those who seen them. He had been found at dawn that morning after the storm, and the fishermen who found him swore they had seen him, in his tattered, too-small clothes, with a mad look in his eyes, shouting incomprehensible words while shaking his bony fist at the sky itself.

Naturally, the man was soon declared mad and since no one knew what else to do with him, they allowed him to take up residence in the abandoned lighthouse, from which he almost never emerged, nor did he associate with others. The man would only venture out briefly, under the cover of night, to gather dead fish, snails, and shells from the rocky border, or to simply stand there in silence, staring into the mist. At first, people were afraid, but soon they learned to ignore him. He never bothered anyone, nor did anyone bother him. He was alone, and he was mad. Simple as that.

While he was still the subject of conversation, they speculated that he was a foreign sailor who had suffered a shipwreck, perhaps losing his crew or a loved one in the process, and only by sheer luck he survived, but with his mind forever altered. He became to them, an irrelevant lunatic.

The inhabitants of the area near the harbor initially found the light the old lighthouse, revived from its long dormancy, quite disturbing, but that lasted only a short time, and no one wanted to mess with the old man anyway.

Sometimes, however, it seemed as though he was signaling someone across the sea, though no one knew to whom? The ships had long since ceased to arrive. The fishing boats came and went in the daytime, always in a hurry with their work. They came to the conclusion that, in his madness and pain, he was trying to call out to his drowned friends. They pitied him, and left him in peace.

As time went on, the old man became almost invisible. He was no longer the subject of conversation, and no one paid attention to the mad lighthouse keeper who signaled with shadows and waves. One night, though, the peculiar old man disappeared. Many believe he drowned in one of his delusional night wanderings. Still... no one cared. He was one less madman in this miserable world. Drunken Obed, however, swore that he had seen the old man standing on the shore… naked. First, he hummed a tune, then he began to dance frenetically. He writhed and twisted, singing louder and louder. For a man of his age, Obed claimed the man's body should not have been able to endure such movements... yet, he had danced on.

Suddenly, he stopped... he began to mutter incomprehensible words, took a sharp seashell, and carved some kind of symbol into his chest. A symbol like the ones they had seen drawn in the sand. Bloodied and disheveled, he headed towards the sea, arms spread wide, laughing as if going to embrace an old friend. At one point, submerged up to his waist, the lunatic's head twisted suddenly to the left, and for the first time, he looked directly at Obed. Even from that distance, Obed would never forget that look. It was a look that crippled him for life. From that moment on, he had tried to drown the memory in alcohol, until one day, when that very alcohol drown him instead.

About a year later, Obed's body was found amidst the limestone rocks on the shore, a bottle clutched in his hand. He had died of a heart attack, but it looked as though he looked as if he had been crying. But... people talk. People love to talk and exaggerate. Especially about things they don't understand. And then they add, change, and insert themselves into the story, until the truth crumbles to pieces, leaving only scraps of it around a great lie. Either way, no one ever heard of the mysterious old man again, and what they found in the lighthouse was enough to seal up the entrance to that cursed place forever.

My eyes widened and my father saw.

"Enough for tonight. Go to bed. And, son, trust only your own judgment... your own eyes and your own ears". Father stood, stretching his massive body. He seemed larger than the room.

"But father", I persisted. "What did they find there?"

"I won't tell you twice. No more questions. It's time for bed. Now, don't make me angry." His deep voice was even deeper now.

I lied down, but I couldn't sleep for a long, long time. When I did fall asleep, I slept deeply. That night, I dreamed of the light, and fish with wings emerging from it. I don't remember the dream, but I remember my mother's worried look when I woke up. She told me that I had been crying in my sleep.

6.

Mother died yesterday. She simply withered away. I found her by the fireplace, her eyes wide open and a smile on her pale face. Her face wasn't the only thing gone cold, however, as father has stopped caring altogether, about me, about the world around him, about everything. Mother is gone, and now it's like she never existed.

The light was still there, however, though it glowed with lesser intensity. It called to me... we still had our secret signals, ones only we understood, but the fear of the unknown held me back from taking that first step. Now, that fear seemed irrational. Father had withdrawn into himself, the lighthouse had gotten to him, and there was nothing left to tie me to this place. There was no more light here. I gathered the courage and made my decision. Tomorrow was a full moon. Tomorrow, I would go toward my light. Right now, I would sleep, and I would dream.

7.

I slept and dreamed of the last true conversation I had had with Father, when he told me the rest of the story about the lighthouse. It was that first night after my mother passed, and although he was going, he wasn't quite all the way gone yet..

"But, Father," I persisted. "What did they find there?"

Father huffed, but then continued on with the second part of the story anyway, even though he was mostly distant and detached as he told it.

The Story of the Lighthouse Keeper

A few days had passed since Obed's burial,and if it hadn't been for Obed's youngest son, no one would have even bothered to enter the lighthouse at all. During the funeral, the boy noticed something strange on his father's hand when taking it to say goodbye. "What's this?" he asked, showing the palm of his dead father to his mother and others. A startled scream filled the air and people soon began to crowd the body. After breaking loose his curled fingers, they discovered that a symbol had been carved into his skin with a shard of glass... some kind of fish with wings. No one knew what it was exactly, but they knew what it reminded them of, and it scared them. It was the same symbol that the mad old man had drawn in the sand. The following day, Dr. White, the butcher, Zeberdie, and a burly fisherman named Net, all voluntarily entered the lighthouse.

Zeberdie was a simple man, a craftsman who had learned the meat trade from his father, who had learned it from his father and so on. He was superhumanly strong and wasn't afraid of anything on God's green earth. If there was one thing he had learned in life, it was that everything could be killed, as long as the axe was sharp enough. Net was an experienced sailor, someone who had seen a lot, with his skin, blackened by prison ink from all sides of the world. He had felt every heat, every rain, and every snow the planet could offer He had also felt cruelty of humans towards their own kind. His scars were proof of that. Net was an old fisherman you didn't want to cross… physically or verbally. Dr. White on the other hand, didn't share the machoism of the other two. He was young and scared. The only thing pushing him forward was the youthful desire to uncover the unknown. After seeing Obed's bloody self-carving, he just felt the urge to enter that devil's nest. He needed to see with his own eyes what could drive a man to do such madness. Insanity? Fear? At least in his case, the fear was slightly mitigated by the physiognomy of his companions.

What Zeberdie described after entering the lighthouse could easily be attributed to delusion., however, hearing the rough voice coming from this enormous man, whilst his jaw trembled, no one dared to contradict him. After that day, however,, he seemed forever more like a big child a shadow of the fearless titan he had once been. Net, they say, sailed away in his fishing boat that same evening. He didn't even contact his lover, and he left all his rods and nets behind, right where he had last used them. No one ever saw him again. As for Dr. White... well, he was the lucky one. After they carried him out of the lighthouse, and after he had regained consciousness, he remembered nothing. The only two residues that stayed with him from that day were that he could no longer sleep without medication, and that his once black, thick hair was now completely white.

Zeberdie's story was later transcribed, and it went something like this, and I remember, I read it many times:

"We had a hard time breaking through the heavy doors of the lighthouse. We don't know how that frail old man had opened them, but the three of us had a good struggle of it. The moment we stepped inside the freezing hallway on the ground floor, we could immediately smell a noxious odor, and we were overwhelmed by an inexplicable fear. We weren't afraid of a living person… this was a fear that resided directly

in our souls. We remained silent, but the looks we exchanged told us clearly that something here wasn't right. Slowly, we started climbing the dilapidated spiral stairs toward the top of the tower. Every now and then, we felt an unexplainable chill, and it felt as if someone were watching us. There were the scribblings all over the walls, pictures the old man had drawn with charcoal and, it seemed, blood of fish or, maybe seagull. From those sacrilegious lines, we felt a spiritual discomfort unlike anything we had ever encountered before. Abstract depictions of fish with bulging eyes, thick lips, and tiny sharp teeth, fish with wings, these drawings, even though they were on the level of childish scribbles, emanated something inhumanly dreadful, which made us physically sick just to look at them.

The stench had also grown stronger with each step. Decay, flesh, algae, salt, and death are just mild descriptions of what flowed through our nostrils as we climbed toward the godless peak of this gangrenous Olympus. Each floor brought new images as well, and each one was more revolting and unsettling than the last. The small windows were blocked by planks and mud, so no light could bring even the faintest breath of life into these sinful, macabre artworks. It felt like an eternity before we reached the end of our journey. When we neared the top of the staircase, however, we heard a scream.

After so many years in the butchering business, Zeberdie had heard many screams. The moment a knife enters soft tissue and the animal realizes the end is here, there is always a final scream. The last curse, the fleeting of the last ounce of hope, and a single, unanswered, final plea, all united in one. But this scream… this scream was something Zeberdie had never heard, and it came directly from Net's lungs. It was at this point that the doctor had fainted, and was now lying unconscious on the wooden floor of that uppermost landing, stiffened from terror, with his hair now as white as snow.

The source of the stench, the source of their fear, now stood before them in all its glorious madness. The drawings that sprawled across the entire inside of the lighthouse were given a single physical form, and it was staring right at them. The grotesque fish with wings was the old man's one and only creation. On a pedestal made of rat and bird bones, it stood,a hideous blasphemy in pure organic form, a repulsive sculpture made of bones, flesh, and the scales of peeled fish, with wings composed of feathers plucked from now dead seagulls. The sculpture exuded with sheer terror. The old man had made sure that every scale, every feather, and every bone had its place in this perversion of godlessness. He had even started to build its interior. Intestines, a liver, and two hearts could be seen inside the unfinished chest cavity. Zeberdie gripped onto the wooden crucifix he wore around his neck. He swears both those hearts were beating.

After the initial recounting of his tale, Zeberdie never spoke of the lighthouse again.

It's unclear who carried out the unconscious doctor, but two days after their 'expedition,' the entrance to the lighthouse was sealed with concrete. The hotbed of evil was extinguished, but the dreams always remained. Zeberdie now works as an assistant to the priest. He has never been able to take a knife or cleaver into his hands again. Rarely, if ever, has he managed to sleep without the aid of medication."

8.

Tonight is the full moon. Tonight, I go toward my lights. I had packed the essentials into a leather bag: some food, binoculars, and a pocket-knife that I had received as a gift from my father. I remember... my mother was against the blade because she thought I was too young for something like that, while my father just laughed.

"Let him have it, let him learn to take care of himself. Look at him... a true man."

I also brought probably my father's most valuable possession. The old carved brass compass that his father, my grandfather, won in a card game.

I had a hard time pushing the small fishing boat into the water. I was slipping in the mud and couldn't find a good foothold. Somehow, I managed to push it out toward the open water and jump in before it drifted away. Although I was small and the oars kept slipping out of my hands, for the first twenty minutes, I was practically spinning in circles. After several failed attempts, I finally managed to figure out the technique and, with hesitation, found the right direction. I didn't have a map, but I didn't need one. The lighthouse would guide me on the right path. I was trembling, both from fear and from anticipation. What would I find beyond the mist?

The little boat rocked on the restless waves of the dark blue water. It seemed as if I had been rowing for hours. The house where I grew up had long since stopped being a dot on the horizon and a possible object of focus through my brass binoculars. Now, all around me was water The only thing guiding me was the faint, flickering light somewhere in the distance.

I hadn't expected the journey to last this long. Though I could clearly see that light from the windows of my house, now, the closer I got to it, the further away it seemed. Every time I pressed the binoculars to my tired eyes, it looked as if it hadn't come any closer at all. It was far away, elusive, untouchable. I was trembling, both from the cold and from dizziness. I wondered what would I find beyond the fog?

9.

I no longer rowed; I had no strength left. I was beginning to lose my mind. At first, it seemed to me that the air was harsh, and that I could smell the stench of dead fish. Then it began to seem like birds were flying beneath my boat. How was that even possible? I saw them circling in flocks around me, waiting to take my body once the last breath of life had left my lungs. But, it seemed, they were not predators. In their eyes, I saw a strange excitement and strange fear, the same fear I felt myself. The water seemed to grow slightly darker around me. For hours, I let the waves carry me toward my destination. I simply gave in. I lied back and looked at the sky. It no longer seemed bright and blue. As the the next day's darkness fell, it took on a dark purple-redish hue, and the waves became denser. The clouds covering the tainted sky had an otherworldly, repulsive appearance.

I had run out of food and water. I couldn't tell how much time had passed since I got into the boat. Hours? Days? Weeks? It seemed like I had fallen into a delirium. I lay curled up in the fetal position, on the bottom of the boat, trembling from dehydration. I could hardly breathe any longer. Fear crept into me, but even if I could cry, would it matter? Who would hear me here? It seemed as though the mysterious sea, which I had idealized so much, had betrayed me. I loved it so much, and now it would be my grave. Then, on the cracked edges of my lips, I felt a drop,, a light touch, and I thought I was dreaming. Then I felt another, and another. It had begun to rain, though the raindrops looked black in the night sky. Cautiously, I stuck out my sponge-dry tongue and let the incoming raindrops bathe it. The sky was black, the water was black. The raindrops were black, and I was saved.

10.

I was wrong. The black rain was sent by the devil himself. I vomited the last food remnants from my stomach, trying to rid myself of the disgusting taste of rot. That act drained the last atom of strength from me, and I fell, holding onto the edge of the boat, terrified that the burgeoning storm would carry me away. The tempest was dreadful, not just because of its ferocity, but because of the sheer depravity it contained. Nothing about it was like anything I had ever seen before. Lightning flashed in explosions, tearing large scars in the battered sky, from which oozed a deep red color, only to merge with the darkness of the clouds. It seemed the darkness was impermeable. Nothing could break it.

The wild waters threw my boat like a crazed dog chasing its prey, but they would not release me from their grip. The sea itself had changed its texture. The black water was now a disgusting, doughy substance. I shoved the oar in and tried to make a stroke, but the swollen matter snatched it from my hands. It had felt as though I had been rowing through a mixture of honey, mud, and glue. The stench, amplified by the black downpour, was almost unbearable. It filled all my senses.

I watched the shadows scream as they flew around me, though my vision was clouded by this disgusting rain of foul ink, so I could only make out the events around me as blurry fragments of this absurd reality. The sky and the sea had become one now, as I sailed through the sticky blackness whose omnipresence was only ever interrupted by the occasional lightning strike. This is the end. Mother, are you waiting for me somewhere? Father? This is the end. The apocalypse revealed its crescendo in the form of a detonation, the force of which shook every fragment of my surroundings, leaving only a piercing buzz inside my head. I began to laugh, giving myself over to the buzzing, and to the black raindrops, allowing the storm to carry me to my death. They say that at the end of life, one sees a white light. A pure lie. There was no white here. Only darkness. Only night.

Do-do-doom... Do-do-doom... Do-do-doom... Do-do-doom...

And again, I was wrong. Death had other plans for me. I opened my eyes and saw a crimson sky stretched above me. I knew I was alive because my battered body hurt too much for it to be any other way. It seemed the apocalypse had calmed. I could hear the beats of my heart. Another good sign. The stench of decaying nature was unbearable. Slowly, I propped myself up and cautiously peeked over the edge of the boat. Everything I had expected to see could not have prepared me for what was around me. The fear that had been smoldering within me until then expanded and screamed out of me, uncontrollably. I squeezed my eyes shut and waited.

Do-do-doom... Do-do-doom... Do-do-doom... Do-do-doom...

I held my chest tightly, as if I could slow the beating of my heart. I was in a place that shouldn't exist. A place that was impossible. Yet, I was here. Paralyzed by an anachronistic fear, I just stood still, staring around me. The landscape was indescribable to anyone who has never seen it. The land was not land... it was a swamp made of tar. When my foot stepped onto the hot, sticky surface, it felt as though it could sense me, it was as if I were stepping onto a living creature, and with each movement, I might awaken it. I observed what appeared to be stunted attempts at vegetation, but there was something inorganic... something unearthly about them. Yet, they was there, before my eyes. The sediment of the earth was made up of a mixture of sand, tar, bones, and fog. The fog itself seemed to be glued to this barren ground, or perhaps it was the vapors of the earth itself, twisting and merging into a foul mixture of sulfur, camphor... and decay. Upon closer inspection, I discovered the source of the stench that had followed me since the abominable rain. The birds were stuck to the ground, their wings pinned by the sticky mess. Some were thrashing about, trying to free themselves, opening their beaks in a plea for salvation. Some had long since lost that battle, as their decaying bodies now pulsed in rhythm with the earth. Others didn't even have beaks. Were these fish? Why did they have wings? I felt nauseous. I wanted to escape. I wanted to get back in my boat and row as far away from this undogmatic place as possible. I just wanted to close my eyes and wake up at home.

Do-do-doom... Do-do-doom... Do-do-doom... Do-do-doom...

Then I heard it. Twice short, then again. How could I have been so foolish? I was exactly where I was meant to be. It had called to me for so long, and now, when I was finally here, I had wanted to leave. My fear was instantly shrouded in a sense of euphoria As I began to move slowly, step by step, towards the sound. Finally, I was under the veil of fog.

11.

The black, spiky stones first appeared only as slight protrusions beneath the layer of tar-like sediment. As I moved forward, however, they became sharper and more jagged. When I reached a small elevation, I first the basalt towers, whose peaks disappeared high into the dense reddish mist. I don't know if I was delirious, but it seemed to me as if the towers and massive stones had their own order and purpose in this chaos. The rumbling grew louder. I was so much closer to my goal. What had been calling me would soon reveal itself in all its grandeur. I began to realize that all of this had been a test. I had been chosen... that's why I was here now.

I couldn't judge properly, but it seemed like I saw a light coming from above, though after being surrounded by darkness for so long, the light almost felt like an error of nature. I continued to walk, feeling the small bones of undefined creatures crackling beneath my bare, blackened feet, and soon saw that the light wasn't just coming from a single source, but that it was on the ground as well, and there were humanoid shapes more dancing a mad dance around it..

The light shone in the familiar rhythm of my secret message, a rhythm I had heard since I was a boy, standing on the beach, lost in daydreams.

I was at the lighthouse, the final point of my search, and It looked exactly as I had always imagined in my dreams, a gigantic black tower of unfathomable proportions that stood before me.

It had the vague shape of some kind of fish, with full lips and rows of small, sharp teeth around the aperture from which the light emanated. Its eyes were smaller sources of light, glowing in the familiar rhythm, twice short, then again. It also appeared to have spread wings, the ends of which vanished somewhere off in the murky distance. A thin stream of water flowed from the corners of its mouth, forming puddles at the base of the tower, which then connected in some sort of unnatural moat.

Enchanted, I approached, guided by some higher force, and the figures, lost in their deranged dance, didn't notice me.

I shambled to the puddle surrounding the base of the tower and leaned over it, hoping to refresh my exhausted body. I took a sip and recoiled. The reflection staring back at me from the depths of the dark water was mine, but twisted. It was smiling. Its eyes stared into mine, and although they were my reflection, they felt only familiar, not mine, strange, cursed...

I was terrified. I wanted to run, but my body didn't obey. I began to panic as I stared at that monstrous reflection, shrouded in some devilish miasma as it approached... closer and closer, until it began to emerge, naked and pure, baptized in the water from the fish-god's mouth. I opened my mouth to scream, but nothing came out. My embodied reflection also opened its mouth, and from it came a whisper and one word:

"Brother."

My eyes widened as I stared at the vision in front of me. My watery reflection, my figure, my body. So foreign, yet so familiar. Something that shouldn't be alive, yet was here, made of flesh and blood. It smiled at me with its arms wide open.

"Brother", it said again. "It's me, why are you afraid?"

I eventually gathered enough strength and spit in my throat to form a sentence. "No. I don't have a brother."

"Of course, you do. Don't you remember? From that day, after the loss of her child, Mother began to lose herself, to smile with emotion,, she stopped eating. She died because all her vital functions shut down. She died with that smile on her face because she saw me. I showed her where I was. While Father... Father faded in another way. When she died, he didn't even notice. And now I see him still. He sits next to the mummified woman, staring into the distance."

"You're lying, I sobbed. I am the only child of my parents. I never had a brother."

"You know that's not true. You always felt me beside you. The light,, I sent it to you. Twice short, then once again. That was our sign since birth. I was the first to dare and take this journey, but you have now arrived.. We are one body with two hearts beating simultaneously. We are one entity from two realms. We are fish with wings, and only together can we see both sides. We shall live both in the sea and in the sky. The land is polluted, dirty, infected. The land is for the dead and the dying. The earth is made of fear and the bones of those who didn't have the courage. You came here to know the truth. You came here to understand. You came to the foot of the monolith of the Black God, and now brother, you and I will be immortal. We will be eternal. We shall be one. Come, brother... allow me to show you. Allow me to show you what only the chosen can see. Come with me into the abyss of heaven, leave hell to burn while madmen dance for the Creator. Only when you embrace Him as the one truth, only then will the sacred monolith open. Only then will God reveal Himself to you in His purest form."

With those words, he grabbed me and gently pulled me down into the puddle of the Black God.

It felt that I was suddenly resisting. It opened its mouth and let out a scream, my own scream, coming from under the water. I ripped myself free from my brother's grasp and started running back toward my boat. I was crying as I ran frantically, not looking back. I shoved the boat away from the tacky shore and jumped in. The figures had stopped dancing and were now somewhere behind me, letting out their inhuman screams. They were the last memory I took with me from that awful place, and they would be forever imprinted in my mind. As the boat lazily drifted away from the sick land, however, my exhausted body slowly forced my mind to fade into unconsciousness.

12.

I first felt a pleasant warmth, then a sharp pain as I was awakened by a prickling sensation in my thighs. A small, ossified crab was trying to tear a piece of skin from me. I swiped it off with my hand and sat up. Fragments of memories from the previous evening swirled in my head like a vortex. Had it all been just a dream? Still... I knew it wasn't. I knew that what I had witnessed was real. I put my hands on my face to wipe away the crust from my eyes and screamed. I looked at my hands... once youthful but now covered in the blotchy skin of an old man. I didn't know how I ended up here, nor why I was so old when the path I followed was a path of a child? Had I been there for years? Had I lived here for years? I didn't know. I didn't remember. With a trembling finger, I drew a sketch in the sand. I didn't even know why . It looked like some grotesque fish with wings. God! It was as if a thought was suppressed somewhere deep in my subconscious.

I looked around. Broken branches, shattered trees, and scattered earth... there must have been a violent storm last night. Then I looked to my right and saw it. A large, stone tower with a glass dome on top, and it stirred up a rush of emotions within me. I closed my eyes and stumbled. I saw the smiling face of the boy from the water, a bird dying in tar, and something else... I don't know what it was, but it was black. Black and terrifying., outside of time. I approached the stone tower with the glass dome., but when I reached the door and looked at the rusted metal plaque. I couldn't make out most of the words, all I could read was "Lighthouse".

With great effort, I entered the structure and was immediately hit by the acrid stench of stagnation. The corpses of rats and insect shells, however, reminded me just how hungry I was, though I knew I wouldn't eat. It felt like eternity as I climbed the winding stairs to the top of the lighthouse with this body on the brink of exhaustion. When I finally reached the top, there was no grand reward awaiting me. There was no magnificent room concealing all the mystery of this world, in fact... there was nothing, only a circular, ring-shaped room, a large tube I thought might be a telescope, an old office desk with covered in radios, and an assortment ofdecaying boxes. In the center, there was the huge lens used to cast light. I approached the desk. I wiped the glass and used the telescope to look through the window. it was then that my heart began to pound like never before.

God! I remembered... I remembered everything.

Somewhere, on the other side of the land, on a gravel spit, stood a boy, staring out at the sea. I looked at the boy, recognizing him. That was me... Where were my parents...? Were they here were they alive? The boy was looking in my direction. He spread and lowered his arms as though he knew I was watching him. Twice short, then once more. Oh yes... I remembered everything. I looked to the right at the yellowed paper and already knew what it said...

Lighthouse keeper's testimony... second scrap.

TODAY! Today is the day when the Black God forgave me. When my brother forgave me. When I forgave myself. Today, I will be united with my lost half. We will be one body with two hearts that beat simultaneously. We will be fish with wings, and we will live forever, both in the sea and in the sky. Wait for me, brother, for I come to you tonight.

I already hear the drums marking my arrival. I see the clouds tearing through the crimson sky. Oh yes... I remember everything.

The Offering

By: Justin Carlos Alcala

It was going to rain today, Captain Garvey thought to himself. It rained every day during the frigid crab season, but that's not what Captain Garvey meant. He wasn't as superstitious as most mariners, but he knew how to read the signs. It was Friday, the crimson moon ran full last night, and at some point this morning, an albatross caught itself in one of the ship's pots, effectively hanging itself. The captain savored the tobacco from his morning cigarette as a chord of loose rigging whipped the bridge's glass window, just feet from his face, cracking it. *It was definitely going to rain today.*

The crew were a half day off course, and treading through rugged ocean waves crowned in brash ice. That didn't trouble Captain Garvey. His vessel stretched over two-hundred feet from stem to stern with a draft of nearly three meters. She could drag ten tons of cargo through choppy waters without batting an eye. It was the crew's mood that pained him. Each hour wasted was money lost, as his crab fishermen only kept a portion of what the SS Melpomene pulled in. Captain Garvey repeated the words his predecessor, Captain Hammond, muttered whenever times were trying.

Steadfast.

Breakfast was a spread of charred toast, overly crisped by the broken toaster, leftover oatmeal, and coffee. The deckhands were up before dawn with little to do besides weld crab pods. Captain Garvey knew they were restless,so he didn't spare any diesel pushing the boat engine as hard as it could go. It was noon when Captain Garvey's first mate, Hewson Kersey, hurried into the bridge. Captain Garvey had worked with the man for twelve years and could read the chief officer like a book. Hewson's expression said that he had bad news. He pursed his lips under his horseshoe mustache while tipping the brim of his yellow rain hat.

"Boys mutinous already?" Captain Garvey grunted, his eyes locked on the hail falling outside.

"Not quite," Hewson replied, his eyes lowered. "Just came to talk."

"Spill it," Captain Garvey ordered.

"What?"

"I've been around you too long, Hewson," Captain Garvey declared. "There's something you want to say."

"Well," Hewson confessed. "It's silly."

"Hewson," Captain Garvey protested, focusing on his brittle first mate.

Hewson swallowed the lump in his throat. Captain Garvey was a middle-aged man with a receding hairline squeezed under his tight fiddler's hat. He was brawny and tall with a flat boxer's nose. His eyes were a jigsaw of grey like shattered mirror glass. He wore a heavy peacoat with gold buttons branded with lion heads. Even after a decade, the cCaptain still intimidated Hewson.

"You know the story we heard at dockside," Hewson stuttered. "The one about the Molly May."

"Aye," Captain Garvey fixed his gaze back on course, wincing at the hairline crack stretching across his bridge's windshield.

"You remember the survivors talking about the drowned woman they saw?"

"Aye."

"Well, you're going to think it's crazy, but one of the boys claims to have seen the same thing. He says he saw a woman under the waves. He's all shaken up about it."

"Who?"

"Danny."

Danny was a greenhorn, only two seasons deep. He was eighteen, with a three-year-old daughter and wife, with another one on the way. Captain Garvey wouldn't regularly take the crew so young, but Danny was Captain Garvey's nephew. After Garvey's brother died, the captain felt obligated to look after his nephew, no matter how dim he might be. Captain Garvey's options were limited, however, and after bailing Danny out of jail twice, he took him on as crew. Since then, Danny had subsided.

Captain Garvey pressed his thick fingers into his brow. "Danny? Where's he now?"

"He's in the galley, Sir."

Captain Garvey traded the wheel with Hewson and made his way to Danny. When he entered the galley, Danny was sitting at a kitchen bench with a steaming mug cradled in his hands. Two of the other men stood cross-armed around him. Static from the radio crackled in the room, spewing out a muffled electric guitar. Captain Garvey twisted the radio switch off.

"Okay, Danny," Captain Garvey announced. "What's all this about then?"

"Danny saw something, Captain," Ben affirmed as he placed himself between the cCaptain and Danny. Ben was a short aboriginal man from the Makah tribe. He caped his hair in a bandana, brandishing the scar running down his forehead from an old bar fight.

"From Danny please," Captain Garvey corrected. Ben took a step back. Danny peered up, his eyes glistening. "Danny."

"I saw it, Uncle," Danny quavered. "A girl in the water, staring up at me, just like the Molly May."

"Danny," Captain Garvey cleared his throat. "I know you saw something, and you think it was something else. The ocean does that. Hell, I've seen boats made of icebergs and ghosts in the mist. Your sea eyes will adjust."

"No," Danny cut in. "I know what I saw, Uncle."

"A lady," the Captain said bluntly.

"Yes," Danny stammered. "Naked and floating along the boat." There was a long pause. Captain Garvey stared down at his nephew. Danny lowered his head, slowly combing his fingers through his ginger hair.

"We'll be back to dropping pods in less than an hour," Captain Garvey assured. "Once we have something to focus on, you'll forget all about this. Now, take what time you need and then get geared up. We have herring to bait." Captain Garvey didn't wait for a reply. He let the brisk air bite at him as he exited the galley, marching to his post.

Once the SS Melpomene returned to her course, the crew's demeanor changed. The deckhands were too busy flipping the car sized traps. There were red king crab to catch. They worked past sunset in the start of a winter storm, whisking around the bow like ants in cold rain. They worked through supper, and by eight o'clock had rescued their schedule, though they were now exhausted and frozen. However, just as the deckhands were turning in to warm up, a cleat from one of the spare pods hung along the port ledge gave way, releasing the seven hundred pound cage into the ocean. The cage sank low, pulling its tail of chord with it. Without hesitation, the men tried to rescue the pod with their bare hands. Captain Garvey watched in disgust as his men tried to pull the pod's chord, splitting their gloves.

"Use the pot hauler, you fool," Captain Garvey shouted into the handheld receiver. He could hear his voice echo over the loudspeaker outside. The crew followed as commanded, fastening the rope on a t-rail before manning the hydraulic arm. The neck of the long machine looked like a sea serpent tugging at the trap's chord. The pod had fallen fifty fathoms and took time to haul up. As the pod reached the surface, Danny, manning the pole-arm in order to hook the pod onto the deck, fell backwards as the trap reached eye level. Captain Garvey watched from behind the cracked glass as Danny pointed to the pot. Captain

Garvey narrowed his eyes and could see a large curled lump knotted along the top of the trap.

"What's going on?" Captain Garvey shouted into the receiver. He watched as Hewson trudged to the bridge, battling the rocking boat as he hurried to report. Meanwhile, the crew gathered around the pod, reaching in to untangle the indistinct bundle. Hewson burst through the metallic door with haste, bringing in the gelid air as he entered.

"Captain," Hewson quavered, "there's a damn woman. There's a damn woman stuck in the pod."

Captain Garvey peered into the darkness, watching as several men wrapped a taxicab colored slicker around the figure. Danny stared over the wall of men, treading backwards. Captain Garvey puffed hot air from his nose like a dragon.

"Hmm," Captain Garvey hummed. "I didn't hear anything over the horn about anyone going overboard. Maybe someone dumped her?"

"Maybe," Hewson shrugged, catching his breath. "She's naked too, Sir."

"Poor girl. Looks like Danny was right. We must've caught her in our rigging and dragged her for miles. Hewson, we'll have to put her in the cooler, respectable like, until we dock, then we'll turn her corpse into the authorities."

"Captain, Sir," Hewson cut in. "I don't know how to tell you this, but she's still alive." The caterpillar like brows on Captain Garvey's forehead raced upwards.

"Impossible."

"No Sir, she's unconscious, but breathing."

There was a long pause. Captain Garvey dug into his pocket and removed a fresh cigarette. He watched as the crew used a raincoat as a stretcher, hauling the girl into the deck spotlight. Captain Garvey could see the woman for the first time. She was tall and lanky with wan skin traced in lavender. If she wasn't dead, she would be soon. Captain Garvey lit his cigarette, appreciating its spiced kiss.

"Make a sick bay out of one of our spare rooms," Captain Garvey commanded through exhaled smoke. "Get her inside, and bring the heat lamps."

Hewson nodded, then exited the wheel house. Captain Garvey lamented. If they could stabilize the woman, he'd need to break from their course in order to get help. He wondered if the Coast Guard could get here in the current storm, but radioed them anyway. As expected, there were questions he couldn't answer. Captain Garvey did his best to report the incident, and was told that aid would try to arrive as soon as possible. Captain Garvey knew what that meant. It would take time. He buttoned the roaring lions along his coat and left for the bilge.

When Captain Garvey entered the once empty cabin, it was booming with activity. Space heaters and hot plates were plugged into every socket surrounding their newest passenger. The nude woman rested along a bunk with hot wet towels pressed along her arms and thighs. Her delicate face parted through a drape of soaked black hair that extended down to her shoulders. She was beautiful, even in her condition. Captain Garvey noticed that her dull teal eyes were open wide, motionless, but gaping. The Captain pushed past Ben, who was trying to boil water on a stove plate, and put his hand across her chest. He could feel shallow breathing.

"Ben," Captain Garvey cleared his throat. "Don't use water. Go get dry compress pads from the first-aid kit and apply them to her neck and chest. Hewson, get her wet hair off her and then layer her in blankets. Bobby and Roland take over on the bridge. Coast Guard has questions I couldn't answer, and they'll need our help to guide them." Captain Garvey paused. "Should they even be able to get someone out here…"

Ben looked for Danny, so did the captain. He was nowhere to be found.

"Where's Danny?"

Hewson chewed his lip. "He's panicked, Captain. Ran to the galley."

"I need him to get the flares on the gangway," Captain Garvey sighed.

"I'll get 'em, Captain," Ben volunteered.

"No," Captain Garvey refused. "I'll go. Let me know if she takes a turn for the worse. If she does, I can tell the Coast Guard to call off their dogs."

Captain Garvey made a beeline for the galley. He remembered that Danny had witnessed his little sister drown ten years ago and was likely rattled. Captain Garvey found Danny standing over the sink in his wet slicker, his arms spread across the counter as if he were trying to catch his balance. *The Wreck of the Edmund Fitzgerald* played through the headphones of an abandoned smartphone along the dinner table. Captain Garvey turned the music off, allowing the boat to moan and groan without interruption.

"Danny," Captain Garvey spoke up. "I owe you an apology. You told me about the girl and I didn't listen. This is my fault, not yours."

Danny raised his head. "Is she dead, then?"

"She's still breathing, but it doesn't look good. I don't think the Coast Guard will get here in time."

"She's alive?"

"Like I said Danny, barely."

"We need to get her off this boat."

Captain Garvey stiffened his back. He took a moment to dig under his coat and tighten his belt before speaking.

"What are you saying, Danny?"

Danny leaned in, as if to tell a secret. "I was the first to see her on that pod, Uncle. I saw what she really is."

"Danny, you're cold, tired and not making sense."

Danny grabbed at Captain Garvey's sleeve, crushing the wool. "Uncle, she wasn't pretty like she is now. She was..." Danny's voice faded, "a demon."

"A demon?"

"I saw it. She had teeth like an anglerfish and her legs looked like a seal's fin."

Captain Garvey ripped his arm away from Danny's grip. "Get a hold of yourself. You sound like a maniac." A grimace spread across Danny's face. "Now, I need you to get some flares from storage. We might have a helicopter coming."

Danny took in his uncle's hard stare. Wordlessly, he zipped up his jacket and left the room. He didn't look back at Captain Garvey or say another word.

"Steadfast," Captain Garvey whispered under his breath.

When Captain Garvey returned to the bridge, Bobby struggled with the helm while Roland shouted into the receiver.

"Angel One," Roland pleaded, his stocking hat folded over his ears. "This is the SS Melpomene. Can you tell me why?"

"What's the matter?" asked Captain Garvey.

Roland scratched his patchy beard. "They're telling us they can't get a bird out here just yet, Captain. Storms are too bad."

"SS Melpomene," a calm female voice on the other end of the radio chirped. "This is Angel One. We need you three miles due south in order to send help."

Roland looked at Captain Garvey for an answer. Captain Garvey nodded. "Angel One," Roland answered. "We are changing course. Meet you there."

The SS Melpomene changed its heading to escape the violent storms. The waves grew tall, causing the vessel to strain through the tides like a heifer scaling across a valley of steep hills. Everyone readied for the rescue.

As they made it through their first mile, Captain Garvey noticed that Danny hadn't reported with the flares. Concerned, he requested that Hewson check up on him. It took Hewson ten minutes to return, but when he did, Captain Garvey didn't like what he saw. Hewson was clenching his jaw tightly, the color drawn from his face.

"Captain," Hewson squeezed the back of his neck. "It's Danny."

"Speak man," Captain Garvey bayed.

"I found him by the girl," Hewson stuttered. "He's not breathing."

"What?"

The pair hurried to Danny. When they entered the makeshift sickbay, the body of the woman lay stripped of her dry packs and blankets. Below her bunk, Danny lay sprawled, his hands clutching the blankets. Captain Garvey flipped him onto his back. Danny's eyes gaped open, his pupils dilated. Captain Garvey checked his pulse. There were no signs of life.

"Jesus," Captain Garvey seethed through clenched teeth, before starting CPR. Hewson and Captain Garvey took turns trying to resuscitate Danny, but their efforts came up empty. There were no markings or other clues as to how Danny might have perished. Captain Garvey, out of breath, tried to wash the thoughts of Danny as a boy out of his head. There was a boat to run and a life that could still be saved. *Steadfast.*

After taking a moment to gather himself, Captain Garvey asked that Hewson prepare both Danny and the woman for the Coast Guard. Hewson didn't argue.

Captain Garvey couldn't remember his trek back to the bridge. He was too busy drowning in memories of his brother and his nephew. When he returned to the wheelhouse, he found Roland crouched studiously over a paper map along the graph table. He was using a ballpoint pen to judge distances between his fingers.

"What are you doing?" Captain Garvey asked in a lifeless tone.

"Captain," Roland bleated. "We're nearly to the coordinates, but we've dropped speeds in order to make sense of things."

"Make sense?"

"Yes," Roland pulled his rolled stocking hat from his head and ran his fingers through his wild hair. "Last I checked, there weren't any islands near here."

"There's not."

"Then what's that lighthouse doing there?" Roland sputtered, pointing towards the nose of the boat. Captain Garvey peered up. Only a short distance away, and smothered in fog, was the dull glow of a magnificent yellow light. The sheen didn't spin as most lighthouse lamps do, but instead beat like a heart, fading on and off. Captain Garvey couldn't make sense of it. He checked the map. No such lighthouse or islands were marked. Roland pressed the radio's receiver.

"Angel One," Roland called out. "This is the SS Melpomene. We are nearing the pickup coordinates, but need to draw out. There's an unmarked lighthouse in the distance giving us warning."

"SS Melpomene," the woman's voice directed, cool and soothing. "That is the pickup location. Please continue the course."

Roland's forehead creased. Captain Garvey held out his burly hand for the receiver. Roland passed it along before returning to the map. Captain Garvey took the helm, trying to feel more in control, while simultaneously working the radio.

"Angel One," Captain Garvey chastised. "This is Captain Garvey of the Melpomene. If you think we can dock, you're mad."

"Understood, Captain Garvey," the tranquil woman's voice interjected. "The pickup will continue as planned. Please move forward at a safe distance. We will pickup from there."

"This is highly irregular," Captain Garvey fumed into the receiver. "I'll move her along a bit further, but I'm not risking my crew nor ship anymore. Also," there was a break in speech. "We have a second person to be picked up. They'll be D.O.A." Roland flipped his head back, but Captain Garvey didn't explain.

"Understood," the woman on the radio echoed.

Captain Garvey drew the boat slowly towards the lighthouse's island, a round island whose shadow loomed through the mist, and the waves began to subside, making his wheel work easier. Captain Garvey watched as Hewson coordinated the crew to convoy Danny and the girl's blanketed bodies towards the bow of the ship as he pulled the boat into a stationary position and waited for a helicopter to appear. The ship went silent as the waters turned placid.

Suddenly, a sound like a low tugboat's horn fused with the cry of a tea kettle pierced Captain Garvey's ears. He covered the sides of his head, his eyes watering. He could see his crew squinting and clawing at their ears as well. Along the bow, the blankets covering the woman fell to the ground. The tall, lanky stranger stood, her hands raised in praise. Captain Garvey could see a muzzle of sharp teeth protruding from her face. All at once, the blinking lighthouse bulb lit like the sun and the island began to rise. Garvey grabbed onto the helm as the bow rose. Ben and Hewson flew from opposite sides of the boat into the water asthe remaining crew and loose equipment were tossed around the vessel.

Garvey strained to grip the now nearly vertical wheel, watching as the island grew before him. The sable shape cut through the fog, revealing a mountainous figure with flesh like coral, raining down water as it breached the ocean's surface. It had no eyes, but a maw large enough to swallow a whale whole, encrusted with rows of serrated teeth. Along the top of its head was a tree-sized stem with a luminous bulb that glowed flaxen. Captain Garvey clenched his teeth as his mighty arms tried to keep his hefty body from spiraling down the boat. He watched as the woman, now covered in fine haired seal skin, crawled like a spider towards port before diving into the water. As the island drew its jaws, ocean water spilled inside. Captain Garvey could feel the boat being drawn in. He stared into the gullet of the beast as the Melpomene was swallowed into the black depths. As the ship's lights flashed off and shadow colored the boat, Captain Garvey swore. He knew it was going to rain today.

The Maw Beneath

By: Denise Landry

Nicholas Mullen heard it again. The sound, a brittle whisper, tangled in static, lost in the tide. He stood rigid, hands rough from salt and storm, gripping the lighthouse window frame. Outside, the fog swallowed the horizon, turning the world into nothing but black water and shifting mist. "Is anyone there?" Nicholas called, voice tight, pressing the radio closer.

The static hissed back. No response. Just that sound. A slow, dragging beat beneath the interference, like breathing…like something alive.

Nicholas swallowed hard. Over the past week the warnings had come one by one. The nets, heaving with half-eaten fish, their bodies torn apart, the boats, gutted against the rocks, their hulls split like bone, even the tides came in unnatural, fevered, pulling farther than they should, as if something beneath the surface was breathing. Waiting.

Nicholas clicked the radio off. Silence settled. Too thick. Too heavy.

It had been years since his leg was torn from him, since the sea tried to take him whole. He told himself what he remembered hadn't been real though. Nothing like that could exist in the deep. But now, he started to feel like he was horribly wrong. He knew he couldn't handle this by himself though, so he turned the radio back on, found a clear channel and once again called out for help.

As Nicholas stepped off the Nova Scotia ferry, he got an eerie feeling that something was watching him, from the ocean, but he thought he was being silly. He walked up the beach to Blackthorn Lighthouse, a battered, salt-crusted guardian against the raging sea. In the dusty, neglected lighthouse, he immediately started his duties as resident caretaker, cleaning up and doing repairs. Once in awhile, his prosthetic leg hurt, but he always just ignored the phantom pains and kept on working, assuring that the automatic beacon functioned properly. He had recently started recording tide patterns, storms, and visibility conditions that could endanger the ships in the area, helping to rescue them when they were in distress. He especially enjoyed keeping up the lighthouse as a heritage site, maintaining old photographs and ledgers, and giving guided tours to visitors. He would tell them all the history of the lighthouse and how many lives it had saved with its light.

"Does that light keep the sea monsters away?" a curious little boy asked one day.

"What sea monsters?" Nicholas asked politely but puzzled.

"Grandpa told me stories about scary creatures that swam around the ocean while he fished around here," the boy said, very sure of himself.

Nicholas smiled, saying, "The ocean is safe. I have never seen any sea monsters around here before." Visitors giggled and they continued on with their tour.

A few days later, Nicholas's old friend, Captain Gail Johns and her crew docked their fishing trawler, The Dawn Star, at the lighthouse dock. The crew was tired after a long day of hauling in their fishing nets. They were happy that Nicholas had invited them for a cozy stew dinner.

The smell of salt, meat, and slow-burning spices curled thick through the kitchen as steaming bowls and beer mugs were placed on the weathered wooden table.

Nicholas sat at the far end, spoon in hand, listening as Gail stretched back in her chair. "You ever think about coming back?" she asked, eyes sharp despite her casual tone. "Fishing, I mean."

Nicholas let out a slow breath. The question wasn't new.

Gail's first mate, Jesse Calloway leaned forward, tearing off a chunk of bread. "Hell, after what happened to him, I wouldn't step foot on a boat again either."

Ship Engineer, Monica Vance, let out a short laugh. "Can you blame him? The whole damn sea tried to take him."

Nicholas exhaled, shaking his head. "It wasn't the sea."

The table quieted.

Gail tilted her head, curious. "Then what was it?"

Nicholas hesitated, turning his spoon in his hand. He didn't know how to explain something he didn't understand. "I don't know," he admitted. "Could've been the waves. The wreck. The dark playing tricks."

The young dockhand, Ezra Boone smirked. "Could've been the Fiend."

Nicholas frowned. "The what?"

Monica grinned. "The Chasm Fiend," she said, leaning forward. "Old sailors say it lives beneath the waves. Something huge, ancient, and waiting for shipwrecks. Waiting for those lost at sea."

"A boy talked about that during the day tour a few days ago," Nicholas scoffed. "It's just a story."

Ship's navigator, Peter Mallory, folded his arms, shaking his head. "That's what we tell ourselves. But there's a reason every generation swears it's real."

Nicholas tried to ignore the creeping chill in his spine. A creature that waits for wrecks. That watches. That feeds… That was just silly, wasn't it?

Ship's cook, an older woman named Lo Hastings, wiped her mouth with a napkin as she spoke with a voice that was quiet but steady. "We laugh about it in daylight," she murmured. "But when the sea goes silent, when the tides shift wrong... tell me it doesn't 'feel' different."

Nicholas sighed, pushing his stew aside.

Outside, the waves crashed against the cliffs. Restless. Waiting.

After dinner, Gail and crew sailed home and Nicholas went to bed, where he had a horrific dream. Aboard The Starling, The

Captain, his mentor Joseph Dane, was at the wheel and a night storm had just started. The ship was caught in an unforeseen squall. The crew fought and the storm raged as a shadow, suddenly freed by the storm and a unexpected shift in the currents, moved gracefully beneath the waves, impossibly large. It was then that tentacles, slick and black, began to entwine the stern. The crew screamed as the vessel tilted. He could just make out the lighthouse's beam, far in the distance. Joseph grabbed Nicholas by the arm, shoving him toward the only lifeboat they had left. "GO!" he roared, but Nicholas refused., That was when one of the tendrils shot across the deck and coiled around his leg. Pain flared through his body. Everything began to fade. The ship sank and the crew were dead…

Nicholas woke up from the dream frightened and sweating but had no choice except to shake it off and continue his day. Everything was fine and he stopped thinking about the dream, that is until strange things started happening. Boats wrecked against rocks, their nets, filled with half-eaten fish, torn apart and ravaged. No one understood what was happening, though some people thought that it was the fiend. Nicholas, head full of weird ideas, just wanted to know what was really happening.

The Dawn Star returned for another night's meal, and Gail believed in the Fiend. "When he was the lighthouse keeper, Grandfather swore that he saw the fiend glowing in the rough seas, with its gigantic tentacles. People thought he was just seeing things though."

Nicholas wondered when the fiend legend started.

"It started eons before the villages around here were settled," Lo said. "Some say it was born from the ocean itself, a predator crafted by the abyss, growing with each storm, each wreck, each soul claimed by the depths. Others believe it was once something else, a hungry, vengeful god which they were to fear. This caused villagers to start sacrificing to it. They called it 'the feeding hour", when the moon dipped low and the waters grew still, when the sea would call for an offering. The villagers, terrified of what might happen if they refused, obeyed. They would sacrifice one of their own, chosen by lot, then dragged to the shore, where their fate sealed beneath the waves. It is said, that on the eve of the offering, the mournful villagers would gather by the shore, and a wooden bowl, filled with smooth black stones, would be passed amongst them. Each person would draw a stone. Most were unmarked. One was carved with a single, deep gouge, running through its surface. Whoever held that stone was chosen. The chosen was led to the water's edge, their wrists bound, before being placed into a small wooden boat, barely seaworthy, and pushed out toward the horizon. By morning, the boat was always gone, and the tide would return to normal. This continued for generations, until a wicked storm struck and a landfall hit the sea. The creature seemed to have disappeared, so the sacrifices eventually stopped… Some think the creature was trapped under rock deep in the sea, or maybe it went back to wherever it came from. The Chasm Fiend name came later, when the story became urban legend, when people found the mysterious underwater chasm near here, the one that some people claim the creature might be found in."

This didn't make Nicholas feel any better, nor did it help figure out what was happening to the sea.

Peter, however, had noticed that most of the attacks actually had occurred around the chasm. "It would be worth investigating," he proposed.

As an emergency response officer, Nicholas felt it was his duty to investigate every possible lead.. It might be useless, but he went on The Dawn Star anyway, performing his duty diligently while white knuckling it the whole way. His leg began to hurt again. "Stop it," he whispered to it. "Everything is going to be fine."

They arrived at the chasm. Nicholas, Peter, Gail, and Jesse all decided to go investigate. They put on wetsuits and brought flashlights, radios, and the rest of the gear they thought they might need. They then dove into deep water, into the chasm, and began to climb along its rocky terrain. The chasm was a deep abyss, a jagged wound carved into the ocean floor, stretching wider than any charted trench. The water was still, the currents sluggish as if something beneath them could dictate their rhythm, as if something was waiting in anticipation.

Even through their diving suits, Nicholas, Peter, Gail, and Jesse felt the pressure bearing down on them. Their radios crackled with static, as no signal got in or out of the chasm, and there was no light down there either. The beams from their flashlights barely pierced the heavy gloom of that murky void.

Something moved. The water shifted. A shadow appeared to bend the darkness around it, the limb of something impossibly large. Then they saw it.

It was the Chasm Fiend.

It emerged slowly, deliberately, its form a grotesque fusion of nightmare and deep-sea horror. Its bioluminescent tendrils pulsed, casting sickly green light through the depths, like a gargantuan, stygian, fishing lure. It was the true epitome of horror, directly below them.

The maw of the Fiend yawned open, not a simple mouth, but a cavity lined with spiraling rows of gnashing teeth, grinding together even when still. Monstrous eyes watched them, unblinking, calculating, remembering. Tentacles writhed, covered in hooked barbs that flexed in anticipation, trailing through the water like searching fingers.

It was just like in Nicholas's dream.

The water lurched, a sudden, violent shift as the Chasm Fiend moved, searching directly toward Nicholas. He barely had time to react before the current slammed into him, sending him tumbling through the abyss. His radio crackled with distant, distorted voices.

Jesse shouted his name, Gail cursed, and Peter tried to track him through the murk., Nicholas could barely tell what happening, all he could hear was the deafening pulse beneath the waves, coming from the hungry fiend. Light bloomed from it as well. Its gnashing teeth ground together, each one large enough to sheer through bone. Tentacles snapped toward him, sensing him, knowing him.

Nicholas fought against the water, against the weight pressing down on him as his breath hitched, as his heart hammered, as every instinct screamed internally that this was the end for him. Then Gail and her crew pulled him away As Jesse and Peter shot flares at the fiend. This gave them their chance, and they swam back to their boat as fast as they could, before speeding straight back to the lighthouse. They would come back in the morning with a plan on how to handle the fiend.

That night, Nicholas tried to relax, but when he looked out the window, he swore he saw the fiend out there, roaring in the sea. Was it searching for him? The lighthouse radio crackled, and he almost had a heart attack. He could hear the fiend roaring and breathing. How? It was then that he realized he must've have dropped his radio in the chasm while trying to fend off the fiend earlier. Now it was stuck on one of its tentacles perhaps, but it was still somehow working! Nicholas couldn't believe it. He called for help on the radio, for The Dawn Star.

—Gail and crew came as fast as they could, quietly docking their ship on the opposite side of the beach so that the fiend wouldn't see them, and once Nicholas got on board, they took off again.

The crew gathered on the deck as the sound of the waves below restlessly whispered against the hull. Nicholas stood across from Peter, arms folded, brow furrowed. Leaning against a crate, watching everyone.

Peter pulled a rusted harpoon launcher from beneath his coat and set it onto the table. "It's not pretty," he said, gripping the metal frame. "But it'll fire. I checked the mechanics, they're old, but they still hold."

Nicholas eyed the battered weapon. "Where did you get it?"

"Came off a sunken wreckage that I explored one weekend," Peter explained. "It's old whaling equipment, meant to bring down beasts bigger than a ship. Normally, it just kills outright, a shot right through the heart, but I'm rigging it for something worse."

Gail raised an eyebrow. "Worse?"

Peter then produced some salvaged deep-sea demolition devices, explosive charges he had salvaged from an abandoned mining outpost. "These aren't meant for hunting," he said, lifting one carefully. "They're designed to take apart rock... To tear open the ocean floor if needed."

Jesse frowned, puzzled, "And you're going to strap that to a harpoon?"

Peter smirked grimly. "That's the plan."

Nicholas leaned forward, scanning the setup. "What's the risk?"

Peter let out a breath. "Everything. If we hit the Fiend and don't place the shot right, it won't kill it, just piss it off. Worse, if the explosion triggers wrong, it could collapse the chasm before it even falls in. We go down with it."

The crew exchanged looks.

Gail drummed her fingers against her knee. "So, we get one chance."

Peter nodded. "One good shot is all I need. We hit it from above and force it down into the chasm, then I fire a second round straight into the abyss. We bury it. Forever."

Silence settled over them.

Nicholas exhaled, steady but uneasy. "You really think this will work?"

Peter shrugged, checking the harpoon's balance. "I think it's all we've got."

Jesse laughed dryly. "Hell, I can't argue with that."

Gail stood, clapping Peter on the shoulder. "Alright, genius. Let's go kill a monster."

The crew moved fast, preparing for the battle ahead. The harpoon launcher stood at the ready, waiting to be used as they knew the Fiend also waited, beneath the waves. It waited for them all, for their deaths, for its dinner. It waited for Nicholas. They knew only had one shot at this, and they intended to make it count.

The ocean suddenly shifted, disturbed by a sudden stillness that made the air feel both thick and heavy, like something vast was about to break through the surface. Nicholas stood on deck, gripping the railing, heart hammering against his ribs. Jesse, Peter, and Gail were beside him, tense, ready. Nothing could have prepared them for what came next, however, as the Fiend emerged, breaching the water in a surge of gargantuan darkness. With its tendrils unfurling, its bioluminescent glow pulsing like a sick heartbeat, and a maw that roared open with its spirals of gnashing, grinding teeth. the leviathan nightmare attacked.

"FIRE!" Gail shouted.

Peter didn't hesitate.

The harpoon gun thundered, launching the explosive-tipped bolt straight toward the creature's core, tearing through its flesh and sending its bioluminescence into a chaotic flickering as the impact of the blast sent a shockwave through its massive body. The Fiend jerked back, its tentacles snapping outward in agony, as it began to fall, its massive form descending down into the chasm below.

Nicholas exhaled sharply, gripping the rail as he watched the abyss swallow the monster whole.

Peter wasn't done, however. "If that thing crawls back out, we're dead," he said as he loaded the second explosive and modded for demolition harpoon into the gun, his weapon now packed with enough force to obliterate whatever lay at the bottom of that abyss and then some.

Nicholas inhaled. Peter fired. The harpoon plunged into the depths, racing toward the Fiend's thrashing body.

When it hit, a rupture tore through the chasm, sending shockwaves through the sea as the explosion ripped into and through rock and flesh alike. They watched as the abyss collapsed, swallowing itself whole and burying the Fiend forever.

Silence came soon after, while the ocean still heaved with the remnants of the blast, while massive waves rolled outward and they struggled to stay afloat. When the sea finally calmed, Nicholas staggered over to the railing, chest tight, and stared down at the water. There was no movement. No glow. No fiend. Just the quiet, empty sea.

Jesse let out a breathless laugh, bent over with his hands on his knees. "It's—It's gone."

Peter collapsed back against the railing, exhaling shakily.

Gail looked at Nicholas, studying his face, the exhaustion, the disbelief, the relief so sharp it almost hurt. "It's over," she murmured.

Nicholas nodded slowly, the weight of the ocean finally lifting from him, maybe for the first time in years. Afterwards, they all returned to the lighthouse and had a great celebration. Lo cooked a grand meal and Nicholas finally started to relax. He pushed the past and the terror out of his mind.

Then the lighthouse radio began to crackle…

The Blue Whale of Catoosa

By: Blake Hoss

Anna Gavigan looked out past the gravel parking lot, across the murky green pond at the Blue Whale of Catoosa and thought about how she needed to be studying. The old concrete whale was beached on one side of the pond and had seen better days. The whale's blue paint had chipped and faded, leaving long white scars like war wounds from past battles with whaling ships or giant concrete squids, but its one visible red eye still looked fresh. Her eyes scanned the whale, starting with its thick, bottle shaped head, looking past the slide hanging limply out beneath the eye like a harpoon, and down to the narrow body just above the water, where several rusty, three rung ladders hung over both sides. At the back, the whale's tail rose and curved around to one side, creating a small cove where several logs, probably fallen trees, bobbed in a logjam. A small white tugboat floated halfway between the whale and the shore, tethered in place by an anchor.

Sitting behind the wheel of his lifted Chevy Tahoe, Teague cracked another warm beer and nodded at the whale. "There she blows," he said through a bulge of dip in his lower lip, before draining half his beer. "Not what you expected?"

Teague reminded her of one of the bad guys from the old westerns her dad and brothers liked to watch. Not the main antagonist, who was usually the greedy owner of a ranch, but one of his hired guns who loped around looking for a fight. He wore a red and white flannel shirt tucked into wrangler jeans held up by a horseshoe belt buckle, that were in turn tucked into a pair of worn brown boots. He kept his sleeves rolled up to the elbow, revealing arms crisscrossed with veins as big as vines and, on his right arm, a brand of the number 44 – his old high school football number – just beneath his elbow.

"You said it was a big blue whale," Anna grabbed her own beer from the cupholder and drained the dregs, crunching the empty can beneath her muscular hand when she finished. "That's a big blue whale."

A few hours ago, sober Anna might have gagged at just the thought of cheap, warm beer, but after splitting a few pitchers, it went down easy.

Maybe a little too easy, Anna thought, resisting the urge to reach for another. She had what her dad and brothers called the 'Gavigan Gift' for throwing back beers. And while the Gavigan Gift earned her brothers, all high school heroes who joined their dad on the force after graduation, nothing but respect – it seemed to frighten people when they saw it in Anna.

"Should we take a closer look?" Teague asked.

A giggle floated up from the back seat and, instinctively, Anna glanced up at the rearview mirror. While an armrest and cupholder combination split the front seat in the middle, keeping Teague and Anna on their respective sides, there was no such obstacle in the backseat preventing Chad from moving in on Anna's roommate, Michelle.

"That whale is so creepy," Michelle said like she just realized where they were, and Anna wondered what she had been doing in the back seat.

"So what? We're just going to sit here in the car?" Anna asked, not waiting for a response. She reached for her door handle.

"Y'all go ahead," Chad said from the backseat, and Michelle giggled again.

Anna pretended not to hear Chad and reached for the back door. The door was locked so Anna pulled on it once, then pretended to stare through the tinted windows and past her own reflection into the back seat at Michelle. A second later, the back door popped open.

"I want to go with them," Michelle said, pretending to pout. "I want to see the blue whale."

One tan leg followed the sound of Michelle's voice through the open door, then another as she hopped down from the lifted car onto the ground. She landed with a surprising amount of grace, before raising her arms up above her head as if she had just landed a perfect dismount in front of a crowd.

Seeing this, Anna smiled. While both girls were out-of-state student athletes, physically, they were opposites. Anna was a swimmer, long and lean and knotted with muscles, with blonde hair cropped in a pixie cut and arms that always felt too long when she was on dry land. Michelle was a pom girl, shorter and curvier, with bouncy brown curls and an endless well of energy. This difference in appearance made it easier for Anna and Michelle to meet guys when they went out, as if guys would be confused if they looked too similar.

"You good?" Anna said, keeping her voice low and speaking directly to Michelle.

"I'm better than good," Michelle said. "I can't wait to take a picture with that whale."

Anna knew why Michelle was so keen on taking a picture. It was the same reason they were out tonight. A month and a half ago, Michelle had met the University of Tulsa's star quarterback at a party and, despite several rumors, red flags, and flat-out warnings to the contrary, believed she could change him.

And, Anna reflected, for a month she had been convinced that Michelle *had* changed him. That he really would settle down. That is until she came back to their dorm room after practice and found Michelle bawling her eyes out.

"You want me to slash his tires? Call my brothers and have them come break his legs? His arms?" Anna had asked between sobs, one long arm thrown around her roommate's shoulders.

"Maybe just his right hand," Michelle said. "He's about to set an AAC passing record."

"You sure? They've got a two for one special when it comes to assholes who break my best friend's heart." Anna managed to elicit a smile from Michelle. "I'll tell them to get on the next plane."

"Good," Michelle said, wiping her eyes. She stopped crying long enough to take a trembling breath and glance around the room. Anna followed her gaze. Despite only dating for a month, pictures of Michelle and her ex covered the walls of the dorm room.

"Let's get out of here," Anna said. "Let's go get drunk."

"Don't you have a test?" Michelle asked.

Anna did have a test on Monday. A test she needed to study for, but she couldn't start studying now anyway. Not right after practice.

It had been an issue all semester. Anna had been able to compartmentalize athletics and academics in high school, but in college, athletics dominated every moment of her life. The practices were not only physically grueling, but also mentally.

Swimming, even on a team, was a lonely sport. One where the athlete spent most of their time underwater, inside their own head, pushing themselves harder and harder. And while in high school, as the star of the team, Anna had been able to afford an off day, now every girl on the team was a former star. So every day Anna pushed herself harder than the last, going deeper and deeper into her own head, and every day she found it a little harder to come back.

"You can always retake a test," Anna said with false confidence. "We're only freshman once."

Michelle looked hopeful, but then she shook her head. "I can't go out on campus. What if we see him. What if we see her?"

Anna found the quarterback's infidelity annoying, but the idea that her friend had traded the quarterback's blue and gold letter jacket for some scarlet letter infuriated her.

"We'll go off campus," Anna said. "What about the casinos?"

Oklahoma, despite a few archaic laws that limited the alcohol content in beer and prevented the sale of liquor on Sundays, was home to several tribal casinos that, from the outside at least, rivaled the casinos of Vegas in size and spectacle. Driving into Tulsa, Anna passed one casino where the parking lot had been covered by a mishmash skyline facade of the biggest American cities, while another had appeared to directly copy the design and aesthetic of Circus Circus. The biggest casino nearby was the Cherokee Hard Rock Casino, which boasted an aesthetic that combined the classic rock vibe of a Hard Rock Cafe with the native American tribal art that permeated through everything in Oklahoma.

"Let's go check out that Cherokee Casino," Anna said. "The one we're always driving by. I'll pay for the uber."

"I've never been to a casino." Michelle's makeup was streaked, but the crying had stopped.

Being raised by a single dad and three older brothers, Anna could remember only two types of vacations growing up:

camping and Vegas. She sometimes forgot that Michelle, one of three daughters in a conservative Texas family, had always gone on more wholesome family trips to places like Disney World and Destin.

"It'll be fun," Anna said. "We'll gamble, have some drinks, meet some guys."

"Good guys?"

Anna hesitated. "Well. We're going to a casino. Not church."

"But not college guys. Not college athletes," Michelle said. "No more college athletes."

Anna doubted it would last, but she was happy enough to have Michelle distracted. Soon Michelle was laughing, trying on different outfits, curling her hair, putting on makeup; all while carefully balancing a glass of vodka and orange juice in one hand. While anything nicer than jeans would have looked out of place in an Oklahoma casino, it still took Michelle the better part of an hour to get ready. Ten minutes after Michelle assured Anna she was ready, Anna ordered an uber.

"You going to try some gambling?" Anna asked. While Michelle certainly wasn't the saintly daughter her pastor father thought she was, her religious background occasionally came out in surprising ways. She used the words 'pot' and 'dope' interchangeably and, despite taking birth control, was adamantly against abortion.

"It's not gambling if you're feeling this lucky," Michelle said.

"Oh, you're feeling lucky?"

"Feeling lucky now," Michelle said. "Getting lucky later."

Anna laughed, but before she could answer, her phone chimed to signal that the uber had arrived. Anna wouldn't say she felt lucky, but there was something in the air. Something big was about to happen and she couldn't help but be excited.

***

The pond that housed the Blue Whale sat barely a mile off Route 66, with a thick wall of trees that shielded all but the top of the whale's head from view. The sound of traffic quickly dwindled to only the occasional passing car, and as the sun began to set, this in turn was drowned out by the rising den chirping of crickets.

"World famous my ass," Teague said, reading from a sign up ahead that said 'WHALE-COME To The World Famous Blue Whale Of Catoosa' in bright red, above a smiling blue whale. As Anna and the others drew closer, gravel crunching under their feet, Teague threw his empty beer can full speed at the sign, scoring a direct hit on the whale and chipping off a piece of paint.

"Nice shot," Chad said, extending a fist for Teague to bump.

Standing next to Teague, Anna found it hard not to compare the two men. Wearing the same good old boy uniform but standing five inches shorter and ten pounds heavier, Chad looked like an obsolete model of the same mold used to cast Teague. Hearing that Anna and Michelle were college girls, the two men had first tried to pass for frat guys, then recently graduated seniors. None of their stories held water, but they kept buying drinks, so Anna hadn't minded. Most people in Oklahoma worked in Oil and Gas in some capacity, and she assumed they were landmen with the night off.

Just past the 'Whale-Come' sign stood an arched entrance, flanked on one side by a post covered in arrows pointing off in ten different directions, each arrow labeled with the name of a major city and a distance, and on the other by a visitor's map. The map divided the park into three main attractions: the Indian Trading Post, the Blue Whale Swimming Hole, and the Reptile Kingdom. Leaning against the Reptile Kingdom, an anthropomorphic crocodile invited guests to "Come see the mighty King Sawgrass and friends!" The friends, presumably, were two hissing anthropomorphic snakes that Anna thought looked both exotic and sexual, with their narrow eyes, curves, and tails beckoning guests forward.

"Wait, reptile kingdom. Like snakes? I hate snakes. Why did it have to be snakes?" Chad's voice took on a different tone as he said the line. Then he looked around at the girls. "Come on. Indiana Jones? Guess you girls aren't movie fans?"

Anna knew Indiana Jones and the line, but Michelle looked genuinely confused.

"That stuff has been closed for years," Teague said. "Just look at the Indian Trading post." Saying this he gestured to the left, where the remains of a wooden structure loomed. Anna thought it looked more like the remains of an old pirate ship than a trading post, but it was in such bad shape it was hard to tell. Most of the wood was rotting away and sections were burnt black, as if they had survived at least one fire. The whole structure looked closed to collapsing, only held up by the silver skeleton of a few metal pipes and the iron turnstiles at the former entrance. "Only thing left is the swimming hole and the Blue Whale," Teague said, drawing attention back to him.

A long, red wooden bar that said: 'Permanently Closed!' stretched across the entrance. Teague examined it, then leaned back and kicked it. The board gave way, splintering and snapping down the middle as it broke apart in two halves, causing both girls to jump. Anna's hands slipped instinctively into her pocket, where she kept her mini key ring pocketknife, along with her dorm and locker key, all on a small pink plastic wrist coil.. She kept pepper spray in her other pocket, nestled next to her phone, so small most people mistook it for an inhaler. Feeling both, Anna shook off any fear.

"What? You thought we'd just turn around and go home?" Teague said, seeing the concerned expressions on Anna and Michelle's faces.

Michelle smiled and shook her head. She was looking at Teague with different eyes than before. It was a look Anna recognized, and she saw Chad notice it too. Michelle might have sworn off football players, but Anna had known it was a promise she wouldn't keep. At least not long term. Michelle's usual type were alpha males with an edge. Teague's edges were a little sharper than most guys on campus, but he fit the bill. She might have started the night by trying something new with Chad, but she was quickly slipping back into old habits.

Or, Anna reflected, she could be thinking about the picture by the whale. Nobody was going to be jealous if they saw Michelle with Chad, but Teague was different. He might not be better looking than most of the football players, but there was no doubt who would win in a fight and that could stir a different kind of jealousy.

"Let's get going," Chad said, squaring his shoulders and stepping past the broken sign first. He wore a wide grin, but Anna thought it looked forced.

The gravel gave way to a dirt path that wound through a garden of porcelain mushrooms towards the pond. Anna wasn't surprised that whoever decided to build a giant blue whale in the middle of a pond in Oklahoma had decorated the surrounding area with mushrooms painted a myriad of psychedelic colors, and she suspected mushrooms might have been involved in the planning, building, and design of the whale itself, back in the sixties.

Teague quickly caught up to and passed Chad, leading them down the dirt path towards the pond. Anna associated most ponds with a foul, rotten egg smell, but instead she smelled only the earthy smell of dirt and grass. She thought maybe it was better described as a lake instead of a pond, but she wasn't exactly sure of the difference. While the murky water wasn't clear, there were no floating lily pads or patches of moss. Aside from the white tugboat raft in the middle of the pond, the only thing floating in the water were a few logs that had drifted free of the tree line on the opposite side of the pond.

"I know it's been said, but this is so weird," Michelle said, holding her phone sideways and snapping a few pictures of the whale. "Like were they on drugs when they made this? I mean, they had to be. Right?"

The sun began its descent behind the tree line, and with it the temperature began to drop too. Anna shivered and crossed her arms.

"Speaking of drugs – are you feeling it yet?" Chad said.

Anna turned and looked at Michelle, who giggled. "I didn't take a whole one."

"A whole what?"

Teague cut her off by lifting his shirt up over his shoulders and tossing it on the ground before reaching for his belt buckle. "I bet nobody has been swimming in here since they shut down." He kicked off his boots and jeans but left his boxers, stopping just short of stripping completely. "At least until tonight."

Anna saw Michelle's eyes light up at the sight of Teague's chest and abs, while behind her Chad frowned.

"We're going swimming?" Michelle said, reaching down to pull up the bottom of her shirt. "But I don't have my swimsuit."

Hearing this, Anna could have thrown up in her mouth.

"Race to the raft. The tugboat," Teague shouted, waving at the white boat halfway between the shore and the blue whale on the opposite side. He waded into the water until it was waist deep then did a half dive into the murky depths.

Anna glanced at Chad and, despite her irritation, could have laughed at the hangdog expression on his face. He watched Michelle strip down to her black lingerie with the same hopeless longing of a Dickensian orphan looking in a toy store window. He seemed to know that, through no fault of his own, Michelle's interest had shifted to Teague and there was nothing he could do. She saw him sigh and turn to appraise her, the leftover girl.

"So, you're a swimmer, right?" Chad asked. He started with his pants instead of his shirt, taking off his belt first.

"What did she take? Should she be swimming?"

Chad looked hurt. "If anything, it'll make swimming even better. You want some?"

Anna glared at him and looked back out at the water. Teague was athletic and making good progress through the water. Behind him, Michelle splashed and slapped at the water, moving at a crawl and listing from side to side.

"You can sit here angry on the shore if you want. But you know," Chad said before turning to run into the water. "You're a lot prettier when you smile."

For the second time that evening, Anna could have thrown up in her mouth. Instead, she took a deep breath and slipped out of her shirt. She reminded herself that Michelle was on the rebound and deserved a certain amount of leeway to be crazier than usual. She was being paranoid because she had heard too many stories from her brothers about dangerous men. It had been Anna's idea to go out. She was the one who picked the casino.

Stripping down to a sports bra and kicking off her jeans, Anna left her pepper spray behind but slipped the band holding her pocketknife and keys around her wrist. Seeing Teague most of the way to the boat, her competitive instincts kicked in and, without another moment's hesitation, she took off at a sprint and dove headfirst into the surprisingly warm water.

Anna couldn't help but take the race seriously. With three older brothers, she was often needed to even up the teams for every backyard sport from basketball to football, and because her brothers always played to win, they never went easy on her. She surfaced expertly, shooting past Chad like a torpedo, her arms cutting smoothly through the water while her legs pushed her forward like a speedboat propeller. Even with limited visibility, she sensed Michelle splashing through the water long before and long after she passed her, and soon it was down to just her and Teague.

Teague was strong, but swimming wasn't just about strength. Anna's coach liked to say that if he had to choose between strength and form, he would choose form every time, and Anna's form was perfect. She slipped easily into her own head and let her swimmer's instincts take over.

When swimming competitively, Anna usually tried to clear her head, to banish all thoughts and any distractions, but this time, whether it was the beer or her frustration with Michelle, Anna found her thoughts wandering back to the casino.

When they had arrived at the casino, the bored bouncer at the front entrance hadn't even bothered to check their IDs. He just handed them wristbands and waived them inside. Stepping into the Cherokee Casino, Anna felt a twinge of nostalgia for those family trips to Vegas. At first, Anna's brothers had taken turns chaperoning her to the pool and different shows while the others drank and bet on sports, but little by little, she was given more autonomy, before eventually being allowed to wander around freely. The price of this autonomy had been several bruising self-defense lessons by her brothers and a promise to always carry pepper spray and a pocketknife, promises she kept to this day, but it had been worth it to wander around the gaming floor and pool, occasionally flirting for free chips and drinks.

Whoever designed the Cherokee Casino had clearly taken their lead from Vegas. The casino lacked any windows, clocks, or clues as to the current time in the outside world, and Anna could have sworn she'd seen the same psychedelic carpet design of neon swoops, circles, and stars at the Cosmopolitan. Despite an ashtray at every machine, the air smelled only faintly of cigarettes, while the hum of constant conversation intermingled with the chimes and bells from the slot machines meant that Anna had to raise her voice to be heard.

"What do you think?"

"Are these all gambling games?" Michelle asked.

Anna had taken Michelle over to the slot machines where they both lost twenty dollars before they decided to try their hand at a few rounds of blackjack. They sat down at the blackjack table and attempted to score a free drink, something Anna remembered her brothers doing in Vegas, only to learn that drinks in the Oklahoma casino weren't free. That was how they met Chad, who swooped in to buy their drinks while Teague laughed and spit into his empty bottle.

"The drinks aren't free and you got to pay a dollar ante every hand," Chad said. "It's all the risk of Vegas and none of the rewards."

Hearing this, Anna could remember the dealer shooting Chad a dirty look.

"Look at him like that again and I'll break your face, and your hands," Teague said, without looking up from his cards.

When the dealer was relieved a hand later, Chad laughed. "Yeah, you better run away."

Anna and Michelle had both giggled. It was, after all, the kind of tough talk they were used to hearing from college guys. College boys were always looking for a fight. Always an insult away from an epic brawl that never came. And these guys seemed the same way, until they were a couple pitchers deep at one of the casino bars, and Chad got up to use the restroom.

Anna hadn't seen what started it, but she saw how Teague finished it. One second Chad was on the ground, looking dazedly up at the dealer from earlier that night. A second later, Teague leapt over Chad's prone body, seized the dealer by the shirt and flung him headfirst into the ground, before stepping back and dealing him one vicious kick across the chest. A crowd quickly gathered but both men knew better than to stick around, so they quickly slipped out.

And, Anna thought, that had seemed like the end of the night. Until they walked outside and Teague's Chevy Tahoe pulled up.

"You girls up for a little adventure?" Chad had said and, without protesting, both girls got in. First Michelle, then Anna.

"So, what kind of adventure?" Michelle had asked.

Teague had passed around warm beers, cracking one before they left the parking lot. "You girls ever heard of the Blue Whale of Catoosa?"

***

Anna caught and passed Teague about ten feet from the tugboat. She sensed him push a little harder, trying to go faster by speeding up his strokes and forgetting about his legs, but it was too late. Anna's hand slapped the side of the wooden tugboat a full beat before Teague.

"You're fast," Teague said with a strained smile, but Anna could tell he wasn't used to losing, especially not to a girl.

They both climbed out of the water and into the tugboat. The tugboat was bigger than Anna thought it would be, but was really just a wooden raft with wooden slats and a tugboat façade built around the front and back. Standing in the middle of the raft, Anna shivered. The sun had sunk beneath the trees, leaving behind a sky streaked with purple and pink. She sensed someone looking at her and turned to see Teague looking her up and down, one eyebrow cocked and a smile tugging at the corner of his lips. Even when she caught him staring, Teague didn't look away, as if it were some sort of compliment.

Feeling more naked without her pepper spray than without her shirt, Anna almost said something when Chad slapped the side of the boat and called for Teague's hand. While Teague helped Chad, Anna looked out across the water at Michelle.

"You got this, Michelle!" Anna shouted, cupping her hands around her mouth to help her voice carry.

"Almost there!" Chad shouted, stepping up next to her.

Michelle chopped at the water for a little longer and then stopped. She spit up a little water.

"I'm feeling weird," Michelle said. "A little dizzy."

Anna felt the muscles in her shoulders tighten into knots. It might have been her imagination, but Michelle's eyes looked big and dark, as if the pupils had dilated to engulf the entire eyeball. She glanced at Chad and saw Teague was also glaring at him.

"Shit," Teague said. "Tell her to swim back."

"She told me she wanted one," Chad said. "I didn't make her take anything."

"You trying to get the cops called? What the hell are you thinking?" Teague said.

"Michelle! Stop!" Anna said, not wanting to get involved. "Can you swim back?"

Michelle blinked, then opened her eyes wide. She licked her lips.

"I feel weird," she repeated.

"Stay there!" Anna said, slipping into the water. "I'm coming to get you!"

She didn't bother telling Chad and Teague that they would be swimming back to the shore. She hoped they could get to the main road before the boys swam back. She had no intention of going anywhere else with them.

Back in the water, Anna started to half swim back towards Michelle, keeping her head above water and her eyes on Michelle. If Michelle slipped beneath the water, Anna wanted to see where she went.

"I'm coming to you, just stay still," Anna called out between strokes.

Anna was so focused on her friend that she didn't notice the log floating towards Michelle until it was almost on top of her.

Only the log wasn't floating, Anna realized. Logs don't float with purpose, and they certainly don't float into ripples. Before

Anna could fully process what was happening and why, the log slipped beneath the water.

Anna's mouth went dry. A warning bell rang shrilly at the back of her mind and panic rose in her stomach.

"Holy shit," Chad yelled from the raft. "Did you see that?"

Then, without warning, Chad began slapping the side of the raft and screaming. Michelle, still treading water, blinked rapidly, then squinted at him. She seemed more confused than frightened until her eyes went wide. "Something touched my leg. Something in the water."

Anna kept swimming, keeping her eyes on Michelle, but panic was already spreading from her stomach and gripping her chest. As she watched, Michelle bobbed once in the water like a cork, dipping in and out so fast she barely had time to register surprise. They locked eyes. Then something dark and scaly washed over Michelle, breaking over her like a reptilian wave and spinning her around, driving her down into the water and leaving behind only a white cap stained with blood.

Anna stopped swimming, her eyes on the spot where Michelle had just floated. A bubble broke the surface, followed by another, then blood poured up as if from an underwater fountain, dying the water around it black with a hint of crimson.

Anna wasn't sure how long she bobbed in the water, staring into nothingness, waiting for Michelle to come back. Then she saw two more smaller logs break the surface. Primal fear overrode Anna's shock, and she turned and swam as fast as she could back to the tugboat. She slapped the side and started to pull herself out when she felt Teague's hands beneath her armpits, lifting her up and out of the water, where they both tumbled down together in a pile of limbs.

Again, Anna's senses abandoned her. A high-pitched ringing filled her ears and the corners of her vision were fuzzy, as if she had stood up too fast. She thought again of Michelle and felt tears spring to her eyes.

When the ringing finally receded, she could hear Chad screaming on the opposite side of the boat.

"Where is she? What the hell was that?" Chad had his hands in his hair. "Oh God. Oh God."

Michelle was gone, Anna realized. And they would be too if they didn't get back to shore.

Anna sat up, looking back at the shore and trying to measure the distance. She found it easier to focus on this problem than to think about Michelle, and she felt her senses returning. She guessed the distance to the shore was about the same as an Olympic size pool, but distance wasn't the problem. By the light of the half-moon she could see several logs drifting between the tugboat and the shore.

Only they aren't logs, Anna reminded herself.

"Oh my god, look at the size of that thing," Chad said.

Anna stood up, just in time to see a crocodile rise up to the surface and push towards them. Up close, there was no mistaking the crocodile for a log, with its long snout full of sharp teeth, its cold reptilian eyes, and that powerful tail swishing through the water. Anna thought it had to be at least fourteen feet long, and she remembered the cartoon crocodile from the sign out front. "Come see King Sawgrass and friends!"

"An alligator," Teague said.

"It's a crocodile," Anna said, recognizing the animal's long narrow snout from the nature documentaries she liked to watch while studying.

"What's the difference?" Teague said.

It's worse, Anna almost said, but nobody needed to hear that crocodiles were fiercer and far more likely to attack humans. Instead, she stood frozen, watching the crocodile swim languidly around the boat, watching them with cold, red eyes. She had never seen one up close before, and without the protection of a fence or a wall, it felt bigger. The crocodile completed another loop, then vanished into the depths.

Anna considered their options. While the front and back of the raft were shielded by the façade of the tugboat, the sides were low enough to practically dip in and out of the water. It wouldn't take much for one of the crocodiles to get on board, which meant they had to escape. She looked at the shore, then out at the blue whale. The whale was only about twenty-five meters away, but the pond was low and the ladders hung high out of the water.

"Shit. She's dead. She's really dead," Chad said. "Shit. If my wife finds out... Shit, and what about the cops? We're on parole man. The judge said no more second chances."

"Calm down, Dave," Teague said, addressing Chad by a different name.

Chad, it was too late for Anna to think of him as a Dave, would not calm down on his own. She recognized the rapid shallow breaths and the wild, unfocused eyes of someone who was hyperventilating.

"Dave," Teague said, clamping a hand down on Chad's shoulder. "Look at me. What did you give the girl?"

"Michelle?" Chad said. His eyes flicked to Anna, then back to Teague. "What do you think I gave her?"

Teague grimaced and stepped away. "That's on you. I ain't taking the fall for that."

Chad looked over at Anna, then back at Teague.

"Will you help me?"

Teague stepped back. "This is your mess."

Chad licked his lips then nodded.

Anna wanted to keep her eyes on the water but turned away from it as Chad stepped forward.

"Don't come any closer," Anna said.

"Look, this is bad. This is real bad. But we don't need to make it any worse," Chad said. He spoke softly, as if Anna were a wild animal, but his eyes were manic. "We need to stick together."

"I won't tell anyone," Anna said quickly, her eyes darting between Chad and the water. "I just want to go home."

Chad nodded as if agreeing, when a splash nearby distracted both of them. Anna turned to see Sawgrass, the giant crocodile, surface nearby. She took a step back and heard the sound of running feet. Turning, she saw Chad rushing towards her, arms outstretched.

He crashed into her, but she had sidestepped at the last moment, so, while the weight of him drove her back, he pushed her away from the edge instead of closer to it. For a moment they fumbled together, dancing awkwardly, then Chad drew his hand back and slapped her with his open palm across the face.

Anna stumbled back. She felt Chad grab her, turning her towards the edge, and realized she needed to do something. She needed to fight back. Swinging her arms up, she knocked his hands aside, then thumped him hard on the chest. Surprised, Chad rocked back a step, giving Anna a second to flick her pocketknife open and hold it up, before he lunged forward again.

Anna hadn't intended to stab Chad, only to ward him off, but when Chad darted forward the blade sank in with surprising ease. She had expected it to be like cutting leather, even steak, but instead the blade slipped into Chad's stomach with barely any resistance, so easily that she jerked in surprise, wrenching the blade down and to the right. Standing before her, Chad's eyes bulged as he wrapped his arms around her shoulders, squeezed once, then released her and stumbled back.

"You stabbed me," Chad exclaimed, looking at her with an expression of surprise and pain, as if in addition to being physically hurt, he also felt betrayed.

Anna stepped back and pressed against the back of the tugboat. She had left the pocketknife in Chad's stomach, and it was now covered in oozing blood. The blood dripped down Chad's stomach, pattering on his feet and between the boards of the raft, into the water below.

"You stabbed me," Chad said again as he pulled the knife from his stomach.

The wound wasn't fatal and, now holding the pocketknife in one hand, Chad looked determined to finish what he had started. He took a step forward when something thumped the boat and, without warning, Chad pitched forward.

Anna could practically hear the calm, measured voice of the narrator from one of her nature documentaries explaining what had just happened. She had seen the same thing happen a hundred times before. A wildebeest would wander too close to a murky river, only for a crocodile to shoot out at blinding speed, wrap its teeth around the poor animal, and yank it off land and down into the water.

Chad landed chest first on the wooden raft, screaming when he saw the jaws of a crocodile where his left leg should be. He kicked once at the animal's head then, when it started to pull him down, he scrambled for purchase on the raft. The wooden boards of the raft, long in need of repair, gave way beneath his hands and the weight of the crocodile, sending water rushing into the boat as it began to break away into two separate pieces.

The smell of blood, recognizable but stronger than she had ever smelled, washed over Anna as the crocodile spun around in a barrel roll, flipping Chad onto his back before yanking him down into the water. Anna glanced up at Teague, who sat pressed against the opposite side of the raft, his eyes wide with fear.

"You killed him," Teague said.

Anna barely registered the words. Instead, she yelped as her piece of the raft began to tilt up. "We're sinking."

Anna wasn't sure if Teague heard her or sensed the same thing. She saw him glance at the churning water nearby and make a decision. While Anna had hesitated when her friend died, Teague didn't make the same mistake, and Anna saw him dive headfirst into the water.

Anna, realizing what Teague was doing, glanced once at the churning water around Chad and then back at the blue whale. She made up her mind and dove into the water.

Her dive was perfect, cutting the distance to the whale in half without wasting a stroke. The water was still warm and, under other circumstances, would have felt pleasant compared with the chilly air. She kicked with her powerful legs and pushed her arms above her head into a triangle. When she breached the surface, she was already mid-stroke, her mind, her arms, and her legs all working together like a well-oiled machine. She wasn't swimming; she was flying.

Fear clawed at her peripheral vision, begging her to stop and glance around to look for the crocodiles, but she pushed it away. She crawled as deep into her head as she could possibly go as she pushed her body to its absolute limits. Today she would have to be fast, faster than she had ever been, or she would die. She found her deepest reserve of strength and she pulled it out. She dug until she hit bedrock, and then she dug deeper.

Anna sensed the whale coming up fast. There were two ladders, one to the left and one to the right. She went right. She came up out of the water at full speed, propelled up by her legs and her will to live. She reached out with one hand, caught the bottom rung of the ladder, and felt it give way in her hands.

For a second, time stopped as she hung suspended in the air, staring at the metal rung in her hands. Then she bounced off the concrete side of the whale, scraping off patches of skin on her arms and head on her way down, before plunging into the water below.

***

Anna sank to the bottom, hand still clenching the metal rung of the ladder. The freshly raw patches of skin on her arms and head burned. She closed her eyes and screamed inwardly, then she forced her eyes open. The pond was shallow here, and she had her back to the concrete. She could see the surface shimmering a few feet above her head, and the other ladder nearby. She was about to kick up when the water changed; the energy was sucked out. Then the water swirled in one direction as straight ahead she saw the white underbelly of the crocodile racing towards her with its mouth open.

Anna acted on instinct. Still holding the metal rung of the ladder, she brought it up and out, catching the crocodile in the soft, white roof of its mouth. The creature exhaled a hiss of bubbles, before swinging its head wildly from side to side and jerking the rung out of Anna's hand.

Anna didn't hesitate. She braced her feet on the bottom of the pond and jumped, narrowly avoiding being struck by the crocodile's thrashing tail as she kicked frantically for the surface.

One more push, Anna promised herself. Just one more time.

She shot out of the water again, catching the bottom rung of the other ladder, and this time it held. She gave a cry of triumph and pulled herself up and over the side of the whale, tumbling down into the middle with a cry of pain.

She lay there breathing heavily for a moment, then pushed herself weakly to her feet. The body of the whale was hollow, but secure from the water and the crocodiles by two tall walls. Looking out over the side, she could see one half of the raft beginning to sink, while a few of the crocodiles drifted aimlessly nearby. She scanned the water between the raft and the shore but saw nothing. There was no sign of Teague.

Anna wasn't sure if she felt relief or just exhaustion. She would have liked to sink back down to the ground, but doubted she would be able to get back up if she did. So, instead, she pushed away from the edge and turned to face the exit.

Michelle had been right. They could have taken some amazing pictures in here, Anna thought. The inside of the whale was hollow, save a few rusted metal poles for support. There was no light, save what little moonlight could slip through the porthole windows that ran along the side, so Anna paused and listened for the sounds of any living animal before stepping forward. The exit from the structure was through the whale's toothy grin and, while a few hours ago she might have found this charming, now it sent a tremor of fear through her body. Finding a last, hidden reserve of energy, she spent it sprinting the final feet through the whale's mouth and back onto dry land, where she almost collapsed again.

Trudging along the shore, but careful to give the water plenty of distance, Anna wondered what she would tell Michelle's parents… That it was her fault their daughter was dead? That she had been the one who suggested going out off campus?

A sob wracked Anna's body and she had to stop until she got her breathing under control.

She would confess, Anna decided. She would tell the truth. Tell them everything. It didn't matter. Nothing mattered. Nothing would bring Michelle back.

Anna reached the spot where they had taken off their clothes and sank to her knees. A part of her brain pointed out that they never had to go in the water, that they could have stayed on dry land the entire time, that the only reason they got into the water in the first place was because Anna was a swimmer and she wanted to show off.

Had that really been the reason? Anna thought. Had they only gone swimming because she wanted to show off? Because she needed to be the best? Her memories were murky, like the water in the lake.

Anna reached for her pile of clothes but couldn't bring herself to look at Michelle's discarded jeans or her clutch purse. She tried to focus on one thing at a time, putting on her shirt before grabbing her jeans and stepping in one foot at a time, then pulling them up. She was so focused on each of these tasks that she never saw Teague coming. She only felt his fist crash into the back of her head, before he lifted her into the air and threw her face first into the ground.

"I hoped the gators would get you," Teague said from somewhere above her. "Hoped I wouldn't have to do this."

Anna blinked to clear the stars from her eyes as she scrambled onto her back. Teague stood a few feet away, still shirtless, his chest heaving. His eyes were red and he looked like he had been crying.

"Wait," Anna said. "I won't tell anyone."

"He was always getting me into trouble," Teague ignored her, and she felt like he was talking to himself as much as to her. "Even tonight at the casino, with that damn guy."

"Please," Anna repeated, scooting back away from him.

"But he was my friend. And you killed him," Teague started forward. "It wouldn't be right. I got to do what's right."

Teague pounced, reminding Anna of the speed with which he attacked the dealer at the casino. She tried to scramble away, but when she felt him drawing close, she grabbed a rock and turned with a wide swing aimed at his head. The blow never landed. Teague batted her arm away with one hand and smacked her across the face with the other, with hands so fast Anna barely registered them as blurs before she felt them. Again she spun around, landing face first on the ground and tasting dirt and blood.

She spat once and tried to catch her breath before pushing up and trying to crawl away. The dirt stung her freshly raw hands, but she kept moving over the rocks and towards the grass until Teague walked up behind her, wrapped an elbow around her neck and yanked back hard, lifting her up.

For a moment, unable to breathe, Anna panicked. She forgot who she was and where she came from. She forgot about her older brothers teaching her how to fight and the self-defense techniques drilled into her by her father.

Then a darker thought flickered across her mind. The idea that maybe, just maybe, she deserved this. That Teague was right, and this was justice. That it wasn't fair that she, Anna, should survive when Michelle didn't.

Then she remembered Michelle. Michelle, the consummate pom girl. Her smile. Her laugh. Her ability to light up an entire football field, not to mention a room.

Michelle wouldn't want Anna to die here. Michelle would want her to live.

Anna kicked her feet up, then swung them back with the force of a wrecking ball into Teague's groin. Something crunched beneath her foot and he groaned, loosening his grip an inch, but an inch was all Anna needed. She cupped her hands and jammed them up and out, slipping beneath Teague's elbow and dropping to the ground in a crouch. She snatched the pepper spray up from her jeans and spun around, pulling the trigger just as Teague came forward again.

Teague screamed, throwing himself back and out of harm's way as he clawed first at his eyes, then at the dirt, and then at his eyes again.

"My eyes," Teague whimpered, crawling backward towards the pond. "You bitch. I'm blind."

He moved towards the sound of water, groping about until he found the pond, where he began splashing water up into his eyes, stopping only when a low hissing filled the air.

Anna saw the crocodile rising out of the water only a few inches from Teague a second before it struck. The crocodile moved with blinding speed, catching Teague's arm and spinning to the side, ripping the arm out at the socket. Another crocodile lunged up and caught Teague around the leg, spinning in the opposite direction and splitting him down the middle, like two children fighting over a toy and pulling it apart at the seams.

Anna blinked and tried to catch her breath, watching as the two crocodiles each claimed their portion of Teague before sinking back beneath the murky water. She wished she could just lay there. Just lay down right there, curl into a ball, and wait for someone to save her. That wasn't who she was though. She could save herself. She had saved herself.

So, Anna kept moving. She pushed up off the ground and grabbed her shoes.

She looked back over her shoulder once, as she reached the gravel parking lot. Despite everything that had happened, the placid scene seemed to have reset. The Blue Whale still grinned on the far side of the pond, and near the back, past the tail with the ladders hanging over the side, the crocodiles bobbed like logs in the water.

The End

They Don't Feel a Thing

By: David McDonald

No one who ever had to deal with Todd Bailey for more than a minute or two would have mistaken him for a sensitive soul. The finer things in life were of little interest to Todd, for his universe rarely extended past the deck of his lobster boat, the Sea Bitch. The only things that he cared about on dry land were whiskey and whores, and he only worked the pots long enough to find the money to acquire more of both. It never seemed to last long, however, and far sooner than he would have liked, he would find himself back out on the sea, braving storm-tossed waves and freezing temperatures. He was not the sort of man who loved the sea, in fact, he hated it and called it a back breaking bitch. But harvesting lobster was all that Todd knew and the boat his father, and his father's father before him, had sailed, was all he had.

He was a tall man, but lean, all the fat burnt off him by long hours hauling heavily laden lobster pots up from the sea floor. Humourless grey eyes gleamed above wind-burnt cheeks and a narrow mouth that seemed permanently compressed into the scowl of man who felt hard done by the world around him. Often, bitterly, he would watch far more expensive and better outfitted boats sail past, their crews laughing as they swapped tall stories of their latest exploits in the port they were now leaving behind. The only time his cracked lips would part in a smile, one that revealed crooked, yellowed teeth, was when he had his hands on a shot glass or a woman made willing by money, or while hauling in a particularly successful catch, his brain automatically converting lobsters into money, and money into drink and debauchery.

While he envied the owners of bigger boats, he knew that the only way he could afford to upgrade would be to take on crew, so he could increase the amount of lobster he could bring in. He was used to his own company, however, and the long silences as he sailed where he willed, following his hunches of where his next catch would be were good times for thinking. He wanted no one to laugh with, or tell tall tales with, and even if he had desired such, he would have had no idea of where or how to start. He had grown accustomed to his solitude, and wore it like a comfortable old pair of shoes, moulded to the shape of his life.

So, he sailed alone, a man of small dreams and desires, content enough to live cheque to cheque, and port to port. Todd Bailey was not a bad man, but neither was he a particularly good one. He cursed the cold of the northern seas but was blind to their splendour, he railed with almost poetic profanity when clouds prevented him setting sail, but did not rejoice at the beauty of the stars on a still, clear night. There was no romance in his solitary soul. Perhaps a more sensitive man might have been better equipped to deal with the strangeness that awaited him, but, chances are, no one would have survived the thing that he pulled out of the sea.

Todd swore bitterly as he pulled another empty pot onto the deck of the Sea Bitch. He had laid out twenty in this particular spot and had recovered ten, and all of them had been completely empty. It made no sense to him; all the signs had pointed to this being a perfect place. Even if he was being too optimistic about its potential, he should have had a least one or two of the bastards to show for his effort. Todd shook his head bitterly. It was just his luck. Habits formed over years of repetitive labour kept his body hauling in pots even as he tried to think of a reason for this disappointing result. He had hoped to return to port that evening, but unless things picked up, it would mean at least another day out on this God forsaken ocean. He was so caught up in these unpleasant thoughts that it took a moment for the change in weight on the end of the rope to register. There was something in this pot!

Irrationally excited, he began to pull it in faster, hand over hand, the thought of actually having something to show for his day spurring him on, even if the weight told him it could only be three or four lobsters at best. Nothing could have prepared him for what he was about to see. As the pot came up over the railing, dripping ice cold water and swaying slightly in the gentle breeze, Todd got a good look at what was inside. He swore and crossed himself, taking an involuntarily step backwards, tripping over a loose piece of rope, and landing flat on his backside. A sharp pain jolted up his spine, but he barely noticed, his eyes locked on the pot which now rested on the deck.

Inside was a solitary lobster, but it was like no lobster he had ever seen in his almost forty years on the boat. It was big, any bigger and it wouldn't have been able been able to enter the pot, but Todd had seen big lobsters before, this wasn't like those., He had never seen a lobster that was a glossy jet black that glimmered in the dull sunlight before, nor one with the reddish swirls that seemed to move in random patterns beneath his startled gaze. Its tiny eyes glowed red, seeming to transfix him with a furious stare. It had antenna twice as long as those of a normal lobster, and they whipped back and forth, seemingly with a life of their own.

As he watched, it raised vicious looking claws and lunged at the wire mesh that trapped it. Todd could see that it had already stripped off the protective layer of plastic, leaving bare metal glittering, scored with the marks of its claws. He was suddenly glad that he had replaced his father's old style pots. He had complained and sulked over the expense at the time, but those clenching pincers would have made short work of the tar coated oak he once used.

"What are you?" Todd muttered, more to himself than to the creature before him.

Strangeness aside, there was something about it that made him deeply uncomfortable, an aura that was strong enough even to penetrate his lack of sensitivity to such things. Todd had attended the bare minimum of school, and while not a stupid man, his vocabulary was functional rather than extensive. If he had been told what the word malevolent meant, however, he would have seized it gladly, because that was what the creature reeked of, a sense of malevolence and unnaturalness. For a moment, he battled the temptation to simply throw the pot overboard and cut the rope, and let the government mandated degradable hinges allow it to escape after he was long gone.

If Todd had a genius, though, it was for working out the value of his catch to the last penny. Where another man might have dreamed of a new species named after him, Todd could only see dollar signs. A discovery like this would be worth the price of a larger boat at least, if not enough to allow him to leave the life he hated and drink and wench his way to his grave in comfort. One of those rare smiles crossed his normally taciturn features at the thought.

It was then that he became aware of the unnatural silence that had enveloped the boat. It took him few minutes to realise what had happened. The sound of hundreds of lobsters crawling over one another in the hold had been a constant background noise, low enough to be on the edge of hearing, a constant susurration that faded into the sounds of the ocean. But now that it was gone, it seemed louder than ever. He cursed and ran across to the hatch, flicking over the bolt. He lifted it, dreading that he would greeted by the unmoving remains of his catch. He stood in the opening for a moment, the only noise the gasp of his indrawn breath as the sight before him slowly registered.

The lobsters were unmoving but very much alive, their tiny eyes staring at him as every lobster faced him with claws raised in an aggressive display. Then, as one, they surged towards him, feet clacking on the boards of the floor, the snap of claws opening and closing as if already rending his flesh. Todd stood frozen, unable to move for what seemed an eternity, but from some previously untapped well of strength, he found control of his muscles just before the first rank engulfed him. He jumped back, slamming the hatch down and flicking the bolt. A few severed, twitching claws littered the planking around him.

Todd hunched forward, hands on his knees, breathing heavily as he considered what had just happened. Never before had he seen such bizarre behaviour, and it took no great mental leap to connect it with the strange animal on his deck, but, where as another man might have been terrified, all Todd could think of was the money he might make when he got it back to land, and brought it to what his father had always disparagingly referred to as "those eggheads up at the university". With happy thoughts of fame and fortune rolling around his head, Todd got back to work. As keen as he was to take his specimen into land, however, he wasn't going to miss out on a single dollar, and that meant collecting the rest of his pots.

He may as well have gone straight back though. The rest of the day proved as fruitless as the morning had been. Every single pot came up empty, and even worse, he began to make rookie mistakes. Lines snarled and he had missed markers he had left out. The last straw was when he cut himself with his belt knife while whittling, something he couldn't remember having done in years.

No matter how hard he concentrated on the tasks at hand, however, he couldn't shake the feeling of being watched, and it wasn't hard to locate the source of his unease. It was coming directly from the freak of nature on the deck. No matter where he went on the boat, its eyes would follow him, and its antennae always seemed to be questing towards him. Finally, he could take no more and threw down his tools with a profane curse. It was close enough to dark, Todd decided, he would catch some sleep.

His cabin below decks was humble enough, a chest of drawers, a mirror, and a single bed, but it suited Todd well enough. His sole luxury was a small porthole that gave him something to look out of if he got bored. It had been his home countless nights, and he was always quick to sleep and quicker to wake. Not this night though, as he tossed and turned trying to get comfortable. The usual noises of the sea at night failed to soothe him, and the creakings and rumblings of timber had an ominous air. Strange scuttlings and slitherings seemed to filter down from the deck above. This ship was as much a part of Todd as his own hands, but tonight it was strange, haunted place.

A faint scratching from the porthole caught his ear and he noticed that the light that should have been pouring in from the full moon was barely coming in at all. Nervously, he walked across the room to the window, gaping at what he found. The glass was a writhing mass of legs and claws as a dozen lobsters clung to anything they could grasp. Todd stood and stared, feeling an intense fear beginning to rise from within him. He might have stood there until morning, but for the realisation that the noises from the deck had grown steadily louder. He knew he had to check it out. What if some passing boat had pulled in alongside, and even now someone was stealing his ticket to riches?

He went straight to the bed and reached underneath. Every lobsterman kept a gun to ward off poachers from their pots, and Todd was no exception. He had seen fisherman with everything from high powered hunting rifles to illegal assault rifles, but a simple pump action shotgun was enough for Todd. He quickly checked the chamber and made sure it was fully loaded, before cocking it as he strode toward the door. He flung it open, a warning shout dying in his throat as the gun dropped from the nerveless fingers.

The scene before him was the stuff of nightmares. The deck was covered in crustaceans of every size and shape, clambering over one another in a careless tangle of clacking exoskeletons. He recognised some of the species; lobsters and king crabs and spiny lobsters, but others he had never seen before. There were things with elongated legs and pincers, pallid shells, and unusually long eye stalks, things that had no business being seen on the surface. There was no apparent order to the unholy collection either, as every spare piece of surface area was covered, with the unlucky ones being pushed overboard by the sheer quantity of their brethren.

All motion ceased as his gun clattered onto the wooden decking. For a moment, every eye and antennae focussed on Todd, and the weight of that inhuman perception turned his blood to ice. Then, they all began to move towards him. Todd felt a warm trickle run down his thigh and he realised that he was urinating himself, his terror was so great he had lost control of his bladder. His legs seemed to weigh a tonne, but the sight of their remorseless advance gave him the strength to slowly retreat back to the illusory safety of his cabin, slamming the door shut behind him and bolting it tightly. Sobbing, he manhandled the cabinet into position against the door before collapsing onto the bed. Just like he had when he was child, he hid himself under the covers, an irrational hope burning in his mind that he might stay safe if only they couldn't see him.

The night seemed to last an eternity, with every noise magnified in the grip of his terror. Hour after hour came a persistent scraping at the door, and his mind's eye conjured up visions of claws digging away at the wood, inch by inch. For a while he screamed, begging that they leave him alone, pleading to every god he had mocked and scorned over his long and chequered life that he be spared, but eventually his voice started to give way, and he was reduced to inarticulate moans. As dawn approached, however, the sounds died away, and as light filtered into his cabin his mood began to change.

Every man who makes his living at the mercy of the arbitrary whims of the ocean must possess an inner core of stubbornness, a reserve of willpower that allows him to face a force far beyond himself. Any man who lacks this trait soon moves on to greener, more rewarding pastures. Todd possessed more than his fair share of stubbornness and resolve, and it began assert itself, with his terror and humiliation coalescing into a rising tide of anger that became white-hot fury.

This was his boat, these were his seas. Yes, he hated them, but he would be damned if any overgrown lobster was going to keep him a prisoner. Gathering his courage, he strode to the door and flung the cabinet aside, not minding the crash of breaking wood. He was lost in a righteous anger that was the strongest emotion he had felt in years. Todd unbolted the lock and yanked open the door, ready for anything he might find, anything, except for the sight that greeted him.

Under the dawn's light the deck was completely bare. Every rope, every tool, every empty pot had disappeared, along with the gun he had dropped the night before, though he could see the marks in the wood where he had dropped it. The only thing that broke the smooth expanse of wood was the pot containing the monstrosity. He had made sure he had chained and padlocked down his prize before retiring to his cabin, and his endeavour had been rewarded. Whatever had swept the deck clean had not been able to shift the pot, or its captive. With an expression on his face halfway between a snarl and a grin, Todd pulled out his belt knife and marched towards it.

"Right, you little bastard, I'm going to gut you like a fish." He giggled nervously at his pun, then stopped, not liking the hint of madness he heard in his laugh.

He circled the pot nervously, almost frightened by the way the beast regarded him. Every time he moved, it would follow him with its crimson eyes, or scuttle around to face him. He half-heartedly reached for the fastenings of the pot, but drew back his hand quickly, as its claws snapped open and shut warningly. As much as he hated to admit it, even to himself, Todd was terrified of this creature and had no desire to put his hands anywhere near it. Even a normal lobster could crush a man's finger, but judging from the marks on the mesh, that thing looked like it would shear them off like it was pruning a rose bush.

Todd hovered uncertainly for a moment, then grinned triumphantly as an idea came to him so suddenly, had he been a cartoon character, a light bulb would have appeared above his head.

"Oh, I have just the thing for you, my friend," he whispered unpleasantly. For the first time, the creatures gaze seemed to waver, as if in fear. Todd liked that, he liked that a lot.

Whistling a long forgotten tune, Todd walked towards the wheelhouse. Underneath was another storage compartment, and inside was a large tub that Todd filled with blocks of ice in the summer, to help keep his catch fresh. When it wasn't serving that purpose, he would often fill it with cool sea water and immerse himself in it to escape the day's heat. Its sides came up well above his knees, and it was three metres by three metres, so he could completely submerge himself when he wanted. He was not planning on using it himself today, however, as he had other plans. Next to this storage compartment was another compartment, where he kept the steam jet he used to clean the decks when the mood took him, which admittedly was not all that often. He dragged it out onto the deck, grinning madly. Perhaps it was for the best Todd could not see himself, because if he had seen the expression he was wearing on a stranger's face, he would have turned and ran as fast as he could, fleeing the madness in his smile as he cheerfully got to work.

The steam cleaner was designed to suck up sea water through a hose that dangled off the side boat, heat it to boiling, then spray it out in a scalding hot stream of vapour that would shift even the most stubborn and filthy stains. Todd was his own mechanic and engineer, and it was easy enough for him to affix the nozzle to the tub, so that the stream sprayed directly onto the surface into one of the corners, quickly condensing into a simmering pool. As he watched, the compartment began to fill rapidly with water that was close enough to boiling as to make no difference.

Leaving it to fill, he walked back to the stern and stood before the cage.

"Soon that water will be nice and deep, and I am going to give you a nice, hot bath," Todd gloated. "I think you will cook up rather nicely. I might even see what you taste like under that pretty shell of yours. That will teach you to mess with Todd Bailey."

The creature hissed, and Todd laughed at the sound. His terror and humiliation of the night before seemed infinitely far away. His laugh cut off, however, as a motion behind the pot caught his eye. Just beyond the railing, two monstrous claws were rising out of the waves, each easily as big as Todd's torso. He whimpered as they clamped down on the railing, wood splintering in their grasp. Slowly but inexorably, a massive lobster began to drag itself up into the boat.

"No. Oh, no," Todd began to moan.

Not daring to take his eyes away from the travesty of nature clambering aboard his vessel, he began to back away slowly, seeking the safety of his cabin, though how long it would protect him was something he didn't dare think about. It was only when he felt something hit against the backs of his legs that he remembered the tub, now full to overflowing with boiling water.

Todd had always scoffed at the idea that in your last moments, your entire life flashed before your eyes. In his years on the treacherous sea, death was something mundane, with no mystery attached. The sea simply took you. Now, as he fought to regain his balance, his weight dragging him backwards, he found that there was one vivid memory that replayed before his eyes.

Todd had received a desperate call from a restauranteur who had somehow found himself running out of live lobsters on the biggest night of his year. After extracting the promise of an exorbitant price from the panicking owner, Todd had agreed to personally deliver a dozen of his finest. After depositing them in the huge tank in the middle of the restaurant, he had paused to admire them, and to think about what he would spend the bonus on. There was a new girl at his favourite cathouse, perhaps he would pay her a visit.

His pleasant reverie was disturbed as he became aware of an older man and young girl of about ten standing next to him, arguing.

"But, Daddy, it's so cruel! They boil them alive!"

The older man, a fairly wealthy businessman judging by his suit, put a comforting hand on her shoulder.

"It's okay, honey. They don't feel pain like we do."

She looked up at him doubtfully. "But, how do you know, Daddy?"

He looked uncomfortable for a moment, then noticed Todd, taking in his working gear with a quick glance, sizing him up.

"Honey, why don't you ask the lobsterman. He would know." He winked at Todd over her head.

The girl looked up at Todd expectantly. "Is that true, mister?"

Todd hesitated, finding the pleading look in her eyes disconcerting. The man must have mistook his hesitation for something else.

"Look, honey, that's a big one!" He pointed at a lobster that seemed no different from the other.

The girl only looked for a moment, but that was long enough for the man to slip a fifty dollar note into Todd's hand, with the practiced ease of a man used to giving bribes. By the time she turned back, Todd had made it disappear just as adroitly.

Todd smiled. "That's right, sweetheart, you don't have to worry. The instant they hit that boiling water it's all over. They don't feel a thing."

He was wrenched back into the present as gravity finally won and he fell backwards, into the tub. As he hit the boiling water, Todd realised just how wrong he had been.

Silence Next The Sea

By: CJ Hooper

It had been a cold February swim two winters ago, at her new home in Cley-Next-The-Sea, which caused the infection that, through perforated eardrums, had resulted in the loss of hearing with the risk of brain damage. The sound of the waves on the North Sea coast had, over the course of the illness, been permanently silenced. Dizziness and nausea replaced the ebb and flow of the sea tides. While the timpani remained flawed, careful showers had replaced bathing, and Nicola would not swim again until they had been repaired by surgery.

From her room over the sandwich bar Nicola could see the sea, and was still thrilled as the waves, whipped up by the wind, crashed against the stony shore, but the absence of noise was distressing and frustrating. The memories of the coastal sounds were still fresh in her mind though, and at night she would try to bring them back as she thought of the sea. It was in dreams that Nicola could hear again, everything was clear and current. While she slept, Nicola was whole once more. The mornings, however, brought with them the crushing realisation that silence was the reality now, and with that came depression. The desire to remain asleep and never wake up was always worse in the early mornings, and daylight brought little relief to the darkness of silence. Silence, however, was a bad description of what Nicola experienced. There was noise, but it was the ring of tinnitus; a constant high-pitched note, accompanied, when she was tired or dehydrated, by a low throb, the echoing of blood pumping around her brain. She had taken up smoking again to get going in the mornings, as some days just felt too tough to get up and write without a 'kick'. She still had to earn a crust, and those articles wouldn't write themselves. As a single woman, an only child, and an orphan, no one could admonish her for her choices. For this she was grateful.

As a freelance writer, Nicola typed at her desk in the bay window, where she smoked, drank coffee in the morning, and hot chocolate from the cafe below as the winter afternoons brought a chill. She had continued her work generally as before the infection and loss of her hearing, however, she now had a new field of experience to write about. Her previous columns on the theatre and literature were now supplemented by the disabled experience, which editors were quick to cash in on. Though how long this morbid, but well meant, interest would last was not known.

The routine of waking, writing, and then walking helped to keep the 'black dog of depression' at bay. The absence of aural stimulus had not increased her other senses, but it had enabled Nicola to appreciate them more. Walking in the early dark of the winter evenings was therefore therapeutic, she could feel the cold and the wind on her face, even the chill in her bones was welcome for a while. When the log fires were roaring, the people of Cley took the places of the day trippers, settling in for drinks and a song. Though unable to join in the songs, Nicola still enjoyed the smell of the fire, the taste of the beer, warmth of the room, and the welcome of her friends in the town. She had not lived there for more than three years but the towners were a mix of old and new inhabitants, all were welcomed, and drinks were shared. Nicola even had a tab and played the 'deaf game' when Randalson, the pub landlord, reminded her that it was due at the end of the month. Nicola had no trouble paying this and did so comfortably.

One cold night in early December, Nicola had gone out for a walk by the marshes just beyond the windmill. She paused in the shelter of the snicket, lit her cigarette, and looked across the low landscape before her. It was a clear night, and the moonlight glistened off the sea in the near distance. There was a gentle movement as unseasonably late geese flew across the marshes and south-east along the coast. She was stubbing her cigarette out on the wall when a hand suddenly landed on her shoulder. Nicola leapt and spun around. She backed out of the alley so that she could see who had accosted her. The face that greeted her was friendly, and familiar. It was Agnes Tuthwright from the village, her white curly hair poking out from under her woollen hat, along with an apologetic look. She turned so that Nicola could see her clearly, so that her lips could be read. Agnes spoke clearly and deliberately, and although Nicola probably would have understood her anyway, the consideration was welcome.

"Sorry Nicola, I didn't know it was you! I was shouting, this explains why you didn't notice me!"

Needlessly, Nicola replied in a similar fashion, which was a common mistake she made, her speech generally unencumbered by her deafness, which is not unusual with those who become deaf later in life.

"It's okay Agnes, I was miles away anyway, flying off with the geese," she grinned.

Agnes laughed,

"Somewhere warmer I expect."

"Yes," Nicola claimed, though she really would rather be nowhere else, except perhaps further along the road. "Are you coming to the pub, Agnes? My shout?"

"I am looking for Ted. He hasn't come home yet. His little boat is back up on the shore over there," she gestured to the stony beach across the marsh. "But I've seen neither hide nor hair of him."

Nicola frowned echoing the old lady's concern.

"Then let's check in the pub, it's possible he's there. I can buy you a drink while you give him a sound telling off in front of his mates!"

"Nothing ventured, my girl, but if he's not there I can't stay, understood?"

Nicola gave a confirming thumbs up before offering Agnes her arm. Together they went back down the alley, and turned towards the George and Dragon public house.

In the snug of the pub, they found quite a crowd, and there by the fire, with a generous whisky in his hand, was Ted. He looked every inch the old sea dog with his white beard, captain's cap, and an unlit pipe in hand. The old man was shivering despite still being in his coat. Both Nicola and Agnes then noticed the water puddling at his feet.

"Ted! You're soaked! Why are you still in those wet clothes? What on earth has happened to you?"

Agnes ran over to him and began to drag his thick, wet coat off him.

"One of you get him a towel or something! He's an old man! How could you just stand there?" Agnes fussed around the shivering old man, muttering to herself darkly. One of the younger men at the table by Ted spoke up in the defence of all the lads close by.

"He's really not been here long Agnes, just long enough for us to get whisky down him and sit him by the fire. Jim's took his boots off, and gone to fetch him a blanket, but he wouldn't let us take his coat. He's not making any sense Agnes, something's happened to him."

This was met with a tut and more fussing. Randalson came in from the door by the bar which led to the living quarters, he had a stack of towels and a blanket. Only then could they get Ted's coat from him, and he was soon wrapped up in towels and properly warming. Randalson even let him smoke his pipe inside the pub,

"Oh Agnes, I was an idiot. I saw summat swim up to the boat. I thought it was a seal, so I leaned over the side. I could have sworn there was summat there. Whatever, it hit the boat, and over I went, into the water. Getting back onto the boat wasn't difficult, I can still swim alright, but I could have sworn that I heard someone laugh." He looked up pathetically, expecting ridicule from the drinkers, but a look from Agnes prevented that.

She put an arm around him, and chided him, "You should have come home, love, not here. And you shouldn't have been out so late on the boat, you should have been back well before dark, long before! You're old enough and wise enough not to mess about when it comes to the sea."

Nicola followed as much of this as she could, and Randalson filled in the gaps for her later.

"I think it may be dementia beginning in Ted's case. He probably thought he was coming home when he came in here, and I think he lost track of himself while he was out there, especially so late. Worse than that, Agnes knows he's losing it. She looked so sad tonight, glad he was safe, but I think this may not be the first incident where he's been odd. I think he may be for a home soon. He's fit as a butcher's dog, but his mind ain't there."

Nicola mouthed a good night to Randalson and left. She looked up and down the street carefully before stepping into the road. The night was clear and bright but the sea wind blowing into town was cold and her breath clouded the air as she marched the short distance back to her flat. She could taste salt in the rising fog that had gradually turned the night opaque. She reached her door and looked out across the marsh once more. The distant beam of the lighthouse at Cromer flashed its slow and familiar sequence. Ted was lucky to have got back to shore. There was another out that night under a streetlight, Evan, the whiskered old man who lived in the windmill on the edge of Cley-next-the-Sea. He seemed to be contemplating the mysteries of the sea. At the sound of her approach, he turned, waved and moved to greet her.

"Evening Nic! You look a pretty picture in the cold tonight. You'll be getting yourself off home then?"

She gave him a half-hearted thumbs up as the fatigue and cold were starting to bite, but he continued stepping before her deliberately, so that she could see and understand.

"I envy you some nights." He glared almost harshly. "You cannot hear the call of the sea. Each night I step out and listen. Each night I resist the yearning to go back out there. You, though, you've not the ears to hear. You'll never feel the call of the sea like the rest of us Cley folk. Oh, I envy you."

The old man sniffed, half weeping, but maybe laughing, Nicola couldn't tell. She was grateful that the talk ended there. She stepped away to her own front door over the road and watched him return to his windmill.

Once she had closed the door on the cold and retreated up to her rooms, Nicola sat in the window looking out over the marsh. The fog was low tonight, and she could now look beyond it, as far as the sea. Though she had initially seen little, she switched off the lamps inside, and her eyes accustomed to the night. Out in the sea there were lights, small and distant, but definite. Grabbing her binoculars she looked out but could make out no further detail. These were just lights, nearly a dozen of them, moving further out to sea.

The morning that followed was equally misty. Nicola had risen early, not long after dawn, and with a dry mouth. She guzzled a bottle of fizzy water from her fridge and gasped for air as soon as she'd finished drinking it all in one go. With a heavy head and throbbing tinnitus, she decided to get dressed and go straight out for her morning walk. It was greatcoat weather out there. Wellington boots and a woolly hat almost completed her armour against the cold, with her gloves having to wait until after she'd lit her first cigarette. It was possible, with caution, to follow the paths across the marsh and over to the stony beach, but Nicola didn't care for this trouble. She followed the road to the turning for the beach which allowed cars to park up close to the sea. There were few people on the road at this time of the morning, though a few anglers were already setting up their rods for the first catch of the day. The tide was high the waves were far from rough, and with luck Nicola would be able to see a seal on its way over to Blakeney Point. A little way off to the west there was Ted's boat, where it had been left the night before, with its short wooden steps hanging off the back. It was being buffeted by the tide, as Ted hadn't been able to pull it completely out of the water's reach. Nicola jogged over to it, then got behind it, her boots sloshing in the water as she tried to push it further up the beach. She made little progress, until a large wave lifted it enough that she was able to give it a hefty shove and move it further up and away from the sea. Taking a step back, she gazed at the old vessel. It needed a new coat of paint and some patching up, but when she looked closer at the rear and side, she could see that some of the surface paint and wood had been torn away. The freshly exposed wood was bright, with no dampening or staining from the elements. The damaged timber had been pulled away from the boat, and not pushed into it, as it would have been, had the boat collided or crashed with a rock. Nicola took off her gloves and used her phone to take careful photographs, from up close and all around. The small sail had been dropped when Ted had reached the shore, but it hadn't been tidied up, just left where it had fallen. Nicola set about organising the boat and leaving it in a fashion likely to be met with grateful smile. She was just taking one last look at the sea, when a familiar shape stepped out of the fog.

"Hello, my dear," waved Agnes. "Thank you for doing that, I was just coming to check on the boat myself. Ted is still in bed. I think yesterday really wore him out!" Again, Agnes was committing to the loud, over expressive speech for the benefit of the deaf woman. Nicola just about contained a laugh.

"No problem, Agnes. How is Ted doing?"

Agnes answered with a shrug and a tired smile. "He's Ted, he's getting old. I don't think he really knows whether he's coming or going anymore. We shan't be letting him sail on his own anymore, I'm afraid, though it'll break his heart. I'd better get back then, thank you for doing this!" Agnes gestured to the tidy boat, and neat sails. "Would you like to join us for a cuppa, love? I think Ted would like to say thank you too!"

This time Agnes offered her arm, Nicola took it, and the two ladies headed back along the road inland and into town.

Agnes and Ted Tuthwright lived in a small cottage which backed onto a ridge overlooking the marsh. It was decorated throughout with nautically themed pictures and postcards. Ted had been in the Merchant Navy and still took Agnes to sea whenever he could. Agnes led Nicola through the hall and into the kitchen, where Ted was sitting at a table by the open back door. The old man's face was wet with tears.

"Agnes, they've been singing again, out there in the mist, I heard them..." He looked up at his wife with pleading in his eyes, but whether he wanted it to stop, or to carry on, Agnes couldn't tell.

Nicola could see that this old ghost of a man was tormented, begging for something that was out of his capability to achieve. She sat down opposite him at the table and took his hand. He turned and faced her.

"Hello Ted," she said, realising that she was using the same voice that Agnes used to talk to her. "I've secured your boat and tied it up neatly. Now, how are you doing?"

Looking up as if the mist had cleared before him, Ted beamed a smile at Nicola, then shook her hands gently.

"Ah, you look like a mermaid my girl, your red hair and red cheeks. You've been out in the cold with my Agnes, haven't you? Let's have some tea, shall we?" he said, getting to his feet.

Ted took Agnes' hands, twirling her as he stepped across the kitchen, dancing with her to a tune Nicola could not hear.

"Woooo!" cooed Agnes as she turned, forgetting the situation for a moment. Her eyes sparkled as the dampness of new tears were replaced with a gleam of joy. At the end of a twirl, the old man stepped aside and took up the kettle to refill it from the tap. With the dance over, Agnes closed the door and began to take her coat and hat off, bidding her guest to do the same before they set about finding cups and the other things for tea.

"Oh, I hadn't heard that tune in years, Nicola," said Agnes, before remembering her guest's disability. "Oh, I'm so careless. Sorry Nic. Ted was just whistling an old sea tune! I hadn't heard it since we were children, it took me right back."

She bustled over to help Ted make the tea. The Tuthwright's made strong cups of tea and swore by having two teaspoons of leaves for each guest as well as the one for the pot. Nicola had to admit she felt strengthened by her cuppa, as well as comforted by it. She often said that she liked her tea like her men; strong and supportive. Not that she was looking for such a mythical being, but it had become an old joke for her by now. With the tea made, the three of them sat down, and Agnes thanked Nicola again for looking out for the boat, and Ted did too once he'd had half of his cup.

"I'm sorry, Nic. It were a shock, that tumble into the water. I'm lucky I ever got back to shore with the boat, thanks for fixing it up the beach."

Signalling her understanding with a simple thumbs up, Nicola smiled and drank her tea.

"Ted," Nicola said, attracting his attention. "What did you see? In the water?"

The old man shivered, as if he felt the cold once more, then looked her up and down.

"It wasn't a seal. I only said that it was so I wasn't laughed at by the lads in the pub. I saw a woman in the water, pale and not old, but not young either. She had long hair like you, and like Ophelia. I had heard her calling, then I realised she was singing." He sang a tune to himself though it had no words. Nicola could not follow it.

"I saw it were a lady drowning, or so I thought. I looked over the side, and she grabbed me, and tore part of the boat as she pulled me in! I swam and I got to the back of the boat, started to scramble back in, terrified I was! But then I heard another one, singing. Just as I got back in, she screamed, she did, both of them screamed at me. The wind was knocking me about and so I dropped sail and made for the oars. Rowed back, I did, as fast as I could. And I heard them laughing at me all the way back."

The cheer had gone from his eyes since he retold the events of last night in plain and simple words, to the deaf woman who was, at least, trying to understand. Agnes, sitting alongside Ted, put her hand on his arm. She hummed something to him, and he laid his head on hers. Nicola patted their joined hands and made her own polite exit.

There was a small crowd out in the single street that formed Cley-next-the-Sea, they were mostly the older townsfolk, and they were shambling towards the path that led to the marsh. Nicola recognised Randalson among them too, and she went to him. The tall man was standing coat-less, shivering and pale, his eyes a lighter blue than they usually looked. Morning mist dampened his beard. As she approached, she noticed his teeth begin to chatter. Taking his face in both hands, she turned him to look directly at her.

"Randalson! Jim! Are you okay?"

He looked down slowly. Realisation dawned on his face and he raised his hand to his forehead to wipe away the moisture that had gathered in the cold morning.

"Morning Nic," he said, then wiped his hand across his mouth, as if trying to remove a bad taste. "What's going on here? Have I been sleepwalking or summat?"

Looking up at him curiously, she shook his face in her hands, then playfully slapped his cheek.

"Jim, you big dodo, you're out in the morning air and without your coat! And all these people with you! Why don't you tell me what's going on?"

Jim turned back to his pub, halfway up the road, then looked back at all the old people shivering away.

"I think I may need to open early today. I need a drink and these folk could do with being warm. Who wants a drink? Come on this way people, I'll have the fire going in no time." With a big wave he gestured all the twitching locals towards the George and Dragon, then turned to Nicola.

"I know its early Nic, so I could make you a coffee, unless you want a drink at this time?"

Nicola gave in to temptation, "Okay, I'll have a coffee, Irish please!"

With a couple of other, younger ladies from the town, Nicola shepherded half a dozen old, confused Cley citizens through the doors of the George and Dragon. Nicola set about lighting the fire as the younger two arranged comfortable chairs around it. Randalson began preparing hot toddies for all those suffering from the cold. From the discussion that followed, it seemed that some of the older folk had felt the need for a walk in the misty morning, while others thought that they were sleepwalking, only to find themselves out in the open and woken by the cold.

Randalson had felt something similar, he'd decided to get up and go for a walk. He'd wanted to go down to the sea, then he was amongst the small crowd in the high street, and then he was looking down at Nicola.

Each of them told their familiar version of the morning's event, but the confusion remained. The local doctor was called and the receptionist said that they'd try and send a doctor out to the pub later that morning, given that these were mostly all high-risk patients. Everything was calm for the next hour or so, the room warmed up and the chatter seemed relaxed after the initial shock of the morning. One of the ladies tending the fire was adding another log when almost everyone turned and rose up from their seats, even Randalson. There were a couple of younger townsfolk with Nicola, who were there to help too, and they were equally taken aback by this behaviour. Nicola went over to Jim Randalson, her friend, and took his face once more. Before his attention came back into focus, he appeared to be singing, as far as Nicola could tell, or at least mouthing the words to something. As the others were brought back to lucidity, they all looked similarly disorientated, and Maeve, who'd been tending the fire, turned and looked up at the young lady next to her.

"I was just remembering an old winter here, from when I was a child. We'd be allowed into the pub for one night, and Dad would give us a small Guinness for health. We would listen to the stories, and we would sing."

Maeve began to hum a tune softly, and one by one the older guests of the public bar turned to listen, then she stopped as she saw them staring at her strangely.

"I'm sorry, I just feel a bit nostalgic, today." She stood and reached for her cooling cup of tea on the mantelpiece. An awkward silence set in as they sat waiting for the doctor. Nicola didn't stick around. Deadlines were beginning to appear on the horizon, and she needed to get cracking on her writing.

It had been a long day, and the articles were not writing themselves, so by five o'clock, when it was starting to get dark, Nicola was grateful to receive a message on her mobile phone that someone was ringing her doorbell. It was Helen Murray, the woman who ran the sandwich bar below Nicola's flat. There was a look of concern on her face, but she still tried to wave a cheery 'hello' as the door opened.

"Hi Nicola," Helen said with exaggerated annunciation. "Sorry to trouble you, but we're all going out looking for Evan, Old Evan Delmar, the chap who lives in the windmill. No one has seen him since that strangeness yesterday, so we thought we should check on him. His post was still hanging out of his door. He's not answered the phone, or his doorbell either. Jim has a key, so he's let himself in and he's not home. So, we're off looking for him."

Nicola pulled on her greatcoat once more, and her hat, then her large heavy boots. The last thing she took from the stand by the door was a packet of cigarettes. It was looking cold again outside as she stepped into the early night. There were a few people out on the street with torches and some searching in the alleys between the old houses. The lights of the George and the Dragon were on full, as if to be a beacon in the night. Nicola explained that she'd seen him the night before and he'd been a bit melancholy, talking about the sea. She and Helen went down the snicket by the windmill, and again, Nicola paused to light her cigarette, then offered one to her friend, who gratefully accepted. It was from here they began looking, following the thin path between the reeds that threaded around the back of the houses and out into the marsh. For once the night was clear, and they could just make out the ridge of stones before it dropped away to the rocky beach. Their torches swept the path for signs that the old man had fallen into the marsh. As they were unable to see each other's faces as they walked, they remained silent, with Helen listening out for any sounds, calling Evan's name sporadically. Moving forward carefully, Nicola shone her torch upon a patch of flattened reeds by a step into shallow ditch. She then called for Helen to join her. It was clear that someone had left the path here and cut across the marsh, there were heavy footprints in the mud before the forced path was immersed under shallow water. Reeds were broken and rent as if someone had clumsily made their way towards the beach. Just as the water and mud became difficult, they pulled up suddenly.

"It's a slipper, a man's slipper," Nicola noted, and she waved it to Helen in the torchlight. "There must be another here somewhere."

Helen's face was grim.

"We've another sleepwalker, and it looks like we may be too late, especially if he's been out this way since morning."

It wasn't difficult to follow the route taken and, though at points they found themselves up to their knees in squelching mud, they sped their way through, afraid of what they may find. The ground became firm once more and pebbled as it became the stony banks of the North Sea shore. There was no further sign of the path from there, at least none that their torches could reveal. Scouring up and down the shore, the two women continued searching for Evan, but could find no trace of where he had gone.

"We'd best go back to the town, Helen! There's no signal here," shouted Nicola. "We'll get help and search again."

Back in the town there were still a few searchers about, and some had been out onto the marsh paths but found nothing. When they gathered back at the George and Dragon, they agreed that the slipper found by Nicola and Helen had been Evan's. It was also agreed that those who could, should get back out to the beach to continue looking, as by the morning it may be too late.

When the morning came, no new clues had been found, and no one knew what more they could do. Then the low tide that brought a gruesome revelation. The body of Old Evan appeared on the shore, half buried by stones and rocks, his face stricken with terror, deathly pale, and covered with cuts.

By the time that the police had arrived and set up a cordon, there was already a large crowd on the beach. Both Nicola and Helen gave statements, then handed over the slipper as evidence. The unusual mass sleepwalking event of the previous day was mentioned to the police by the ladies present, by Randalson, and by a couple of the others who had witnessed it, but the police were not entertaining the idea that this was within their remit. They deferred to the doctor who had stated that, despite some risk of colds, none of the somnambulists were worse off for their experience, and that he couldn't put it down to anything specific, just 'one of those things.' He did suggest that with the exception of Randalson, they had all been old people, who would probably be better off in nursing homes by now anyway. The doctor then despaired of their seemingly non-existent families and conceded that the state should have some way of dealing with these people who were perceivably a nuisance and a menace. Helen tutted audibly at the doctor at this point, before walking way, and Nicola, oblivious to his comments, had noticed Randalson's hackles rising. She led him away before he turned violent.

Leading him into his own pub, Nicola sat Randalson down in his favourite chair, near the fire. The coffee machine behind the bar was switched on, and quicker than boiling a kettle, so she made him a latte with extra sugar to calm him down. This worked for the most part, though if conversation strayed back to the doctor, Nicola knew she would see his temper rise.

After several attempts to placate Jim, she sent him out to the woodshed to split logs for the fire. The pub would open soon, and it was cold outside, so the place would need to be as warm as possible for its guests. 'The snug' of the pub became so cosy that

Nicola decided to work there for the day, quickly disappearing home to get her computer and her purse. Today's vice would be coffee until six o'clock, when she would close her laptop and stash it somewhere safe in Jim's room. She would then see if they needed help behind the bar, as lip reading was a leveller in a noisy pub, if not an advantage, and she knew that Jim was short staffed at the moment. she worked hard, and eventually the shift ended as all good nights should, with just two mates and a bottle of whisky. The front doors had been locked, and the last drinker had finally been shoved out the door in the direction of their bed. Only now did Jim Randalson feel that he could forget about being the landlord and just be 'a bloke'.

"Thanks for helping Nic, you're a star. It's been a tough day and Evan was a good mate. Been a weird few days here, hasn't it?"

Nicola nodded wearily, clutching her dram close.

"I've still got the keys to Ev's windmill. Let's go up and toast him properly, that fire'll die out soon and I think we should drink to Ev' on high."

Jim was looking wistful but determined. Nicola was too tired to argue and didn't want to leave her best friend when he was feeling like this. With a smile she raised her glass, then drained it.

"Okay Jim, but it had better be warm up there, and quickly so. And bring that bottle just in case it's not."

She extended her arm up to the big man and he practically lifted her out of the chair, then caught her as she nearly toppled over.

"Come on girl, while you can still manage the stairs."

Nic didn't notice this remark, as she was regaining her balance. Taking their coats and hats, slipping into their boots without doing them up properly, they stepped out of the back door, carrying the best part of a bottle of Glenlivet with them.

The mist was coming in low over the marshes again tonight, but Nicola's shiver was only partially due to the cold. In the short time it took to cross the road and walk up to the windmill on the edge of the town, the mist had become thick fog. They were both damp now with the wet air, and Nicola had given up trying to light cigarette.

"Smoke inside, Nic," said Jim. "Evan won't mind, and I doubt anyone will live here for a while. I might even scrounge one myself if that's alright."

Taking her by the hand, he dragged her through the door and up the curving stairs to the living area on the second floor. This was a wide round room with an electric fire, which Jim switched on as soon as he stepped off the stairs. The room was cold but warming quickly. A balcony neatly encompassed this level of the windmill. From there you could see the marshes as far as Wells-next-the-Sea and Sheringham, but also out across the sea. Tonight, the fog was below the level of the balcony and clinging to the town and the marshes. The sea, in the clear distance, was dashing against the stone shore, and a strange wind blew, though it didn't shift the fog, or cause it to even move. The two friends poured large drinks and toasted, "to Evan, who art in heaven," then with less respect shown to the whisky, they necked their drinks.

"Time for a top up already," declared Randalson, as he made to refill both glasses. Nicola was feeling bad for smoking inside the house and wanted to go out onto the balcony. She opened the large double doors and a stiff wind blew in, making them both shiver. Nicola turned to relight her cigarette, which had quickly gone out. Randalson was standing, holding the two glasses, now full again, as he looked out to the north.

"Careful now," she giggled.

As he stepped past Nicola, she took her glass from him. Jim didn't react at all. His eyes had paled, and his lips moved as if singing. He stepped out onto the balcony, dropping his drink as he did so. Tapping his hand, she got no response from him, so she took his face in her hands, as she had done before, and though he turned to look at her, there was no recognition or focus in his eyes. He continued singing, though Nicola had no idea what song it was and could not read the words on his lips. With a bit more force, she was able to push Jim back into the room and close the doors behind them. With the wind, marshes, and smell of the sea locked outside, Randalson began to return to his senses.

"It happened again, didn't it?" he asked looking directly at Nicola. "I felt the need to go out there towards the beach, to see the waves. There was that song again."

Nicola tried to follow his words and gently pressed him for more. "How many times has this happened before Jim?" She moved him over to the sofa and sat him down. He shuddered, then sighed. For the first time, she saw Jim show fear.

"It's happened a few times: three times before today, when the nights started drawing in. Twice I've found myself out there in the street, though you found me one of those times. Then there was when Maeve began to sing that old song in the bar. It's a folk song, you know, the sort that grandparents sing, all the old families around here know it. All the old families in these parts are from sailing, or fishing families, especially at Cley. I couldn't remember any of the words until Maeve sang a bit though. It's about lost loves, and a wedding beneath the waves. I'll need another drink."

Nicola left the dropped glass out on the balcony and fetched another from inside, then poured her friend a large whisky. Jim sipped his drink and his eyes began to droop. Not wishing to leave him alone, Nicola looked around for something to read while she kept a vigil on the potential sleepwalker. On the next floor up, she found a small collection of books, *Moby Dick* was there and *Tales of Smuggling,* a collection of boys own adventures it seemed. On Evan's desk, she found a diary, it was this year's, so she took this back down to read through while she tried to stay awake. Evan had been keeping a journal, a record of a relatively quiet life, though two days ago, he had written much more than usual. This included a list of names; Maeve Seward, Ted Tuthwright, Agnes Murray, Lawrence Culvert, Ella Irwin, Doris Bosun, Inga Helsdottir, Thomas Wolson, James Randalson, and his own name, Evan Delmar. Amongst these names were the six sleepwalkers from the day before, and Ted.

She hadn't before realised that Agnes was a 'Murray' and was probably related to Helen. On the day before, there was an entry

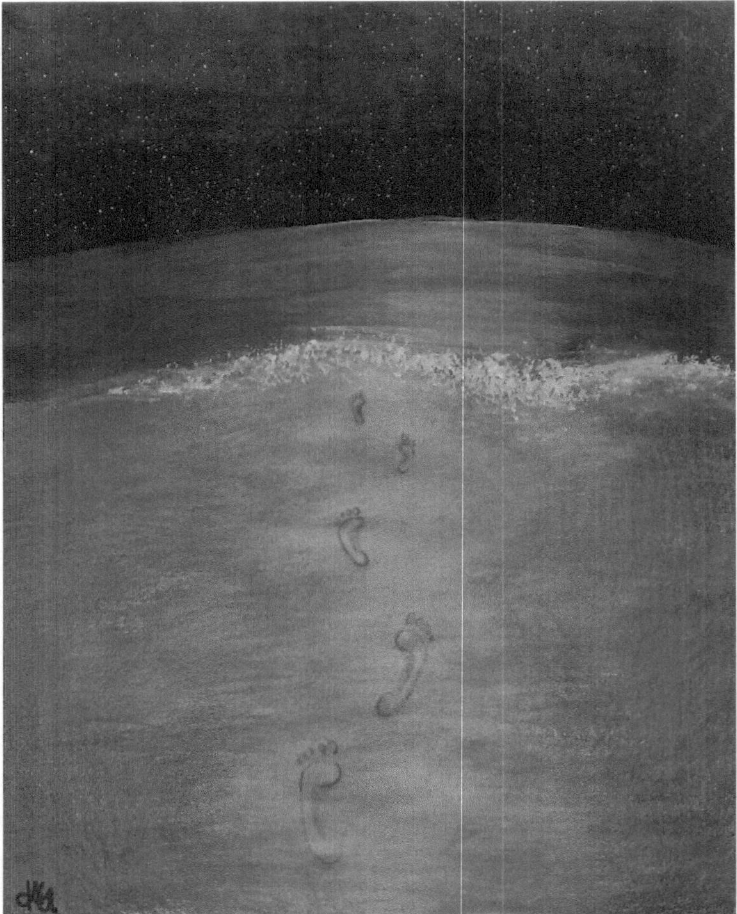

which stood out even more, for the opposite reason. It simply said that 'the song has been sung again, the sirens are calling from the sea.

I will go to join them this time I'm sure, but I don't want to go.' Nicola recalled what Evan had said two nights ago, and had she not seen the sleepwalkers, or experienced Ted's strange behaviour, she may have thought nothing of this, but that wasn't the case. She wished that Jim was sober right now or, at least, awake. Nicola needed to talk to someone. She considered calling Helen, but it was well into the small hours, and would have to wait. With nothing further that she could do, she took up the old copy of Moby Dick and settled into a comfortable chair next to the sofa, where she began to read. "Chapter One, Loomings…"

Nicola was shaken awake with the book on her lap, and the smell of coffee just under her nose. Randalson was up and looking fresher than he had any right to. He'd borrowed a jumper from Evan's wardrobe. He looked every inch a lighthouse keeper and had it not been for the great wind sails outside the windows, he may well have been one.

"I don't think the old man would mind, but I've made you some breakfast out of what he had left in the fridge. I hope you like kippers."

Nicola was unnerved at how chipper Jim was being this morning. She threw off the blanket he'd placed over her at some point and rose to join him in the kitchen, on the ground floor, taking Evan's diary down with her.

"I think you should look at this Jim," Nic said as she presented the diary before him. "That list of names, you and the other sleepwalkers are on it."

He took the diary and looked over it, unsure of what to make of it.

"Well, this is creepy. We should check on all of these people to see if they are alright. Maybe they went for a walk last night too."

"How are you feeling, Jim?" Nicola asked, still curious about his apparent good mood.

He served up two plates of kippers and poured himself another coffee.

"I'm good, thanks. I slept well, and don't have a hangover it seems, but maybe it'll catch up with me. I don't know what's going on, but mass somnambulism is weird. All the old people too."

"And you Jim, you're not that old, what are you? Fifty?"

Randalson laughed. "That's very kind of you. I'm fifty-six, and I'm glad you think I look young." Nicola smiled too at this.

"I was just being polite. You always take ten years off what you think. How old do you think I am?"

Placing his coffee mug down to have hard stare at his friend, he stroked his stubble in mock thought,

"Oh, I don't know, thirty-two? Thirty-three?"

In victory she pointed a kipper laden fork at him,

"Cheeky, you know I'm forty-three and that proves my point!"

Once they finished breakfast, they tidied up the mess they made and left the windmill as they had found it. The day outside was foggy again, and they began their walk to the various houses of the others named in the diary. Most of the towners had suffered from a disturbed sleep, but were otherwise accounted for. Only Thomas Wolson wasn't answering his door. They went around to the back of his cottage and rapped upon the kitchen window frame. There was no sign of him inside and the doors were locked.

"I think we have to assume that he's away or still asleep. His house wouldn't be locked up if he'd gone walking in the night," Jim suggested. "I don't think we can break in just yet. Let's ask around."

They agreed to leave it until later, though neither Nicola nor Jim were comfortable about this. As lunchtime approached, Jim had to open the pub and prepare for the day's custom, as it was Saturday, and likely to be busy.

Nicola decided not to write today. She put on her wellington boots and went to explore the marshes instead, though her growing unease was heightened by the thick fog, and, although she was sticking to the clear paths, she felt unsure of her surroundings. Still, she Kept an eye out for signs of anyone leaving the paths, or of anything that suggested a lone, nighttime walker. There were a few dog walkers out, keeping their animals on short leads in the fog, but none said that they had seen any old men around looking disorientated. Communication had been difficult due to the low visibility, though hand gestures to convey Nicola's deafness had made some of the conversations easier. The ground became stony, and the fog began to clear as Nicola neared the beach. In the fog she saw a figure ahead of her and could make out a woman with red hair, standing on the slight ridge over the beach. Nicola stepped forward and called out at what she hoped was an appropriate volume.

"Hello!" There was no response, so she tried again, but there was still no reply. A cloud of fog blew between them and then the woman was gone. Nicola stepped forward to where she had seen the lady, then jumped in shock as a hand touched her elbow.

"Jesus!" She turned suddenly. Before her was a young woman, with deep red hair and what looked like a linen skirt in dark green, with a loose shirt over it. Nicola stood square before her and spoke clearly.

"Aren't you cold? It's freezing out here!"

The woman laughed and shook her head. Despite her youthful looks, her smile revealed stained teeth, like those of a lifelong, heavy smoker.

"No," she spoke, enunciating her words, but whether it was for Nicola's benefit or not, she was clearly understood. Unblinking, she continued, "I am used to the cold, this is just a breeze."

Nicola found this hard to believe, as she was wearing several layers but could still feel the chill.

"I'm looking for someone," Nicola said. "An old man, with grey hair, and a moustache, possibly a bit confused. Have you seen anyone like that?"

The stranger smiled strangely nodded before adding. "Yes, I did. He seemed sweet, he was over there," she pointed further east along the shore. "It was a while ago. I think he was heading over to the town."

The woman almost smirked, and Nicola could have swung for her.

"This is serious. Was he okay? Was he definitely heading to the town?"

This time the woman openly smirked, laughing as she replied, "Oh, he was fine. He gave me a little wave, then went that way, which I think is back to the town. How would I know? I'm not from around here!"

Enraged at this display of flippancy, Nicola erupted, "Well piss off home then! Bloody tourist!" She turned and headed in the direction of where Thomas had allegedly been seen. She was fuming, and with her back to the strange woman, Nicola had no idea how she had reacted, nor could she hear the soft shanty now being sung.

The lady in green gave Nicola a curious look, still singing as she walked back towards the sea.

Thomas had not been found by the time it got dark, and many of the rescue party had decided to give up searching until the morning. The Cromer lifeboat crew had been out, but they had found nothing. Despondently, the townsfolk went to their homes, or to the pub, to respectively commiserate or drown their daily sorrows.

The public bar of the George and Dragon, however, was lively, as bright lights and the smell of people in close proximity confronted Nicola the moment she opened the door. There were quite a few young people in there today, day trippers and hippies she judged, by the looks of them. There were also those who had second homes in the town, who at least helped support the local pub and the shops in the town. Nicola could see that some of these people were singing, and even the old piano had been wheeled out of the corner, where Maeve, of all people, appeared to be playing it.

Pushing her way to the bar wasn't easy, as the crowds of young people were proving to be annoying, seeming completely oblivious to Nicola as she tried to pass. When she reached the bar, she was shocked to see Jim at the far end, apparently flirting, or at least being flirted with, by two young ladies. The one nearest to her had long, brown, wavy hair that went most of the way down her back and flowed down behind her as she rocked back with laughter at something Jim said. This movement revealed the second girl to be the cocky redhead that she'd met earlier, the one 'not from around here.'

Immediately angered, Nicola rapped her knuckles on the bar to get Jim's attention, and when this didn't work, she threw a stray peanut at him. It bounced off his cheek and he made as if to brush away a fly before finally noticing Nicola. He waved at her to come over, but she made very definite signs that she would not, and that he should come to her. With reluctance, Jim whispered something to the girls, who giggled, before sidling over to his friend.

"Cheer up Nic, it's nice to have a busy pub for once, and we could all do with some cheering up."

Nicola scowled at him with a face that she hoped conjured up a disappointed teacher.

She mouthed, "We still haven't found Thomas. He could be out there freezing to death or already dead in a ditch. That red headed bitch said she'd seen him coming back into town, but where the bloody hell is he?"

Jim tried to look placatory as he poured Nicola a large rum, but he seemed unfocused, and if she didn't know better, she'd had wondered if he was drunk. He tried to soothe the matter.

"She probably made a mistake. She's on holiday, what would she know?"

"She should know better than to piss around when it comes to a man's life!"

Unable to always appropriately pitch the volume of her voice, most of the drinkers near the bar heard this outburst, and the two young ladies who'd held Jim's attention a moment before certainly had. They turned to look at them, their broad grins and filthy teeth sickening Nicola. She wanted more than anything to go over to them and put their heads through the bar.

As Nicola made to move, Jim took her by the wrist, and clearly mouthed the words, "They're not worth it Nic. Orlaith and Bridget will be gone by the morning, and we will continue to look after our own," and then with a stronger, more enunciated expression, "leave it."

That was when the girls had made their way over to them instead. They were attractive girls, but for their teeth, with hair that was unkempt but looked naturally conditioned, and clothes that seemed rather simple.

"I'm sorry girls," Nicola spoke, controlling her voice. "You're not tourists, you're fucking tramps."

The two young women laughed, then replied with soft, but cleverly pronounced words, so that only the deaf lady understood.

"You're right, we're not tourists," said Orlaith, the redhead. "But we are regular visitors, and the people here know us in their hearts, unlike you. You're new to the town."

"Evan certainly knew us, he knew us of old, and he died happy," spoke Bridget with a mocking grin, displaying her sharp rotting teeth behind her glossy red lips.

Jim saw the movement, but was too late to intervene as Nicola brought her glass into contact with the side of Orlaith's head. Customers screamed as the glass shattered, before Nicola was bundled away from the girls by a couple of younger men. Jim came round from behind the bar, his face full of anger.

"Right Nicola, go home! Don't be surprised if you don't get a visit from the police after this! What's got into you?"

The two women were quickly to gain either side of Jim.

"It's okay Jim, Orlaith isn't hurt. Look there's no blood..." Bridget gestured to her friend. "And there'll be no need for the police."

"That's right," opined Orlaith, running her hands through her hair. "The only offence caused was the waste of a good drink."

Sickened by this display, and by the passive attitudes of the locals, Nicola stormed out of the pub.

"Bloody bitches!"

Chain smoking by her window, Nicola had some wine, drinking straight from the bottle in agitation. Her mood was not improved by her drinking, however. She could see lights out at sea, drifting erratically. As time drew by, the fog thinned and began moving out towards the sea. Half-cut, Nicola watched it, glad to see it leave. It was then that she noticed the figures that were moving with it, groups of twos and threes, shambling north into the marshes and towards the sea. She leapt to her feet and immediately made her way to the stairs, barely taking the time to grab her greatcoat, and pulling on her boots without tying them, before rushing out the door and taking the quickest line to where she had last seen the figures moving north.

She sloshed onto the wet paths, missing her footing, then rejoined the firmer ground, seeking the fastest and safest way to where she'd seen people moving. These were sleepwalkers, but more than she'd previously seen. Right now, she had to reach them before it was too late, and without killing herself in the dark. Her torch was little use and her missteps were frequent. Occasionally, she would see figures moving ahead of her and she'd try to make her way to them, but would end up tripping in the reeds, water as she did. Once she reached the stones of the shore, she could make out the sleepwalkers in ones and twos, each accompanied by one of the younger people she'd seen in the pub, the tramps and the hippies. They were leading the somnambulant old folk into the water. There was also Jim. He was with Orlaith and Bridget, up to their waists in the sea, with the waves breaking gently against them. Nicola ran to them in a rage and took Orlaith's arm. She tried to pull it away from Jim, But the arm was cold, and it felt like stone. Orlaith's face turned towards her, the teeth were still filthy but this time they were longer and sharper looking. In the moonlight, Nicola could see gills in Orlaith's neck, thin slits in her pale flesh that appeared to open and close. Nicola continued pulling at that immovable arm and then beating it with her fists, but she proved impotent against this horrid thing that was before her. Bridget left Jim's side, moved toward Nicola. In a flash, she grabbed Nicola's arms, facing her, baring her teeth, her gills glistening in the night, pulling her prey deeper into the water.

"Look! Watch them!"

She turned Nicola's face from hers and towards the other townsfolk in the water. She saw Maeve, and some of the other old singers from the pub, all moving further out into, and then under, the water. Agnes was following Ted, wearing the same expression that she'd worn when they were dancing in the kitchen to the old folk tune. Others had the appearance of dancing, and some were singing too. The bedraggled young folk were leading them, seeming to become more fish-like as they neared the water, growing webbed hands, as well as gills, and grinning with teeth like serrated razors. Wrestling in vain against

Bridget's uncanny strength, Nicola tried to scream, to break whatever it was that Jim could hear but she couldn't. Bridget's hand silenced the scream, and she looked directly into Nicola's eyes. She spoke with clear menace.

"Every few years we come by and see how the old families are, the ones with sea blood still in their veins. We drain those who are old, and need moving on, guilt free. This year it's looking busy, with quite a few ready to drop. Granted, Jim isn't old, but we fancy him, not everything has to be vintage. And you, Nicola, well, you've seen it all now, so you're coming too."

Their victim couldn't hear the 'song of the sea', so the Sirens took her forcibly by the hands and pulled her into the cold waves, following where her friend, Jim Randalson, had disappeared just moments before. Unable to feel the rapture that had charmed the other townsfolk into the depths, where they had gone willingly to meet their doom, Nicola felt only terror as the ocean claimed another orphan.

Seaweed Folk

By: Pip Pinkerton

Lulu Attenborough was eighteen years old, having just graduated high school, an A honor roll student, but instead of trying to get into a rich, pretentious school in a different state, her plan was to take a year off, go to Community College in the next town over, get her general's done as cheaply as possible, then probably go to the university in the city, a forty five minute drive from her house, that is if she still wanted to continue her education at that point, or if she even still wanted to be a veterinarian, or possibly an archaeologist. She was glad she could experiment affordably in Community College.

That was for next year though, this year she was going to take off, but not to travel or party, but to say goodbye to her childhood. She won that freedom for one year, and her parents agreed, but after a year, if she wasn't in college, they were going to make her start paying rent.

The Attenboroughs lived in a modest house, at the top of a hill, with lakefront property. It was the former cabin of Wayne Attenborough, Lulu's grandfather, who had it converted into a house, then later paid to have the extra room added on for Lulu.

Dave and Corrine Attenborough weren't rich, but they definitely weren't poor, and they taught Lulu how to be frugal. They also taught her how to hunt and fish, being as Dave was an avid outdoorsman and had no sons.

Lulu didn't care. She loved the outdoors. She felt bad killing deer, but they didn't waste anything they could use, and it fed the whole family for the for most of the year, if not the whole year, as long as they froze most of the meat and put it in the deep freeze. Lulu loved everything about fishing though, fish weren't warm like deer, they didn't cry out, or spurt blood, they barely even seemed to know they were dead. That, and she never fished for sport, only to eat, and she loved the taste of fish, especially walleye. That was why she was fairly enthused about her boyfriend, Daniel, coming over after breakfast so they could spend the whole day out on the lake.

Daniel arrived a little after nine that morning. "Hi Mr. And Mrs. A. Did you guys make bacon?"

"The smell is that strong?" Corrine Attenborough asked.

"Yeah, your whole house smells delicious," Daniel replied.

"Have some," Corrine told him.

"Here," Lulu said, emerging from the kitchen with three strips of bacon in their hand. "Let's go."

"All righty," Daniel said with a slightly intimidated shrug, before Lulu toward the back door and away from her family.

"Bye Mom, bye Dad," Lulu called back as she led Daniel the rest of the way outside. It always made her nervous when her parents and her boyfriend conversed, and she often tried to rush their encounters.

"Bye," Lulu's parents called simultaneously in return.

"Bye," Daniel called back as Lulu pulled him the rest of the way outside, before quickly reaching past him and closing the door.

"Anxious to get out of the out on the water, are we?" Daniel asked.

"I don't want you guys to start talking about cars. It's boring... And how friendly you are with my parents weirds me out."

"They're good people. Besides, bad boys go nowhere in life. I am simply networking and building lasting friendships," Daniel replied, jokingly.

"You're such a nerd. Now, let's go," Lulu said as she walked down through her family's lightly wooded backyard to their mildly secluded dock. Lulu was carrying the poles while Daniel hauled the tackle box. When they reached the boat, Lulu climbed on deck and set the poles carefully against the back row of seats. As soon as they had both boarded, she untied them from the dock and pushed them out into the water.

Daniel grabbed the oars and began to row, waiting until they were all the way clear of the shallows and weeds before starting the motor.

"I hate seaweed," Lulu said with a shiver. "It's like slimy fingers coming out of the ground to grab you." She looked over the side of the boat, into the water, and just beneath the surface of the lake, she saw endless seaweed, awful green-black tendrils that looked like an amalgamation of rotten spinach and dead snakes. It was the reason Daniel had to row out right now with the oars, so the motor didn't clog with the stuff.

Daniel rowed out about thirty or forty feet, before he finally withdrew the oars and dropped the engine into the water.

The pair then spent that morning hitting up all their favorite fishing spots and catching a great many fish, even though most were on the small side, so they hadn't caught any they could keep yet.

At one point, when fishing was getting slower, Daniel opened his tackle box and started rummaging around inside.

"You know, I can kick this up a notch and make sure we get some of those big fish," Daniel told Lulu, pulling a dark red M-80 firecracker out of his tackle box. His expression showed that he was only kidding though.

"Yeah! They're coming right for us," Lulu replied with a chuckle, being as she kind of remembered Uncle Jimbo doing the whole explosive fishing thing in an episode of *South Park*.

"My uncle really did it once," Daniel told her, before looking reflectively off into the distance. "I would never really do it. I just like to mess with people. It does actually work though."

"So does flashlight fishing, from what I hear, but fish already have it hard enough. Could you imagine a hook going through your face?"

"I said I wouldn't actually do it," Daniel replied, then proceeded to change the subject as they continued on their way

They mostly just had fun that whole morning, trying different baits and seeing what kind of fish they could catch. Lulu caught a small-mouth bass, which they decided to keep, and Daniel caught a large dogfish. He had caught it when Lulu had been changing her bait, and she had noticed the M-80 in his tackle box. She looked at the dogfish and the thought of blowing it up briefly crossed her mind, but it went away just as quickly.

They came in for lunch at about twelve thirty. Lulu's father had made hamburgers on the grill, and they each ate two. After lunch, Lulu immediately wanted to get back out on the lake again. She grabbed her gray hoodie, just in case, as the day was still a little crisp, especially with the breeze, and put it on, while swiftly bidding her parents farewell as she headed back in the direction of the boat. Corrine Attenborough handed Daniel a brown bag with a couple of pre-made peanut butter and Jelly sandwiches in it, then waved him goodbye as he turned and rushed to catch up with Lulu.

Once they were back out on the water again, after applying the same initial departing method with the oars as before, Daniel shot Lulu a glance that told her there was something he both did and didn't want to say.

"Just spill it", Lulu told him. "Stop beating around the bush."

"Okay. I know this spot on Kassir Lake. It's a hidden patch of water, just beyond lily pads, perfect for walleye. My uncle once showed me."

"I don't want to go to Kassir Lake. That's like two hours away, and we'd have to go all the way across my lake, under the dam, then all the way across Sparrow Lake before we get to Kassir."

"Well, generally you'd be right, but last year, me and Gary went through the swamp land behind the Connors, and it connects to Hockley Swamp, which you only have to be on for about ten minutes, then you hook to the left, take the small inlet, and it curves around and takes you straight to Kassir. Forty minutes tops. We can be there by one thirty.

Lulu looked at him with great trepidation. She hated the lily pad and cattail riddled swampy marsh that connected to the bottom of Corner Lake, the lake her family lived on. She hated lily pads, cattails, frogs, and everything about the swamp, especially the seaweed. Most of all the seaweed, but Daniel was so excited. The look on his face was one of pure enthusiasm.

"Okay, I guess," Lulu conceded, with great reluctance.

"You're the best girlfriend ever!"

"I know."

Daniel drove Lulu's family's boat a quarter of the way across the lake, before turning sharply around the peninsula on which the Conners lived. They only made it a little way back before they had to pull the motor, as they rapidly entered into Hockley Swamp.

After Daniel had pulled up the main motor, he put down the much smaller trolling motor, which was the only way they could hope to get across the swamp without seaweed clogging up the propellers. Even with the trolling motor though, he wouldn't have been surprised if he still had to row, but he would bear that burden if it came to it. As soon as he finished getting everything situated, Daniel turned to Lulu, a devious expression on his face.

"You've heard the legends of the lakes around here, haven't you?" Daniel asked, almost dramatically, then waited for a response. He was trying to build suspense.

Lulu looked at him curiously. She hadn't heard the legends, not really, but she was hesitant on whether she wanted to bite at his line of dialogue. She thought Daniel might be trying to scare her, or at least creep her out, but in the end, curiosity won, and ultimately, she decided that she did want to know the legends, even if they were scary, or stupid. "Go on."

"They say Kassir, Sparrow Lake, and Corner Lake have a lot more drownings and missing boaters than any other similar lakes of their size… They say things live in these lakes, especially in the swampy areas…"

"Yeah, bullshit," Lulu replied, although she did know of at least two people who had gone missing on one of the three lakes, and neither body had ever been recovered as far as she knew.

"They say it's the seaweed-" Daniel started, but was cut off.

"Fuck you. You know I hate that shit. Seaweed creeps me the hell out," Lulu told him, embellishing her level of offense, even though she really was terrified of seaweed. She kind of liked being scared though, especially when she knew she was actually safe. She had been on lakes her whole life, and although the seaweed always crept her out, making her think of small, strong, wet, hands, forever trying to pull her down into their soggy, smothering darkness, if she wasn't actually touching them, she wasn't really afraid. Besides, she and Daniel were both experienced boaters, so there was almost no chance they would fall in or even get stuck.

"I know it does. That's why I am telling you this tale as we travel through the swamp. I didn't make it up though, but I will stop if you need me to… If you are too scared," Daniel said, egging her on.

Lulu scowled at him, but there was no real malice in the expression. "Go ahead asshole," she replied, followed by an overly dramatic eye roll.

"So, the story goes, these lakes date back to prehistoric times. They are so old, scientists can't even properly date them, but they also don't care that much. Back in the sixties there was a huge fossil rush, and these lakes got hit hard, but the bone prospectors ultimately ended up with nothing, except for a bunch of drowned fossil hunters."

"Is this supposed to be a scary story or history lesson?" Lulu asked. "I didn't know there'd be school today."

"Quiet you, I'm getting there."

Lulu rolled her eyes for a second time.

"Anyway, the old timers say that both the prospectors and the scientists were looking for the wrong stuff. They say it's the flora of the lake that ought to be studied, not the fauna, or what's left of it. At least that's how my granddad used to put it."

"Flora? Fauna?" Lulu asked.

"Flora are the plants and fauna are the animals. I only know because I had asked gramps when he first told me."

"Okay... Go on."

"So, they say, and not just my grandfather either, that it's the seaweed that's taking people. It's the seaweed that's responsible for all the missing boaters and swimmers."

"Yeah, my parents used to tell me that garbage too. You'll get snagged in the seaweed, and it will pull you under. I used to believe it was like quicksand in the water. I think that's probably why I'm so damn scared of this stuff," Lulu told him. "My parents drilled it in hard."

"No. Listen. This shit even freaks me out. So, they say, the seaweed here is sentient."

"Like it's alive?"

"Yes. They say the seaweed can think."

"Okay, so, living seaweed, quite possibly the worst thing imaginable… Well, now that I'm going to have nightmares until I'm forty anyway... Go on, I guess."

"Okay, so the old timers believe that the seaweed-"

"Let me guess, the seaweed snatches people down so it can eat them," Lulu interrupted. "Yeah, that's original."

"No. You didn't let me finish, the seaweed doesn't really eat people, not like that, it saves people-"

"So, now it's heroic seaweed?"

"No. It doesn't save people so they can survive and live their lives. No, it saves people like we save leftovers."

"What are you talking about? What for?"

"From what I've heard, the seaweed in these lakes once lived. It was the dominant species in this area, and it could form itself into a rough imitation of a person, or any creature that entered its domain. They say the seaweed could live both on land and in the water."

"Yeah, that sounds believable," Lulu mocked, even though she was actually starting to become legitimately afraid.

"Anyway, the seaweed people used to rule these parts, and some say they still do. They say they take the people who fall in the swamp. They take them, and drown them, and then they drag their bodies all the way down to the bottom of the lake, where they encase the corpses and begin to fill them. The seaweed stores the bodies as it slowly suckles away their nutrients, feeding itself for weeks at a time. It is said that once the bodies have been picked clean, the seaweed then uses them as scaffolding, reincarnating them as hideous, amphibious, man-plant-animal monstrosities. They say that's the real reason why the seaweed folk can look like people."

"Stop! That is so fucked up Daniel. Why are you telling me this? That is taking it too far."

"Calm down. You're overreacting. I'm just telling you exactly as I had heard it," Daniel replied, unintentionally defensive. "You didn't even let me finish."

"You know seaweed creeps me the fuck out. Did you really have to tell me that story while we are floating through a shadowy swamp?" Lulu didn't mean to be angry, but she really was scared.

"Okay," Daniel said, defeatedly. "I can stop. I guess. Are you sure though? You really don't want to hear the end?"

"No. I really fucking don't," Lulu said, knowing she was overreacting. She didn't know why the story was making her so frightened, and she didn't like being unable to control her fear, especially when she knew it was irrational.

"I'm sorry," Daniel said. "I only meant to play... I was just telling you what they told me."

Lulu scowled at him, but she also felt bad. She knew he was only trying to get a rise out of her, but she could see he was also starting to scare himself a little, and that made her feel just a bit better.

"What do you want to talk about then?" Daniel asked, trying to make a peace offering.

"Just fucking tell me the ending," Lulu said with an exasperated sigh. "Fuck!"

Daniel's smile returned. "If you insist... So, the seaweed folk live under the lily pads. That's where they wait. It's their time to hunt now. They know they need enough bodies to get them through the long winter. They just need to wait for somebody to fall in... There are potentially dozens, maybe even hundreds of seaweed folk down there right now, patiently waiting at the bottom of any of these three lakes, especially within their swamps, waiting for more victims, waiting for someone to fall in and have their foot tangled in seaweed, just enough to keep them under."

"That is terrifying. I already hated seaweed before, but now that I have that pleasant story in my mind, that'll be nightmare fuel for the next decade."

"Come on. It's not even that scary, and it probably isn't even true."

"Shut up, Daniel," Lulu said, a little harsher than she had meant to. "Why would you say probably? Seaweed folk, or seaweed people, or whatever you call them, living things made of living seaweed are definitely not real."

"Well, those are the actual details from actual stories that I heard from my dad, my grandpa, and a couple of their fishermen friends, mostly after they've had some drinks in them."

Lulu exhaled loudly. She had heard similar stories herself, but had usually walked away before the storyteller got to any of the scary bits. Lulu couldn't and wouldn't believe that anything like that was even remotely possible.

"Looks like we're about halfway through," Daniel told her, snapping her back into reality as he stood up and looked around the swamp, gauging their position.

"Good," Lulu said, also looking around. "Can we go any faster?"

No sooner had she spoke; the trolling motor started to make a strained whirring sound. Daniel rushed to the back of the boat and lifted the small motor out of the water. Completely encasing all its propellers were thick strands of green-black seaweed. They were wrapped tightly around every blade, in a way that was going to take several minutes to remove.

"Damn. I hate when this happens," Daniel complained as he began picking the thick, soggy, clumps of seaweed from the propellor.

"Looks like you might just have to row," Lulu said with a slight chuckle, her way of saying I told you so.

"I'll get it… So, it might be a little closer to an hour instead of forty minutes, we'll still get there with lots of time to spare."

"Just hurry," Lulu sighed, trying to make it sound like she was irritated, when, in fact, she was frightened. Even though it was the middle of the day, it was still cloudy, and with sun currently hidden behind a bank of clouds right now, their sense of seclusion was extreme, that, combining with lengthening the shadows of all the trees surrounding the swamp, the area permeated an almost ominous atmosphere that would have given Lulu chills even if Daniel hadn't just told that story.

It also didn't help that the breeze had completely died in the swamp, and with all the lily pads standing so still, it seemed like they were frozen in time. That was when Lulu noticed she no longer heard any wildlife, or anything else at all for that matter. There was only complete silence surrounding them. It was incredibly unnerving.

"Hey, Daniel, would you maybe want to row?" Lulu asked nervously. "I won't give you any more shit."

"Come on, Lulu," Daniel started to say, but when he looked at her and saw real fear in her eyes, he stopped. He looked at the motor, two thirds free from the seaweed, then back at Lulu. "Give me one more minute, please? If I can't get this going after that, I'll row. I promise."

Lulu reluctantly agreed, though she was extremely nervous and agitated. She would have rowed herself, but the thought never even crossed her mind.

Daniel finished removing the last strands of seaweed off the third and final propeller just over a minute later. "All right, we should be good to go," he said as he finished the job.

Lulu watched as Daniel put the trolling motor back into the water, then pulled the cord to get it started. The motor instantly sputtered into life, and they even started to move again, but they only made it about five yards before the motor stopped for a second time, only now, instead of a strained whirring, there was a loud crunching, like the propeller had smashed against a boulder. In the top part, where the actual engine was, the trolling motor started to smoke.

"Shit," Daniel called as he tried to pull the motor up again, only this time, the propellers wouldn't come out of the water.

"What in the hell?" Daniel exclaimed in confusion as he reached down to get a better grip.

"What's going on?" Lulu asked uncertainly, trying not to be nervous.

"Don't know. I've never had this happen before. Maybe we are caught up in a floating, abandoned anchor line or something," Daniel told her as he began to try to pull the trolling motor back out of the water again, using all his might to do so this time. Just as the first propeller blade was about to penetrate the surface of the water, the whole bottom of the motor was suddenly yanked forcefully back down from below, hard enough to smash the motor against the back of the boat, and also to send Daniel, who had been expecting no such thing, somersaulting right into the lake with a large splash.

Daniel's head emerged from the water a moment later, and Lulu instantly moved to help him back on board.

"What the hell happened?" Lulu asked, extending her hand out for her boyfriend to grasp.

"I don't know," Daniel replied, swimming swiftly towards her. "Let's just get the hell out of here. I don't even care, I'll row."

Daniel was just about to reach Lulu's hand, when a dark, slick-looking clump of seaweed bobbed up right behind him. It was disgusting just looking at it, like something the lake had coughed up, and it made Lulu's stomach queasy… and that was before she began to smell the noisome odor that seemed to permeate from the death-green, clumpy mass.

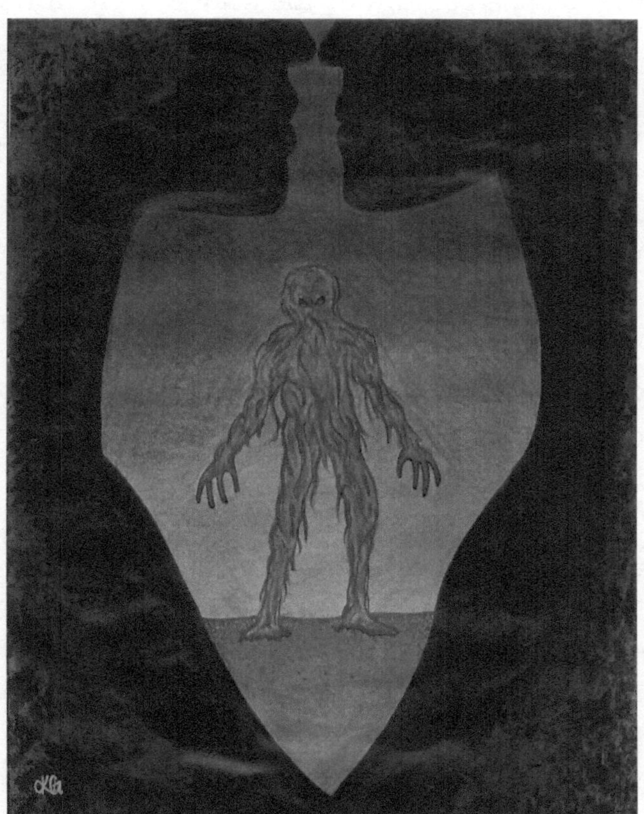

Lulu was watching the repulsive seaweed as Daniel took her hand. Unfortunately, however, in that first contact, their hands, one wet from the swamp, the other coated in a sheen of nervous sweat, did not connect in a firm grip, and both sets of fingers slipped easily off of and away from one another.

Daniel reached out again, but a loud splash from directly behind him instantly made him turn around. There, seeming more to slog through the water than to swim, was what looked like a large man in an old, soaking wet, extra dark ghillie suit. It kind of reminded Daniel of Jordy Verrill from *Creepshow* for a moment. That was his last sane thought before absolute terror set in.

"Hurry! Hurry! Hurry!" Lulu screamed loudly, still extending her arm over to Daniel, only she was jumpy, like a child trying to feed an animal they fear might bite them.

Daniel immediately turned from the horrifying swamp aberration and tried once again for his girlfriend's grasp.

Lulu extended her arm out as far as she dared, but as she reached out for Daniel, the thing behind her boyfriend reached out for him as well. Lulu felt Daniel's hand in her own, she grabbed him as tightly as she could, but the seaweed creature behind Daniel had reached its soggy arms, thick and strong as logs, around the poor boy at the same time, gripping him in an adamantium bear hug as the monstrosity pulled backwards and down, deep into the swamp, ripping Daniel's hand out of her own, ripping her lover out of her life forever. Lulu fell backwards into the middle of the boat, as she had been pulling with all her might, and hit her funny bone on Daniel's metal tackle box, sending a shooting pain up and down her arm, mapping every agonized tingle from her shoulder to her fingertips. She also hit her hip against one of the chairs, and her fall had caused the boat to start rocking wildly.

Lulu was terrified. She wanted something to protect herself with, in case the boat did tip. Playing through the pain, Lulu quickly rose and opened the tackle box, then frantically rummaged through it for either the fillet knife or Daniel's buck knife, which he mostly used to cut snagged line.

Lulu found both knives with ease, and in the process came across two M-80s, one of which Daniel had shown her earlier, along with his Pink Floyd Zippo. She grabbed everything and shoved it all into the pockets of her hoodie. That is when she noticed movement just a few feet away from her.

In the several seconds it had taken her to plunder the tackle box, half a dozen seaweed monsters had surrounded the boat and were now slowly starting to reach up and cling onto the sides.

Lulu's screams echoed loudly through the still swamp, not even answered by the birds, and the scariest scenario she could ever possibly imagine was currently unfolding upon her like a personalized living nightmare. Her fight or flight reflex kicked in, and immediately she began to process that there could be no flight without fight.

Lulu quickly flipped open the buck knife and unsheathed the fillet knife. She took a weapon in each hand, like some sort of Mephistophelian butcher, and began to hack and stab at her attackers in an adrenaline-charged, tremor-fueled rage. She stabbed the closest of the seaweed creatures in the head with both knives, feeling them slide, with relatively ease, straight into the monstrosity's rotted skull, or what was left of it.

After several downward thrusts, it became clear that her assault wasn't deterring the creatures in the slightest. Even when she tried with all her might, all it did was lose her of the fillet knife, as she had embedded it too deeply into one of the creature's heads for her to remove. The knives were useless anyway. Even so, she quickly closed the buck knife and shoved it into her pocket, not willingly allowing herself to throw away a weapon, before pulling out one of the M-80's and the lighter. Lulu knew what she had to do, and she knew she had to time everything perfectly.

Lulu flicked open the Zippo and lit the wick of the first firework. She then set the lit M-80 down in one of the top compartments in the tackle box, being as the boat was rocking wildly, as the creatures began getting their arms and heads up over the side of the gunnel. She was somewhat thankful that they were coming from both sides, however, because although the boat was rocking wildly, the relatively even distribution of weight kept it from tipping. She just needed it to stay that way for just a couple more seconds...

Lulu grabbed one of the oars and commenced a brief round of whack-a-mole on the heads of the seaweed people, focusing her aggression on the side of the boat closest to shore, which was maybe forty feet away, trying to dwindle down the onslaught on that side as much as possible.

The boat was rocking so wildly now, Lulu had to crouch down not to fall. The wick of the first M-80 was almost out, and the creatures, at least on the swamp side, we're starting to get their midsections over the side of the boat, progressively tipping the boat in that direction and pulling it down, closer into the water.

Lulu grabbed the lighter and the second M-80 from her hoodie pocket, spun the wheel with her thumb to produce flame, and lit the second M-80, holding it tightly in her hand even though the sparks from the fuse were starting to burn her skin. Lulu then dropped the Zippo, quickly picked up and tossed the first, almost wickless M-80 into the water, and waited.

Her timing had been close, too close for comfort, but it had worked perfectly. The M-80 had exploded no more than two feet down, right in the middle of a cadre of horrendous swamp people. She watched as the shockwave rippled through the water, through the seaweed people, rattling their pieces apart into myriad large clumps of disgusting offal.

Lulu watched in horror as the clumps began to make their way disturbingly back toward one another, recombining seemingly at random. She only watched for half a moment though, before she took a deep breath, threw the second lit M-80 out in front of her, then jumped into the swamp after it, on the side closest to the shore.

The water was cold and slimy, like being in a frog's mouth, and she instantly felt both claustrophobic and suffocated by all the lily pads. They were everywhere, and she could feel their stocks under water as they tried to entangle her.

Lulu swam faster and harder than she had ever swam before, swimming for dear life, literally, and swimming against an opposing swamp and her heavy clothing, for she was wearing no life jacket. She fought for every inch of swamp conquered.

There was a large cluster of branches, the top of a fallen tree that had landed horizontally in the water, and they were only about thirty feet or so away from where she now struggled. Lulu locked in on those branches and swam.

She made it only five feet, however, before she felt rotting fingers, seemingly as strong as steel cables, take hold of her ankle. Lulu only screamed once before she was pulled down under the murky water.

It was dark under the surface. Lulu couldn't see a thing, but could still feel herself being pulled down, quicker now as she felt more and more of the creatures closing in upon her. She consider letting herself drown. It was a better fate than whatever they were about to do to her. It was as if all her worst nightmares were coming true.

Unable to just give up, however, Lulu reached into her pocket, thankful she had kept the buck knife after all, and blindly worked open the blade. Her lungs were already starting to burn when she plunged the knife into the creature's arm and began to saw, hoping to de-limb the abomination, though she immediately saw that it was useless. There was no way she could saw through all them, not when she was struggling just to saw through one. Not while she was drowning. Hope was fading fast as Lulu's lungs began to throb painfully, forcing a dry, abrasive, regurgitative pulse up her throat, burning her esophagus as she felt her consciousness begin to grow dark. It was then that a large explosion from almost directly below her, the result of the second

M-80, not only made all the creatures release her, but rocketed Lulu's drowning form right up to the surface.

Lulu gasped desperately for breath when she breached the water, but she also immediately began trying to assess her location as well. She wanted to start swimming the moment air touched her flesh, to start heading for land even if she couldn't yet breathe.

By some miracle, the blast had blown her even closer to the fallen tree, so close that she was maybe only fifteen feet away from its gnarled branches. Lulu torpedoed forward, taking tiny breaths where she could, but focusing solely on her speed, on reaching that tree.

Her fingers brushed against the branches only a few moments later, and she immediately grasped onto the dead wood, beginning to climb the moment she had a good hold. Lulu knew the tree was dead, and she knew it might not hold her, but she was in such a hurry, such a panic, she hadn't even thought to check branches. In her frantic flight up the dead tree, one of the branches snapped in her hand, and Lulu was instantly plunged backwards, right back into the swamp.

Something between unconsciously determined, terror-directed reflexes and an adrenaline-fueled blackout was responsible for Lulu's movements over the next few seconds. She pulled herself rapidly back out of the water, scrambling up, over, and through the dead branches that poked at and scratched her with every move, drawing their own taste of blood, and hauled herself through their deciduous ganlet like a half-drowned squirrel with its tail on fire.

When she was almost through the branch cluster, one of her calves slipped back into the water for just a moment as she maneuvered around a thick tree limb, and Lulu suddenly felt something slick and powerful grasp onto her foot. She kicked wildly, flailing so intensely she almost dislocated her knee. In the end, however, it was worth it. Her shoe came off in the monster's hand and she was allowed to finish her painful ascent the rest of the way through the abusive branches without pause. Lulu didn't look back, not even when she reached the main portion of the trunk, which was covered in slippery, slimy moss. Lulu straddled the tree trunk, shimmying across those last few feet to freedom, hoping she didn't get pulled from to one side or the other. It was like scaling across a giant, wet, carpeted tongue.

Lulu finally made it onto solid, albeit incredibly muddy land, and even though her thighs were scraped bloody, and the branches had cut and stabbed her just about everywhere, she was ecstatic. She was out of the water. Lulu knew there was no time to savor the moment, however, and instantly started moving. She scrambled the rest of the way out of the up the muddy, sludgy, bank, like crawling through grassy, pancake batter as it was still wet from last night's rain, before finally making it up onto mostly dry and level ground. Even though she had to once again fight against the weight of her sopping-wet clothes, and was already starting to get lightheaded, Lulu immediately started to run.

Just as she crossed the threshold into the potential safety of the trees, there began a sloshy cacophony of viscous splashing, intermixed with the squelching of heavy, spongy bodies and mucky limbs squishing against one another in the mud.

Lulu risked a single look back, only to find two dozen or more of the seaweed folk slogging out of the swamp, trudging determinately from the muck and heading in her direction, at least for the most part. Lulu snapped her head back around and increased her speed, even though she was already running on empty.

She knew Old Highway 61 was in this direction, maybe a block or two away, and she could already hear the cars. Even if she didn't make it to the highway, there were plenty of houses around here, safety was almost within her grasp.

That was the mantra Lulu played over and over again in her head for her entire excursion through the woods, until, a short time later, she finally did come upon Old Highway 61. Lulu immediately started walking toward town, travelling on the shoulder and hoping a car would drive by soon and pick her. She was constantly looking back, and even though she hadn't seen a single seaweed person since the lake, she still didn't feel safe.

It was ten minutes later, after three cars had passed her by, not picking her up because she not only looked wet and covered in mud, but also because she was severely disheveled and looked half-crazed, when she finally saw the flashing lights.

A cop pulled up behind her a moment later. The officer got out of the vehicle, immediately went to his trunk to grab Lulu a towel and a blanket, then rushed over and covered her up, before ushering her into the back of his cruiser.

"Hi, my name is Miles Garaka– Officer Garaka. Are you okay? Wait right here, I'm calling this in right now," Officer Garaka said as he helped Lulu into her seat. He then went to the front seat of his squad car and began to radio to headquarters, but before he could say anything into the receiver, a loud hissing static came through instead, followed by a panicked, young male voice.

"Backup needed immediately! Any officers near Kassir Hospital, get here now, we have an attack by multiple assailants in ghillie suits. None of them seemed armed, but it looks like this might be a PCP type situation. Please, proceed with caution."

"What the hell is going on?" Officer Garaka asked, turning back to look at Lulu.

"It's the seaweed folk. The seaweed folk are here to get us," Lulu told him, then began to make a sound that even she wasn't sure whether it was laughing or crying.

The End

Propagating Wave

By: Dino Parenti

Tess guns the Chevy Tahoe around mountain curves, panic-laughing at not yet having careened through a guardrail and plunged to her death.

But death, nevertheless, is still coming.

Even a paralegal career hasn't prepared her to handle the information overload of the past nine days. After all the variables and calamities of last-minute detection—that it was hidden in the sun's glare, been knocked off an otherwise benign orbit by another body into a collision course with Earth—the asteroid finally slammed into the Pacific, 650 miles off the Southern California coast.

4SKY had relayed this three minutes earlier, and soon his languid baritone resumes over Drew's police scanner.

"...updated estimates, folks. The shockwave's anywhere from twenty-to-thirty minutes away..."

Tess guesstimates she's still about twenty-minutes from her late parents' cabin, and her right foot presses a bit harder on the gas.

Because 400mph winds are no joke.

Being between mountains *should* dampen the effects, but underground shelter is greatly preferred according to 4SKY—former JPL astrophysicist and current ham-radio fiend, offering play-by-play of a planet-killing asteroid's game.

Amongst the ensuing salvos of partial-information and blatant misinformation outlets following the asteroid's detection, it was 4SKY that Drew had turned her onto, after his LAPD cohorts had done so for him.

Not surprisingly, Drew left out that 4SKY was also one of the loudest of the conspiracy theorists, rambling between computations that the asteroid had been deliberately shifted into a collision course by rogue government elements. New World Order nonsense, Accelerationism Theory advocates, eugenics champions, etcetera, etcetera.

But 4SKY knows his stuff regarding the physics and order of events, and right now, that's enough for Tess.

A stalled car appears suddenly around the next tight hairpin, and Tess yanks a hard left.

"Jesus-shit, fuck, fuck, fuck!" she cries, her front bumper clipping the rear of the Mini Cooper belching steam from its gaping hood.

Tess brakes, eyes toggling in the rearview. The car's empty, thankfully, its owners on foot along the shoulder, necks craned as if looking for something.

As her mind screams to keep driving, her body autopilots her into reverse until she's abreast of the pair, whereupon she rolls down her window.

"You two okay?"

The couple—in their late thirties like she and Drew—squint perplexed gazes her way before resuming their search, seemingly not caring that she'd hit their car, the man calling for "Mookie" in high-pitched baby tones.

A dog trembles in the brush.

"It just hit the ocean," says Tess. "I can...take you up the mountain."

The woman, scowling suddenly with cornered rage, bats a hand at Tess.

"There's no fucking asteroid, bitch! You've been fucking lied to!"

In the ensuing pause, the man's eyes meet Tess's, all unfocused, unsure terror.

Tess rolls up the window and drives on.

Rock Doubters. What the media labeled asteroid deniers. But most believed. Some even sensed what to do, if not knew via solid information. Most, however, still wait in their homes even now, praying the least catastrophizing voices from their social media feeds are the right ones. But the animals understand. Even minutes before the impact, Tess had noted their odd behavior, as if stymied by some primordial foresight. Coyotes gazing at the sky from under dipped, twisted heads. Racoons, in broad daylight, slouching in circles in the middle of climbing lanes. Hawks divebombing behind tree-lines and not resurfacing.

Even Mookie knew what to do.

"…any minute now," 4SKY's calm lilt crackles through.

Tess's eyes flutter. How long had she been daydreaming? Because the tunnel's close now. She'd been to her parents' cabin many times as a girl, and though it's been years since, the familiar twists-and-turns of the mountain will forever hum in her DNA.

"…you'll hear the shockwave in advance, like a stampede. Get underground. Get against the east face of a mountain. Do not *hold your breath. Pressure equalization is crucial…"*

Almost on cue, the tunnel's opening sweeps into view just as the rumble of some colossal, abyssal thing thrums in her ears, reverberating the SUV's chassis to the molecules.

Tess glances in the rearview, to the secure life nestled the San Fernando Valley she'd just bolted from, but the spreading bruise around her eye swats away any intrusive reservations. She sees then a living mirage as wide as the horizon rushing in from the coast, vaporizing all clouds.

Darting into the tunnel, she cuts the engine and swaddles herself beneath comforters to dampen the 150db roar that can rupture eardrums.

Through the tunnel's rear, she glimpses everything not anchored down getting progressively slammed against the mountain side as if teed off by a line of goliath slicers.

The roar is the agony of a planet splitting in two, and everything goes black.

***

Tess announced her pregnancy to Drew nine days ago, right after news broke of the impactor.

As Asteroid 2023-DF16 approached the atmosphere—nicknamed FOMO for "Fear of Making Orbit"—Drew simmered in silent rage.

Raging at the government, who was surely responsible, he'd just gotten off the phone with Brett, his LAPD partner. They're going to start a Reddit board about it tonight. Blame shadow US cells for conspiring with China and Russia.

Then he raged at Tess.

Raged at her for choosing a moment of abject terror to divulge a thing that should've been revealed without provocation during a park stroll, or across shared sundaes.

None of this surprised Tess. It's what their six-month trial separation was about: Drew's anger issues. His anger at the world. His anger at the *other*.

Anger at *her* inability to make a baby…

…Tess's eyes flutter open.

Through the windshield, brown choking dust swirls about the tunnel. It's so abruptly quiet that she can hear grit pinging against the car.

The scanner frizzles and pops.

"…best hurry now…"

4SKY. His mic spikes with feedback.

Tess turns the ignition. The engine hitches initially but soon catches.

The radio keeps breaking up. The tunnel in cahoots with 4SKY being on a different mountain range. The Santa Barbara's, she thinks. Somewhere closer to the coast.

Closer, as suggested in the quaver of his otherwise bucolic voice, to know what's coming next.

She putters towards the opposite light blur, at length creeping out of the tunnel to dissipating dust.

Her breath catches in her throat.

Century-old trees lay canted and splintered against the entire west face of the mountain.

"…it ain't over, folks. Back-of-the-napkin calcs so far, but… Just a moment…"

A *moment,* Tess ponders. What it took to say *I do,* make a baby, lose a baby, destroy a planet.

Moments as long as lifetimes.

An audible swallow from the scanner. Tess likewise gulps.

"Tsunami inbound. Twelve-hundred feet of seawater, give-or-take. ETA, seventy-to-eighty minutes. Those still listening, get to higher ground ASAP…"

Tess floors the gas, pupils swinging like compass needles passed over magnets.

***

She takes the turnoff road to the cabin and only then does it hit her that the place might not even be standing after the shockwave.

A chuckle coughs out, her first expression of mirth in weeks. Because the cabin isn't some charming, rickety thing cobbled from salvaged wood. Her parents were Cold-War babies. Mushroom-cloud futures prompted them to build a stone-and-timber fortress into the side of a granite outcrop. At most, she might have to plywood over shattered windows.

As she slaloms up the gravel drive around blown-over branches and pinecones bursting under her tires like party poppers, she wonders how Drew would've appreciated the cabin and its reason for being. It's why she never brought him up here. He would've suggested they move there. He'd always wanted to live someplace *less gentrifying and crime-riddled.*

Tess was always quick to cite the incongruity of his reasoning.

"You just crave cultural homogeneity," she'd said. *"I'm not leaving civilization to feed your lunatic isolation jones."*

Once out, *isolation* and *homogeneity* became buzzwords—grenades to lob between Drew's feet whenever he suggested they separate themselves from the general *riffraff*.

Persistent squabbling, coupled with a second miscarriage—the one she kept from an escalating Drew—led to the six-month separation, followed by ponderous soul-searching, a shaky reconciliation, a third pregnancy that seemed to take.

Then FOMO's arrival.

She rounds the massive boulder against which the driveway gate is anchored—a gate swung fully open that should've been locked.

Before her parents' cabin is parked an open van teeming with AV gear. Beyond, a half-dozen college-aged kids mill about on the observation terrace, setting up cameras and gear.

***

"What's going on?" Tess calls, stepping out of the car. The question tastes bitter in her mouth, like bringing up the weather to someone weeping over a loved one at a funeral.

One of the youths, a tatted-to-the-nines and sporting enough piercings to generate her own gravity, approaches Tess, a cautionary hand extended as if this is *her* place and Tess's the interloper. "Whoa there, lady. Are you hurt? We have water and snacks. A nice sectional to chill on before you—"

"I'm well aware of what I have," replies Tess, smiling, holding her cool. "This is my cabin and this *is* private property."

Another of the youngsters steps forward, tall and rangy, fiddling with some camera adapter mount. A coma-shaped swath of jet-black hair obscures half his face. "Yo, *amiga,*" he says, a voice too resonant for such a scrawny torso, "No such thing as private property anymore. In case you're not hip to current events."

Tess grins away his snark before addressing the girl. "What are you all doing here?"

"I'm Abby," she replies, scowling, as if failure of introduction had just violated some Geneva Convention statute. There's a sexiness in her cool, Tess notes. She seems someone easy to follow. Easy to like. "This is Rah. Over there are Olivia, Micha, and Bran."

"I'm Tess."

A muffled radio plays where the others are setting up shots. Some newscaster. Something about it rings familiar.

A nerdy ginger sidles up to Abby and hands her a headset. The one Abby called Bran. The guy nods warily at Tess before returning to his work, glancing a quick I-think-I'm-in-love-with-you grin at Abby.

"We're live-streaming FOMO," says the tall one, Rah. "The clusterfuck the government has unleashed. And this cabin's a primo vista for it."

Abby glares at Rah as if he'd just demanded that Tess donate an egg to the pro-life movement. "Documenting everything to the cloud for posterity," she tells Tess. "We assumed the place was…abandoned, all things considered."

And it hits Tess then: the others are also listening to 4SKY. Their radio and Drew's scanner Doppler the broadcast between her ears like speaker delay. She snags bits of it—4SKY blathering about previous Earth civilizations, undersea denizens, Silurian Hypothesis crap.

No wonder JPL shit-canned him years ago.

The wind, which had vanished with the shockwave, emerges again, gusting east.

"Look, lady…sorry, Tess?" says Abby. "We only care about live-streaming this. After that, we're out this bitch."

Tess is trapped between a head shake and a nod before blinking away all remaining misgivings. "Whatever. Stay as long as you want. Where else are you gonna go?"

She grabs the first couple of bags within reach from the SUV before traversing a debris-strewn driveway to the side kitchen door while 4SKY continues raving on about midnight zones and eldritch nightmares.

***

Dropping the bags on the center island, she steps to the large panorama window in the den and spies the mess of cables, tripods, and cameras set up on the observation terrace. Despite the quality equipment, the others are still shooting everything through cellphones. One's a tanned beach-bum in a Social Distortion tee, ripped jean shorts, and black Doc Martens.

Micah.

The other girl, immensely pregnant and in matching Docs, scrunches her forehead over a laptop while absently twining jet-black locks.

Olivia.

Tess glances right and spies the long, rectangular mirror above the fireplace. She steps up to it and probes at her blackening eye. She's glad nobody pointed it out, especially Abby, for whom a detail like that wouldn't go unnoticed.

Her face was spotless just forty-eight hours ago, before informing Drew the baby wasn't his.

That she had used donor sperm.

They were stuffing the Tahoe with supplies in preparation to leave for Drew's brother's place in Palomar when she was struck by a need to speak her mind—not to Drew, necessarily, but to herself.

Drew's response to her candor was extreme but not surprising to Tess. He hauled back and punched her, his eye-whites glowing with fury.

Like the news of FOMO, all normal expectations simply stopped applying after that, so as soon as Drew retreated to the patio to drink off his anger, Tess took the Tahoe, after kicking his shit onto the curb, and stayed in a motel overnight to think things through.

Her parents' cabin was her only choice. Though Drew knew about it, he didn't know where it was and she doubted he would look for her anyway. Not after what she'd confessed. In his eyes, she's spoiled goods.

A voice flutters past her ears as if from underwater. At first, she assumes it's 4SKY, but it's younger, deeper.

The tall kid outside with the hair swoop. Rah.

"It's coming. Sweet Jesus, it's coming."

4SKY, with surging manic energy, is blabbering much the same through the radio.

Tess huffs it upstairs two steps at a time.

The main bedroom window has been shattered by the shockwave. The sky beyond has changed color. A hazy, submarine nimbus dappled by speckled movement.

Every bird in creation, seemingly, is flapping eastward.

Tess smells the air. Minerally, like brackish water, hot with ozone and power. And then the rumbling earth—different than with the shockwave.

It's how she imagines the fluttering heart at the core of their world as it's about to give out.

By the window sits a cheap telescope her mother once used for stargazing. Tess moves the tripod onto the balcony.

"...it's...amazing..." 4SKY says from below. *"...watching the Point Magu beaches through my binoculars..."*

Before Tess's eyes, the horizon swells. Even thirty miles out, the impossible wall of water is undeniable.

A giggle from 4SKY. Indecipherable mumbles. He's starting to lose it.

"...did these idiots think it was only going to be some ankle-deep swell? It's fucking swallowing *them whole..."*

Some on the terrace below scream, some cheer. Tess glimpses their leader, Abby, frantically relaying to an audience what she sees into a headset mic while filming with a camcorder.

Tess, eyes distended fully at the approaching wall of water, nestles into the telescope's eyepiece, as if somehow lenses will dilute the terror.

Even after focusing, she keeps readjusting. What she sees, her brain won't fully grasp.

Entire buildings, streets, and scrambling crowds of people are swallowed under the advancing swell. A push-broom of rabid water against ants.

"...once every two-million-years, this happens..."

A helicopter flying too low over Van Nuys gets broadsided and enveloped as it tries, too late, to climb over the frothing mass.

"...they return to spawn..."

Within the advancing edifice of water, Tess makes out vague shapes tumbling through. Debris being agitated, ablated, annihilated.

"...they return to feed..."

Strobing pinpricks of arcing light at the wave's base: transformers across the valley short-circuiting.

The countless splash curtains as surging ocean careens against buildings, hillsides, mountains.

She steps away from the telescope and looks down.

None of the kids are laughing or cheering anymore. Their eyes and lenses are fixed wide on the ocean rushing continuously to the east.

"...all thanks to FOMO..."

One of her hands instinctively crabs against her still flat belly.

"...FOMO was brought here to reveal the truth...*"*

A sharp report as a power plant at the mouth of the Newhall Pass explodes.

"…they're emerging! See? See? *They're plucking people off boats! Plucking them off mountain tops!…"*

Tess quivers as she watches the mad water cataract into the valleys and hollows of the foothills, breaking over one another like hands groping madly for higher ledges, blending smashed structures and cars in a mounting, foaming roil, consuming hundred-foot Ponderosa Pines in seconds.

"…they're coming for me now, folks. They're coming for us all…"

South towards the basin, Downtown LA is almost gone from view but for a few skyscrapers teething through the churn.

"…it's been a trip, ladies and gents…"

A lone 747 circles slowly over where LAX once awaited.

A single gunshot from the radio below, followed by static.

Screaming from the terrace shudders Tess back to the present. To the massive column rising from waters below.

***

This is a monster, Tess thinks. Real and in-the-flesh—or whatever passes for its brown, mottled hide still shedding water. This tentacle's skin.

She sprints back downstairs. Back to the den.

Through the window she sees Rah double-fisting cell phones at the tentacle as if they were crucifixes warding off vampires.

A slamming to her right. The window by the bar area.

The tentacle's end, thick as a mature oak trunk, probes the glass. What look like a dozen eyes, black and globular, circumscribe the opening, squelching and suctioning against the pane. Deeper in the tentacle's maw, more rings of eyes, like barrel rifling, vanishing into pitch-blackness.

The eyes closest to the surface roll back, then invert, like the pupils of great white sharks about to bite, only instead of a caul of flesh, hooked, translucent teeth rotate around, snapping against the window, spidering the glass.

More screams from outside, but Tess can't see. The panoramic window is now fully blotted by the tentacle's girth.

She drops behind the sectional couch and crawls frantically towards the kitchen.

At the center island, the screaming outside reaches a new, hellacious pitch. Tess cowers against the island and covers her ears.

***

She's unsure of how much time passes. A trembling hand rubs her belly, feeling for her still unformed baby. She'd wanted to test Drew, to see if he still would've helped raise a baby not of his making, because despite her fear of being alone—of raising a child solo following a cataclysm==she needed to *not* feel apprehension about any choice she made.

Despite the violent form it assumed, she was thankful for Drew's irrefutable clarity.

She hears tapping, and at first, assumes the tentacle is back at the window, but it's a softer, more subdued rap, and it's coming from the side.

From the kitchen door.

Has the tentacle moved there?

"Tess? It's Abby. Are you there?"

Is it fucking talking now, too?

A firmer knock, followed again by Abby's voice.

No, Tess thinks. That's a bridge too fucking far, and she rolls onto all fours and crawls to the door.

Before she can fully open it, Abby reaches in and hauls her out, pressing a shushing finger to her lips. Bran takes her other hand, and all three skitter towards the SUV.

Tess looks back. Despite her trepidation, she needs to see.

As if piggybacking onto her frequency, Abby and Bran do likewise.

The tentacle has partially retreated into the still-rising water, its remaining portion swaying like a cobra. Bands of bioluminescence radiate down its length and between its hardened segments in coppers and teals, intensifying until it's almost too bright to look at.

Tess notices blood on the observation deck just as she's ushered into the back seat of her truck. Abby takes the wheel and slowly eases them away from the cabin until they're back on the main road, whereupon she guns it.

***

The ocean has stopped rising, or so Tess hopes.

They just passed Ravenna, heading northeast towards Acton. Elevation signs say they're over 2,400 feet above sea level.

Over 40 miles inland, and along the last canyon pass, the invading Pacific Ocean still churns less than fifty feet below their tires.

At least they've seen nothing of the tentacle for the last half-hour.

Tess's gaze fixes between the backs of Bran's and Abby's heads, the latter driving. She'd just met them forty-five minutes earlier, and she's now a passenger in the SUV she'd commandeered from her husband. How things have changed. The *world* has changed, in the blink of an eye, she's being ferried by strangers from her cabin outside Lang to a different cabin on Mt. Gleason.

Abby said her uncle awaits them there, ready to fly them to higher elevations near Mammoth Lake in a helicopter he'd commandeered from NBC news.

Tess's hands have stopped shaking, at least, and after several flexes, she picks up Abby's camcorder in the seat beside her. A similar SONY to the one Drew uses. Or *used,* rather, as her husband was now surely dead, along with countless millions of others.

Shoving those horrors aside, she pops in the earbuds and scrubs back the video feed. Abby had filmed everything, all the more specific horrors Tess had missed entirely while huddling in the cabin with her eyes shut so hard her head still aches from the effort.

But she'd heard it. She heard every godawful sound.

Noting a shift in perspective on the video—Abby shooting from her back on the ground instead of standing—Tess stops rewinding, then hits PLAY.

Beyond the sound of the tentacle coiling towards the camera, its hard segmented rings clacking like a million maracas, it's Abby's heavy but controlled breaths that Tess hears the loudest. A Lamaze compelled more to dampen fear than pain.

The orifice at the tentacle's end begins to twist and swivel like a camera iris, like a closed mouth swishing masticated food.

A moment later it swirls open and a secondary tentacle slithers forth, a fleshy, serpentine appendage compared to the knurled, umber carapace that houses it. It whips the air in an elegant sine wave before its tip drops onto Abby's belly, its end splitting into digits that grip around her torso and hold.

A quick yelp issues from Abby's throat, but she holds the camcorder steady, maintaining her measured breathing, which is escalating slightly as, over the span of the next ten-seconds, a nodule sprouts from the slick surface of the inner tentacle a few feet beyond her, and an unusual form begins to grow.

Tess finds herself moving the viewfinder farther from her eyes as the shape carves and etches itself into a perfect, marbleized replica of Abby, right down to her facial rings.

It then starts breathing in perfect cadence with the supine woman, this doppelganger molded from glistening flesh the color of spoiling cantaloupe.

Beyond this very alien, startling connection, it's Abby's bravery and composure that Tess most marvels at, for she knows she would've been a shrieking, thrashing mess had it been her.

A male voice screams out of frame, and Abby swings her lens to the right.

Another tentacle, or as Tess realizes, a branching segment from the same fleshy appendage that holds down Abby, now has Rah by the legs.

Rah, who threw the shittiest shade upon Tess arriving at *her* cabin. Abby's camera captures him being hoisted into the air by the tentacle segment, having swallowed his legs to the waist.

His falsetto wails betray his otherwise deep basso. He beats angrily and uselessly against his captor with his fists.

From some nebulous place within it, the thing issues a sound—an ungodly blend of whale song and theremin that crackles through the earbuds, and Tess wonders if it sounds even creepier underwater.

"It gets…ugly," Abby says—not the recorded version, but the one driving. She's looking solemnly at Tess through the rearview, probably has been since she picked up the camera.

Tess nods, feeling the acidic slosh of looming horror in her belly, but she watches anyway. She may have liked Rah the least of all in the group, but he didn't deserve to die. None of them did.

New *limbs* elongate from the tentacle beneath where Rah's feet are. They hook upwards and rapidly latch onto each of Rah's hands, slurping them up to his shoulders like linguini.

Rah growls and struggles against them until the area around his knees starts distending, swooping up in a parabola and, like with Abby, assuming his perfectly mimicked form before him.

The tentacle double starts blubbering, or mimicking some alien translation of human sniveling.

Wrath flares from Rah's eyes, and he spits and curses at his slick binary—this stygian claymation—until suddenly his eyes blast open in baffled shock.

The tentacles holding his arms quickly draw apart, ripping meat and flesh from both limbs.

A girl—Olivia—screams out of frame.

Even Abby, capturing it all with a seasoned war correspondent's aplomb, issues a suppressed squeal.

At this point, it's only reflex that has a shocked Rah wobbly beating at the tentacle with red, mealy bones.

All the flesh and muscle from his arms have been degloved from the shoulders down.

Olivia's screams pitch even higher as Rah's fading body is then glugged the rest of the way down the tentacle, bulging along the appendage like a snake's swallowed lump, until finally disappearing into the hardshell source.

Turning the camera left, Abby focuses on another tentacle segment pinning Olivia down. Cute, aloof, and pregnant Olivia. The tentacle incarnates her completely, right down to her expectant state.

The double shivers, shifting its gaze about like some cagey critter.

When Olivia's mirrored pregnant belly begins changing shape, everyone starts screaming, including Abby.

Tess watches Olivia claw with black acrylics at the gruesome twin shivering above her—watches specifically the twin's pregnant belly morphing into her fetus's face which then twists into a mask of despair.

Thoughts flood Tess mind: the tentacle mimics its quarry, but does it also think? Does it merely reflect its prey with its "smart-flesh" as a way to stun it, or is there a deeper motive involved? Why is it throwing back a prey's own panic, the way it's doing to Olivia? Is it malevolent???

"How the fuck could you be so calm during this?" Tess blurts out suddenly to the back of Abby's head.

Abby shrugs. "Years of Herzog films? Years of whiskey? Years of AA? It's where we all met. In meditation class. Called ourselves the Rum Journos. Fuck, whatever…"

Bran gently squeezes her shoulder. Abby forearms away quiet tears and snot.

Tess turns to the screen in time to witness the tentacle smother the real Olivia's belly. Watches as Olivia's eyes widen in unspeakable horror and pain as the tentacle kneads against flesh, muscle, and placenta until a lump traverses the intestinal appendage from her belly and into that of her alien twin's—doubling its belly size momentarily before Olivia's own stomach collapses back in on itself, at which point the shrieking girl is suctioned down its gullet like it had done with Rah.

A howling *Noooooo!* erupts left of the camera, and Abby swings it to the source: Olivia's boyfriend, Micah, who up till then hadn't uttered a peep, even as a tentacle segment has him pinned to the terrace floor by his crotch.

Micah. The spicy-but-quiet type. Standoffish like Olivia, haughty like Rah.

His avatar studying him from above through curious, terrier cants of the head. Would he have survived had he not fished out a gun from his back waistband and emptied the clip into his twin seconds after it had devoured Olivia and his unborn baby?

Tess doubts it. Nor could she blame him, mouthing a silent prayer for his soul as his double, upon absorbing the bullets like pebbles dropped into a bowl of pudding, proceeds to embrace the original, and within thirty seconds, shreds a screaming Micah into itself.

Only then does Abby's camera seek out the last of the Rum Journos: Bran.

Bran, a tentacle offshoot pressing him by the chest against the terrace's ledgestone wall, comes into focus in Abby's camera, just past the blood smear left on the concrete that was Micah only seconds earlier.

He, like Abby, breathes in focused, measured breaths.

So does Bran's twin, sprouted from the tentacle like some ambulatory tumor.

As the tentacles hold Abby and Bran on camera, Tess catches bits of conversation from their present versions in front of the SUV.

They're comparing notes, positing about the tentacle.

Bran: "It felt…what I felt…"

Abby, nodding: "If we started to panic, I *felt* it in the tentacle. In my…avatar."

In hindsight, it makes a certain sense to Tess, and as if hearing her thoughts in the video, the tentacles simultaneously release Abby and Bran, their twins absorbed back into the smart-flesh before withdrawing into its harder outer shell.

Bran, in the flesh: "Like they're triggered by sudden adrenaline and cortisol release…"

Abby nodding: "If you match its aggression, it sees you as a threat and…"

Bran: "…and it eats your ass."

They go on, but Tess starts fading. She needs sleep, even if it comes with nightmares.

***

It is indeed a channel 4 NBC News helicopter they find upon arriving at Mt. Gleason an hour later.

Abby hops out and hugs the white-haired man doing final flight checks. Introductions are hastily made. Uncle Ethan fiercely hugs Bran and Tess as if they're also family. At this point and in this world, you're either family, or you're a threat.

Within five minutes, they're in the air.

***

Uncle Ethan performs a final swoop towards the LA basin before turning north, but it's enough for them to see. The Pacific has swept well past the Inland Empire, but that's not what gives them the most pause.

Filaments of glowing russet and aquamarine branch out from where the coast used to start, likely originating just past the continental shelf. It's a webwork of tentacles, stretching, branching for miles inland from something ancient and forgotten under the world, now awakened by a rock from space.

Tess is sure that if she opens a window, she'll hear the screams over the chop of the rotors. Not of the people, but of their doubles. Doubles revealing to their prey-hosts all their animal panic, simian unpleasantness, and primeval dreads that slavish repetition to modernity haven't fully scarred over.

She takes slow, deep breaths, and tries to think up names for a child about to enter a new world where old fears and furies will still kill.

Whatever Happened to Jonathan Obrero?

By: Don Anelli

Jonathan had spent the last three years waiting for this moment, ever since his father, anthropologist Dr. Neil Obrero, disappeared in the area, looking for the elusive Wandersnatch Indian tribe, just off the coast of what would one day become known as Goosepoint, Oregon. Jonathan had been searching for the tribe himself, trying to figure out what happened to his father.

Now, he finally could do it, thanks to the help of a local Tillamook guide, who investigated what happened with Neil and the Wandersnatch Indians. The legend his guide, Kilchis, told him, though, made no sense at all. There was no way for any of it to be true.

According to Kilchis, the Wandersnatch were an outcast tribe of numerous interbred individuals from local tribes who banded together to place their trust and worship in a savage sea creature that prowled the nearby waters. They described a creature so hideous, so cruel and powerful, no one had ever laid eyes on it and lived to tell the tale. They say that to see it would be akin to setting your soul on fire, that it freezes your blood to the point of immobility, rendering you the perfect prey.

The Wandersnatch's worship of this creature had long been a source of concern between the tribes, leading to many in the area being hesitant to talk or even interact with them at all. This was why so little was known about them. How they should be dealt with, however, was the cause of a great many wars and disputes.

Fortunately, Jonathan had found someone who would lead him to where Neil had last been seen, in a secluded cove, just outside the farthest reaches of Tillamook influence. Kilchis would go no further, refusing to leave Tillamook land, though he agreed to wait at that spot for one day. Jonathan continued to search through the woods by himself, trying desperately to find some clue to his father's disappearance.

After following his guide's directions to the cove, it wasn't long before Jonathan spotted something odd sticking out of from between some rocks along the shore. After staring at it for a few moments, he walked over to find his father's belongings buried in a haphazardly constructed outcropping of rocks. Jonathan retrieved all of his father's belongings, but most importantly, he had found his father's diary.

Jonathan met Kilchis again, and they made camp that night, with Kilchis setting up as Jonathan began poring over the notes in the diary, hoping to uncover his father's fate. Page after page gave detailed descriptions of his father's interactions with the Wandersnatch, with numerous observations about their customs and rituals, or confrontations with wildlife. It was all fascinating, but nothing gave Jonathan any insight about what had happened to the man.

Finally, just before the end, he found something interesting. He found a series of ruminations about what his father was leaving behind to go chasing after the Wandersnatch's feared and elusive God. It all came out of nowhere, with no build-up in the rest of the diary, making it all the weirder.

Could that be what happened to his dad? He went off chasing after this strange God that this tribe was worshipping? It was something he had to figure out.

That evening, Kilchis brought him to the nearest village, where he was able to procure a small canoe for a pocket knife and a bottle cap. The next day, Jonathan returned to the very spot where he had found his father's journal, by the rocky cove, determined to figure out what happened to him. He launched the small canoe into the water and headed out into the cove, where a map his father had sketched in his diary indicated the giant creature the Wandersnatch worshipped may reside.

It took a few minutes of rowing to reach a point in the middle of the lake where he was able to look out on the entire area around him. At the point of the breakers, where he was floating on the water, where the inlet turned over to the ocean. With the woods behind him and a large rocky outcropping to his left, atop the cliffs coming partway into the sea, Jonathan looked out over the water.

It was quiet. There were no bird calls, no rustling nature, only the gentle lapping of water against the outer skin of the canoe.

The serene environment would have been hypnotizing and captivating, if it weren't for the fact that his missing father was out there somewhere. Jonathan couldn't enjoy the moment; he had to concentrate and focus on finding his father.

Beneath him, gliding silently, unseen, and unnoticed, a shadow circled under the boat, curious about the strange, new intruder in its domain.

Jonathan canoed closer to the rocky outcropping jutting out into the cove. After a few paddle strokes, however, a splash of water erupted behind him, spraying his head and back with salty seawater. Jonathan immediately looked back over his shoulder, only to spot foamy water that signaled something had just submerged.

He waited for a few seconds, to see if whatever had made that splash was still around, before continuing on with his investigation of the large outcroppings to which he was previously headed. That's when he first witnessed the Wandersnatch tribe along the shore, looking out to sea at him, several tribe members expressing a look of concern.

As he decided to head back to the shore and meet with them, Jonathan was surprised to see that several of the Wandersnatch tribe members getting in their own crafts and paddling out to meet him. The rest of the tribe, including the elders, headed back into the woods, following a small trail hidden away on the side of the mountain.

Unsure of what was happening, Jonathan tried to make peaceful gestures at the approaching Wandersnatch, but they seemed indifferent as they pulled up alongside his canoe. The men grabbed him, pulling him into one of their own canoes with little difficulty, then holding him at spearpoint. They remained where they were, however, looking up at the outcropping on the side of the cliff, waiting almost ceremoniously.

Jonathan looked up at the spot on the side of the outcropping that of the tribe members were eyeing. The elder from earlier, and with several other highly adorned tribe members appeared on the side of the mountain, at a structure Jonathan had just now noticed, a structure that looked a lot like a ceremonial altar.

The Chief, carrying what appeared to be a ceremonial staff, approached the edge of the outcropping, before motioning with the staff as he looked down at Jonathan, still being held by the tribesmen. In a language he couldn't understand, the Chief began to speak rapidly but with purpose, as if praying or chanting. The tribesmen holding Jonathan hostage began to get anxious, as if they were anticipating something special.

The Chief concluded his speech by chanting 'Wandersnatch! Wandersnatch! Wandersnatch!' They crowd joined him. The entire experience was immensely confusing and momentarily made Jonathan forget he was being threatened, as he wondered why they chanted their name.

Before he could consider further, he was grabbed around the waist and lifted to his feet, before being presented to the back of the canoe, whose front end was facing out towards the ocean. The ocean's surface, normally calm and tranquil, started to bubble and foam. It was as if something large was stirring underneath its surface.

Fearing for his life, Jonathan looked around at the tribesmen holding him, still wondering if the Wandersnatch was really the name of the tribe, or something else. He received his answer when the source of the disturbance on the water revealed itself before him. It truly was a monstrous sea creature!

Jonathan couldn't believe what was looking down at him!

It was large, and that was just what he could see, as more of it lurked below the surface. It was dark in color, a blueish-brown nightmare that glared down at Jonathan, towering over his six-foot-tall frame. It appeared slick, streamlined, and built for speed, yet it looked like it incredibly powerful. With a large, horse-like face that featured a mouth filled with vicious teeth, a sleek flap on the top of its head, and a growth of barnacles starting along the side of its face and trailing down his back, it left quite the hellish impression on his senses.

The fact that Jonathan couldn't see the body or get a full-size look at the strange creature made it all the more frightening.

Again, over his shoulder from behind him, Jonathan heard the Chief once again begin chanting the name "Wandersnatch", as the creature slowly started floating over towards Jonathan's canoe. The name of the tribe wasn't Wandersnatch. It was the creature!

With a bellowing roar, the Wandersnatch lunged forward, using its large neck to reach down into the canoe. Jonathan frantically tried to escape, as breaking into a fit of violent jerking and hoping he could get free of the grip of the tribesmen holding him. Even though they had been expecting some struggle, the force that Jonathan unleashed took his captors by surprise. They tripped over each other trying to subdue him and everyone, Jonathan included, fell over the side of the boat, splashing into the water as the rest of the tribe watched with surprise that quickly evolved into frantic panic as the sea monster had not secured its prey.

The Wandersnatch was furious, and it took out its anger on the tribesmen still in their canoes. It flailed about so wildly that before long, everyone got dumped into the water. With so many options, the enormous creature stuck its neck down into the water at random, plucking someone up into its jaws before disappearing back down beneath the water, its screaming prey darkening its submersion point with as it descended.

When Jonathan finally surfaced, he quickly looked around and tried to determine his next course of action. There was panic throughout the entire tribe, both those watching from the outcrop above them as well as the others floating in the water with him. The Chief and the rest of the elders on the cliff were frantically yelling and trying to get down to the water. Meanwhile, the tribesmen on the water were desperately trying to pull themselves and their friends and family out of the water, away from the Wandersnatch, who could resurface at any moment.

Jonathan knew this was his one chance to get away, right now, with everyone distracted.

Jonathan dove back underwater, and once fully submerged, he paddled as fast as he could back to shore.

After a few strokes, however, he felt a hand grab his boot and try to pull back. One of the tribe members who had been holding him hostage had caught up to Jonathan and grabbed him, apparently still trying to hold him for the Wandersnatch. Yelling in his native language to the one of the canoes with people inside, the tribe member kept a bear-like hold on Jonathan's foot, to prevent him from fleeing, yet with both men floating in the middle of the deep water, he didn't have enough strength or leverage to pull him.

They struggled fruitlessly as a surge of water nearby indicated that the Wandersnatch was now returning to the surface, likely to continue feasting on victims. It burst forth from the water with a vengeful cry, before charging down at where Jonathan was struggling to free himself. It struck the water fiercely, only to attack the tribe member who had still been trying to hold him captive, whom it then began to consume whole. A terrifying series of crunches and screams were emitted as the body was quickly devoured.

Once it had swallowed, it returned its attention back to Jonathan, who had begun to frantically swim away. The Wandersnatch's massive body charged through the water, send a large wake crashing into the tribesmen who were still trying to climb aboard their canoes. The creature made a beeline straight for Jonathan.

Even though he was swimming and kicking as fast as he could, his efforts proved futile, as the massive Wandersnatch covered that same distant in an instant, before grabbing Jonathan out of the water, then bringing him back down beneath it, in a haze of foam and blood.

If there were any silver lining to Jonathan's fate, it would be that he was not the last victim of the Wandersnatch. The creature went on a rampage, attacking the tribesmen both in the canoes and those still in the water, devouring them all in turn or in small masses, soon leaving the Chief and tribe elders as the sole survivors of their tribe. They fell to their knees and began to weep. Their God, the creature they had prayed to for centuries, to whom they had fed all of their enemies, had just wiped out most of its worshippers. The Chief was shocked, crestfallen, in utter disbelief.

After that day, what remained of the tribe, the few elders and the woman and children who had stayed home, all abandoned the cove, eventually settling in a new spot further up the coast, away from the vicious sea creature that had just, in one unsanctimonious act, massacred and betrayed them.

Kilchis left when Jonathan did not return, and to this day, no one knows what happened to that tribe, nor even their true name and identity. They remain a mystery and perhaps always will, just like the legend of the Wandersnatch itself, who had supposedly survived undiscovered and unknown possibly since the time of the dinosaurs, just like the mystery surrounding the death of Neil Obrero and his son, Jonathan.

Dillena's Dragon

By: Matthew Chabin

Rhain was strong, and no fool about it. When the boy who tended the flock reported that the *Llamhygin Y Dwr* had taken another sheep, he took some wool for barter and went to see Mermin, the old trader who lived at the edge of town, and who was known to sometimes keep weapons in discreet areas of his shop. Sometimes they were killing instruments salvaged from battlefields and sometimes they were crude things he forged himself. Rhain came back with a good ash spear, steel-tipped and well balanced. I watched him go up on the hill behind our house and practice with it, his thrusts angled up, as if he were bailing hay. Already, I could see what he had in mind.

When he came back down, he went to the shed, put on rawhide gloves, and rubbed the spear-shaft with pitch. "It's called a Water Leaper," he said, grinning. "Let it leap onto this!" He went back up and trained until supper.

Father, lame since the war, kept house as our mother would have, had she survived the fever that carried her off along with forty other souls that same disastrous year. "You plan to fight it alone?" he asked as we sat around the hearth.

"How else?" asked Rhain. "Dillena is a girl; she can be no help. And the boy is even weaker than she is. You want us ask our neighbors to help fight for *our* sheep?"

Father nodded in that way of his that did not always signal agreement. "Strength alone rarely determines an outcome," he said. We knew by the way he puffed his pipe and leaned back, eyes to the rafters, that he was in a story-telling frame of mind. He'd been a soldier and a poet before he was a sheep farmer, and he knew all our local tales, as well as many from the faraway places he'd been.

"When Beulf, the Geat, fought that killer of men called Grindle, he went bare-handed and alone. Why?"

We knew the Beulf stories well. Father had learned them as a prisoner of Saxon pirates on the isle of Alderney, and they were great favorites of his on dark winter nights.

"He wanted honor for his king," said Rhain. "In any case, he wagered his strength was equal to the task."

"Correct," said Father. "But when that same hero went to fight the dragon, he went in armor, and brought his sword and friends to help him. Why?"

I knew the question was for my brother, so I kept silent. He was a bit slower in answering.

"The dragon was a stronger enemy. He wanted to win."

"And even so, he lost his life."

Rhain absorbed this, then shook his head and laughed. "The boy says the Leaper is hardly bigger than a sheep."

"And yet, it preys on sheep," said Father. "It kills things its own size, and perhaps bigger. Have you ever killed anything bigger than yourself?"

Rhain scowled and became serious again. He explained how he planned to do it. I aided his cause by saying he looked capable with the spear.

"I'll go at sunup," he said. "It's eaten recently. That may slow it down."

Again, Father nodded, though I sensed he was not at ease.

Good as his word, Rhain set out early for the bogs, where the sheep often strayed and the Leaper wallowed. When he noticed me following, he made some token attempts to send me back, but he didn't put in much effort. He planned to win. He wanted a witness.

We entered the marshes. The morning mists lay below the trees, and several times Rhain led us onto tapering fingers of ground, and we had to backtrack. We knew we had found the spot we were looking for when we saw the sheep carcass hanging in a tree. A sorry thing, just a head and a gutted hide, wedged in the fork of the tree trunk, as though it were flung there. Below it, the bushes opened up onto the bank, with the water's reaches hidden in mist. There was an old firepit, with stones imported from some rockier place, whether by a fisher, anchorite, or warlock, who could say? Rhain went to the water's edge and crouched down, spear braced at his hip, as he peered out into the mist.

He sat like that for a long while, but apparently saw nothing. He muttered a curse, stood, picked out a large rock from the firepit, then heaved it into the water. The water gulped the rock, and Rhain shouted, "Kill my sheep? Steal from us? Come fight me!" Nothing answered, but the tiny noises of the swamp, of which I had hardly been aware, all seemed to fall into a portentous silence.

"Dillena," he said. "Get back." I already was some distance behind him, and my instinct was rather to move up and see what he was looking at. I saw only an arrowing wave in the water, however, like a waterbird's wake, though it was swifter, and larger, but with no bird preceding it.

"Back, Dillena!"

He didn't get a chance to say it again. The leaper exploded out of the water with a ripping double-flap, flying right at him. In that instant it seemed to be all mouth and purple gullet: a gaping frog-like head, a pair of membranous wings, and a long tail that quivered rigidly in flight and ended in a fat barb. The boy had said nothing of that tail—perhaps he was too shocked to notice. Shocked as *I* was, I did not immediately realize its import either.

The creature hit him like a spat wad of gristle and set him staggering, as it wrapped him in its wings. The spear had missed the thing's body by inches, tearing almost uselessly through a wing instead. It croaked, a guttural, expectorating sound—*holph!-holloph*—as it heaved its mouth like an open sack at my brother's head. Its cartilaginous frame showed through the jelly-like hide as it cinched its embrace tighter. Rhain's backpedaling legs tripped over his spear shaft and he went down.

I screamed his name and started towards him, thinking to grab the spear, pull it loose, stick that awful thing with it.

"Get back, Dillena!"

His voice cracked, yet I could tell he still expected to win. He even laughed once, as he would when wrestling another boy or a stubborn ram. He kicked out, forcing the thing to roll with him, forcing space with his elbow while the other hand reached for the firepit, for a rock to bash it with.

He'd wrenched his head mostly out of its mouth, and now it gnawed at his shoulder and part of his neck. I hadn't seen any teeth, but Rhain's shirt was stained red. Its eyes—oblong black pupils in golden orbs—dilated at the taste of blood.

"Rhain…?" I paced, starting to cry.

"Back!" he panted, grinning intently. His fingers searched the stones, questing for a good grip. He almost had one.

It was then that the creature's barbed tail coiled around and dug into the space he'd opened with his arm. It wriggled and gouged, and Rhain screamed. His arm collapsed against his chest, trapping the stinger to its hateful work. It wormed and dug. Rhain shrieked and thrashed, panicky kicks that found little purchase in the wet grass, and now its mouth was back around the top of his head.

"Run! Go now!" Those were his last articulate words, and then he was vomiting white foam. I screamed. I picked up a rock and threw it. I missed. His eyes rolled, and his kicks became spastic. He looked at me, and perhaps there was an imputation there, a last command to save myself, and perhaps he was already seeing Heaven.

I ran.

***

In lieu of burial, we went into town and offered prayers at the church for Rhain's soul. When we got home, Father sent the boy to his shed so we could be alone with our loss. We also had to think of our circumstances.

"I'll work harder," I said. "I'll make up Rhain's share." I knew this sounded ridiculous, considering how hard Rhain had worked, but I felt obligated to say it and somehow make it true.

Father shook his head. The Water Leaper, he explained, would kill again. This place was no good. We would have to use our remaining sheep to buy our way onto another farm, one of the larger ones up-land. We would live then as the boy did now, working for meals and lodging. We had to make the deal quickly, before we lost any more sheep, or we'd end up begging on the road.

We then spoke about Rhain and his life, and finally, how bravely he'd died.

"It wasn't like the stories," I said, wiping away tears. "It was awful."

Of course, many of the tales told of similarly awful events. I meant, I suppose, that it was uglier than I could have imagined, lacking any note of poetic grace. I certainly didn't mean it as a rebuke to Father, but I saw in his eyes that he took it as such. He went out back then and wept, and would take no supper.

The next day I went into town, charged with negotiating our employment. Instead, I went to see Mermin. I didn't tell him what had happened to Rhain; I told him that my brother had sent me after the thing I wanted. I had seen it years previous, amongst the junk of his shop, and after inquiring about it, Mermin wasn't even sure it was still in his possession. He allowed me to search of the back room, and after some minutes, finally it appeared, though looking less impressive than I remembered.

"For bear hunting," said Mermin, fingering the hinged, steel collar with its star configuration of spikes. "That's what the fellow said anyway. A funny, tough little man from the north, and he looked just about crazy enough to fight a bear in this."

I saw that it was indeed crafted for a small man, but would still be quite bulky on me. Nonetheless, he showed me the straps that tightened the fittings. "It should fit Rhain well," he said. I promised him payment upon our next sale of wool (not knowing if there would ever be one).

I bundled the suit with its helmet and gauntlets and carried it home, where I left it at the edge of our field. I went into the house. Father was taking his afternoon nap. I lit a fire in the hearth and ate a quick meal of bread and cheese. Then I scooped some coals into a ram's horn, took two short logs and some sticks of kindling, and slipped out just as Father was beginning to stir and mutter in his cot. Outside, I tied the wood to the bundled suit, and with the smoldering horn, went into the woods and down the hill to the edge of the marsh.

I stopped in the shade of a wych elm and donned the armor, cinching the straps as tight as I could without cutting off the blood. The iron plates had been wrapped with leather in such a way that the spikes poked through the seams in bristling rows. It was heavy, and the helmet—designed to cover the whole head with narrow slits for eyes and mouth—allowed me to see only what was right in front of me. I moved like a clumsy child in that thing, but I wasn't planning on being fast or strong. Only clever.

I added some sticks to the horn and blew through a hole in the side until the coals were glowing hot. I made for the pond. The sun was below the treetops when I arrived at the bank. Rhain's body—his torso anyway—was tangled in the tree beside the tatters of the sheep, dark against the falling light. Flies covered him in a moving shroud, and his hair hung down, sparing me a look at his eyes. Anger put my fear to route. I wanted my brother back. Barring that, I wanted to take the life of filthy thing that killed him.

I crouched by the ring of stones and set about making a fire, keeping an eye on the water as I worked. Soon I noticed a vague, drifting shape about a stone's throw from the bank. It might have been mistaken for a cast-off garment or lichen-draped branch, but for the arrowing wake and the zigzag route it cut.

"See you," I whispered, and stoked the fire.

It wasn't coming in fast like before. Maybe it smelled the fire, or maybe it wondered at the small, spiny creature tending it. I knew this was probably my last chance to run. The flames were crackling. I stood up and spat in its direction. Instantly, it changed its course. It was coming!

This time I had a better view of its leap—how it slapped the water with its wings to gain lift, and the second, cracking beat that launched its arc. I set my knee to the ground and grabbed my helmet, arms covering my face, as I braced for impact. Even so, it knocked me flat.

Stunned, blind, leveled, I struggled in its cold, sticky embrace. A smell like rotten fish overwhelmed me, and I gagged. *Holph!*_that phlegmy, murderous croak; I screamed in answer, and everything went dark.

Through the gap between my arms, I saw only a glistening pocket of receding, fleshy spandrels, dark at its core but letting the late-day light through the stretched, purple membranes. It had fit its big, loose-jawed mouth over my head, just as it had done with Rhain, and I was looking down the damnable thing's throat. Meanwhile, I could feel something like a stout child's fist punching randomly at my armored legs, hips, and ribs. It was trying to sting me and eat me at the same time.

I planted my feet and pitched back with all my strength. Hard rocks and hot coals received my weight, and suddenly there was light. *Holough! Holough!* it barked, and the pain in its cry was sweet to me. I arched my back and rolled my shoulders in the smoking bed, protected from the heat by the armor and the embrace of the creature's wings. I rolled and twisted, feeling the spikes grit against the rocks through its flesh. Its grip on me loosened. I levered my arms out and sucked a great breath of air, realizing too late my mistake (hadn't I seen Rhain do the same thing?), when the flickering shadow crossed my face.

The stinger point grazed my cheek and lodged in my armor just under my chin. Invisible fire blossomed in its track. I howled. Blistering pain wrapped my head and raced down my neck. The barb wriggled and began working its way into the gap between the plates. I could feel the pressure of its wicked point through the leather. I knew if it penetrated, I was finished. I wrenched my head so that the helmet came half off my face and clamped the gristly, worming organ in my teeth, just above the barb. I tucked my head, trapping the stinger at a blunt angle against my chest, barely registering the awful taste against the pain that raged in my face.

The Leaper emitted wheezy honks as it mouthed my head and shoulders. Our struggles had rolled us out of the firepit, but I kicked hard and rolled us back in. Rotten *cooking* fish, the smoke of the stifled coals, and the smell of my own burning hair packed my airways as its foul blood filled my mouth. I coughed and gagged, but managed to keep my teeth clamped as the stinger flexed dangerously close to my neck.

Suddenly, the leaper released its hold. It bucked and scrambled under me, trying to get away. I rolled it clear and released its tail. The stinger slapped at me, but there was no compression in the strike, and it went wide. It hissed and wheezed as it paddled the grass with its punctured wings, turning away from me and going for the water. I crawled after it. The left side of my face was a hardening mask of torment; the eye squeezed shut, the tightness was working its way into my throat. Hard to breathe. Hard to say, just then, who had killed whom. Then my hand found a rock.

It hissed in fear as I stood up, looming over the thing, and the sight of it filled me with a queasy mix of fear, pity, and exultation. I saw it was no devil, no shadowwalker, not a thing of evil, but a creature that wanted to live, just like me. I fell on it with the rock. I beat the broad, flat head until something wetly broke inside, and it oozed thin, fish-like blood and lay still. I crawled down to the bank then, just as it had tried to do, where I vomited in the reeds and scooped mud onto my burning face.

It was dark by the time I found the strength to climb the tree and pull Rhain's body down. Working half-blind, I buckled what was left of him inside the suit of armor and dragged it by the straps like a sled. It was hard labor getting it out of the marshes, where the spikes snagged the grass, and even more work getting it up the hill to the edge of our field. Father was sitting out on the step and stood as I stumbled out of the trees. He'd later tell me he thought I'd died and returned to him a revenant. All the same, he hobbled to me as fast as he could and caught me in his arms.

The next day, he took the boy and went to bury Rhain in the town's churchyard. I was in no condition to go with them. The swelling was down, but my right eye was blind and runny, half my hair was burned off, and I could barely move from all the aches and stiffness. Several times I staggered out to wash myself in the tub behind the shed. I kept smelling the thing on my skin—its blood and venom. For a long time after that, I'd dream of Rhain screaming through the fog and that awful sound—*holph-hollolph!*

That night, Father applied a salve to my face. We watched the fire, he smoked his pipe, and we talked. "The stories tell of great heroes," he said. "When common folk get mixed up in such matters, they're likely to be killed or badly hurt."

I reminded him of his fighting years.

"I gave it up," he said. "Life is too precious."

"Was it wrong, then, what I did?"

"No," he admitted. "You've won a victory and likely saved us from penury." He asked, then, if I wanted anything.

I almost laughed. I was sixteen years old, a poor, disfigured country girl with the keep of eighteen sheep. My work would be twice as hard and my marriage prospects half as good, and I would never again be able to go near standing water without breaking into gooseflesh and a chill sweat. My good eye was weeping now, too. I wanted my brother back and nothing else.

"Tell me a story," I said, as the fire crackled, the pain throbbed, and the rain began to fall on the roof. "Tell me something fine."

Cotton Eyed Joe

By: Kasey Hill

"There's no such thing as a catfish as big as a pontoon boat!" Nick exclaimed as he lifted a beer to his lips and took a swig.

"I'm telling you! It was as big as a pontoon boat!" DJ exclaimed with arms extended, holding a beet and wide eyes. "It jerked my pole out of my hands, and I nearly fell in. Lost my damn lantern at the same time, and as it slipped through the water, I saw its face! Had I been in a kayak, it would have knocked me out of it when it hit the bass boat!"

"Bullshit!" Nick rebutted. "You were drunk as a skunk and seeing shit!"

"Naw, man," Alvin butted in as he hit the joint they were passing around. "Y'all heard about that catfish they found over at Smith Mountain Lake Dam, right? Big as a Volkswagen. Ate two of the welders in the water."

"Y'all need to stop drinking the water 'round here," Nick laughed, taking another swig of beer. "They're slipping crack into it now, and you two dumbasses are proof."

"Motherfucker, I ain't no damn crackhead," DJ laughed as he hit the joint passed to him. "Pops told us the stories about Smith Mountain Lake and how it used to be a town and how it's so deep all the fish do is eat and eat and grow that big. They're at Smith Mountain Lake and Philpot. Swear to God I saw one!"

"Whatever, man," Nick replied, hitting the joint after DJ passed it to him. "I'll believe it when I see it." He paused and looked at the joint. "What is this?"

"That, my friend, is genuine, homegrown, kick your dick in the dirt Holy Ghost," DJ rambled off, grinning ear to ear.

"Why's it called Holy Ghost?" Alvin asked, poking at the fire with a stick.

"What planet are you guys from?" DJ muttered. "Ole Miss Emma Lynn grows it. You think you're going to see Jesus after smoking it."

"Great. Just what we need," Nick began. "More hallucinations."

"Eat me!" DJ spat with a chuckle.

I remained silent as the fire crackled, a piece of wood split, releasing moisture from its core. The four of us were camping out at Philpot Lake's Salthouse Branch Campground, enjoying a weekend of fishing, swimming, and just hanging out. It had been a hot minute since we all had been able to hang out together due to work schedules and the inability to get a babysitter, but the time finally arrived where we all synced up, and we booked the first available spot to tent camp. Philpot Lake was just as popular as Smith Mountain Lake, except quieter and more peaceful.

Of course, we all had heard the tales from Pops growing up. That man spent every chance he could fishing on Smith Mountain Lake in his pontoon boat. DJ was always with him, but I wasn't allowed to go but a few times. Pops didn't like to take me because one, I was a girl. He didn't like having to control his language all the time because of "women being present." The other reason was that I was an impatient fisherman, and he hated having to recast my pole all the time. But those few times I went with him, he told the stories, and we all listened intently. According to the state, it was just a tall tale what had happened to the town before Smith Mountain Lake was created, but the old timers that lived around here, long since dead, corrected their "facts." According to them, the state bought out a bunch of people's land and houses, businesses, everything. Once everyone was relocated, they began the long and arduous process of making the man-made lake into the prestigious landmark it is now. Pops said they didn't even bother demolishing anything and just pumped the water through the entire building, trees, power poles, houses, and all were flooded out, so there's an entire town preserved beneath the placid waters.

While we sat and fished, he told us about the fish and what he had witnessed himself. Huge bass and huge catfish lurked deep beneath the surface of the lakes. Old fish that had escaped capture during all the fishing and tournaments hosted throughout the years. He said you had to be careful swimming out in the deep waters where boats zipped, not only because you could be hit by a boat not seeing you in the water, but because those fish would eat you whole. Again, the fish in Smith Mountain Lake and Philpot being the size of cars were also chalked up as tall tales. But every time I was out on those waters, I could only feel the impending doom of the urban legend silently waiting in the depths for someone to fall in for a meal.

The Roanoke River Basin was the origin for both Smith Mountain Lake and Philpot Lake, which was also a constructed lake to help ease the floods that tore through the area every year. Philpot Dam and Smith Mountain Dam were both erected to control the flow of the waters, and just as Smith Mountain Lake slowly swept away Virginia history, Philpot did as well. The water system was interchangeable, not by a single river, but by the basin itself. Many Native American archeological sites were eaten up by the expanding Philpot waters, leaving just one site still accessible, just below the dam. Smith Mountain Lake covered approximately thirty-five sites along the Roanoke and Blackwater rivers. We lost a lot of history with those lakes just so we could control waterways for hydroelectric dams. It was quite possible that the way that lost history fought back was by growing unimaginable dangers in the water as revenge.

"I believe you," I said as I took the joint from Nick and hit it a few times before passing it on. "I mean, it's Native American land we drowned creating the lakes. Philpot also had some graveyards. Those waters are haunted by who knows what, and those haints could very well feed them damn fish."

"You don't count," Nick laughed, tipping his beer at me. "You're certified crazy, so we all know everything you say is crackpot talk."

I flipped him the middle finger while Alvin and DJ laughed. "Yuck it up," I muttered, taking a drink from my own beer can. "You won't be laughing when you're being dragged to the bottom of the lake and declared a 'tragic drowning victim' in the paper when it was those monsters in the water that got ya."

"I will take you up on the bet," Nick replied, rising to his feet. "DJ, drop the boat in the water. Let's go do some night swimming."

I rolled my eyes. "I don't swim, and you know it."

"You mean you can't swim?" Alvin shot back with a chuckle.

"Same damn thing. I don't do boats, either," I growled.

"Pussy," Nick spat.

"Ain't anything to do with being a pussy. If you can't swim, naturally, you don't want to get on a boat to drown," I sassed back. "I ain't stupid. Mama didn't raise no fool."

"There's life jackets," DJ offered, holding up a vest for me. "Besides, if the fish do try to eat ya, they'll just spit you back out. You're too sour for them, you sourpuss."

"Fine," I muttered, snatching the vest from his outstretched hand. "Do you even remember where you were when you saw the damn thing?"

"Yeah, I had it on my GPS radar," DJ replied, fishing it out of his pocket. "I saved the coordinates."

"Well then, let's go," I huffed, jumping up from my seat and putting the life jacket on. "You morons need to put one on, too. Can't have you drowning because you're too high and drunk to swim."

"I ain't any of those things," DJ refuted, crossing his arms. "I don't need one."

"Well, when the game warden pulls up and you ain't got one on, that's your ticket," I spat, grabbing a life jacket and tossing it at Alvin. "Put yours on."

"Yes, ma'am," Alvin mocked, donning his life jacket.

Alvin and I waited on the dock while DJ and Nick dropped the boat back in the water. After DJ parked his truck, we all climbed into the boat, and DJ maneuvered it away from the dock and out into the open water before opening the boat up to full speed.

"Would you slow down?!" I shouted over the roar of the boat engine. "You're going to get a ticket!"

"You're just scared you're going to fall in!" DJ laughed back, opening the throttle more.

We hit some turbulent water from another passing boat, and it nearly tossed me into the water. DJ looked back at me with an "oh shit" look and throttled the motor down as I glared at him. We were moving across the lake for about thirty minutes before DJ throttled the motor to a crawl and shut the engine off, tossing an anchor into the water.

"This is the spot," he called out, looking over the side of the boat.

We all looked quietly, half-nervous and half-excited from the thrill. Nick picked up a flashlight and shone it into the water, but you couldn't really see anything through the murky green that surrounded the boat. We all grabbed a flashlight and stood at different parts of the boat, looking in, coming up with nothing. For a brief moment, I saw a shadow pass under my light, but it was quick, and I passed it off as a school of fish drawn to the light like moths. Many people don't know that fish like the light as well and will follow it. Seasoned fishermen will use it as a tactic to draw them up to the surface, making them think it's daylight outside. The shadow reappeared and lingered for a moment before disappearing again like before.

"There's something over here," I whispered so I wouldn't spook it. Yes, fish can hear through vibrations of the water, which was another reason Pops stopped taking me fishing. I wouldn't shut up. I used to think it was because he just didn't want to listen to me. It's most likely still partly true, but I also learned that they have a line running along their sides that picks up vibrations in the water, allowing them to hear.

Everyone walked carefully over to my side of the boat so as not to cause much turbulence with the water bouncing around on it. The boat leaned slightly from the weight, and my anxiety crept up, fearing I would topple in. We all silently watched the water, waiting for the shadow to reappear.

"You sure you saw something?" Nick asked, watching the water for any signs of movement.

"Yes, I saw it twice," I hissed, annoyed he didn't believe me.

Briefly, the shadow appeared and once more disappeared just as quickly. "See," I gloated. "A shadow."

"That could be anything," Nick snorted. "Probably a school of fish."

Just as the words left his mouth, something knocked against the bottom of the boat hard. DJ, Nick, and Alvin pitched over the side while I barely kept my footing and thumped backward onto the boat floor. I scrambled up to look over the side of the boat, holding my breath and waiting for them to resurface. There was no way I could save them from drowning since I couldn't swim. I grabbed the buoy with a rope, tossed it over into the water, and waited for them to resurface. Alvin was the first to pop up, and I breathed out in relief. I scanned the water for Nick and DJ, but they still hadn't emerged on either side of the boat.

"Do you see them?!" I asked, panicked.

Alvin dove back under the water for a moment and popped back up, wiping the water from his eyes. "No, I can't see shit in here."

A loud, thrashing sound cut through the silence of the water, and both Alvin and I jerked our heads in the direction from which we heard it. I shone my flashlight, and about fifty yards out, Nick had emerged to the surface. Another thrashing sound quickly followed by a short, "Help!" had me jerking my flashlight behind the boat. About one hundred yards back, DJ was struggling to stay above the water. Alvin started swimming his way as I fished the buoy from the water to toss it his way. There was no way Alvin could drag him back to the boat without help.

"Is he okay?" Nick called out as he paddled as fast as he could to the boat, arm over arm in the water.

"I don't know!" I answered, keeping my flashlight trained on Alvin and DJ. Alvin had almost made it over to him. "Alvin is almost to him."

I flung the buoy as far as I could, and it landed about twenty yards from DJ. Alvin had finally reached him and was struggling to drag him back to the boat. DJ grabbed the buoy, and I quickly pulled the rope to bring him in while Alvin swam beside him. "I've got him," I called out to Nick. I was met with silence. "Nick?" I asked, looking over my shoulder as I continued pulling the rope in. He wasn't anywhere to be seen. "Nick!" I screamed.

Nick thrashed to the surface of the water, sputtering and gasping. "Get out of the water!" he bellowed before being sucked back under again.

"Alvin!" I screamed as I pulled as quickly as I could on the rope to draw DJ in. "Swim faster!"

Nick popped back up to the surface again, kicking and sputtering, and began swimming as fast as he could. Alvin picked up his speed, and DJ helped me drag him in, kicking his feet as fast as he could. DJ disappeared beneath the water and came back up coughing.

"Get me in the fucking boat now!" he ordered, pushing as hard as he could with his feet and kicking at something.

Alvin made it to the boat first and dragged his body over the side, thudding in the bottom. He quickly jumped up and took over, pulling the rope in. I turned around to watch Nick as he swam with every ounce of energy he had left in his body. Once more, he disappeared beneath the water.

"Nick!" I screamed, running to the front of the boat and shining my light around in the water. Just barely, I could make out his body. I fell back in sheer terror as my light hit the shadow he fought with. It was massive, just like DJ had claimed.

"Babe! I need help!" Alvin shouted as he struggled to haul the rope in.

I ran over to him and shone the light in the water, hearing DJ thrashing and cussing. His foot was caught by something, and it kept dragging him under. The only thing keeping him coming back to the surface was Alvin's hold on the rope. I dropped the flashlight and grabbed the rope behind Alvin and pulled with all my might. Inch by inch, we slowly dragged DJ over to us.

"Don't let me go!" he pleaded as he kicked.

"Help me!" Nick shouted from the other side of the boat.

He had finally made it to the boat and was holding onto the bow while something tried eagerly to drag him down. Tears brimmed behind my eyes as I struggled to keep a hold on the rope.

"What do we do?" I whispered to Alvin. "We can't save them both. If I let go, DJ is dragged under. Nick can't hold on much longer."

"Tie the rope off on the side of the boat and go help Nick!" Alvin ordered, straining against the pull of the rope.

I did as told and wrapped the rope tightly around the horn cleat on the side of the boat and ran over to the bow of the boat. Nick struggled to keep his grip on the boat while trying to kick off whatever had hold of his other leg. I pulled on his body, but whatever had his leg had a good grip, and I couldn't pull him up from the water. The boat began to turn and be dragged as whatever had a hold of DJ moved through the water. Nick's body began to drift in the other direction as whatever had a hold of him went the opposite way. He howled in pain as his muscles tensed.

"The rope is starting to break!" Alvin shouted, his feet up against the back of the boat and holding tight to the rope.

Before we could do anything else, I heard a howling scream as Nick's leg was ripped from his body. Blood coated the water, but he was finally free to drag himself into the boat. I hauled him in with all my might, and he thudded to the bottom of the boat. I quickly sprang into action and snatched his belt from his pants and fastened it as tight as it could go around his leg, just above his knee, to staunch the bleeding. I quickly jumped up and ran to the end of the boat. DJ was just within arm's reach of me. I held my hand out, trying desperately to grab his hand. We made contact several times, but the slick water caused me to lose grip.

"Don't let me die!" he cried, kicking and flailing.

For just a moment, the beast in the water let his leg go, and the tension went slack. He kicked hard, closing the distance between him and the boat, and just as he was about to grab my outstretched hand, the creature in the water jumped from the water, and I fell back in terror. As it came back down into the water, the monstrous catfish opened its mouth and sucked DJ in as it went back under, snapping the rope Alvin held onto. The boat tipped from the force and was nearly at a 45-degree angle, and just as I was about to topple into the water, Alvin snagged my life jacket and yanked me down to the bottom of the boat. The boat thudded back down onto the surface of the water with a loud splash, and silence filled the air.

"DJ?" I whispered in sobs.

"We need to get back to land," Alvin urged, taking control of the situation.

He jumped up and ran to the captain's chair and tried to turn the motor over. The engine sputtered and died.

"Fuck!" he seethed. "The engine must be flooded."

"The CB radio!" I garbled. "Call the game warden!"

Alvin picked up the headset and pressed the button. "Mayday, mayday. We have a man with serious and critical injuries that needs to be taken to a hospital immediately."

"Game warden. What's your location?" the voice answered.

"We are just outside of Deer Island. Please, be quick. He's losing a lot of blood."

I looked over at Nick, who was pale and breathing shallow as blood pooled around him in the boat. I ran over to him and refastened the belt again, tighter to get it under control.

"DJ?" he gasped and looked up at me.

I swallowed the lump in my throat and shook my head. "I couldn't save him," I choked out.

It didn't take long for the game warden to show up, and within minutes, Nick was being airlifted out by Lifeguard-10 while Alvin and I stood on the banks of Philpot Lake explaining to the game warden what had happened.

"A catfish?" he asked, pen paused, staring at us. "The size of a pontoon boat?"

"Yes!" I hissed.

He snorted as he wrote down what we told him.

"It's not a joke!" Alvin growled.

"You know it's dangerous to drink, smoke, and boat, right?" the game warden asked, cocking an eyebrow.

"I am telling you!" I shouted way too loudly. "It was a fucking catfish!"

"What's going on?" another game warden asked, walking up to see if his partner needed help.

"These two claim a catfish ripped the one boy's leg off and ate the other boy who was with them," the game warden chuckled. "Can you believe it?"

"And you saw it?" the other game warden asked, intrigued. "You saw Cotton Eyed Joe?"

"You have a name for it?!" I hissed.

"My pa told me there was a catfish that's been in this lake for a long time, just getting bigger and bigger. Size of a pontoon boat now. They named him Cotton Eyed Joe because you don't know where he came from or where he goes," he answered.

"Horseshit," the first game warden spat. "Quit going on with your tall tales from your damn Pa."

"It's not horseshit!" he refuted. "My pa saw it!"

The game warden who took our statement huffed and walked away. The one left behind turned toward us with apologetic eyes. "Sorry about that. He's an old coot. Tomorrow, we will drag the lake for the other boy who was on the boat."

"You won't find him," I sniffled, rubbing my arms in the cool night's breeze.

"Maybe, maybe not. Pa said they usually get spit out, and those bodies are just counted off as drowning victims. No one knows any better as to how they really died because there aren't any others around to attest to it being Cotton Eyed Joe."

"Well, your pa was wrong on some information," I mumbled, staring off into the placid waters that swallowed my nephew whole.

"Oh yeah?" he asked, looking out alongside me.

"Yeah," Alvin answered, grabbing me by my shoulders and tugging me into his chest. "Cotton Eyed Joe is out there, but he ain't alone."

"Not alone?" the game warden asked, confused.

"No. There's two of them now."

Broken Bridge

By: DJ Tyrer

George blessed the storm. For most folk in Cumbria, it was a disaster, but for him and Bill it was a source of riches. The two of them sat in the cab of the rented van, wrapped up against the winter chill. Rain lashed against the windscreen, making visibility poor in the early-morning light.

The white van ploughed a furrow through the flooded lane, sending waves sloshing over the hedgerows before the waters crashed back down behind them, and rippled back into stillness. Overhead, the sky was a slate grey. Dark clouds glowered on the horizon, threatening worse. Most people were hoping they held snow that would fall upon the higher ground instead, and offer the sodden county some respite, but Bill and George were hoping otherwise. The longer the rains fell, the more villages they could loot.

"Remember," said George, glancing at Bill, "just take small things – jewellery, electronic gadgets, that sort of thing. Stuff you can hide in your clothes. If someone spots you hauling a widescreen TV down the street, they'll know you're up to something."

"I ain't stupid," Bill replied. George didn't bother to correct him.

They were almost at their destination. The village had been evacuated after the bridge connecting its two halves had collapsed into the white, frothing torrent that had replaced its usually docile river.

"You sure it's safe?" Bill asked, clutching the dashboard, as the van splashed down towards the cluster of houses, the water rising up its doors and dribbling in about their feet.

"'Course it is." George slowed to a crawl, no longer able to discern what hazards the water might conceal.

"That's odd," Bill said, after a moment, pointing.

"What is?"

"The bridge."

"What about it?" George was more concerned with keeping the van on the road.

"Look at it. It looks as if it exploded. There are chunks of it all over the show."

"That's the force of the water for you," George replied as he parked the van in a shallower area of water. "Right, let's get out there and fill up. Come on."

"Gah, it's freezing," Bill exclaimed as he climbed down into the water.

"Keep your mind on the prize."

"Will do."

They had to clamber over the sandbags that were piled up in the doorways of houses. While originally intended to keep the homes dry, the sandbags had been overwhelmed by the rising waters and now served to dam the waters in. As they splashed their way inside, they saw various knickknacks and household items, things that made a house a home, floating by on the pooled waters. Even heavy pieces of furniture – tables and fallen shelving units – floated about like so much driftwood. There was a sink of sewage in the air.

They climbed the stairs. The homeowners had carried up as much as they could of value, conveniently laying the goods out for them to pick over. Once finished with these items, they proceeded to grub through the bedroom drawers, and anything of worth was slipped into the many voluminous pockets of the coats they wore.

"Good haul," George commented with a grin as they headed back down the stairs.

Suddenly, he paused and put a hand on Bill's shoulder. "What was that?"

"What was what?"

"I thought I heard..."

"I didn't hear anything."

They were silent a moment. It was unlikely any rescue workers would be about, but it paid to be careful.

"Nah, it was probably nothing," decided George, and they continued on their way.

After a few houses, having picked them all clean of trinkets of any value, the two men trudged back to the van and divested themselves of everything they had stuffed into their pockets. In the back of the van were a number of plastic bins, which allowed them to sort the items by type. Once unloaded, they waded off down the street to the next set of houses.

"Hey, this one looks as if something crashed into it," Bill said, gesturing towards one building that had been halved in size.

"Probably the water caused it to collapse," said George as they went inside and began to look about the ruins. He sighed, annoyed. "I don't think we're going to find anything here. It's too much of a wreck. Let's move on to the next one."

They climbed back down the piled rubble and began to once again splash their way along the street.

Suddenly, they were bowled over as the building just ahead of them exploded, as if it had been struck by an artillery shell. It happened so fast, they couldn't even register whether it was the blast, or the wave that had caught them. They plunged beneath the filthy, frigid waters, then, quickly broke the surface again, spluttering in terror and confusion.

"Help!" shrieked Bill. "I can't swim!"

"Shut it, you muppet. It's not that deep: you can stand." George helped him to his feet, then looked about and said, "What the hell just happened?"

Bill just shook his head.

"Houses collapse inwards," said George. "They don't explode outwards."

"Didn't the news say something about the risk of a gas explosion?"

"They've turned it off. I doubt it's that."

"Then, what was it?"

They were interrupted by the splash of an oar and a demanding voice. "What are you doing here? Don't you know it's dangerous?" A man in a kayak was paddling towards them along the flooded street.

"Just checking on our house," George lied, easily.

"You're not from around here," the man countered. He was probably a local, and he likely knew all his neighbours by sight.

"I meant our aunt's place. She got out ahead of the flood, so we thought we'd best check how it was."

"Really?" The man was silent for a moment, then said, "Still, whatever you're doing here, it's dangerous. Especially if you're motives aren't entirely pure."

George ignored that last jibe and said, "Sure, I can see that. That house just collapsed."

The kayaker laughed. "Collapsed… Yeah."

Soaked through and feeling frozen, George found the man's tone irksome. "What's that supposed to mean?"

"Nothing. Just that it's dangerous here."

"No, come on, what do you mean?"

"Just that you really ought to get out of here, assuming you want to live."

Although Bill shifted nervously, sending ripples out across the waist-deep water, George snorted and said, "Really? Is that meant to be a threat, or are you talking about the weather, cause the forecast says we won't get another band of heavy rain till this evening. Things aren't going to get any worse."

"Floodwaters are the least of our concern."

"Come on," said George, turning to go and gesturing for Bill to follow him. "Man's a loony."

"Evil has been set free here," the man called after them.

"Loony."

There was the crash of another house being torn apart.

"Best get out of here," George muttered. "The flood must be getting worse, after all."

They didn't make it far before they stopped dead and stared out in horror. Something large and black loomed into view, having just crashed through another building. Brickwork tumbled off it as if being shrugged away, and water ran off it in rivulets. The size of a hill, they could barely comprehend its form: it had bulk and they were given the impression of numerous legs, but beyond that, it might have been a shapeless mass.

Bill swore. George gave a shriek.

"What is it?" Bill demanded as they continued to stare.

"Evil," called the man in the kayak from behind them, maintaining his distance.

The *thing* began to turn towards them.

"Run!" shouted George, pulling at Bill's shoulder.

The kayaker was already paddling swiftly away.

Between waist and chest deep in the water, George and Bill could barely make much speed at all.

Behind them, the enormous bulk lumbered slowly but steadily after them. They attempted to pick up speed, but even actions intensified by fear could only achieve so much.

"This way," called the kayaker, appearing again from down a side street. They gave up on getting back to their van and followed as best they could.

"What is it?" George shouted after him.

"Evil – bound here for six-hundred winters within the bridge. When the floodwaters tore the bridge away, it was freed once more. You need to leave this place. Leave if you want to live."

"We'll find a different way back to the van," said George.

Unfortunately, despise George's words, their only means of escape was back the way they had just come, past the creature that threatened them.

There were more crashes, more houses being destroyed as the creature moved closer.

Taking their chances, they clambered over rubble, slipped around debris and, finally, returned to the van. The man in the kayak stayed bobbing close by.

"You should hide," he said. "If you leave now, it will follow your van. It might come for you anyway, evil calls for evil, but there is a chance: My grandmother taught me the old chants that bound it before. I'll try to bind it once again, if I can. You should be able to escape then, whatever happens. If I fail, perhaps the wind will change direction and blow in some truly icy Siberian air. Maybe that will freeze it in the waters long enough that I can find a way to deal with it, or someone else can."

"Well, I'm not hanging around to find out," said George, climbing into the driver's seat. He looked at Bill, who was hesitating at the passenger door. "You okay?"

"I didn't want to come," he replied. "I'm going to find somewhere to hide." With all the rubble about, there were plenty of options, and he quickly jogged off to secrete himself, hoping it was a wise move.

George decided not to wait. Leave the kayaker to his crazy plan, he decided. Leave Bill too. He turned the key but the van didn't start. He swore.

The waters shook all around him as he tried again, but still there was nothing.

Then, an enormous leg, like a pillar of slick, black stone, came down immediately in front of the van. A moment later its twin crashed down upon the van's roof. George didn't even have the opportunity to register what had happened before he was dead.

Bill trembled where he hid. He was certain it was getting colder, that winter was suddenly here with great ferocity. He wasn't sure where the man in the kayak had gone, but he could hear him declaiming loudly somewhere within the confines of the devastated town. Bill wondered if it really was possible for the man to bind that *thing,* as he said his ancestors had, then he had a horrible feeling that they were all going to die together here in this godforsaken place.

Chill winds blew in and the voice of the man rose in pitch as he cried out again and again for the thing that had escaped the bridge to obey his words. But, wondered Bill, what was there to bind it within?

Maybe, Bill thought, if it followed the man long enough, he might have a chance to get away, but on the other hand, perhaps with the temperature dropping, they would all die here of the chill. Bill certainly felt as if he might.

The thing and voice of the man in the kayak were starting to grow nearer.

Bill made up his mind and started to run, splashing desperately along the flooded street.

He might just make it, he thought.

That was when he heard the pillar-like legs crash down into the water just behind him, sending up a spray that fell upon him like a torrent of stinging darts of rain.

He wouldn't make it.

Something seized him by the waist and he felt himself being raised up into the air. For a brief moment, Bill got a clear view of the devastation wrought upon the village. His final thought was to wonder if they had deserved their fate, as the man had implied. Was this all some hideous punishment? He then ceased to wonder and was dead.

The rain continued to fall and, slowly, the floodwaters continued to rise. The weather remained indifferent to the horror it had released.

Ends

Narrative of the HMS Verdigris

By: Miguel Fliguer

BEING THREE ANNOTATED FRAGMENTS CONCERNING THE DREADFUL ENCOUNTER BETWEEN THE CREW OF THE HMS *VERDIGRIS,* AND AN UNIDENTIFIED CREATURE, PURPORTEDLY FROM THE DEEP SEA ABYSSES, WHICH HAPPENED IN THE VAST EXPANSES OF THE PACIFIC OCEAN, AT AN APPROXIMATE LATITUDE 48 SOUTH AND LONGITUDE 127 WEST[1], ON THE DAY OF ST. SWITHIN[2] IN THE YEAR OF OUR LORD 1791, AND WHICH WERE RECORDED IN THE AFTERMATH BY THE SHIP'S SURGEON, DR. HENRY COLERIDGE, WHO IN HIS DIARY CONSIGNED HIS FIRSTHAND RECOLLECTIONS OF THE EVENT, AS WELL AS INTERVIEWS CONDUCTED IN THE SUBSEQUENT DAYS, THUS PROVIDING A VIVID, HARROWING ACCOUNT OF THE EXPERIENCE BASED ON THE TESTIMONIES OF THOSE WHO WITNESSED FIRST HAND, THE AFOREMENTIONED MONSTROUS ENTITY, ITS ALLEGED HEIGHT AS IT TOWERED NEXT TO THE *VERDIGRIS,* AND HOW ITS MYRIAD OF BULBOUS EYES REGARDED THE HUMANS ABOARD WITH A MIXTURE OF EVIL CONTEMPT AND SUPREME INDIFFERENCE, SPARKING A COLLECTIVE BOUT OF INSANITY AMONG SEVERAL CREW MATES, WHOM SUDDENLY JUMPED OVERBOARD WHILE SINGING AN ODIOUS CHANT IN A TONGUE NONE OF THOSE PRESENT COULD RECOGNIZE OR UNDERSTAND, UNTIL THE HOLLERING OF THE CAPTAIN MADE THE REMAINING CREW MATES RETURN TO THEIR SENSES, THOUGH NONE COULD REMEMBER

WHY THEY HAD ACTED THAT WAY, NOR DID ANY KNOW WHAT LANGUAGE THEY HAD BEEN SPEAKING; IT IS MIRACULOUS THAT THE CREW WAS ABLE TO CORAGEUSLY MANEUVER THE SHIP TO TRAIN THEIR STARBOARD CANNON BATTERIES AGAINST THE STRANGE FOE FROM THE DEEP AND FIRE SEVERAL VOLLEYS OF HEAVY PROJECTILES WHICH, ALTHOUGH DID NOT SEEM TO CAUSE DISCERNIBLE PHYSICAL HARM TO THE AQUATIC COLOSSUS, IT APPEARED TO BE ENOUGH OF A NUISANCE TO CAUSE THE CREATURE TO SUBMERGE UNDER THE FURIOUS WAVES AND RETURN INTO THE ABYSSES OF THE UNDERWATER HELL FROM WHENCE IT HAD COME, CAUSING GREAT REJOICE AMONG THE CREW AND THE OFFICERS, WHICH LATER CELEBRATED THEIR VICTORY WITH EXTRA RATIONS OF FOOD AND ALE, A FACT THAT MAY OR MAY NOT HAVE BEEN A FACTOR RESULTING IN THE BONE-CHILLING NIGHTMARES THAT DISRUPTED THE SLUMBER OF MANY OF THOSE SAILORS THAT EVENING, PARTICULARLY THOSE WHO HAD HAD THE CLOSEST AND MOST TERRIFYING VIEW OF THAT UNNAMABLE OCEANIC BEAST.

One – Excerpt from the recollection of Dr. Henry Coleridge[3]

I was resting in my cabin when I heard screams coming from the upper deck. Thinking one of the sailors had suffered an accident, I ran onto the deck toward starboard but froze in terror when I saw the thing before me. Its barnacle-covered, misshapen form was still rising from the depths, but what was already above water was enormous, taller than our main mast by a good thirty feet[4]. It towered over our main sail like an evil portent. It did not have a face… only a massive bulk of grey flesh, with thousands of cilia where its mouth should have been, and a head shaped like an octopus but the size of our ship, with hundreds of yellowish eyes scattered across its abhorrent visage… It was something not of this Earth, dwarfing our ship… indifferent, as if our vessel was just a bit of floating debris. I pray someday I can forget its sight, which has come to me in my dreams every night since. Laudanum[5] helps, barely.

Two – From the testimony of Alfred Shaw[6]

Aye, doc, it was absolutely 'orrible. I've whale-hunted in the North Atlantic and seen all manner of sea beasts, up close like I am from you now. There are some ugly bastards down there in the deep, I assure you, but nothing like that thing we all saw yesterday. 'Twas some Leviathan that our Lord forgot, when He created the abyss. If I didn't know that all the crew saw it too, I'd be tempted to think it was all an evil dream from the spiced rum[7]. Could we all have dreamed[8] it, doc?

Three – Excerpt from the journal of Captain John Wilkins[9]

I was studying a chart in my cabin when I heard the commotion at starboard, and I thought a man had fallen overboard. As I ran to aid or at least assess the situation, the panicked screams soon turned into animal-like whimpering. I continued onward towards the strange noises, turned a corner, and saw the thing rising… not like a whale breaching… more like a crouching giant getting up with slow, deliberate movements, as if it had just woken from a long slumber. It almost drove me senseless… I knew the bottom was at more than 500 fathoms[10]… Was this thing standing on the ocean floor?

Suddenly, three sailors went mad and, screaming in a strange tongue, they all jumped overboard, instantly disappearing beneath the waves. I realized at once that if more men followed those poor wretches to their end, we wouldn't have crew to man the ship[11]*, so I barked furious orders for everybody to retreat to the starboard cannon deck.*

My decisive call to action seemed to restore some sanity to the crew, but that was enough. When they opened the cannon hatches, we saw the beast close to starboard, and I ordered to fire two volleys of round and chain shot[12]*, point blank, from the eight cannons*[13] *that faced the monster. Astonished, we saw the beast appeared unscathed*[14]*! It seemed we were merely a nuisance to the creature, like an insect that wasn't even worth the effort to crush, for we watched it slowly submerge back into the deep, without giving us another glance. In a matter of minutes it was gone, not a trace of it remaining amongst the churning waves.*

There were cheers of joy from the whole crew, myself included, and I gave orders for extra rations of food and ale to be served at supper that night. Everybody joined in prayer of gratitude for our deliverance. The night gave way to merriment, and with numerous cheers we dedicated our victory to Britain and our King.

That very night, the nightmares began. Oh Lord, the visions! Have mercy!

Several days have passed since we witnessed that ungodly aberration[15]*. The nightmares never cease. All the crew suffer them too. Everybody's afraid of sleeping and Dr. Coleridge's laudanum supply has run out. The men do their work around the ship in a stupor, gazing at the sea with vacuous eyes. I fear for us. I fear for our souls.*[16]

---

1. There are reasons to believe this particular geographic information has been obfuscated and the real coordinates of the incident were several miles away.

2. July 15th. In traditional folklore, if it rains on St. Swithin's Day, it will rain for 40 days, Conversely, fair weather means 40 days of fair weather will follow. Some interpretations of this

belief postulate that if something horrible happens on that day, 40 days of horror could follow.

[3] The HMS *Verdigris'* medic, bloodletter, and apothecary. An Oxford graduate with over 20 years of practice at sea.

[4] There are notable discrepancies between testimonies regarding the height of the monster, probably due to the relative position of the different observers. Although a mirage-like visual aberration cannot be disregarded.

[5] A common opium-based narcotic tincture or potion.

[6] A sailor, served over ten years under Captain Wilkins. This was his second journey on the HMS *Verdigris*.

[7] An exquisite, highly sought-after spiced rum distillate, originally from the former colony of Pennsylvania, and widely known for its superb flavor and its potent vision-inducing properties.

[8] The hypothesis of a collective hallucination cannot be dismissed. There have been recorded instances of mass delusions aboard ships at sea, a frequent phenomenon among crews in the Sargasso Sea, and some have attributed it to a possible noxious influence from the abundant seaweed.

[9] Decorated officer of the Royal Navy, with a long, distinguished career commanding several warships and merchant vessels.

[10] About 3,000 feet deep. This is a very conservative estimation by Captain Wilkins, probably based on the maximum length of the ship's weighted rope. Recent measurements have established the ocean depth in those regions at about three times Captain Wilkins' calculations. This makes the prospect of a crouching beast supported by the sea bed exponentially more terrifying.

[11] Unlikely. Period ships like the HMS *Verdigris* had a crew of between 60 and 90 sailors, and about 130 soldiers and officers. So the loss of even ten men could have been manageable. But in all justice, Captain Wilkins acted prudently here.

[12.] Period cannons could fire, among several types of ammunition, regular five-inch caliber roud shot–the common cannonballs-and chain-shot, two pieces of round artillery linked by a length of heavy chain. This was a type of projectile designed to create devastation upon the upper decks and masts of the enemy ships, especially at close range when they were more accurate.

[13.] A sizeable fraction of the ship's firepower, which can be estimated between 24 and 30 guns in its only cannon deck.

[14.] The fact that those devastating chain-shot projectiles didn't inflict any damage on the monster suggests exceedingly peculiar hypotheses about its material –or immaterial- nature.

[15.] A page was ripped from the journal before this entry.

[16.] This is the final entry from Captain Wilkins' journal, which was found, along with Dr. xvii. Coleridge's diary, about four months after their alleged encounter with the unidentified creature. The HMS Verdigris was recovered three hundred miles off the coast of Alta California, derelict, without a soul aboard, and listing heavily from about four feet of seawater on the bilge. The ship's two pinasses were still attached to the port side, so the crew hadn't been used them to abandon the vessel. After long discussions among Navy investigators, the agreed upon conclusion by the Royal Board of Inquiry was that a creeping madness, likely induced by the terrible encounter with the monster, eventually claimed the entire crew of the HMS Verdigris. When and where exactly they jumped to their burials at sea, remains a mystery.

Persy

By: Thomas Folske

"Happy Birthday!!!" Cici's parents hollered as soon as she came down the stairs for breakfast

Christian Cameron, Cici for short, named after her great uncle, the adventurer, smiled as she walked into the kitchen, following the beckoning aroma of sizzling bacon and fresh from the tree maple syrup.

Her mother, Maxine Cameron, had made Cici's favorite breakfast for her this morning, which consisted of lots and lots of bacon, French toast, scrambled eggs, and hash browns drenched in syrup, with strawberry crepes for if there was room, and Cici always made room for strawberry crepes. They were her favorite breakfast food ever, especially when her mom loaded them as full as they would go without spilling out of the sides with fresh strawberries that they had picked up at the farmer's market, where they also bought their syrup.

Cici sat down at the opposite end of the table as her father's seat, right between her mother and her four-year-old sister Brynn, and started to heap delicious smelling strips of bacon onto her plate.

"Thank you everyone. Thanks for breakfast mom, this all smells really great," Cici said as she shoved the first piece of bacon into her mouth and practically swallowed it whole.

"Of course, honey. Your birthday only comes but once a year," Maxine replied with a proud grin.

"Yeah, and your sweet sixteen only comes once in a lifetime," Tom Cameron, Maxine's father, said as he entered the room and started to pour himself a cup of coffee.

"Happy birfday, Cici," Brynn said as she looked up from her plate with a mouthful of French toast. She had both of her two front teeth missing and she had a problem with her TH's.

"Thank you Pebbles," Cici replied with a smile. Everyone in the immediate family called Brynn Pebbles, ever since she was little, because she looked almost exactly like Pebbles from *The Flintstones*.

Brynn giggled and spit bits of food up all over table.

"Pebbles!" Maxine said. "Cover your mouth."

A look of "Ooops!" spread across Brynn's face as she quickly put her small hand in front of her lips and tried to stifle her giggles.

"I'm glad I have a sister that isn't a brat," Cici commented as she leaned over and rubbed the top of Brynn's head playfully.

Brynn glared up at her older sister, stuck out her bottom lip in a pout, and snorted, only it was followed by a quickly trailing cough.

"Oh no, is Pebbles sick?" Cici asked in an imitation child's voice.

"No, I'm not," Brynn cried as she swiped the sleeve of her sweater across her nose to wipe away the trail of snot that had just begun leaking from her nostril.

"Yeah. I heard her earlier this morning. I was hoping it was a false alarm, but that's the third time I've heard her cough since she woke up," Maxine said with a look of concern.

"Oh no," Cici said. "Poor Pebbles."

"I'll be okay," Brynn assured them, right before beginning a small coughing fit.

"Cici, I think we're gonna have to schedule our annual Birthday lunch for a different day," Maxine said as she walked over to feel Brynn's forehead.

"It's okay. I'll get over it," Cici said, trying to hide her relief. Cici loved her mom, but sometimes the woman was way too much of a mom, and overprotected both her and Brynn.

Fortunately, Brynn more so since she was the baby, but still enough for Cici to get a little embarrassed when they went out together in public, though she would never say anything.

"Don't get too excited there, Christian," Tom Cameron told his oldest child as he walked into the living room and turned on the weather channel.

"What? I was not," Cici replied quickly and defensively.

"No. I wanna go wiff Cici," Brynn cried through congested sinuses.

"How about if I let you blow out the candles on my cake when we get back. Hopefully you'll be feeling better by then," Cici offered.

Brynn smiled satisfactorily.

"Thank you Cici," Maxine said.

"It's cool," Cici said as she began shoveling bacon into her mouth again.

After breakfast, Cici ran upstairs to begin getting ready for the day. They had planned out the details of the day's festivities last night just after dinner. The plan was to have breakfast, get ready, meet up with Whitney Townsend, pick up Sandra and Pamela Hynes, and then head up to the family's cabin up on Lake Persephone, an hour-and-twenty-minute drive away from Cici's house. Having her mother and sister staying home from the trip didn't alter plans in any detrimental way, and really only affected Cici in the fact that she would now be riding shotgun.

Tom Cameron was already ready to go for the day. He had set his alarm for six thirty that morning. It was almost nine. He sat in his recliner in the living room watching for the third time that morning to see what the weather was supposed to be like for that afternoon. All signs pointed to a beautiful, bright, and sunny day.

Cici came downstairs in a pair of capris and a blue silk blouse she wore over her bathing suit. She had sunglasses resting on top of her head and was chewing bubblegum, a towel in one hand, and her purse in the other.

"Alright Dad," Cici yelled. "I'm ready to go."

"Did you remember sunscreen?" her mother asked as she poked her head out of Brynn's room.

"It's in my purse," Cici answered, with a small sigh.

"Let's go," she lipped to her father as soon as he stood up from his chair.

"Bye Honey, bye Pebbles, I love you guys," Tom Cameron called up the stairs.

"Bye Mom, bye Pebbles, I also love you," Cici called up after him.

"Bye, we love you too," Both Maxine and Pebbles called back down.

Cici and Tom walked outside, closing and locking the door behind them on their way out.

Their first stop was Whitney Townsend's house, which was located a block and a half down, but on the same road. Tom and Cici Cameron pulled up to the Townsend residence and honked once. Whitney came running out the door with the bright pink backpack she used at school full of all her lake and beach supplies.

"What up Gangsta?" Whitney asked her friend, as Tom started to pull out of the driveway.

"Not much. Just picking up my sister from another mister and now I'm ready to go to the em-efffin beach. Yeeeahh-Boi!" Cici said, imitating a party girl.

Both girls giggled.

"Wow," Tom Cameron said while shaking his head incredulously. Kids grew up too fast.

"You know we're just messing around," Cici told her father.

"Well, maybe. Depends. Got any booze Mr. C? I was thinking we could get drunk and invite over some boys," Whitney replied humorously.

"Hmm... Getting drunk with a bunch of underage teenagers... I think I'll pass this time. Besides, I don't think the boys would like me very much"

"Damn. No booze. No boys. I will just have to take what I can get... Cici, you ever want to try the other side?"

"Never gonna happen," Cici replied with a smile, which she covered with her hand as she began to blush.

"How about you, Mr. C., did you bring your Speedo?" Whitney joked.

"Nah. It shrank in the dryer. I had to bring my shorts instead," Tom retorted in similar jest.

"That's a damn shame. You could've worn them anyway."

"Okay. That's enough. I think I'm gonna ralph," Cici broke in. "Besides, we're at Sandra and Pamela's anyway."

Tom Cameron pulled his truck up to the curb and honked.

"I hope they aren't lame this time," Whitney complained from the back. Last time they all went out to a lake together Pamela stopped going into the water halfway through the day because "it was too cold", and Sandra would not stop passive-aggressively complaining about mosquitoes, even though they all had bug spray on and they even had one of those Off burning coil candles.

"I hope not," Cici said. "I'll get on Pamela's case if she starts bitching."

"Good," Whit replied.

"Do I sense some pent-up hostility there, Whitney?" Tom Cameron asked with his eyebrows raised.

"No. I like them well enough. They are both cool sometimes, I just hate it when they get all girly and shit, well, mostly Pamela, but still..." Whitney answered.

Before anyone could reply, Pamela and Sandra pulled open the back sliding door and entered the vehicle.

"What up girlfriends?" Pamela asked, mostly looking at Cici.

"You ready for an amazing day of fun and sun and maybe some cute boys?" Cici asked in answer.

"You better believe it," Pamela said as she took a seat behind Whitney.

"Hey guys," Sandra said in a mellow tone as she quickly climbed in, closed the down, then sat down next to her sister.

"Everyone all buckled?" Tom Cameron asked as he pulled back out onto the road.

The eighty-minute drive to the Cameron family cabin went smoothly enough. Whitney slowly eased into conversation with the Hynes sisters and magically remembered that she didn't hate them after all, just like she did every time she hung out with them, while Cici and Tom talked about when they had come up here just two weekends ago, and what they were gonna do today. Cici told her father that she had grabbed a bunch of girly movies and candy for a "Slumber party", and how he had to stay in his room upstairs for the whole night and not come down unless it was for food or if the cabin was on fire.

When they finally pulled into the driveway of the cabin, everyone aboard, except for Sandra, was so immersed in their conversations, it was almost two minutes before Tom finally got out of the SUV and started to bring things into the cabin. Then, with everyone sharing the labor, the truck was unloaded in a matter of minutes.

"Alright girls, I'm gonna go launch the boat into the lake," Tom Cameron told them. "You coming with, Whit?"

"Of course," Whitney exclaimed. "Who else do you think could handle driving *The Beast*?"

The Beast was what Whitney alone called the Cameron family's SUV, and since she was six months older than Cici and already had her license, Tom often let her drive it, as well as all their other vehicles. He had mostly been the one to teach her how to drive. Whitney and Cici had been friends since they were three and Whitney's father had died when she was seven, after an explosion at the power plant where he worked. Tom Cameron had been there for Whitney ever since, and he treated her and Cici liked sisters. Whitney saw him as a father, and he saw her as a daughter.

"Okay. I'm gonna start lunch while you guys are gone," Cici said before Tom and Whitney started off toward the boat launch, about three quarters of a mile away from the cabin.

The three remaining girls started to make food with Cici instructions as to what they were to do, and where all the dishes were located. Twenty minutes later, Whit pulled back up to the cabin and Tom pulled up to the dock about two minutes after that. When both Tom and Whitney got back inside the house, Sandra and Pamela were just finishing up setting out all the silverware and glasses as Cici emerged from the kitchen, holding Velveeta macaroni and cheese in one hand and a pot full of boiled hot dogs in the other.

"Someone wanna grab buns and condiments?" Cici asked as she set the food down on the table.

"Sure," Sandra said as she scurried back into the kitchen to retrieve what Cici had asked for.

"Grab the milk too please," Cici called after her.

Sandra came back out of the kitchen with her hands literally full. She was trying to hold the gallon of milk and the ketchup and mustard between her arms while trying precariously to balance the hot dog buns on the top without smooshing them.

Whitney quickly rushed to help her.

"Thank you," Sandra said. "I have small arms."

"It's all good," Whitney told her. "You don't have to work so hard you know, we're already your friends, you know."

"I know, but I thought I could get it all, and I didn't wanna make two trips."

"If you say so… Let's eat."

Cici Cameron, her father Tom, and all of her friends enjoyed their home-cooked lunch while laughing and having a good time. Not one of them had the slightest idea that this would be the very last time they would all share a meal together.

After they finished lunch, all the girls stripped down until they were only in their bikinis and shorts. Tom Cameron went into the bathroom and changed into his swim trunks, though he kept his T-shirt on. Within minutes, everyone had traveled across the backyard, up over the dock, and had nestled themselves comfortably into one of the seats in Tom's boat, life jackets and all. Tom sat down in the captain's chair, stuck the key into the ignition, and slowly started to pull his boat away from the dock.

It wasn't long before he had the big blue speedboat zipping across the lake, skipping like a stone across the surface of the water, and leaving two monstrous waves in its wake.

"Faster! Faster!" Both Cici and Whitney shouted. Cici was in the seat to the left of her dad and Whitney was sitting in the curved area at the front of the boat. Pamela was seated behind Tom, her eyes wide and a look of distress on her face, like she might fly out of the boat at any second, while Sandra sat opposite her sister, looking as though she wanted to cheer and holler with the other two girls, but was afraid to allow herself to do so. Tom Cameron drove the boat even faster, however, and Sandra could no longer help but cheer, even though her cheers were swallowed up by the sound of the motor cruising along the lake. They drove for a good six or seven minutes before Tom slowed the boat down to a creep, in approximately the middle of the lake.

Tom turned on the fish finder just before finally stopping the engine completely.

"What's going on? Why are we stopped?" Pamela asked, a little nervously.

"I'm getting to that," Tom told her as if he had just been talking and she had interrupted him. All eyes turned their attention to Cici's father.

"Did I ever tell you girls the story of Persy?" Tom Cameron said in a foreboding voice.

Cici and Whitney smiled. They had heard the story before, but Pamela and Sandra had not. The sisters were scared before the tale even began.

"It goes way, way back, to frontier times. When my grandpa's grandpa was alive. In fact, he was one of the founders of this town. He's the one who named the lake Persephone.

Anyway, my three-times great grandfather built this cabin, the one you girls are going to being staying in tonight, and he lived there with my three-times great grandmother. Now, he claims that one night, after him and a few of his of his friends had drunk a few beers, they decided they would all jump in the water for a swim. Now this is where the story gets strange... My three-times great grandfather claimed that when he was in the lake, swimming with his friends, he felt

something graze his foot, something enormous, right before that same
something yanked his friend, Chris Colman, right down under the water.

He said that everyone started swimming back to the shore, but a boy named Tony Dimincko and a girl named Leslie Spence didn't make it. He said that Persy got them.

"They reported it to the authorities immediately, and there was an investigation, but it yielded almost no results. My great grandfather and all of his friends that did make it back to shore that night never set foot in lake Persephone again."

Everyone looked frightened, most of all Pamela.

"Yeah, there are caverns under this lake," Cici added, making her father smile. "There are underground paths that could lead to almost anywhere, and we're not too far from the ocean. They're also a great place for some enormous creature to get enough food from all the surrounding lakes, not to mention a place to hide where no human would ever be able to find them."

"You didn't tell them how even though this is a huge lake, it has three times the disappearance rate of most other lakes its size," Whitney chimed in. "That even creeps me out."

"Wanna be creeped out? Look at the depth finder," Tom Cameron told them.

All eyes turned to the depth finder. Whitney even got up and moved by Cici so she could see it. It read 183 ft.

"Wow," Whitney said.

"Wow is right," Tom said, "But this is the deepest part of the lake. If we go over by the island, it's like twelve- or thirteen-feet tops."

"Well, we should go there," Pamela said, almost pleadingly.

"Okay. Fine. You getting a little scared there, Pamela?" Tom asked with a smile.

"No. I just don't like the idea of having one hundred and eighty-three feet below me that I can't see," Pamela replied.

"I was just giving you shit," Tom said. "We can head to the island."

Tom started up the boat again and turned off the fish finder as he did so. A second before the screen shut off, however, he swore he saw a humungous shape moving in toward the boat from the right. He reached forward to turn the fish finder back on.

"Hurry," Pamela said with fright in her voice.

"Alright," Tom said, and instead of turning the fish finder back on, he turned the wheel of the boat until they were facing shallower waters while simultaneously pushing the shifter forward and getting the boat moving again. They were soon heading toward the eastern portion of the lake.

"I didn't mean to scare you so bad," Tom yelled over the roar of the engine.

"It's fine," Pamela yelled back. "I'm good as long as…"

BBBAAAAASSSSHHH!!!!

The boat smashed hard into something in the water and the engine suddenly killed.

"What the fuck was that?" Tom Cameron shouted as he tried to start the engine again. It wouldn't turn over. He tried again. Still no go. It was almost like there was something caught in the motor.

Pamela and Sandra both looked terrified. Cici and Whitney were even frightened, though they were doing a much better job of hiding it.

"I think something might be caught in the motor," Tom Cameron said as he walked toward the back of the boat. "We probably hit a clump of seaweed, or maybe we hit a stick and got tangled in one of the branches."

"You need some help?" Cici asked as she stood up and started to walk towards her father.

"Nah. I think I got it," Tom answered as he pulled the head of the motor up into the boat, so the propeller was out of the water and exposed. One of the propeller's fins were bent and the engine couldn't make a full revolution because of it. Tom considered trying to find his big pliers, but instead just grabbed the utility tool off his belt, unfolded it into the long nose pliers, and started trying to bend the propeller back into place. It took a lot of muscle, and he almost wasn't able to get it. He also almost broke the pliers, twice.

"How's it looking?" Cici asked after a few moments.

"I think it's good, but I just wanna be sure," Tom Cameron said before turning back to face his daughter. "Will you see if you can find me a real pliers anywhere, I know I had one in the boat at one point."

"Sure," Cici said, but as she turned to start searching, something in the water caught her eye.

"AHHHHHHH!!!! DAD!!! WATCH OUT!!!" Cici screamed as she started to run toward her father.

Tom Cameron turned around just in time to see a large, scaly, bird-like head, attached to a long, thin, serpentine neck, swoop down from above and swallow the majority of his right arm.

The creature pulled away, ten feet up into the air, and with it went Tom's arm. He didn't even feel any pain.

Everyone on the boat started screaming, everyone except Tom, who just stared quizzically at his truncated arm, looking almost as if someone had just insulted him.

"Start the boat!" Cici yelled as she ran over to her dad and slammed the motor back down into the water.

Whitney, quicker than lightening, jumped into the captain's chair and started the engine. It started on the first go and Whitney took off as fast as she could away from the monster.

As soon as they were speeding away from the aquatic monstrosity, Cici began taking off the belt around her shorts and getting ready to use it as a tourniquet.

"You guys! You guys! It's going back under!" Sandra yelled. Cici could see out of the corner of her eye that Sandra was jumping around frantically, but all her attention was focused on her father. She wrapped the belt around his upper arm, but too much of it was missing and she had to tighten it at an odd angle.

"Christian," Tom whispered, barely audibly.

"Yes Dad?"

"Christian, I love you."

"I love you too, Dad. Don't say that. You're gonna be alright," Cici said as her eyes suddenly began to fill with tears. Tom had lost a lot of blood and his face had gone a ghostly pale.

"Christian," Tom said again, this time barely moving his lips. Cici held her head close to him to hear. "Christian, take care of Brynn and your mother. You're strong Christian. Much stronger than you realize."

"Stop talking like that. Save your strength. We're almost to shore," Cici commanded, holding her father in her arms. She was lying though. Lake Persephone was a huge lake, and she couldn't see the shoreline in any direction.

BBBBAAAAAMMMMMM!!!

There was another loud crash. Tom released a bloodcurdling scream of pain that sent Cici into a fresh burst of tears. Pamela and Sandra each started a new screaming fit. Whitney scrambled for the ignition… The engine had stopped again.

"What the hell is going?" Cici shouted, turning away from her father and focusing on Whitney, but mostly because he was much too hard to look at right now.

"I'm trying. I'm trying," Whitney shouted in a panic.

As Cici started to turn back around, Sandra let out a scream so loud that you'd think glass would have shattered, then Cici was knocked over, flat onto her face. She could instantly feel her chin turn warm and tingly and knew that there would be blood, but that didn't concern right her now. As Cici rolled onto her back, she was just in time to see her father's body, only visible from the waist down, soar high up into the air above her.

"NNNNOOOOOOO!!!!!!!!" Cici screamed as she leapt to her feet and ran frantically to the side of the boat to rip one of the oars out from its velcro strapping. She moved just as quickly to the back of the boat and began swinging at the creature's throat, which was just in range of the oar. After the first strike, however, the creature jerked its head forcefully downward and to the left, looping back into the water, meaning to submerge itself again with Tom's body secure in its mouth. Before it could submerge itself completely, Cici took a bounding step toward where it was aimed and bashed her oar directly into its face, connecting perfectly with its eyeball, an instant before it disappeared below the surface of the water, her father's body still dangling from its jaws.

The Hynes sisters stopped screaming. Whitney stopped trying to start the engine. Everyone just sat silently, staring at Cici and trying to process what had just taken place. Awe and sorrow began to show on their faces while Cici's face remained utterly vacant as she stared into the dark and deep waters that now served as a cemetery to the man who had created and raised her.

No one said anything for almost two minutes. It seemed that even the creature was giving them a moment's reprieve. Cici slowly autopiloted herself back to a chair, where she sat and stared at all the spattered blood in the place her father had just been moments before. Sandra and Pamela looked at each other with frightened expressions, not sure what they should be doing right now and not yet fully understanding what has happening. Whitney's heart sank into her small intestine. She wished to go to Cici and hug her. She wished for Cici to come to her and to give her a hug. She wished to be out of this situation and safe at home in front of the TV. Most of all, she wished hadn't had to lose another dad.

Whitney forced herself to move again. She wiped the tears out of her eyes then reached forward to turn the key over in the ignition, when their boat was suddenly assaulted again. Sandra almost flew over the side and Whitney was thrown out of the captain's seat so violently, she bit her tongue. Everyone started screaming again.

As if on cue, the monster reemerged from beneath the surface of the lake.

The creature appeared on the right side of the boat, next to Cici and Whitney, across from where Pamela and Sandra were now seated, and just hovered there for a moment like a snake deciding which egg it wanted to steal from a nest.

All of the girls were too terrified to scream, move, or even breathe. Except Cici, who just stared blankly up at the monster as if it didn't matter and she was just in the middle of some cheesy horror movie. She slowly turned her head to look around at the other actors. They were doing a great job of being terrified. Pamela even had a dark spot slowly forming on the crotch of her pants. Cici looked back at the monster.

Just as her gaze reach the monster's face, it lunged forward, into boat, coming right at her. Well, at least Cici thought that it was coming right at her, but the creature's neck made too wide of an arc and instead of eating her, which she didn't think she would have even resisted, the monster grabbed up Pamela instead. It pierced into her shoulder, making a good portion of her arm and chest, fully including one of her breasts, disappear completely into its jaws. Then it was gone and so was Pamela.

Cici sat up slightly and watched as the last bit of her friend's legs disappeared under the dark, consuming waters of Lake Persephone.

"PPPPAAAMMMMEEELLLLAAA!!!!!!!!!!" Sandra yelled as her sister was pulled down into the flat, glass-like abyss, just like Alice through the looking glass.

The creature appeared again almost instantly, its teeth dripping with the young girl's blood, only this time it was on the left side of the boat, just feet away from Cici. Sandra turned red with rage. She picked up the oar off the floor, which Cici had dropped, and ran toward the creature, rocking the boat violently as she did so. Sandra began batting at the monster, bashing it in the throat multiple times as hard as she could. Though it appeared that she was hurting the monster, at least a little bit, Sandra was soon consumed by her fury and began to swing erratically. Whitney was quick and able-minded enough to get out of the way. Cici on the other hand, stared right at the paddle of the oar as it soared through the air and directly into her forehead, instantly knocking her unconscious.

Pain…

Cici's head hurt and she couldn't quite remember why. She put her hand up to her forehead and started to mumble when she suddenly felt weight on top of her and a hand over her mouth. Cici's eyes shot wide open and she began to struggle.

"Shut up, you idiot. Shut the fuck up," Whitney yell/whispered into Cici's ear.

Cici stopped struggling.

Whitney took her hand off of Cici's mouth.

Cici stared at her confusedly for few moments as all the day's events rushed back to her. She began to sob.

Whitney slapped her. "Crying time is later on. Right now we have to focus on staying alive so we can make it out of here."

"I'm good…" Cici whispered, regulating her breathing, "I'm okay."

"Good," Whitney said quietly. "It got Sandra while you were out. Now it's just us two."

"How long have I been out?"

"Somewhere around four or five minutes probably, but it's hard to tell, I'm scared shitless."

"When's the last time you seen the monster?"

"It disappeared with Sandra and it hasn't come back up again… That was right after you got knocked out."

"Maybe it's full."

"Or maybe it's setting a trap."

"Well, we have to do something, sitting here waiting to die while the monster is who knows where…" Cici started, but was cut off by Whitney.

"You're a genius. I love you," Whitney said and quickly kissed Cici on the cheek.

Cici raised an eyebrow.

Whitney curled herself into a squatting position and began moving extremely slowly toward the captain's chair.

"What are you doing?" Cici yell/whispered, raising herself into a crouch as well.

Whitney didn't turn around. Instead, she kept on going until she was right next to the driver's seat. Cici thought she was going to start the engine and was about to come over there, when Whitney instead turned on the fish finder.

There was a loud beep as the machine came to life and both Whitney and Cici nearly jumped out of their skins. They both held their breaths, waiting for the creature to emerge again and eat one of them.

It didn't.

The girls continued to hold their breath for the entire time it took the fish finder to calculate depth, where the fish (or monsters) were, and everything else it showed on the screen. They exhaled slowly when the monitor showed that the monster was nowhere to be seen.

Cici picked up the now bloody oar off the floor next to her before moving as carefully and meticulously as she could into the chair across the aisle from the driver's seat. Whitney moved her fingers onto the key still inserted into the ignition, trying to make as little noise as possible. Before she attempted to start the engine, however, they both looked again at the fish finder.

Still no monster.

"You ready to do this?" Whitney asked.

"As ready as I'll ever be," Cici answered, tightening her fists around the oar like a baseball bat.

"We'll get the cops, and the feds, and the army over here when we get back. That thing is gonna pay. All we have to do is survive."

"I love you, Whitney."

"I love You, Cici."

All eyes went to the fish finder as Whitney turned the key in the ignition.

The boat struggled to turn over, acting like it wasn't going to start again, making Cici's blood run cold as she dreadfully contemplated pulling the motor back up, but then the engine fired into a slow roar. The fish finder's screen remaining mostly blank, with the exception of a few aimlessly wandering fish, so Whitney pushed the shifter forward, making the boat creep slowly along the surface of the lake.

"I think this is the way to the island," Whitney said.

"I'm almost positive it is," Cici agreed. "But I wanna get to land…"

"We're in the middle of the fucking lake Cici. We're way closer to the island. I'm surprised we don't see it yet. If we get to the island, all we have to do is wait until tomorrow night and help will come get us. Hell, they know exactly where we are."

"I don't want to sleep on a fuckin island. We need to get the fuck back to shore. We need to get help right away. We need to rescue them," Cici cried.

"It's alright. It's gonna be alright," Whitney said consolingly as she reached over and hugged her best friend.

Cici and Whitney held each other for only a moment before Whitney, this time, caught something out of the corner of her eye, something in the fish finder, something large and heading in their direction.

"Oh fuck!" Whitney yelled as she quickly pulled away from Cici and threw the shifter forward as far as it would go.

The boat took off with a roar and both girls were slammed into their seats by the sudden increase in velocity. Cici tilted her head to look over at the fish finder and also now saw the large, ovular shape heading right towards them.

"Oh fuck. Oh fuck. Oh fuck," Cici cried out as they tore across the lake. She began to feel nauseous and knew that the oar she held would be no help. She swallowed hard and focused on keeping the contents of her stomach where they belonged and on trying to keep herself calm herself, when Whitney suddenly jumped up in her chair and started to shout. It almost gave her a heart attack.

"Land. I see the island. Look Cici. Look," Whitney hollered joyfully.

Seeing salvation so close at hand gave Cici renewed courage. She stood up and turned, planting her legs wide as she took position and raised the oar over her shoulder. She readied herself to swing, and no matter how effective or ineffective her blows ended up being, Cici Cameron was ready fight.

There was nothing. Yet. But Cici wasn't deceived. She knew the creature was there, rushing toward them, ready to pop its murderous head out of the water at any second to eat one of them.

It wasn't long before Cici's fears were realized. The creature's head burst forth from the water at the back, righthand corner of the boat, popping up out of the lake like a rocket. It screeched intimidatingly, but Cici stood her ground. All the fear in her body was suddenly replaced by anger and vengeance. Here, before her, was the thing that killed her father. Cici squeezed the oar so tightly that her fingers turned pure white. Adrenaline surged through her veins. The creature lunged forward right at Cici's chest.

Cici swung the oar as hard as she could, connecting perfectly with the monster's lower jaw and busting the oar into splinters. The creature stopped following them for a moment as it let out another screech, though this one was different than the first, this one was a screech of agony.

"Did you get it? Is it hurt?" Whitney asked, not daring to look back at this speed.

Cici ignored her question and instead took advantage of the monster's temporary distance; she looked down at the broken oar in her hand and began to prepare for her next combat. The oar was mostly destroyed, but fortunately, the remaining bits of wood were jagged and sharp. It could now be used as a stabbing tool.

The creature started towards them again, only it moved much faster this time. It was beyond irate now.

"Drive Whitney. Fucking drive!" Cici shouted.

"I am driving. We're almost there," Whitney hollered back.

The creature was gaining on them.

Cici raised what remained of the oar into the air, holding it like a spear, with her left hand on the shaft and her right hand on the grip, her pose reminiscent of Captain Ahab getting ready to harpoon Moby Dick.

The monster was on them in no time flat. It was horribly, savagely enraged. Cici started to shiver and shake with fear. The monster went right for her with lightning speed just as Cici thrusted the oar forward, through the air, and with an incredibly lucky strike, she hit the creature right in the back of the throat.

The monster pulled away from the boat with the oar lodged in its gullet as it began to gag, right before Cici was thrown off balance and fell forward onto her knees.

"HANG ON!" Whitney yelled as the boat crashed violently into the sandy beach of the island.

Cici went flying from the boat and landed hard in the sand, scraping up her side and back, getting the wind knocked out of her, and maybe even breaking a few ribs. Still, she rose instantly.

"Whitney?" Cici cried faintly between gasps as she struggled not only to stay standing, but also to catch her breath. "Whitney?"

She cried out again, louder this time as she looked toward the lake and saw that the monster had once again disappeared from view. She looked back toward the boat, desperately trying to find her friend. "Whitney!"

"Oh fuck. My fucking face!" Whitney moaned loudly, though it sounded as though she had something covering her mouth.

Cici ran toward the boat, toward her friend's voice, completely ignoring the pain in her torso, when Whitney suddenly popped up, right in the middle of the beached vessel. Cici screamed at the sight of her.

"That bad huh?" Whitney managed with a mumble.

It was terrible. It was one of the worse things Cici had ever seen. Whitney's face had been smashed so violently into the steering wheel, her nose had been smooshed almost flat, and both of her cheeks were already purple and swollen. Also, it looked like the bones below her eyes were broken. That wasn't part that bothered Cici most, however, as the worst injury to Cici's face was right below her nose. There, her upper lip was fat, bloody, purple, and partially severed. It hung down limply and fell into Whitney's mouth, going much too far in, accentuating the fact that she was now missing most of her upper row of teeth.

"Here let me help you," Cici cried, running to her friend.

"It's okay. I got it," Whitney said as she started to step over the side of the boat and onto the shore, though she would have fallen flat on her already maimed face if Cici hadn't been there to catch her. Fortunately, Cici successfully helped her friend out of the boat and down onto the sand.

"Where is it? Where did it go?" Whitney asked.

"I don't know. Let's just get the hell away from the water," Cici told her.

Whitney nodded.

They took each other's hands and started to walk toward the center of the island when there was a sudden, loud splash right behind them. Cici turned around just as Whitney was being pulled away from her by the sea-monster. It had the girl by the legs. Whitney screamed in fear and pain. Cici reached out and grabbed her other hand and pulled as hard as she could, but it was no use. Whitney's entire lower half was in the monster's mouth. Not knowing what else to do, Cici pulled harder still. She knew she couldn't let go, not even when she started to rise into the air, suspended by Whitney's arms as Whitney was suspended by the creature's large maw and horrendous, sharply pointed teeth. Cici still didn't let go. She wouldn't let go, not even if the monster pulled them both into the water. She hadn't had to face that situation, however, as the monster bit down hard, completely ripping her best friend in half, just below the ribs, and sending Cici and the majority of Whitney's torso flying backwards.

Cici and the upper half of Whitney landed hard, but as soon Cici hit the ground, she was back on her feet just as quickly, with Whitney still held tightly in her arms. She scrambled into the trees until she was definitely sure she was out of the monster's reach, then propped what she had left of Whitney's body against a soft looking stump.

Whitney looked up into Cici's eyes and smiled. She never moved again after that.

Cici held Whitney in her arms and cried.

Epilogue:

Christian Cameron was found two days later. There had been a search party sent after none of the girls showed up back home the second night, and they located her almost immediately.

The rescuers found Cici covered in blood and cradling Whitney's lifeless corpse in her arms, shaking and afraid. It was the most horrific scene any of them had ever encountered. They approached had the frightened girl carefully, but she was practically catatonic as the paramedics began tending to her wounds. The cops asked her questions and the only thing Cici managed to say was one sentence.

"He's real, Persy is real."

The paramedics took her away before the cops or anyone else could question her any further, but when they attempted to put her on a boat to bring her back to shore, Cici thrashed so violently that she knocked over the stretcher and they had to sedate her to calm her down. It took three fairly muscular paramedics to hold her down to administer the shot.

When Cici woke up in the hospital the next day, she told the cops the entire story of what had occurred at Lake Persephone.

No one believed her, of course, but they also didn't have enough evidence to prove anything to the contrary. Cici was released from the hospital two days later, with only minor injuries, including two broken ribs and a sprained wrist. Although she was suspected by some in the disappearance of her father and all her friends, she was never charged with a crime. The lake was dragged, but the bodies of Tom Cameron, Sandra and Pamela Hynes, and the lower half of Whitney Townsend were never found. Neither was the creature. The case remains officially unsolved to this day.

Jacob's Dragon

(Adapted from a chapter in Michael Mortimer's novel, *The Town Crier*)
By: Michael Mortimer

I leaned on the railing of the high dive and looked out over the lake. There was no moon. House lights shimmered on the surface, dulled by wisps of June mist. I reached into my pocket and pulled out my lucky rock. It was about three inches wide and shaped like a gibbous moon, thin and very smooth. In the vapid light it looked dark green, like the lake water below the surface. I tossed it up and down a few times.

The "high dive" was a rust-smattered, metal-framed platform ten feet above the water at the end of a concrete slab. The thick wooden planks under my bare feet had been worn smooth and free of splinters over the years. They felt as sturdy as ever. The dark brown house on the lot had always been boarded up, but back in the resort days there would've been a bunch of rich folks here jumping off this diving board. In my time, there was no actual board, but you could still see the holes where it had been attached. At some point, the platform was inherited by a bunch of lake-reeking kids. A point of bliss in the summer, my friends and I sometimes had it all to ourselves for a while, but more often there'd be a whole gaggle of kids and teens — sometimes enough that the cops would swing by and chase us off. Older kids would leap off the railing for an extra few feet of drop. Really brave ones would do a flip or a sailor's dive. Later on, in high school, it was an occasional destination for night swimming, beer, and skinny-dipping.

I could just barely see a wooden dock floating a little ways out. I faded back to times when my friends and I had epic games of King of the Dock. Fourteen-year-old boys, hours of tussling and swimming… I couldn't even imagine the energy we had. At fifty, my energy supplies were running low. Fifty. Jesus. Where did fifty come from? Snuck up on me, that's for sure. A great resignation had settled over me awhile back, the realization that I was running out of days. What had I done with my life? Not much. Who did I have? I was married once, for a minute, but now I couldn't buy a girlfriend if I tried… Not many friends at all, certainly no good ones. Parents gone and buried, no family anymore that I was close to. I put the rock back in my pocket, took off my clothes, and dropped them to the concrete below. I stepped towards the edge of the platform and leapt off. My breath sucked in; I smiled as I splashed below. I paddled on the surface of the warm, thick water for a few moments. A fish jumped behind me. I kicked my legs up and dove under. I swam deeper down for maybe ten feet, eyes open — murky blackness everywhere, but it didn't scare me.

I swam to the ladder and climbed out. After I pulled my shorts up, I took my lucky rock out of my pocket and moved to the water's edge. I held it in my open palm and did something I hadn't done since I was a kid. I made a wish. I wished on my rock that something would happen in my life. Something extraordinary. Something that would shake me loose from the inexorable gravity pulling me down into an early grave. I sidearm skipped the smooth rock into the lake, and although I only saw a few splashes before it disappeared into the darkness, I knew it was a good skip. I heard it go for quite a while. Of course, none of my wishes as a kid ever came true, so there was no reason for me to believe this one would either.

Two nights later, Adam, Dave, Mike, and Ed readied themselves for a night of adventure.

It was just after midnight and the four fifteen-year-olds were in the Shack — a hideout in the woods they recently built behind Adam's house. They had entered the beer drinking phase earlier that summer, at a post-freshman-year party, with varying degrees of success. They were all eager to try it again. Finding older people willing to hook them up though, was proving unusually tough, so the acquisition of beer became the order of the night.

Adam had a brilliantly exciting, even dangerous, notion one day on the lake in his canoe — he noticed that The Beach House restaurant had a couple old wood-framed crawlspace windows on the lake side. A basement. What would a restaurant/bar keep in its basement? Cases of beer perhaps?

Adam had rowed over solo a few nights later to reconnoiter the accessibility of the windows. He managed to jimmy the old sash lock with a simple flick of his pocketknife. He swung the window out and up and held it open, his heart pounding. After a good minute, he lowered it back into place, then darted down to the canoe and pushed out. Once far enough away, he stopped paddling and drifted for a half hour, watching to see if any police responded to an alarm. There was nothing.

Go time.

Adam codenamed the outing "Operation: Beer Bandits" and developed a simple plan: row a canoe across the lake to the beach behind the restaurant. Adam would enter through a window and feed out cases to Mike and Ed, who would then rush them down to the waiting canoe where Dave would be on lookout. Assembly line-style. Three cases seemed like a good number, not too much, not too little. Maybe the restaurant wouldn't even notice.

Other than the crunch of their footsteps and the relentless wall of insect noise, it was very quiet as they moved down the dirt road behind the Shack, towards Lakeside Drive. They wore dark hoodies, looking very much like teenagers up to no good, but they made it to the dock without issue. Dave's dad owned the biggest canoe, so earlier that day, Dave pocketed the key to the lock. Now he unlocked it. He pulled the chain through the eyehook, making such a clanking racket that Adam hissed at him, "Dude, shut the fuck up!"

A short time later, they were on the water, with Adam and Dave paddling slowly towards The Beach House. Mike and Ed kept their eyes and ears on alert. All was quiet. They skidded onto the beach.

The restaurant hadn't even locked the window from the last time Adam was here. He slipped in (very bravely, the others noted), turned on his headlamp, and returned about thirty seconds later with a case of Yuengling. One more case of Yuengling and a case of Keystone later, they were back in the canoe and heading for the far side of the lake. They planned to stash the beer in the trees near the lake's other bar, the Casino. Then they would paddle the canoe back to Dave's dock, lock it up as before, and simply walk over and grab the beer. They could bolt straight up the hill and back to the Shack with it and no one would ever be the wiser.

The water quietly slapping against the metal canoe lulled them into post-adrenaline contemplations. Then, mid-row, Adam gasped. He couldn't believe it — a cop cruiser pulling into the Casino parking lot, headlights off.

"Oh, fuck," Ed said.

Dave tightened his hood around his face and ducked. The others did the same.

"What do we do?" Mike whispered frantically.

"Dump the beer! Dump the beer!" Ed pleaded.

"Don't fucking touch the beer!" Adam hissed. He thought for a moment. "Back! Row back, now!" He had his paddle in the water, and they started to spin. Then Dave paddled and they righted. The cruiser slowed to a stop as they moved towards the middle of the lake.

"I don't think he saw us," Adam whispered. "Must be a routine patrol. Probably getting ready for a nap. We'll wait it out."

"Fuuuck..." Ed's breathing was unsteady. Dave stifled a laugh with a hand over his mouth as they floated back and drifted. Mike snorted. Then, as kids are prone to do in a scary situation, they had a full on crack up. They kept it quiet though.

When it passed Mike said, "We have three fuckin' cases of beer!"

"Shh!" Adam said, with an eye on the cruiser. "We aren't out of the woods yet."

They felt it before they heard it. The canoe was jostled as something scraped against the bottom.

"What was that?" Ed asked.

"I don't know. Maybe a log," Adam answered, not believing his own words.

Dave leaned his head over the water to see what he could see. Adam peered out into the water and swore he saw something large and spiky break the surface, briefly, maybe fifteen feet away.

"What was that?" Adam mumbled, more to himself.

"What?" Ed's voice was getting high pitched.

Something exploded from the water where Dave was leaning over. Blinded by water spray and their own fear, the boys couldn't fathom what was happening. Dave's body flopped back into the boat, missing its head.

Ed began screaming.

Mike stared, slack jawed, as the body twitched. Blood squirted in gushes. Adam grabbed his paddle and rowed hard towards the cop. He didn't get far before the canoe was blasted from below and lifted off the water, jolting to one side. Dave's body tumbled out. The cases of beer too. Mike was thrown sideways into the water. The boat came back down hard, as a panicked Mike came to the surface a few feet away and thrashed back to its side.

"Help me!"

Ed sat frozen but Adam lunged. He grabbed Mike's arms and pulled. Mike was halfway in, bent over at the waist, when he was yanked from Adam's grasp. Mike wheezed in pain as he disappeared underwater, the canoe nearly tipping over with him.

Adam was paralyzed, but only for a moment. He grabbed his paddle and shouted at the cop car — "Help! We need help!" Ed snapped out of his own fear-induced paralysis and started screaming too.

Just as the officer opened his car door, the sound of tearing metal came from the bow. The stern lifted a couple feet off the water then slapped back down. Water gurgled in through a gaping hole in the bottom of the boat. Within seconds, it was half-filled and sinking.

The cop turned on his spotlight, shining it on the lake just in time to see Adam dive from the vanishing boat and swim like a madman towards shore. Ed screamed in the stern as the bow went down. Finally, he tumbled into the water, swimming twenty yards behind Adam.

The cop had his light on them. "What's going on out there!"

Adam reached the point where his feet touched the bottom. He ran. On the beach he turned and shouted to Ed. "Swim! Faster! Come on!"

Ed was only fifty feet from shore when he was pulled below.

I was in a booth at Nino's Pizzeria, eating lunch, when I heard the news. The guy from the vacuum store came in and ordered a slice, then casually mentioned that a few kids were missing up at Mountain Lake. No one was sure what happened, but another kid who was with them apparently blamed it on a monster in the lake.

I was out the door and in my pick-up before he even finished his sentence.

Figuring it would be a circus down there, I parked my truck at home, then grabbed my bike and headed down the hill. I rode to the fork, went right, towards the Casino, and saw that it was a circus indeed. Cars lined the road and people were all over the place, searching the trees and the waterline for any sign of the boys.

There were a ton of boats out on the water. I suppose Sunday is a great day for a search party, because everyone was out. The cops were in the Casino parking lot. I leaned my bike on a fence post and moved past a news van towards the action, passing a couple guys donning scuba gear in the back of a pick-up. A group of four, early twenty-somethings, recorded the action with their phones — imagining fame as documentarians, I'm sure.

Sarge Taylor, my friend from high school, was there, off-duty no less, judging by the street clothes. He was conferring with some staties but saw me coming and met me halfway.

"What's going on?" I asked.

"All we know is that four boys were in a canoe late last night, and only one of them came to shore. He told an officer that something attacked their boat and took the other three under."

"That's insane."

"Tell me about it. But the patrolman who was parked here turned his spotlight on the lake…" He shifted uneasily. "He saw one of the boys swimming to shore go under."

"Go under?"

"Yeah, as if pulled…" A chill went through my body as I looked out at the rippling water. "Remember Mandy Hendershot?" Taylor asked, nodding towards a huddled group of crying women.

"Sure." I'd gone to grade and high schools with her. I saw her in the group, tissue to her nose, comforted by the other women.

"Her youngest son is one of the missing boys."

There was a sudden commotion as a man emerged from the grove of trees next to the parking lot, carrying a sopping wet, black sweatshirt. He held it up to the cops — it was shredded. Mandy Hendershot screamed. Taylor rushed off as I tried to figure out what to do next. They didn't need my help in the search, so I went to the bar.

The Casino was crowded, the hub for gossip and misinformation. I could tell who the regulars were — they were irked by the interruption of their monotony. A stubble-ridden old guy, gray-haired and haggard, sat at the bar with a cocktail in front of him, looking at me. I had a glimmer of recognition but couldn't place him. After the harried bartender gave me my beer, I went to find a table that looked out over the lake.

The kid's claim of a monster seemed absurd, but, I couldn't shake a nagging sense…

A uniformed statie rowed the scuba guys out two hundred feet from shore. The water was green and murky in this lake, but where they were, it was only about fifteen feet deep, so finding a canoe wouldn't be a problem. The divers lowered their masks, inserted their regulators, picked up their flashlights, and splashed below.

As soon as they went under, it was as if the scene outside went motionless, becoming like the painting of a lake. The only minute movements I could discern were sparkling ripples and diminutive waves; nothing else seemed to move. Then I felt it, and the chattering of all the people in the bar became a low, incomprehensible murmur that drifted through some distant part of my mind. I was suddenly in a stasis of anticipation — something inside me seemed to know that the fabric of perception was about to be shredded, like the sweatshirt found by the shore.

Then bubbles hit the surface. They were not the bubbles one might expect from basic scuba activity, however, but a violent surge of air, as if one of the air tanks had exploded underwater. A faint shade of red tinted the water as the bubbles dissipated. Ten seconds after the bubbles, one of the divers broke the surface twenty-five feet from the boat. He ripped his regulator out and gestured frantically, first at the shore, then at the boat, all the while shouting words I couldn't make out. His body language was clear: "GET ME OUT OF THE WATER!".

The cop in the boat grabbed the oars and started towards him. The scuba guy freestyle-stroked to help close the distance. He was five feet from the boat, and I was on my feet, head pressed against the window, when the inevitable finally happened.

I've known snapping turtles very well in my life. There is a family of snapping turtles living in my pond, at least three of them. I have witnessed, on several occasions, two of them rolling on the surface, entwined, so I assume that there have been many more, hatching, living, and dying over the years. They've been there at least as long as I have. I've encountered them many times, walking alongside the pond, and I presume there's a nest nearby. I always move in for a better look at this creature that to me was as close to a prehistoric monster as I could ever hope to find. Of course, as a kid, I also couldn't resist poking them with a stick (a long one). I'd marvel at the vicious hissing, and the way the long neck would crane out, twisting so it could snap its dreadful beak at any nearby danger. This wasn't a turtle whose first instinct was to hide in its shell. When taking a dip in the pond, I always silently hoped I didn't lose a toe. I did research years ago to learn more about this fascinating animal — Chelydra Serpentina, that could live to be a hundred-years-old. Interesting fact, a snapper will swim to the bottom of a lake or pond or river, partially bury itself in the muck, then open its mouth wide and let its worm-like tongue float and sway, attracting hungry, doomed fish. They hold their breath for hours at a time and even absorb oxygen directly from the water itself. In the winter, they hibernate under the ice. The biggest ones inhabiting my pond were the size of large watermelons.

What I saw that day at Mountain Lake, the thing that took that diver down, was closer to the size of a small car.

I gasped as the massive, jagged shell broke the surface. The head rose from the depths, swiveling at the end of a neck as thick as an oak tree. The beak opened and clamped down on the diver, instantly forcing him under, a dead man for sure. Its clawed rear feet and spiky tail cleared the water as it submerged again, its tail thwapping down once before disappearing, soaking the cop in the boat.

Other than the roiling water that rocked his boat, the cop himself had gone immobile. I heard a moaning sound, actually thought it was the cop for a moment, even though he was much too far away, then realized it was me. I silenced it and turned away from the window. One couple, also by the window, were babbling, arguing about what they'd just seen. The old guy who had been watching me at the bar was next to me, against the window. He put a shaking hand to his mouth and turned to me. No one else in the bar had witnessed any of it. I bolted for the door.

Outside, I rushed towards the beach and called to Taylor. "Not now!" he barked, in crisis mode. I understood. A cop squawked through a bullhorn, trying to clear the boats off the water. Other officers were pushing everyone back away from the beach. I ignored them and moved forward to the water's edge. This lake where I'd grown up, swam countless times, that was always a place of comfort, suddenly took on a sinister aura of the unknown.

I felt a hand on my shoulder. "You're Corbin Hoffman's son, aren't you?"

I turned to the old guy from the bar. I remembered him — Kyle Beatty, my dad's friend who was around all the time when I was a kid. I hadn't seen him since the funeral thirty-five years ago. He seemed pretty drunk, then and now. "Yeah."

"Do you remember me?"

"Yes."

His hazy eyes filled with emotion. He seemed on the verge of getting something off his chest but thought better of it. He said, "Why don't you come with me up the hill to my house."

I looked back at the lake just as a young officer stepped towards us. "You guys have to clear off the beach right now."

I stayed a few paces behind Kyle as we walked up the hill in front of the Casino, past the old inn. We reached Lewis Lane and entered his yard. The house was beat down, with peeling white paint. He trudged up the concrete steps, opened the screechy screen door leading to the screened-in porch, and held it for me. I went in. I waited for him to pass and open the wooden main door, then followed him inside.

I remembered coming into this house when I was little; I envisioned my dad, younger, laughing. I felt the past swelling up here, tangible — I knew Kyle felt it too. He was staring at me again, searching me to find my dad, his friend that he lost so long ago. And maybe the self that died with him.

I noticed a woman in her sixties lying on her side on the couch, looking at a tablet. She wore pajama pants and a sleeveless Allman Brothers concert shirt, revealing faded tattoos on her upper arms. She raised her eyes to me. "Hi, sweetie."

Kyle shifted awkwardly. "Oh, sorry. This is Katie."

"I'm Cobb."

She smiled and asked, "What's going on down there?"

I replied, "Something in the lake attacked the divers."

"What do you mean, 'something'?"

"Giant snapping turtle, looked like to me," I said.

She screwed up her face and said, "Jesus." She blinked and went back to her device with a, "...hmm."

Kyle again looked as if he wanted to say something important, maybe profound. "You want a beer?"

"Sure, thanks," I said, thinking that was about the most profound thing he could have said right then. He went into the kitchen.

The house was sparsely decorated and smelled faintly of cannabis and heavily of a lifelong bachelor. But it was tidy and dust-free, probably thanks to Katie. A battered acoustic guitar leaned in the corner next to a record player and an impressive vinyl collection. Probably nothing past 1990, I figured. I remembered music playing here, on that record player: Neil Young's "Down by the River" on one occasion, and Van Morrison's "And It Stoned Me" on another. The *phhhts* of two bottles opening brought me round again as Kyle came in holding out a brown bottle of Yuengling. I took it.

"Well, cheers." He tilted his bottle in my direction and took a swig. I did the same. "Why don't you sit down?" he said as he dropped onto the couch, tapping Katie's legs out of the way. She curled them up.

I sat down in an old, frayed, but super-comfortable chair. To help us out of the awkward silence that soon followed, I said, "Some scene down there, huh?."

He said, "No shit. The Hendershot lady and her boy live just two doors down from me. The boy who survived is right next to them. All teenagers are assholes, but they seemed all right. Just boys."

"Did you see it? The thing in the water?"

He swallowed hard. "My eyes ain't the best right now. What did you see?"

I exhaled deeply. "I read once about the Stupendemys Geographicus, the largest turtle to ever live, as far as they know. It was the size of a compact car and supposedly went extinct ten million years ago. What I saw today would make me argue that."

Kyle took this in, his eyes going hazy again. "You always were a smart kid."

"Kinda dumb, actually. In most ways."

"Yeah? That makes two of us." He pulled deeply off his beer and rubbed a hand on his forehead. He smiled weakly. I felt it again, the weight of the past. It must have been especially heavy for Kyle because he seemed about to crumble under it. He cleared his throat and finally said the thing weighing him down. "I'm sorry, you know?... Sorry that I never checked up on you after your dad died. I should've. We were real close, me and your dad. Your mom never liked me much, but I should've..." Katie got up and tiptoed out of the room as Kyle trailed off.

I could tell this was important for him. It was irrelevant to me at this point, but if I could offer some feeble absolution to an old man, then why not? "No worries, I did all right."

"I'm glad to hear that. But that's not the point…"

"It's okay."

A silence hung heavy for a while, but I don't think either of us minded.

He said, "So strange… As boys, your grandfather told us stories about this area… stories of a giant snapping turtle living in the lake. How Indians and Dutch colonists used to battle it."

I thought back to my games of King of the Dock as a boy, how occasionally I or someone else would mock anyone tossed into the water that they better watch out for the giant snapper. Was this because my dad told me the story at some point? I didn't remember. Maybe it something that we just knew? A reality that became a myth that lived in the water, waiting for us to soak it up…

Kyle continued, "He told us that in the Lenape days, this creature was seen quite a bit. Anyone fishing in the lake had to be cautious. Even in the last couple hundred years there have been more than a handful of missing persons. Supposedly drowned but never found." He took another pull off his bottle, then perked up a little. "I remember making wooden swords and shields with your dad and tramping around these woods like regular Knights of the Round Table, searching the swamps for the dreaded dragon to slay. Guess it wasn't just a myth after all."

"I guess not."

I felt better when I left Kyle's place a little while later, and I think he did too. When I got back to my bike, however, the chaos still ensuing on the beach planted a troubling thought in my mind. I rode around the lake, heading home, unable to shake a steadily growing sense of responsibility. I wasn't blind to the fact that the appearance of the monster coincided almost perfectly with me skipping that wish-laden stone into the middle of the lake.

Nino's Pizzeria was not where I wanted to be the next day, but I'd agreed to help Nino with the lunch shift deliveries. I leaned on the customer side of the counter as he kneaded a dough ball.

"I saw it. It was a legit lake monster. A giant snapping turtle."

"Bullshit!" he snorted.

"I saw it, plain as day. It took down a scuba diver."

"You didn't see nuthin'! Shit like that don't happen."

I shrugged. The bell above the door jingled. One of Nino's poker buddies, Lou, came rushing in, his phone held out in front of him, eyes wide. "Did you guys see the footage?"

"Footage of what?" Nino asked, laying the stretched dough on the peel.

"A fucking monster in Mountain Lake. They recorded it taking down a scuba diver."

"Jesus Christ, not you too! Let me see this bullshit."

I smirked – apparently the documentarians on the beach hit paydirt.

Lou went behind the counter. "It's gone viral. It's all over the news." His hand was shaking as he held the phone up to Nino's face. Nino was mid-movement ladling sauce onto the dough, acting as if put out, bored by the whole thing, dripping ladle hovering just above the dough surface. Lou hit play. Nino squinted a little and leaned in. After maybe ten seconds, his eyes went wide and he gasped, his body jolting as if electrocuted.

"Jesus Christ!"

The ladle flew up and spun around, sending sauce all over Lou and everything else in the vicinity. By the time it clattered to the ground, Nino was already in the back room, cursing. He flung his apron across the room as onions rolled across the floor, spilled from a box he had knocked over along the way.

"Fuckin' bullshit! It's AI!"

Lou turned towards me, sauce dripping off his face and phone. I went around the counter, dodging the puddles of sauce, to hand him a towel. He asked if I wanted to see the clip. I shook my head —I didn't need to see any damn video to confirm what I'd seen. It was seared into my brain.

Nino pulled himself together enough to finish the lunch orders, though he was uncharacteristically quiet. Probably shaken to the core, I figured. A lot of people must be feeling the same. I spent the next couple hours delivering pizza. Lou's "viral" comment irked me, as did the notion that all this would somehow put Mountain Lake and Hackettstown on the map in a big way. My mind roiled, trying to figure out what in the hell it had to do with me.

Eighty-one-year-old Silas Leonard lived in a small, shabby house on Tamarack Road, just across from the vast swamp that spills off the south end of Mountain Lake. He couldn't figure out why J.D. wouldn't quit barking at the woods.

"What's going on, girl?"

The ten-year-old German Shepard was against the screen door, hackles up, growling with her teeth bared. She turned to Silas briefly, then barked furiously at the trees, butting her nose against the fraying screen. Silas pulled her back by the collar.

"Easy, girl. What the hell's gotten into you?"

Silas had always been a bit of a loner, usually chasing away anyone who ever started to care about him, though there weren't many of those to begin with, and that suited him just fine. He enjoyed watching

YouTube videos at night, and fishing or deer and turkey hunting with J.D. in the preserve across the street. He always got along better with dogs than people anyhow.

The problem was, though he lived less than a mile from the lake, Silas was just isolated enough that he hadn't yet heard about the situation going on over there. The house next to him was now owned by a family he didn't know and had never even talked to. He had no way of knowing that a large creature in the lake would have fled from the ensuing tumult and sought refuge in a more isolated area. If he'd known, he would have realized that a bog was the perfect place for a humongous snapping turtle to hide.

Silas flicked up the hook holding the door in place and pushed past J.D. He shoved the door closed in her face as she barked again. He slid the hook into the eye on the outside to keep her in.

"Stay put."

She jumped up and pushed at the door with her front feet, then continued to bark.

"Hush now," he barked back. He put a saluting hand on his forehead to shield out the sun and stared with crinkled eyes at the tree line across Tamarack. He saw no movement. "What do you smell out there, girl?" He took some steps forward until he reached the gravel on the side of the road. A car whizzed by, surprising him, as Tamarack usually wasn't that busy of a road. The forest was dense around the swamp where the lake let out, and Silas couldn't see past a hundred feet in. Probably a bear, he figured.

J.D. though, named after Silas's favorite drink, knew what bear smelled like, and everything else in the bog, for that matter. She'd been roaming around in there since Silas got her as a puppy ten years ago, and she claimed some dominion over the land across the road. What she smelled now was something else — something strange, unknown, primeval. It was so overpowering that it drove her mad. The idea that the man who'd always been so kind to her would cross over and enter the woods with that smell, without her, was too much.

Silas, who had no intention of going into the woods at all, spun around as J.D. exploded through the screen door. Barking furiously, she bolted towards him, then into the road.

"J.D.!"

A car screeched to a halt to avoid hitting her as she darted across the road, then down the slope towards the bog. The driver shouted at Silas, who briefly wondered why there was so much traffic, but Silas just waved him off, and the car moved on. The dog's barking grew fainter as the woods quickly swallowed her.

"J.D.! Come back here, girl!" Silas said as he took a step to follow, but, gritting his teeth, turned back to the house instead.

He did his aching-bodied best to rush inside and grab his twelve-gauge shotgun from the rack on the wall. He always kept it loaded, so he knew it was ready to go, but he opened a drawer and put some extra shells in his back pocket, just in case. Well, *he thought,* if it's gonna be a bear that kills me, fuck it.

Silas moved, panting and sweating, through the grove of tamarack trees and past the big old white oak, until he felt the sphagnum moss under his feet. He was close to the brook now. He knew this forest better than the back of his wrinkled hand. The dog's barking grew steadily louder, so Silas knew she'd stopped running. Her bark became more repetitive, less hysterical. She must've found what she was looking for.

Finally, J.D. came into view at the edge of a swampy area where the creek turns west. She stood crouched with her forelegs low and straight, hindquarters up. He stopped to catch his breath twenty feet from her. She was next to a large, jagged tree stump, growling towards the cluster of skunk cabbage in the water. Silas couldn't see what she was looking at, his view obscured by a deteriorating, fallen tree.

"J.D.!" Silas gasped for air. "Come over here, girl."

She looked at him, then amped up her ferocity. Silas's heart thundered in his chest. He thought, with a chill, that he may just topple over right there. The dog continued barking and growling, then Silas heard a splash.

Something in the water, *he thought, as he raised his gun to his shoulder and crept forward. He couldn't fathom what had his dog so fired up. When he cleared the stump and stood next to J.D., he lowered his gun and just stared in bewilderment.*

A foot-long pink worm protruded from the water ten feet away. It was just wiggling around and splashing about.

Well, shit, *Silas thought,* at eighty-one I am seeing something I ain't never seen before.

J.D. was frenzied as Silas stepped closer and leaned in, trying to figure out just what in the hell... The worm dropped below, down into darkness as something massive, the color of swamp muck, erupted from the morass. The last thing Silas Leonard ever saw was a gaping maw twisting sideways, just before the beak clamped down on his body.

It was deep into the night, a 3 a.m. feel. The clear sky was densely peppered with planets and stars — the vastness so evident, I had to turn away if I gazed too long. The moon was nowhere to be found. I'd been in a camping chair at the edge of my pond for hours, chewing things over as I watched the lightning bugs and listened to the frogs. Then, with crystal clarity, I realized what I had to do. And it terrified me to the point of tears.

That night I dreamed that I felt myself deteriorating, one atom at a time, and I was okay with it. I had decided to give up the endless, futile battle against gravity and lie down on the ground to let the Earth reclaim me. Eventually the husk of my body blew away and my bones rose up, and I was just a skeleton — a skeleton that ran through the woods, and swam in the pond. A skeleton that stood on the deck, bone arms outstretched to the sky, silently screaming with joy because I was free.

I woke up in the chair, in the moments before sunrise. I barely moved as I watched as the night slip back into the shadows, then, painfully, I pried my stiff body up and out of the chair. I cracked my back and stretched my arms and legs, trying to get things flowing right as my joints snapped and popped in protest. I took off my clothes and dove into the chilly pond to shock my system, then I went inside to brew some coffee.

I had a big day ahead of me.

I rode my bike down to the lake around eight that morning, wanting to scope out the scene. When I reached the Lakeside Drive fork, it was worse than I'd imagined — cars were backed up going both ways. I turned left towards the firehouse, which I assumed was the base of operations. Cars lined the road along my route, to the point that traffic barely flowed. Horns blared everywhere, as residents shouted at visiting gawkers and monster seekers to get the hell out of the way and stop blocking driveways.

People crowded the beach of the Beach House, as well as the grass area on the west side. I braked and looked out across the lake. A dozen metal boats drifted around on its surface. Behind them, the Casino beach was even more packed. At least two news vans were over there. I reached the firehouse, and I was right — home base for the cops. The lot was full of vehicles from Belvidere PD, State Police, Sheriff's Department, and Fish and Game. If Sarge Taylor was here to help out, I could maybe get a scoop on what was going on. And maybe, just maybe, he'd tell me something that meant my big day didn't have to be so big after all. I inquired with a Belvidere cop I knew a little, and sure enough, Taylor was there.

"Can you believe this shit?" he said when he met me out front, wired on too much coffee.

"Not really," I answered.

He told me that the boats on the lake were using fish-finders, dangling hunks of raw meat on big hooks, and trawling with nets. I looked out at the water again with a sinking feeling. With that much activity on the water, even a large creature would want to find somewhere safe and quiet. I glanced behind the firehouse, where the lake let out into Mountain Lake Brook, creating a big swamp called the Bog Preserve. I bid Taylor farewell, then made my way around to the other side of the lake, where I walked up the hill to Kyle's house.

I wasn't sure why I was going there. Melville once wrote that, "Few men's courage is proof against protracted meditation unrelieved by action", and I figured I was out to prove him right. Or maybe I was hoping Kyle would talk me out of my asinine plan. Still, some trace of my certainty from last night hadn't yet evaporated in the harsh light of the sun. As crazy as it seemed, it somehow didn't seem that crazy at all. Not yet anyway.

Katie answered from the porch when I knocked on the screen. "Hi, sweetie. Come on in." I stepped in. Katie hollered, "Kyle!" then went back to the couch and her tablet. When he walked into the living room, Kyle seemed surprised, then touched to see me standing there.

"You want a beer?"

"I better not."

"Okay. What can I do for you?"

"Mind if I sit?"

"No. Go ahead."

I sat in the same chair and Kyle sat next to Katie. I wasn't sure where to begin. I saw the guitar and said, "I remember you were really good."

He blinked a few times, then nodded. "Ah, not bad… Shit, bring a lady up here, play 'Stairway to Heaven' or 'Wild Horses'... that kind of thing is a great panty remover."

"Jesus, really?" Katie said, then once again got up and left the room.

Kyle called after her playfully, "That's how I got you, if I recall."

A unseen door slammed.

"You and Katie been together long?"

"Christ, I don't know. I brought her up here for a night and she never left. She's all right, though. Tidies up…" He got back to the music. "Me and your dad wrote a handful of songs together, back in the day. We had plans… we were gonna have a band. Corbin was a good songwriter, man, a poet for sure. We would've gotten good if we'd have stuck with it."

"Quite a circus down there," I said after a moment, with a gesture towards the lake.

"That's for sure."

"Turtles by nature are shy animals."

Kyle tilted his head slightly, confused. "I guess."

"I'm just saying maybe the bog is a better place to look."

"Ok… I suppose that makes a bit of sense."

Finally, I sighed and sat back. "What if I told you that I may be responsible for what's happening now?"

Kyle took a minute, then leaned forward, wincing from his bad back. "I'd say that's kinda hard to believe."

I told him about my wish, how I skipped my rock into the lake, and how it was just after that when the monster appeared. Kyle's dewy eyes stared at me, betraying no emotion. Certainly not disbelief. He sipped his beer and grunted. "Well, that's quite a story. Forgive an old timer like me if I can't quite get my feeble mind around it…" He sipped and ruminated. "Then again, before the other day, I'd never have believed any of this was possible either…" He waved a hand towards the lake. "Even so, what are you getting at?"

"I think I need to take care of this myself, before anyone else dies."

He blinked several times. "You can't be serious." When I didn't answer, he continued. "If you want to do something, go tell the law down there your thoughts on where the damned thing might be hiding. They have plenty of firepower. That's what they're paid to do."

"I'm not convinced bullets will do anything against what I saw… And what if someone else gets killed trying?"

"It's more likely that you'll get killed. It's a fool's errand. Go the hell home and don't even think about it anymore. Or stay here and drink beer with me for a while. They'll have this all wrapped up pretty soon."

Despite the truth in each of his points, I knew with a renewed sense of purpose that I was going into the bog today. "You don't by any chance have a real sword, do you?"

"A what now?"

"You mentioned that you and my dad used to take wooden swords on quests."

Kyle was quiet for a long while. He sighed and stood up. "Well, no. But I may have something else."

After rummaging and clanking around in his shed for a couple minutes, Kyle came out with a six foot long, square iron rod, maybe an inch and half thick. One end had been grinded to a rough point, battered by use. He brushed some webs off it and held it out. "I used this for aerating my lawn and prying out rocks and whatnot. I don't know if it's quite what you're looking for..."

I took it and looked it over. It was heavy, but my years of house painting had given me a solid core of strength. "It's perfect."

"Why don't we get out my grinder and sharpen it up a bit?"

After he finished, the iron rod was dangerously sharp. Kyle surprised me by grabbing a can of kerosene from the shed and filling four empty beer bottles with it, then stuffing old rags into the mouths of each, thus creating some good ol' fashioned Molotov cocktails. He stuffed them into a tattered, army-green shoulder bag and handed it to me. He said, "I still don't think you should go, but you're a grown man, and your dad would appreciate me doing my best to make sure you come out alive."

He reached into the breast pocket of his shirt and handed me an old flip-top lighter.

"This is probably really dumb," I said.

Kyle considered this. He said, "All I know anymore is that there's a grave waiting for us all somewhere."

I pushed through his screen door and walked down the steps into his yard, feeling the weight of the lance each time my foot hit the ground. Kyle called from behind me, "Be careful, Jacob."

"Okay, will do."

"Come back and see me sometime."

No one paid me any mind as I rode back around towards the firehouse, despite the metal rod resting awkwardly on my shoulder and the bag of clanking explosives. When the firehouse came into view, I stopped my bike and considered what Kyle said. I could easily track down Taylor and tell him my thoughts on where the monster might be hiding, and since the bog was directly behind the firehouse, it would be easy enough to send a team in there to search it out. Instead, I made a right onto Knoll Dr. and rode to the edge of the woods where there weren't any houses. I pulled my bike into the underbrush and walked into the copse of pines where, as teenagers, we had many a paintball battle. The swamp was to my left.

The Bog Preserve was a mystical (some said haunted) place when we were kids, mainly because of the generally unexplorable nature of it. We would move far enough in that we could see the vast, primordial, forbidden land beyond, then turn back in silence, inherently aware of its many dangers. This time though, I didn't stop at the edge. I looked to where the creek flowed into the bog, swallowed my fear in a cartoonish gulp, then dropped down the slope and followed the stream.

I scanned for a sign of anything that might help me on my quest as I walked, and it wasn't long before I saw something of interest — a large, muddy area at a bend in the brook, where the summer waters had receded, which was heavily disturbed and churned. Although I could easily identify prints left behind by deer, bear, mountain lions, and racoon when I saw them, this was totally foreign to me. There was a wide swath of pressed down mud, with thick claw scrapes on either side. Right down the middle was a steady gash through the mud. Like a dragging tail. I was no genius, but it wasn't hard to imagine a gigantic turtle leaving a trail just like this.

Dammit.

What had seemed like a fool's errand suddenly morphed into a suicide mission. Was that my ultimate goal, blundering into a bog to battle a dragon? There had to be easier ways of pulling it off than being eaten alive. *But it certainly is original,* I thought.

The dark, fetid power of the place held me fully in its thrall, as I realized that all our forebodings as children were well-founded. I gripped the pole tightly and tried to step as quietly as possible in the direction the tracks led, but the slurping suction of my boots in the mud was devastatingly loud. I came to where the brook turned hard west, and there, across the creek, next to a fallen tree, I saw color. Green, gray, and brown dominated the palate here, but this was an out-of-place red, though it was probably just fabric or plastic. The water here wasn't deep enough to conceal something the size of the creature, so I moved into the brook and made my way across, stepping on rocks most of the way. On the other side, I clambered up the embankment and found what was indeed fabric, of the flannel kind. I stepped closer.

There was an arm inside the sleeve, severed above the elbow, clutching a shotgun in its rigid, pallid hand. The ghastly sight sent fear crashing over me. I leaned the lance on the stump and carefully unshouldered the bag of bottles.

I heard a squishy splashing, mixed with the sound of suctioning air on my left.

There it was, in all its terrifying glory: a monster right out of a fairy tale, lumbering through the mud some forty feet away, perpendicular to me. It was the most incredible thing I'd ever seen. Its massive shell had three rows of spikes, like mountain ranges, and spikes all around the edges. The legs were scaly and covered in thorns; the long tail dragged behind it, truly something that belonged on a dragon. Its over-sized head was like a block of water-rotted wood, with beady reptilian eyes, mostly hidden under a rough membrane. With a downward slashing mouth that culminated in a dagger-like, overbite beak, it was as if a giant hunk of deep, dank earth had broken loose and come to life.

I cursed myself for not bringing a camera instead of these feeble weapons, as I knew what I had brought stood no chance against this creature. I decided to wait until it passed, then flee to the firehouse, where I'd tell law enforcement to gather as many explosives as they could and call the National Guard.

I'm not sure if it smelled me or what, but the moment I thought to flee, it stopped abruptly, and pushed its four legs out completely to their highest length, lifting its shell away from the ground. Its wickedly long neck stretched out as far as it could go, transforming what had at first looked rather clumsy and oafish into something lethal. The head swiveled back and forth in search of danger, while its tail whisked around, almost canine-like, in anticipation. I considered that its vision might be based on movement, and hoped that if I stood completely still, it wouldn't see me. Then I thought of Schrödinger's Cat and wondered if I could maybe close my eyes and make the monster cease to exist altogether. So I did. I closed my eyes tight and froze in place. I've never in my life been so still. It was working too, because with my eyes clamped shut, the thing disappeared into the vaporous blackness behind my eyelids.

Then it hissed.

When I opened my eyes, its head was swiveled directly at me, its own eyes much wider than before, and demonic with hatred. It opened its mouth absurdly wide and wiggled its footlong pink tongue grotesquely.

I may have pissed myself I can't be sure, as the thing turned slowly on its axis until facing right at me. We stared at each other, two gunslingers in a quick-draw shootout. Only, I had no intention of drawing or shooting anything. I merely trembled, waiting for either my brutal demise or for a miracle in which it decided I didn't look appetizing enough to eat, and went on about its business. Ultimately, I must have looked pretty tasty, because the beast began to rock its body back and forth, hissing and snapping its beak with brutal clacks — a preview of what it held in store. But it didn't advance.

I had resigned myself to death, thinking I would simply kneel and accept my fate as a meal for this fucking dinosaur, but then remembered the shotgun. I looked over my shoulder: the arm was only five feet away. I took a step back. The snapper hissed, pulled its neck in, and shot it back out. Snap! But still, it didn't advance. I took a couple steps back and I was at the gun. Dammit if the thing didn't cock its head knowingly before charging.

I spun and lifted the gun, the dead hand still clinging to it. I shook it off and the arm flopped to the ground. The gun was an old double barrel, just like one of my dad's. One I had fired many times at clay pigeons. I had about ten seconds, just enough time to check the safety and see if it was loaded. I cracked it open: two shells. I checked one: unfired. I clacked it shut. Safety off, I lifted the gun and nestled the butt against my shoulder. I aimed at the charging snapper's head with a clarity that surprised me. I even waited until the mouth opened before I pulled the trigger.

Click.

Water-logged and useless. I slumped my shoulders. The snapper made its final five-foot lunge. I tossed the shotgun horizontally into the gaping maw, diving to the left. It missed me by millimeters. I rolled away as the turtle snapped the gun like a twig. It then made a large arc and charged again.

I scampered around the stump to grab Kyle's lance, then continued circling the stump, figuring something that huge would be awkward in that game. I was wrong. Its elastic neck whipped around. The beak snapped, missing me, but just barely.

I smelled its pungent, swampy breath as I stumbled backwards and fell, coming to the sudden realization that I was, in fact, the awkward one. I slid myself backward until I was up against the partially submerged fallen tree. I climbed on top of it and balanced my way out forty feet where I reached the end. I was trapped.

The snapper waded into the shallow water and made its way towards me. It had me dead to rights. I thought about dropping into the water on the other side of the log, but I knew I would've become stuck in the mud for sure. I held the metal pole in shaking hands as the thing closed in, moving more like a snake than a turtle.

At first, I only noticed a harsh noise, just on the other side of the adrenaline roaring in my head. Then it registered as a dog barking, angry and loud.

A big German Shepherd charged past the stump and splashed into the water. Growling, it pounced forward and bit the snapper's swaying tail. The snapper turned its head away from me and hissed. The dog backed away, towards the forest, and the snapper followed. The creature reached solid ground and charged the dog. They circled each other, the dog making up for its lack of size with pure noise and frenzy.

The idea of this heroic canine falling prey after saving my life was too much to bear. I got mad, angry that I let my firmness of purpose once again disintegrate into cowardice. Angry at the idea of being lunch. I teetered back along the fallen tree to the stump where my bag waited.

I dropped the lance to pull one of the bottles from the bag, finding hope in the pungent gas fumes. I took Kyle's lighter from my pocket and lit the rag. It went up with a *whoosh,* the heat intense on my face. I cocked my arm back, set my feet, and waited for the snapper to circle around and create the largest target. I tossed the bomb.

It hit true. The glass shattered, spreading flaming gas over the creature's shell. The flames dripped down onto its legs and head.

I had never heard a turtle scream before and hope I never will again. It was a guttural, high-pitched hissing, and it filled me with grim satisfaction. The beast twisted towards me in furious confusion as I drew another cocktail from my bag. It moved to charge me, but the dog lunged and bit its tail again, giving me the time I needed to light the rag. I tossed it. This time it broke on the edge of the shell, towards the back legs. It did the trick though, as the fire spread along the creature's legs and tail, and under its shell.

Recognizing me as the cause of its pain, it charged hard. My cockiness vanished. Neither the dog nor another Molotov could save me now. I gritted my teeth and grabbed the lance. I held it out, snarling — it was dull-end forward.

The flaming snapper bore down upon me.

I groaned, and with barely enough time to act, I spun the point end around as I took two involuntary steps back and hit the stump. *Welp, this is it…* I thought, my nostrils filling with the scent of burning flesh as it made its final lunge, mouth open to the max, seemingly ready to split itself open if it meant fitting me inside.

I put the whole force of my existence behind the thrust. Every feeling of frustration I ever had, every unbearable regret I ever suffered under. The rod struck the giant turtle directly in the mouth, plunging in deep, and as the butt-end of the lance hit the stump, there was nothing for the snapper to do but swallow the pointed instrument of death whole. I lurched to the side as it came to a halt, its head mere inches from my face. It was essentially on a spit. It couldn't move its mouth or turn its head at all as its four legs thrashed and clawed at the mud. Blood began leaking from its mouth as it started to spasm and sputter, life slowly draining from its eyes. The pink worm-tongue flopped out of its mouth and dangled useless against its bottom jaw.

My knees quivered and I fell back onto my ass on the wet and muddy ground. I stared with wonder at the smoldering monster as the remaining kerosine slowly burned off. I'd forgotten the dog until it ran up and nuzzled my face — I grabbed the fur on its neck with both hands and hugged it tightly. The dog whimpered. I checked the tag on its collar: J.D.

"What are you doing out here J.D.?"

As if to answer, the dog ran to the severed arm and sniffed it. It whimpered again and looked at me, wagging its tail a few times. I understood.

The dog took off into the woods towards Tamarack Road as I got up and did a slow circle around the snapper. I ran my hand over the contours of its shell, committing the whole remarkable creature to memory.

I looked like a mud-slathered, primordial thing myself when I walked out of the woods and into the firehouse parking lot, judging by the looks I got from the cops and firemen, and the various loiterers who were pretending to be cops and firemen. I considered just going home and forgetting all about everything — I didn't want the attention. And maybe it wouldn't be such a bad thing if these people were stuck thinking there was a monster in the lake. Then Taylor rushed up to me.

"What in the hell happened to you, Cobb?"

"I killed the monster. Back in the swamp a ways."

I took a small group of cops out there and watched with quiet glee as they all freaked the fuck out. Seeing people have their minds blown is a very satisfying thing, especially when they're a bunch of hard-ass men. I then told a couple Belvidere cops the details of what had happened.

One of them said, "J.D.? That's old Silas Leonard's dog."

The other one looked down at the severed arm and said, "We'd better go check on him."

Things got pretty crazy for a while after that. The townsfolk had a different glint in their eye when they saw me, and people who knew me a little couldn't fucking believe it.

Nino said, "There must be some kind of mistake! This guy barely says a word for twenty years, then this shit!"

Needless to say, not too many people went swimming for the rest of the summer, only kids jumping in on the occasional dare. A memorial for the victims was set up in the grassy area next to the Beach House, and a horde of outsiders flocked to the area, some for the victims, but mostly to see the remains of the creature, before it was removed to be studied for scientific research. We made national news and I became somewhat of a celebrity for a minute, even doing interviews for a couple TV news stations and multiple newspapers. I gave most of the credit to J.D., however, ensuring that the dog found a nice home to live out the rest of her days. A bullshit show about paranormal research/monster hunting came around and did an episode, which they asked me to participate in, and I managed to get laid out of it, which was cool, but after that I decided I was done. I stopped by to see Kyle, like I said I would, and we had a couple beers and a few laughs over the whole thing, while he told me some cool stories about my dad.

The rest of summer flew by like a dragonfly. Fall came on quick, and with it came a portentous sense that, despite everything that had already happened, all of this was just beginning for me.

Little did I know that on Halloween night, three more snappers would come crawling out of the lake…

Something in the Water

By: Margaret Eve

The *Windswept* wasn't a logical choice for stowaways, nor was the Middle of the North Sea, hours away from any other vessel, a logical place for them to board. Yet Simon's flashlight glinted off a set of neat, wet footprints on the deck, marching away from the railing.

"Terry," he said into his radio." Seen something not quite right. Just going to check it out."

"Duly noted," came the crackly reply. Simon winced at a sharp snap right in his ear. The static was really bad tonight. "Report in when you get back to your normal route."

"Right you are, sir!"

The prints didn't go anywhere interesting. Simon followed them along the deck and down the stairs into the processing area beneath the main hatch. They only went a few yards further before stopping abruptly, like someone had swung a mop round the corner, took care of the last couple footprints, then ignored the rest of the corridor. Simon stuck his head round to take a quick look down the passageway, but there was nothing to see. He lifted the radio back to his mouth.

"Couldn't find anything," he reported. "Heading back up on deck now."

"What caught your attention anyway?" Terry asked. His voice was heavily distorted, the static making him almost impossible to understand. Signal could get patchy out here, but they both knew that their equipment ought to have been better than this.

"I found bare footprints coming away from the railing, near the stern. They go down below and then just stop right before the conveyer. Weird huh?"

"Very weird." Terry sounded troubled. "You stick with your rounds. Keep your eyes peeled. I'm going to report this to the captain."

"Sir," he said by way of acknowledgment, comforted now that the unflappable older man was on the case., As he turned to go back to his post, he noticed the water was starting to fade, evaporating away in the warmth. When Simon returned to the deck, he saw that those prints were doing the same thing, despite the frigid air. His imagination perhaps? Or the wind? The weather had died down, but there was just enough of a breeze left to blow the water around and distort the footsteps.

Next stop on his tour: the stern port side lifeboat. Proper checks were done first thing every morning, so this was just a precautionary once over, to make sure nothing looked to have come loose or been put back incorrectly.

Upon arrival at the lifeboat, Simon was shocked to find more footprints patterning the deck here, concentrated around the winch that released the small boat into the sea. Simon checked frantically to see if anything had been tampered with, then, when he found nothing wrong, he checked again a great deal more slowly and methodically.

Everything was just fine. Whatever had left them had apparently done nothing but look. Simon breathed a sigh of relief.

"Terry? You with the captain yet?" he asked into his radio. "I've found more prints." A blast of static was his only response. He thought he could hear a voice speaking through it but couldn't make out any words. "Terry?" Still nothing he could make out. He wasn't even sure he could hear speaking on the other end anymore. Simon glanced back at the lifeboat.

Fuck it, he could come back and finish things here when he'd made sure Terry was all right. "Terry, I can't hear a thing over the radio so I'm coming to you," He said, hoping he would find the other man waiting for him, a pissed off expression on his face and a broken radio in his hand.

The room was empty. Terry was gone. His headset dangled on its cord a few inches above the floor. It was possible he could have already left to report to the captain...but then why hadn't he put his equipment away properly? Terry always put things back, a leftover habit from his navy days. Maybe he had just been so worried about what Simon had told him that he had become distracted and forgot. But there were stories about how Terry had found the time to pack up cleanly when under fire in the Gulf. An unusual message during nightly rounds should not have been enough to make him lose his cool.

Since there was no one to object to it, Simon collapsed down onto Terry's chair. He hopped straight up again with a yelp. The seat was soaked! A small pool of water had gathered around the feet of the chair, it had been squeezed out of the fabric when Simon had sat down. He looked upwards just in time to see a drop fall from the ceiling, a ceiling with absolutely no cracks to indicate a leak, and no plumbing or anything up there that could possibly *cause* water to come through.

Simon stared up at it, trying to deaden the growing sense of unease in his stomach.

He needed to think about this sensibly. There was probably a perfectly good, normal reason for Terry to have left his station in such a state of disarray, and as for the water dripping from the ceiling, until he found out what that was, he needed to just keep his head and do his job. The captain needed to be informed of the situation, and since he had no way of telling if Terry had gone to do it, he knew he would have to go himself. He took a deep, steadying breath, and told himself he was just overreacting, that the captain would have already been informed, by Terry, and he would just be sent back to complete his rounds.

Simon wiped the cold sweat clamming up his hands onto his pants as he steeled himself to leave. Another drop fell from the ceiling onto Simon's head, causing him to all but run out the door.

***

"And you're quite sure he said he was coming to me?" Captain Richards asked, pacing along the back wall of his cabin.

"Quite sure sir," Simon said. There was nothing more relaxing than having a problem passed over to someone with more experience and authority, someone that had sailed and captained vessels since before Simon had ever even seen the sea.

"Very well, thank you for apprising me of the situation," Richards said, clearly making some sort of decision as he paused mid-stride, then returned to his desk. "Return to your rounds and keep me apprised of anything else you spot that looks even remotely unusual. Can't be too careful out here."

"No sir," Simon said. "Thank you, sir." He'd only gone a few steps down the corridor when the lifeboat problem popped into his head. He'd completely forgotten to tell the captain about it! He turned on his heel and headed back to the small office. "One more thing sir," he said. "There were more footsteps up on deck by the stern, port side lifeboat. The mechanism didn't look to have been tampered with, but I didn't get the chance to investigate the rest of it before all this happened. I just thought you should know."

Captain Richards looked up at this new interruption, his steely blue gaze above his bristling beard pinning Simon to the wall .

"Duly noted, lad," Richards said, bending back to his work after staring into and through Simon's skull. "I trust you'll get to it. But finish your standard rounds before you do. I want to make sure nothing else unusual is going on first."

Simon nodded and scuttled off to do as he'd been instructed. He needed to stay calm, focused, and level-headed. This was no time to give in to paranoia and flights of fancy.

What was that dripping sound?

Simon shook his head. That last thought was not meant to be drifting into his calm and composed mind. They were at sea. Watery noises were to be expected. Just because there had been damp, inexplicable footprints and some unexplained dripping, that was no reason to start panicking over every little drop of water he now came across.

He squashed down the unease and continued back up to the deck, making a point to keep an eye out for anything out of the ordinary. He'd managed to get all the way back to the lifeboat before the small thought that had been trying to make itself known finally stumbled into the forefront of his mind.

Captain Richards had brown eyes. Warm, brown eyes and a gruff manner that reminded him of his granddad. The eyes he'd had back in the office were about as far from that warm brown as he could imagine. They were almost like the sea on a perfectly clear day...

Now, he was just being ridiculous. Eye color didn't just change like that. It had to have been a trick of the light. He pushed the thought out of his mind as he carried out his orders, which were very sensible, even if he, personally, would have made sure the lifeboat was secure before he did anything else. He also couldn't stop thinking about that sound of dripping water, deep within the bowels of the ship, where any leaks would have been found and reported immediately...

He was going to go get one of his mates to help him. He was sure the captain would understand, just so long as he didn't pull anyone else off active duty to do it.

***

"Please tell me you're not serious," James said, finally looking up from his crossword. "You actually expect me to willingly do work, off shift, just because you've been reading too many horror stories?"

"Come on Jim, please?" Simon begged, wishing he didn't sound quite so much like a little kid when the words came out. "When do I ever ask for favors? You know I wouldn't ask if it wasn't important."

James gave him a considering look, weighing up his options, and then sighed, pushing the small book across to him.

"Help me with seven across and you've got a deal. It's been bugging me all day."

Simon glanced down. "Peanuts," he said promptly. "Definitely peanuts."

James pulled the book back. "Damn." He scribbled down the suggestion and closed the book with another sigh." Oh well, let's get this over with then. It's the port side ones, right?"

"Yeah, at the stern."

"Fair enough. At least this won't take long." He begrudgingly hauled himself out of his bunk and grabbed his jacket. "You owe me one though. Especially if 'peanuts' throws off the rest of my clues."

"If the rest of the clues go wrong, it's because you got them wrong," Simon said. "That one really can't be anything else – wait...do you hear something?" They'd just pulled level with one of the other bunk doors. Simon paused to listen. There was a faint *drip drip drip* coming from beyond the door. "I can hear water through there," he said, nerves starting to build again. "Maybe we should take a look."

"Oh, for God's sake!" James said. "Man up, will you! It's probably just a leaky tap. I'm not wasting my down time playing nanny for the others. If you want to check the taps, you can do it when I've finished babysitting you on your rounds."

Simon gave the door a wary look before reluctantly turning away to follow after James. He *was* just overreacting. He had to be. Still, having James for company made him feel better, even if it did mean he was going to have the piss ripped out of him in the mess tomorrow. And likely, for the rest of the voyage.

***

"You *have* been watching too many horror movies," James said when they got back to the lifeboat. "There's nothing bloody here!"

Simon just shrugged uncomfortably. The footprints were all gone. An over-active imagination was one thing but his eyes playing tricks on him was quite another. He *knew* he'd seen them, just like he knew he'd seen the ones going below deck. Just because there was probably a perfectly good reason for them to be gone now didn't mean they hadn't been there before, or that they weren't cause for concern.

James's mood didn't improve as they continued along Simon's rounds. It thankfully didn't get any worse, but it didn't make for good conversation. Sullen silence or not, Simon was still glad for his friend's presence. It was far easier to operate sensibly and calmly, secure in the knowledge that he wasn't alone, and with the reinforcement that this wasn't as much of a problem as he'd feared. He'd relaxed enough that he had no issues carrying on alone for a bit when James disappeared off to take a piss.

Of course, the nerves and doubts set in again the minute he was by himself, but Simon squashed them back down, trusting that they'd go away when his company returned. As he continued onward, a cold drop of water landed on his nose, causing him to flinch and stifle a gasp. Simon's heart was just about beating out of his chest as he looked up, only for him to become almost weak with relief at what he saw. It was just condensation, perfectly normal, absolutely nothing to worry about. Except...James had been gone a fair while now. Granted it might have just been his nerves causing time to seem slower than he thought, and although he knew James really wouldn't appreciate it if Simon came barging in just as he was doing up his pants, that it would open him up to even more mocking, he paused, agonized with indecision for a moment, before finally turning on his heel toward the lavatories. One more mocking story on top of all the other ribbing he'd be taking already wouldn't dent his pride too much further. The consequences of his actual fears coming true were far more dire.

Rather than barrel straight in, Simon gently pushed open the door. .

"Jim? Jim you in here?" he called. No response. There was no one at the urinals and the stalls were standing open. Shallow pools of water decorated the gray floor, swaying slightly with the motion of the ship. Had he just got tired of Simon's nerves and gone back to bed without telling him, to teach him a lesson? It hadn't been long enough for Jim to get back to his locker yet, so he would still have his radio. Simon flicked his own into life to try and contact him.

"Jim, if this is your attempt to freak me out even further, it isn't working," he lied. He'd been about to continue, when he experienced the unnaturally odd sensation of hearing his own words being parroted back to him, heavy with static, from one of the stalls.

James's radio was lying on the floor, in a puddle of water. Simon felt like his heart was going to burst out of his chest and rupture his eardrums. Even if James was annoyed with him, even if he was angry for some reason, he wouldn't have just left his radio here. He'd have been the one logged as taking it out, so he'd be the one in trouble for not returning it. Surely his irritation wasn't worth *that*!

Simon had to find someone, *anyone,* and let them know something very weird and *very* bad was happening here. He had to tell Head Office and he had to let any other ships in their vicinity know that they needed help.

He spun to run back out and crashed straight into James's damp form.

"Where's the fire, kid?" he asked, steadying the pair of them. "I was just heading back to meet you, when I realized I'd forgotten my radio." He flashed a disarming smile. "Wasn't trying to scare you more. Scouts honor. Genuine accident is all."

"You just...forgot your radio?" Simon said with a frown, his heart still beating a mile a minute, seeming to be asking him why he wasn't running for his life as planned. "And then we just happened to somehow miss each other as I came here and you went back to the gantry?"

"Well...yeah. Guess that must be it," James said, friendly smile still in place. "I mean, what else could have happened. I was there, you're now here, and we didn't see each other in the middle." He gave a fluid shrug.

"I would have seen you," Simon contested stubbornly. "It's not that big of a boat. There's not many ways you could have gone for us to miss each other." His mind was going through every possible route when he noticed an odd thing. His friend's irritation seemed to have completely vanished.

"I took the scenic route," James said, words flippant but with irritation starting to soak into his voice. "Come on now, kid, I think this imagination of yours is starting to cause a few problems. Tell you what, you head to bed, I'll finish off your rounds, and you can owe me one. Deal?"

Simon took a step back. "I would have seen you… Or at least heard you." James's smile started to melt into a frown. That was when Simon noticed that his eyes had changed too, the blue tinged gray of a stormy sea was gone, replaced with vivid cerulean. "Unless you were still in here and I just couldn't see you… The floor's not looking as wet as it did a minute ago."

The smile was back now, but rather than his friend's charming, easy grin, it was a cold turning of the lips and baring of teeth. A shark's smile.

"You've been reading too many horror stories, kid," James said in a voice that sounded very little like him. "You should have just accepted my offer and just gone to bed. Believe me, this is so much easier for all concerned when you don't see it coming."

That was all the warning Simon got. It was just enough. He ducked round James's arm and made a break for the door, just as his friend puffed up and burst into water droplets. The spray showered over where Simon had just been standing. Simon escaped with just a wet foot and damp pants.

He pounded along the deck, crouching behind the base of the gantry when he reached it. It was somewhere he could stay out of sight while he caught his breath and collected his thoughts. What the hell was he going to do now? The captain was one of them, his best friend had turned into a puddle and attacked him, and who knew who else on board had been infected. Terry, the guys in the bunk he'd heard dripping from earlier, but who else? Was there anyone else left on the ship he could turn to? Either way, he needed to make a move soon, or the thing pretending to be James would catch up with him.

Although a few moments had passed, and there were no sounds of anyone coming along the deck, Simon peered cautiously out from behind the gantry crane. No one was coming, and the only sound he could hear above the engine was a faint dripping.

Simon leapt out of his hiding place when a drop of water landed on his head. How could he have been so stupid! Of course, James wouldn't follow by normal means. In the bathroom he had easy, immediate access to the pipes; he could go absolutely anywhere on the ship! Jesus Christ what was he going to do?

He'd keep moving. For now, he'd just keep moving, and he'd avoid anywhere that sounded like dripping water while he thought of what the hell he should do! Monster invasion hadn't been in the fishing company's handbook!

He had to get a message back home, to tell them something bad was going on. He had to warn them that getting another ship involved might just cause the problem to spread. That meant heading back to Terry's workstation in the wheelhouse. Simon's heart sank when he thought of the water dripping from the ceiling and the soaking chair. Whatever had attacked James had taken Terry too. It might still be there, waiting for him. He had little choice in the matter though. He had to do *something*.

***

There was no wind, but the sea was getting rougher. The deck pitched and rolled, making Simon stumble. The sound of water dripping from somewhere unseen stayed his constant companion as he continued along, and it was loud enough to hear clearly over the roar of the waves. The spray felt like freezing nails, piercing any exposed skin they could find. Despite his fears, Simon was grateful to stagger up the stairs to the wheelhouse and slam the door closed behind him, shutting out the weather.

The patch of damp in the ceiling had gone. It had apparently moved on, he thought. The chair looked to be equally dry, but Simon wasn't going to risk sitting in it.

"This is the *Windswept*, of the West Maritime Fishing Company" he called into the microphone, hitting the button to relay his message. "The ship has been attacked. The captain is dead, as are some of the crew. I don't know how many of us are left." The dripping that had been following him across the ship started up again to his left, it was in the room with him. Simon shifted to keep an eye on it. "No demands have been issued." No attempts at communication at all, in fact, outside of promises of oblivion. "Approach with extreme caution. I repeat: approach with extreme caution." The dripping grew louder. "Does anybody read me?"

His only response was the same static that had disrupted his conversation with Terry earlier. His heart sank even further. It was not the response he'd been hoping for, and he knew he didn't have the time to try again. All he could do was hope that someone would hear it.

The water seeping through the ceiling was increasing, becoming a steady fall of rain pattering into the room. The puddle was spreading, filling the wheelhouse and leaving Simon pressed against the window. Getting back to the door meant walking through it. The damp hem of his pants from James's attack was as close as he wanted to get to this stuff. He had no idea what getting drenched would involve, but he did not want to find out.

His only real escape option was out the window. Simon grabbed the chair and swung it at the glass as hard as he could, trying to smash his way free before the encroaching puddle was able to cut him off. A large crack appeared across the surface, but the window stayed intact. He swung again and the crack splintered further. He readjusted his grip for a third swing.

The chair hadn't been completely dry. As it moved through the air towards the window, water started seeping out of the cushion. It coalesced into the shape of a face, a maniacal grin rippling across the surface as it lunged forward. It splashed across Simon's wide staring eyes and into his mouth, opened with the beginnings of a scream.

This time the window shattered, spraying glittering shards of glass out into the night. Simon spat at the floor, trying to get the water out of his mouth, when the rain falling from the ceiling suddenly swept over him.

"It doesn't have to be this way, laddie," Terry said, slouching against the doorframe, so different from his typical ramrod posture. Beneath his sodden cap, rivulets of water ran from his red hair across his serene face. "Just stop fighting. Let the water wash your cares away. It'll make life so much easier. The ship is ours. You might as well accept it."

Like hell he was going to do that! Blinking hard and rubbing away the droplets trying to creep into his eyes, Simon flung himself out the window, not caring that he tore both his hands on the jagged glass in the bottom of the frame.

"What do you think you can do anyway?" Terry called after him. "You're the only one left! It's over!"

A wave of helplessness flooded through Simon. Just what could he do against these things? Try and sink the ship? Even if he could think of a way how, he doubted more water was the answer. The hold storage freezers? For all he knew that would make them stronger, give them a more solid form to attack with. And it would involve going down below. Who knew where the rest of the corrupted crew were? He knew he'd never make it. There was only one thing left for him to do: try to make it off the ship so that at least they wouldn't be able to get *him*!

Simon scrambled to his feet and started to run. Something gripped tight around his ankles and pulled. His feet skidded on the slippery combination of glass and water, and he came back down with a painful crash. He twisted on the ground, glass digging through his pants and cutting into his skin with each movement. James was oozing out of the chair cushion, grin still firmly in place, sharp blue eyes glittering with malice.

"Come on mate, just give it up!" he said, as if they were having a friendly conversation back in their bunk, not fighting for Simon's life on the deck, amid broken glass. "If you don't fight, it really is just like going to sleep."

Simon kicked out frantically, aiming for the things face. To his horror, after a moment's resistance, his foot sank in up to the ankle. James's grin grew wider. His fist flowed along the deck, half-limb, half-liquid, solidifying to engulf Simon's other ankle, creeping up his body until the entirety of his lower leg was gone. Cold stabbed into his skin like ice. "Poor James here...he struggled. Turned just in time to see me coming. For him it was more like drowning."

Simon redoubled his efforts to get free, his bloody hands sliding across the wet surface as he tried to find a dry enough patch of deck to gain purchase. James crawled up his body, inch by damp inch, the slow, inevitable creep of a deadly glacier. Panic started to set in. His breathing began to come in short, sharp pants.

His foot slid free from one of his boots, free from its watery entrapment, and with three unencumbered limbs, he ripped his other leg out of James's grip with a wet sucking noise. Both were stunned, but Simon recovered from the surprise faster. He leapt to his feet and ran, glass stabbing into the soles of his feet with each step, but he never once slowed down. There was a bubbling scream of rage from behind him as he pounded along the deck. Pursuit wouldn't be long in coming. He needed to get to a lifeboat. He needed to find something to hurt or distract these things, even if only for a moment, just long enough so he could launch the boat and get away.

The ship pitched violently, sending him crashing into the deck fuse box. Electricity! Of course! He wasn't certain it would work, but it seemed like his best and probably only chance. He looked round and didn't see anyone coming, so he yanked open the panel, revealing the rainbow of wires that lay behind it. He didn't know what the fuse box connected to, and he didn't care, so long as it had electricity and live wires. Simon rapidly started pulling them out of place, ripping them free of their casing. Sparks flickered and crackled in the air as the wheelhouse lights died. Simon turned to the sight of movement off to his left, but before he could do anything, he was slammed back against the wall with a cold wet fist around his throat.

"This is getting tiresome, mate," the thing that looked like James told him. "We want you to join us, but if you keep kicking up such a fuss, we're just going to have to kill you. So…" His fingers tightened, choking off Simon's air flow. "What's it going to be?"

All thoughts of a plan went out of Simon's head. His world narrowed down to the false James' tight, damp, grasp, and how he might loosen that terrible hold. He clawed at the grip that had now formed a seamless ring around his neck. It got tighter still, making it even harder to drag air into his lungs.

"This isn't the calm surrender I was hoping for, you know," James said as Simon struggled and gasped. "All your shipmates are here. A crew should stay together. For comfort. You don't want to abandon them, do you?"

Simon glared at the thing that had stolen his friend's shape, but it just looked back at him with minor irritation, then moved in even closer. Simon could feel the chill radiating off it as the pressure at his throat increased, and he wondered how much longer it would be until it crushed his windpipe.

"Fine," James said coldly. "If that's how you want it..." His face started melting away, turning back to water. Sparks flew through the air by their heads.

This is going to hurt Simon thought as he dragged himself sideways, into the path of the sparking wires. There was a loud crack, followed by searing pain across his entire body, then everything went dark.

***

The wires were still sparking when Simon came round. He sat up slowly, limbs twitching, wincing at the burning pain firing across every nerve. The sea was still. James was gone but Simon didn't know for how long, or if Terry and the others had been taken out as well.

Now was his chance to get to the lifeboat.

It hurt to move. The glass shards digging into his feet left bloody footprints as he walked, and his fried nerves objected to every movement. The minutes dragged by slowly as he forced his way towards the lifeboat. He could no longer hear dripping water, only the waves slapping against the side of the ship. The puddles he passed by remained still, rippling only when the wind blew.

He reached the lifeboat unmolested. Nothing stopped him as he lowered it into the water, or as he pushed away from the ship. His heart sank as the *Windswept* grew smaller. It went against every instinct he had as a sailor to abandon ship while she still floated. He tried to quash the feeling of guilt. There was nothing more he could do. His best bet was to find help and come back.

Turning away, Simon sank down to the bottom of the boat, letting his sore, weary muscles rest. He lifted one foot to try and assess the damage, and to remove some of the glass. He pulled out a long, needle-like splinter with gritted teeth, before letting it drop to the bottom of the boat. A small wave brushed over the gory glass shard, washing away the blood. Simon stared down at it. There hadn't been any water when he'd lowered the vessel off the *Windswept*. It occurred to him now that he'd never got round to completing his checks on the lifeboat.

Laughter bubbled up from below him, as the water started to creep slowly up his leg.

Afterword: Depth of a Nightmare

Depth of a Nightmare

In my bed, where I lay at night,
You always come; you give me such fright.
Water seeps in, the room silently fills,
Just the thought of you, gives me the chills.

A dorsal fin glides in; I know that you're here.
I don't want to look; how you fill me with fear.
A shark in my room, I know you're just in my head,
But that doesn't stop you from causing me dread.

You swim all around, waiting for me to look.
I feel like a worm, at the end of a hook.
I can't go to sleep, for fear that you'll eat me.
I don't want to get up, not for a drink, not to pee.

I just wish that you would leave me alone,
Go back to the ocean, for that is your home.
My bedroom is no place for a shark to be,
Though it still seems my mattress is surrounded by sea.

This is a poem I wrote about what I used to imagine almost every night before bed. I would sit up, watching *Hercules* and *Xena* on broadcast television, and I would try to go to sleep, but my imagination almost always had a different idea.

Since I can remember, I have held not only a great fear, but also a great reverence for the sea and the secrets it holds. My earliest known memory of being afraid of the water and want lived within occurred when I was two or three years old. My dad was finishing off the side of the boat we were on, when his line went taut and he knew he had a big one. He proceeded to reel in a Northern Pike. If you have ever seen a Northern Pike, then you know that they are a terrifying fish. They are long and sleek, and their mouths contain myriad, sharp, needle-like teeth. They also have beady little eyes that look naturally fierce and angry. It was my first concept of a sea monster, because even though it was only a fish, the thing terrified me to the core, especially being that it was longer than I was tall. When I was a kid, I used to remember every detail of this incident, but as an adult, even though most of the memory has faded away, my fear of sea and sea creatures has not. Thalassophobia has been part of my existence ever since.

To add to my growing terror of all that is aquatic, I watched one of the *Jaws* at far too young of an age, and after watching someone get eaten by a shark, oceans started to scare me even more than lakes. On top of that, we owned a copy of Time Life's *Mysteries of the Unknown: Mysterious Creatures,* which I probably shouldn't have read. The pictures it contained within, those of the Kraken in particular, surfacing alongside a small boat, haunted my nightmares for years to come. Also, when I was seven or eight years old, we had a cabin where we would go fishing off the dock, and sometimes, when we left the fish on the stringer, we would pull them back up and only their heads would remain. My parents told me that it was probably a snapping turtle, which was a little scary, but never having seen it, I could cope... Until the day I pulled up the stringer up so we could add another fish, and to my surprise, when I pulled that thin rope out of the water, there was a giant snapping turtle head staring back at me, less than two feet away from my face, and less than a foot away from my hand. Needless to say, I dropped the stringer and screamed.

All these events culminated in a deep fear and fascination for the sea and the mysteries it contains within. I have read many of Peter Benchley's, Steve Alten's, and Micheal Cole's novels about deep sea terror, I have read *20,000 Leagues Under the Sea,* Nick

Cutter's *The Deep,* and every other sea monster book I could get my hands on, as well as watching as many sea monster movies as I could find, from *Lake Placid* to *Leviathan* to *Underwater* to *Piranha DD.* I simply can't get enough sea monster stuff in my life, which is why I chose to create this anthology. My hope is that you love each of these stories as much as I do, and maybe, just maybe, your thirst for terror on and under the seas will be quelled, if only for a short while.

Yours Truly,
Thomas Folske

Picture Index

Author Bios

Stephen A. Roddewig:

Stephen A. Roddewig is an author from Arlington, Virginia. Cutting back from four to two cups of coffee a day has convinced him that he is superhuman, and his Horror Writers Association membership hasn't disproved that belief. When not pushing the bounds of human endurance, he has published three novels and fifty short stories, including an appearance on The NoSleep Podcast. Mostly, though, he spends his time reading incredible war fiction from William Peter Grasso while cycling in the gym and cooking like his savings depend on it. You can find more of his speculative fiction and comedy at stephenaroddewig.com

Jeff Parsons:

In addition to Jeff's two short story collections, *The Captivating Flames of Madness* and *Algorithm of Nightmares*, he is published in *The Horror Zine* ezine and also in many of their anthologies. He has also been published in *Aphelion Webzine, Dark Gothic Resurrected Magazine, Fireburst: The Inner Circle Writers' Group, Amazing Stories Tales of Galactic Pest Control, Beautiful Tragedies 5*, and in many other anthologies. He is currently seeking a publisher for his first full-length novel titled *Tomorrow Will End*, a sci-fi/ horror adventure.

Charles Reis:

Charles was born and raised in Coventry, Rhode Island, but currently lives in West Warwick. He graduated from the University of Rhode Island with a BA in English Literature in 2012. Currently, he works as a museum tour guide. He's had numerous short stories and poems published, with several appearing in various books such as One Night in Salem, Eldritch Investigations, and More Lore for the Mythos. Besides writing, he also has an interest in travel, history, horror films, the outdoors, and the paranormal.

Facebook Author Page: www.facebook.com/CharlesCthulhu

Instagram: https://www.instagram.com/cthulhudawn1979

Amazon Author Page: https://www.amazon.com/stores/Charles-Reis/author/B077C563HK

Lillian Csernica:

Lillian Csernica writes fantasy, romance, and horror. Her short stories have appeared in *Weird Tales, Fantastic Stories,* and *Jewels of Darkover*. Her Kyoto Steampunk stories can be found in the Clockwork Alchemy anthologies *Twelve Hours Later, Thirty Days Later, Some Time Later* and *Last Stop on the #13. SHIP OF DREAMS,* an historical romance, is set in the Caribbean of 1725 during the Golden Age of piracy, is available through Digital Fiction Publishing. A genuine California native, Lillian resides in the Santa Cruz mountains with her sons and two cats.

Visit her at:
lillian888.wordpress.com and https://www.facebook.com/lillian.csernica.

Claire Davon:

USA Today Bestselling author Claire Davon has written for most of her life, starting with fan fiction when she was very young. She writes across a wide range of genres, and does not consider any of it off limits. Her novels can be found in the paranormal romance and contemporary romance sections, while her short stories run the gamut. If a story calls to her, she will write it. She currently lives in Los Angeles and spends her free time writing novels and short stories, as well as doing animal rescue and enjoying the sunshine.

Claire's website: www.clairedavon.com.
Facebook: https://www.facebook.com/ClaireDavonindieauthor/
Instagram: https://www.instagram.com/clairedavon/
Newsletter signup: https://clairedavon.com/newsletter/
Pinterest: https://www.pinterest.com/bibimarlowe/
Goodreads: https://www.goodreads.com/author/show/7915840.Claire_Davon
Amazon Author Central: https://www.amazon.com/-/e/B00IMP2KSU

LJ Jacobs

LJ Jacobs was born in Chester, England and raised in North Wales. He lives in a small Welsh hamlet and enjoys the quiet life with his lovely family. He enjoys playing and listening to music as well as writing. He's contributed to numerous anthologies and online journals with publishers such as Mind's Eye Publications, Wicked Shadow Press, redrosethorns, New Edition, *Unsplatterpunk!* and Culture Cult.

He hopes to collect his work for his own anthology one day.

Mawr Gorshin:

Mawr Gorshin was born Martin Gross in Timmins, Ontario, in 1969. He moved to Taiwan ROC in the summer of 1996, where he's lived ever since, teaching English as a second language. In his spare time, he has composed and recorded music (classical and pop), which can be found on the Jamendo website, under both his original (the classical music) and pen names (the pop music). Over the past fifteen years or so, he has focused on writing, much of which can be found on his blog, 'Infinite Ocean' (poetry, prose, analyses of literature, film, and music--mostly from a Marxist or psychoanalytic perspective--and writing on narcissistic abuse). Below are his blog, Facebook links, and Jamendo link:

https://www.jamendo.com/artist/362453/mawr-gorshin
https://mawrgorshin.com/
https://www.facebook.com/mawrgorshinwriter/
https://www.facebook.com/mawr.gorshin

Milan Simić:

Milan Simić was born in 1988 in Belgrade, Serbia. He would divide his life into two parts up until a certain moment. Art and music. His fascination with the ninth art (comics) led him to start drawing and painting at a young age. He graduated in graphic design, which he still occasionally do today (as much as time allows). The aforementioned moment came when writing entered his life. He is the author and creator of the blog "Vault of Chaos" which represents his virtual form of personal expression and the CV from which it all began. In addition to his own blog, he is a regular collaborator for the portal "Helly Cherry." where he writes reviews and articles.

His short-term goal is to publish his first book and comic, while his long-term goal is to one day leave the daily grind of his current job and dedicate all his energy to writing, painting, and playing music.

His bibliography currently consists of several short stories, published in several horror and SF book collections.

Justin Carlos Alcala:

Justin Carlos Alcala (he/him) is an award-winning Mexican-American novelist & short story writer. His works are most notable for their appearance in Publisher's Weekly, the SLF Foundation Awards, and the University of British Columbia project archives. Justin is a folklore fanatic, a history nerd, a tabletop gamer, and a time traveler. Alcala's sixty-plus short stories, novellas, and novels can be found in anthologies, magazines, journals, podcasts, and commercial publications. He currently resides with his dark queen, Mallory, their fey daughter, Lily, changeling son, Ronan, goblin-toddler, Asher, and hounds of Ragnarök, Fenrir and Hilda, in Bigfoot's domain. Where his mind might be is anyone's guess.

Website: www.justinalcala.com
Instagram: Justin.alcala

Denise Landry:

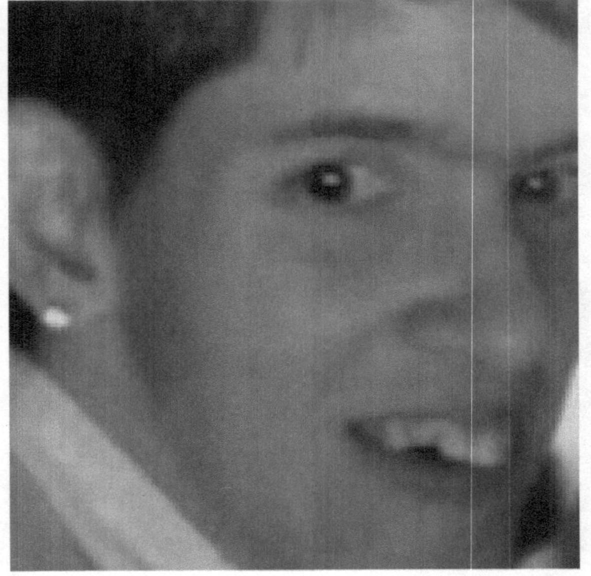

Denise Landry is a disabled writer living in Montreal Canada. She has several poems and short stories published in several magazines and small press anthologies. Publishers include (Sweetycat Press/ Steve Carr 2022). Written Tales Chapbooks, (2023&2024) and Wicked Shadow Press (2023-26), Pen and Paw International 2024 River City Siren Press 2024. Micromance magazine (2024-2026) Beaches and Trails Publishing (2025) VerseveZINE Blackout: Alice in Wonderland (2025)

https://deniselandryauthor.tumblr.com

Blake Hoss:

Harold Hoss is a film producer and attorney born in Oklahoma. When he isn't reading or watching movies, he enjoys swimming (preferably in areas that aren't infested with crocodiles) and walking with his dogs Margot and Texas Chainsaw Massacre (or Tex for short).

David McDonald:

David McDonald is a mild mannered editor by night, and a wild eyed writer by day. In 2013 he won the Ditmar Award for Best New Talent, and in 2014 won the William J. Atheling Jr. Award for Criticism or Review and was shortlisted for the WSFA Small Press Award. His short fiction has appeared in anthologies from publishers such as Moonstone Books, Crazy 8 Press, and Fablecroft Publishing. In 2015, his first movie novelisation, Backcountry, was released by Harper Collins, and his first Marvel novel—Guardians of the Galaxy:Castaways—was published in August 2016. David is a member of Science Fiction and Fantasy Writers of America, the Horror Writers Association, and the International Association of Media Tie-In Writers.

http://www.davidmcdonaldspage.com
bsky: sercamaris.bsky.social

CJ Hooper:

CJ Hooper is deaf author from Hertfordshire in England. He has a background in history, archaeology, mythology and performance. Each of his tales has a strong sense of the historic environment drawing upon the atmosphere of the familiar, then making it unfamiliar. Silence Next The Sea is also the title story of his first collection of weird tales. The tales vary in style, some will haunt, others terrify, yet others are heartwarming, though still spooky. His first novel, "After Babalon" will be published later in 2026 (all being well).

Pip Pinkerton:

Pip Pinkerton was born and raised in Oakdale, Minnesota. Pip is a wanderer and a dreamer. He loves writing short stories, poetry, and screenplays. A former theatre student and current guitar player, Pip currently co-manages a record shop. When he is not writing or jamming, he is spending time with his trusty rottweiler Shrimp. Pip has been published on the Monstrous Femme website, as well as with HorrorAddicts.net, Wicked Shadow Press, Sometimes Hilarious Horror, Theaker Quarterly Fiction, J. Manfred Weichsel, Pawsitively Creepy, and Ink'd Publishing. He has upcoming work to be featured in anthologies by Red Cape Publishing, Xpress Publishing, and Alien Buddha Press.

https://www.amazon.com/stores/Pip-Pinkerton/author/B0DZTYJVZ6

Dino Parenti:

Dino Parenti is a writer of dark, speculative fiction. Author of the novella, *Bitter Breed,* as well as the Imadjinn Award Finalist short-fiction collection, *Dead Reckoning and Other Stories,* he also won the first annual *Lascaux Review* flash fiction contest and was featured in the Anthony Award winning anthology *Blood on the Bayou*. He lives in Los Angeles.

Facebook: Dino Parenti | Facebook
Instagram: Dino Parenti (@dinoparenti) • Instagram photos and videos
Twitter (X): Dino Parenti (@DinoParenti) / Twitter
Bluesky: Dino Parenti (@dparenti.bsky.social) — Bluesky

Don Anelli:

Don grew into horror as he got older, becoming a fan by the time of his teenage years after dabbling in the genre for years but never making the jump into out-and-out fandom. By the time of his 20s, he spent most of his time watching and reading as much as he could before finally deciding to try writing it, which led to a slew of short stories and flash fiction written more for himself than anyone else. After failed submissions in several different styles and publications, "Whatever Happened to Jonathan Oberero?" is his first stab at sharing anything beyond his laptop.

Matthew Chabin:

Matthew Chabin hails from Portland, Oregon. He worked as a journalist in the Navy, as a teacher in the Czech Republic, and in several volunteer capacities with the Tibetan community in Dharamsala, India. He currently lives with his family in Japan, where he teaches full-time. His work has appeared in a number of journals and anthologies.

I Please see his Face Book writer's page, 'Matt's Dark Places,' for more information and links to published material.

DJ Tyrer:

DJ Tyrer dwells on the misty northern shore of the Thames estuary, close to the world's longest pleasure pier in the decaying seaside resort of Southend-on-Sea, and is the person behind *Atlantean Publishing*. They studied history at the University of Wales at Aberystwyth and have worked in the fields of education and public relations. DJ has been widely published in anthologies and magazines around the world, such as *Alone in the Borderland* (Belanger Books), *Chilling Horror Short Stories* (Flame Tree), *All The Petty Myths* (18th Wall), *Steampunk Cthulhu* (Chaosium), *What Dwells Below* (Sirens Call), *The Horror Zine's Book of Ghost Stories* (Hellbound Books), and *EOM: Equal Opportunity Madness* (Otter Libris), and issues of *Sirens Call, Hypnos, Occult Detective Magazine, parABnormal,* and *Weirdbook,* and in addition, has a novella available in paperback and on the Kindle, *The Yellow House* (Dunhams Manor).

DJ Tyrer's website is at https://djtyrer.blogspot.co.uk/

DJ Tyrer's Facebook page is at:
https://www.facebook.com/DJTyrerwriter/

The Atlantean Publishing website is at:
https://atlanteanpublishing.wordpress.com/

Miguel Fliguer:

Miguel Fliguer (b. 1961) lives in Buenos Aires, Argentina. His first book, *Cooking With Lovecraft* (2017), is a collection of gastronomical weird tales. His short stories — many in collaboration with Mike Slater (*NecroNomNomNom*)—are featured in several weird fiction anthologies, among them: *Weird Tails, Ancestors and Descendants, Corridors, Portraits of Terror,* and *The Pickman Papers* (Innsmouth Gold Press); *Arithmophobia* (Polymath Press); *Once Upon a Future Time* (The Brothers Uber); *NecronomiRomCom* and *Atlas of Deep Ones* (Obsidian Butterfly); *Vastarien* (Grimscribe Press); *Strange Aeon 2022* (Thorncroft); and the recent, self-published collection *Splinters of Azathoth.*

Miguel dwells on Instagram as @cookingwithlovecraft, and as himself in the Book of Faces.

Thomas Folske:

Thomas Folske lives in Minnesota, USA, with his wife, five kids, and three black cats. He holds a BA in Creative Writing, an AA in Liberal Arts, an AS in Education, and a certificate in Creative Writing. He has had over 80 short stories published by various publishers over the last ten years, most in the last five years. This in the first anthology he has ever curated. See more at: https://tfolske1987.wixsite.com/mysite and https://www.amazon.com/-/e/B00UKTWZ6I.

Michael Mortimer:

Michael Mortimer is an award-winning writer and filmmaker living with his wife and son in Phoenix. He self-published his first novel, THE TOWN CRIER, in 2023.

https://www.instagram.com/the_town_crier_book/

Margaret Eve:

Margaret Eve is an author of short horror fiction, with publications in Midnight Street Press, Piker Press, and Horror Tree's Trembling with Fear. She is a member of the British Fantasy Society and a regular attendee of FantasyCon. When not writing she works as a biomedical scientist in South East England and lives with her husband, daughter, and cat.

Rob Tannahill

Rob Tannahill is the author of Prince Junkie, Mirrorball Road, and The Girl in the Galactic Glory Hole and Other Tales. He is also the editor and curator of Last Christmas and Confessions from the Think Tank. He's been writing songs, so before long, you'll probably see them. Find him on Amazon authors/robtannahill

Kasey Hill

Kasey Hill is a critically acclaimed, versatile writer from Franklin County, VA, known for her work in several genres, including urban fantasy, horror, thriller, paranormal romance, and metaphysical/New Age topics. She has authored both fiction and non-fiction, with a particular interest in Wicca.

Her fiction often dives into the supernatural and the macabre, blending mythological elements with modern storytelling. She has published multiple novels, poetry collections, and short stories. Notable works include her *Guardians of Light* series in the mythology fantasy genre and her poetry, which has received recognition for its depth and emotional resonance. As she grows in the horror genre, she has a particular penchant for Southern Gothic/Appalachian Gothic storytelling, such as her Adult Horror novel *Devil's Claw* and her Young Adult horror series, *The Whispering Spirits,* featuring *The Haunting at Foxwood Village* and *Dark Coven.* She has several Horror short stories circulating for anthologies and Ezines, featuring her unique style of worldbuilding.

www.kaseyhillauthor.com

www.facebook.com/kaseyhillauthor
www.instagram.com/kaseyhillauthor
www.tiktok.com/kaseyhillauthor
www.amazon.com/stores/Kasey-Hill/author/B00O2WT210

Artist Bios

Alhiya Hoffman and Olivia Davis:

Alhiya Hoffman and Olivia Davis are two high school students with promising artistic futures. They designed and drew the initial cover, then turned it over to Mia Folske to color and finalize. Both girls love art, are constant drawers, and both are aspiring artists. This is the first time either Alhiya or Olivia have ever been published, but both intend to continue making art and refining their skills. Both girls are also considering pursuing art degrees after graduation.

Ben Merk:

Ben Merk is a talented young artist with a passion for horror movies. He has been drawing and making art since he can remember, but he feels like he really started to consider himself an artist at about seven years old. He is currently in high school and wants to be a continue creating after he graduates, possibly considering a career as a tattoo artist. This is his first published piece of artwork, though he has sold his art in the past, and is looking to broaden his audience by selling at craft fairs, or possibly submitting pieces to future anthologies.

Kelsey Grimmell:

Kelsey Grimmell is a mixed media artist based in St. Paul, Minnesota. While painting is her main passion, she dabbles in many forms of artistic expression. With a deep passion for nature, she draws inspiration from the world around her. Her artwork blends the whimsical vibes of mossy forests with gothic, witchy elements. When she's not exploring outdoors, Kelsey finds comfort staying in with her partner and their dog, Amos.

Mia Folske:

Mia Folske is a professional plumber as well as an aspiring artist, with a background in computer design. She has loved drawing since she can remember and has had her work featured in magazines as well as in promotional material for local bands. She has also done artwork for short stories and has had her artwork displayed and sold in local galleries. She is a proud mother and is currently living in Minnesota, USA with her fiancée.

Michelle Hanson:

Michelle Hanson lives in Minnesota with her three cats, Lola, Chloe, and Moe. She has art in her blood, though she is somewhat of a dabbler. She has created everything from a resin lamp and resin figures to professional grade make-up jobs to amazing paintings and rhinestone artwork that has sold for hundreds of dollars. This is Michelle's first piece of published artwork.

Sidney Shiv:

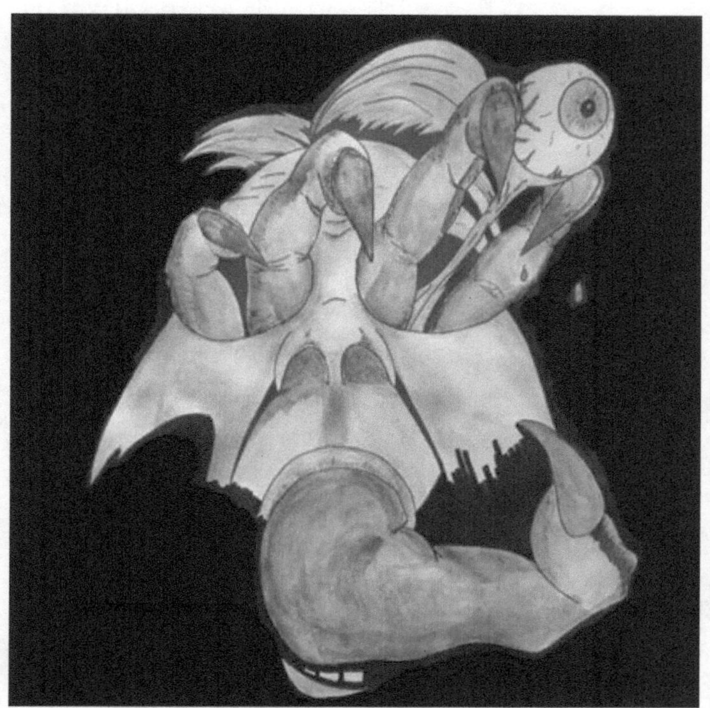

Sidney Shiv is a horror author, editor, and cover artist. In 2025, he won a Splatterpunk Award for best anthology for his role in co-editing *Splatology 2.0*. His short story, 'Fulfillment,' from his collection, *Where Devils Dance*, also received a nomination. Besides writing, Sidney enjoys curating, editing, and illustrating horror anthologies.

Warren Muzak:

Warren Muzak is an Ontario, Canada–based illustrator specializing in horror and sci-fi imagery. A seasoned, self-taught professional, he has created artwork for numerous horror and science fiction anthologies, earning a reputation as a visual storyteller who brings mood, movement, and emotion to every piece. Inspired by legendary artists like Bernie Wrightson, Wally Wood, Jack Davis, and Arthur Rackham, as well as classic horror publications such as Creepy, Eerie, and 1950s EC comics like Tales from the Crypt, his work combines vintage atmosphere with dynamic, contemporary energy. He's known for flowing lines, dramatic perspectives, and richly layered organic textures—rock, wood, bark, and dirt often find their way into his richly detailed worlds. Whether working in pen and ink, watercolor, and pencil, or digitally with a WACOM Cintiq and Krita, Warren seamlessly blends traditional craft with modern digital techniques. When he's not crafting dark, otherworldly scenes, he's likely hunting for vintage comics or expanding his collection of classic Lionel trains. https://warrenmuzak.weebly.com/ for my complete portfolio.

Instagram: https://www.instagram.com/warrenmuzak/

LinkedIN: https://www.linkedin.com/in/warrenmuzak

Facebook: https://www.facebook.com/warmuzak

Todor Gotchkov:

Todor Gotchkov is a game concept artist and Illustrator based in Bulgaria, focused on horror & dark fantasy design and visual storytelling. His work has appeared in various indie games and on numerous book covers.

Featured Authors:
Blake Hoss
Charles Reis
CJ Hooper
Claire Davon
David McDonald
Denise Landry
Dino Parenti
DJ Tyrer
Don Anelli
Jeff Parsons
Justin Carlos Alcala
Kasey Hill
Lillian Csernica
LJ Jacobs
Margaret Eve
Matthew Chabin
Michael Mortimer
Miguel Fliguer
Milan Simić
Pip Pinkerton
Rob Tannahill
Stephen A. Roddewig
Thomas Folske
Featured Artists:
Alhiya Hoffman
Amelia Folske
Ben Merk
Blake Hoss
Kelsey Grimmell
Michelle Hanson
Milan Simić
Olivia Davis
Sidney Shiv
Todor Gotchkov
Warren Muzak

www.ingramcontent.com/pod-product-compliance
Lightning Source LLC
LaVergne TN
LVHW041058080826
845145LV00007B/1624